The Bookseller's Son

The Bookseller's Son

A Novel

by

Bob Seay

2025

ISBN: 979-8-9867587-2-5

First Edition: 2025

This is a work of fiction. Names, characters, places, and incidents are either products of the author's imagination or are used fictitiously. Any resemblance to actual persons, living or dead, events, or locales is entirely coincidental.

Self-Published

Printed in the United States of America

Dedicated to the writers whose books have been banned.
Your truth speaks, even in your absence.

Contents

1

Back in 1972, when men wore polyester suits and joined civic clubs and sat children on their laps behind the steering wheels of station wagons as they drove home from church; when the Supreme Court said they knew obscenity when they saw it; way back before God became a Republican, Jeremiah Malone, the nineteen-year-old manager of Clear Spring Books & Electronics, was certain of only one thing:

God was *not* on his side.

Despite this certainty, Jeremiah made his way to the Clear Spring Church of Christ three times a week, not to gain karmic points with an angry god but to, as he called it, "console and comfort" any female members of the congregation whose boyfriends, fiancés, or husbands might be serving overseas in the United States military.

Jeremiah had charmed his way into the bed of one of the sopranos of the church one cold Sunday evening when he heard the front door rattle.

He froze in full pushup position.

"You're married?" he asked, realizing it was a little late for that type of question.

"What?" Mary Olson raised her head only enough to see Jeremiah's face. "No."

Jeremiah jumped out of bed when an unmistakably male voice called Mary's name.

"Engaged?" Jeremiah whispered as he scrambled to find his pants.

"No." Mary fumbled with the buttons on her red blouse. She'd buttoned it wrong; one side of the blouse was hanging lower than the other, leaving one bare shoulder exposed.

Suddenly, her eyes dilated and her jaw dropped. She bit her lower lip.

"I gave my boyfriend a key when he shipped out for Vietnam," she said in a very rushed whisper. She decided the half buttoned blouse was good enough and searched for her pants. "We met two weeks before he left," she said. "I didn't want him to forget me."

"I'm sure he won't," Jeremiah said.

Jeremiah had one leg in his pants and was struggling with the other leg when Private First Class Delbert Courville of the United States Marine Corps threw open the bedroom door and announced that he was home from the war.

"What the…?"

The surprised Marine applied his hand-to-hand combat training to Jeremiah's face, upper body, and groin. Then he threw Jeremiah over his shoulder, carried him down the hall, and threw him into the street beside the trash can.

PFC Courville looked back at Mary as she stood on her front porch. Tousled hair, shirt askew. She still hadn't found her pants. He tossed the house key in her general direction. It landed somewhere in the tall grass of the yard.

"I'm going home," the Marine announced. His voice was calm, more resigned than angry, as if this was just one more disappointment in what was already a disappointing existence. PFC Courville picked up his duffel bag, gave Jeremiah one last kick to his stomach, and walked away. Jeremiah heard the screen door slam as Mary went back inside.

Jeremiah rolled onto his back and stared at the stars in a moonless winter sky. He'd had close calls before, but this was his first face-to-fist encounter with a Marine who'd come home from the war. He remembered seeing the name tag on the black dress uniform, but he could not remember the name. Then he realized he didn't know Mary's last name either.

He thought about how his life had come to this. There wasn't much to reflect upon.

He was there because of sin.

2

Sin had been a dominant theme in Jeremiah's life for as long as he could remember. Clear Spring Books & Electronics, owned and operated for fifteen years by George and Tammy Malone, was known for selling books like Miller's *Tropic of Cancer* (banned for obscenity and sexually explicit content), Ginsberg's *Howl* (banned for sexual content, profanity, and drug use), and other books that were banned somewhere for one reason or another. They were, by local standards, *sinful* books. According to Millicent Spate, Clear Spring's most vocal authority on such matters, this meant the Malones and their bookstore profited directly from sin. In the all-or-nothing, black-or-white morality of the Bible Belt, this meant that everything George, Tammy, and, by extension, Jeremiah did was tainted by this original sin.

This was not always the case. Millicent was one of the first people to greet the Malones when they moved to Clear Spring from Hollywood. This was fifteen, maybe sixteen, years before Jeremiah's encounter with PFC Courville. George and Tammy were not particularly religious people, but George felt it was important for them to become part of the community, and the Clear Spring community included church. They attended the church closest to their bookstore on a Sunday morning soon after their arrival.

Always ready to welcome newcomers and potential church members, Millicent visited the Malones at their new business the next day, on Monday, to welcome George, Tammy, and three-year-old

Jeremiah to town. George was alone at the counter when she came in. Millicent started inspecting the inventory while they were still exchanging the usual introductory pleasantries.

"I don't really care for the new Bibles," Millicent told George as she admired the leather cover on the New American Standard Bible resting on a display near the front counter.

George grinned. "That translation was published in 1901," he said. "It's not exactly new."

"I just prefer the original King James." Millicent said. Her eyes narrowed as one side of her mouth curled into a half-smile. She laid the Bible on the counter.

"Bookstores are so important, don't you think?" she asked.

"I hope so," George said. "If they're not, then I just wasted a lot of money." He ignored Tammy's arched eyebrows and quiet laughter behind the bookshelf.

"They are," Millicent leaned on the counter as she continued. George noticed the small, kid-sized grape jelly fingerprints on the shoulder of her shirt.

"You have a huge responsibility, providing books for people," she said. "If they read the wrong things, they get wrong ideas. They do bad things. Before you know it, the entire country is on the wrong track."

"Uh huh," George said. He straightened the Bible on the rack, even though it didn't need straightening. He looked at his visitor.

"Don't you think people should be allowed to decide for themselves what they want to read?" he asked.

"They can decide," Millicent said. "We just need to make sure they decide to read the right things."

Young Jeremiah witnessed this conversation from behind a wall of Lincoln Logs he'd built on the floor near the front counter—a wall he was certain rendered him completely invisible, even if it stood less than a foot high. He was too young to follow everything the adults were saying (or not saying), but old enough to decide that this woman, with the deep lines around her thin-lipped smile, was not nice. And she didn't seem to like the same books as his parents. From his hiding place, he inhaled the woody smell of the Lincoln logs and tried not to breathe too loud.

The Malone family attended a different church that Sunday. Millicent dismissed them as unfaithful church hoppers and did not visit the store again for a long time.

Despite their fall from Millicent's grace, the Malones eventually became faithful members of the Clear Spring Church of Christ. Tammy enjoyed that denomination's tradition of acapella music with actual four-part vocal harmony, unlike so many other churches where everyone sang in unison while the piano pounded out chords. George disagreed with some of the Church of Christ teachings but decided they were less objectionable than other churches in town. The lesser of several evils, as it were.

The preacher and church elders seemed to understand that the same First Amendment that recognized their freedom of religion also recognized the Malones' right to decide which books they would sell in their store. If they didn't understand that, then they certainly understood George and Tammy's healthy contribution to the collection plate every Sunday.

Morally, Jeremiah was a child of two worlds: the Hollywood values of his relocated parents, in which sin was little more than an abstract philosophical concept, and the strict "you were born a sinner" values of the rural Arkansas community in which he was raised. When something went wrong, he tended to think it was because he had sinned.

Jeremiah had worked in his parents' bookstore since he was three, when he knocked over a bookshelf as he was climbing and was told to put the books back where they belonged. He was stocking shelves by himself when he was six and was running the cash register by age twelve. By the time he was in high school, Jeremiah was deciding which TVs and stereos should be sold on the electronics side of the store. It wasn't long after that when Jeremiah started managing the store himself on weekends when his parents were out of town.

George and Tammy were so confident in their son's managerial skills that they made plans to retire and move to Florida when Jeremiah turned eighteen. It would be their "Third Act", as George called it, following Act One: Screenwriters and Act Two:

Bookstore Owners/First Amendment Activists. As writers, the Malones tended to think in three-act structures.

George and Tammy informed Jeremiah of their plans on Christmas during his junior year of high school, when he was still just sixteen.

They made these plans, as did all families of young men at the time, with the understanding that everything could change in an instant if Jeremiah was drafted and sent to Vietnam. The war colored everyone's plans, but none more so than the plans of young men.

The prospect of a guaranteed job for life in a place where jobs were not that easy to come by was exciting to sixteen and even seventeen-year-old Jeremiah. But as July and his eighteenth birthday got closer, he began to wonder if the bookstore was part of the life he wanted. He was tired of fights about book bans, censorship, and the whole First Amendment problem of free speech. He was tired of working all the time.

George and Tammy left Jeremiah to manage the store alone almost every weekend of his senior year. They were always off speaking at some save-the-books protest or some conference about free speech and were often out of the state for days at a time. Jeremiah was exhausted by his parents' activism, even if his only contribution had been to stay behind and mind the store.

He wanted to do *something else* with his life. He just wasn't exactly sure what that would be. He only knew that living and dying in a bookstore while fighting with the spiritual progeny of Millicent Spate was not it. He'd watched his parents long enough to know that no matter where they went, it was always the same fight. George always started his talks the same way:

"I'm George Malone and I want to talk about books."

3

The Clear Spring High School Class of 1970 graduated in May. George and Tammy were already packed and ready to move before Jeremiah received his diploma. They simply had to wait for Jeremiah to turn 18 in July because, as Tammy noted, "We can at least wait until he's officially an adult."

Jeremiah was also ready to move on. He just couldn't figure out how to make that happen. Rather than seeing his eighteenth birthday as the beginning of his independence, Jeremiah saw it as the beginning of his incarceration.

His parents mistakenly interpreted his low enthusiasm for his pre-destined future as a lack of confidence in his ability to do the job.

"Don't worry. You can do this," George told Jeremiah between bites of birthday cake.

"Congratulations." Tammy beamed and put her hand on top of Jeremiah's.

"You've earned it."

Jeremiah smiled and questioned what he must have done to have earned such a depressing fate.

As required by law, Jeremiah registered for the draft the day after his eighteenth birthday. Registration was a rite of passage for young men in the 1970s, perhaps even more so for young men in the rural South. Other parts of the country may have been burning in anti-war protests and seething in civil unrest, but the rural South, where patriotism and religion have always been conflated, provided more than its share of proud military personnel, volunteer and otherwise. For young men from poor families in the South, military service was practically inevitable.

In Clear Spring, Arkansas, to speak against the war was to be unpatriotic. To be unpatriotic was to be against God. To be against God was un-American.

War is holy when you're a true believer.

Beyond the legal requirement to register, Jeremiah saw the military as his way out of the bookstore. Military service, whether it be volunteer or because he'd been drafted, would be an honorable escape from a permanent future in Clear Spring. It removed the need for any explanation or apologies for not taking over the family business. Being in the Army would erase the stigma of having liberal parents in a conservative rural community.

It was also a better fit for how Jeremiah saw himself. Every young man thinks he's a badass. The military was a chance to prove it.

On the Friday after his birthday, George and Tammy watched the store one last time while Jeremiah took the day off. Jeremiah celebrated his last day of freedom by registering for the draft and then enjoying his first legally purchased adult beverages while water skiing at the lake with some friends.

The pilot of the boat—a lanky, long-haired, eighteen-year-old boy called "Skipper"—climbed behind the steering wheel while

Jeremiah got ready for his run. Jeremiah wrapped the ski rope loosely around his wrist as he pushed his feet into the skis. He was adjusting his swimsuit when a speedboat rushed by, exceeding the 35 mile per hour speed limit by at least 30 miles per hour and creating a tsunami-level wave in its wake. The surge lurched Skipper's boat forward. Skipper lost his balance and stumbled. As he struggled to regain his footing, he tripped over something and stomped the gas pedal to the floor. The engine roared, the skis popped off, and the ski rope snapped taut around Jeremiah's wrist with a loud popping sound like the crack of a whip.

Jeremiah's severed hand fell into about ten feet of muddy lake water.

In shock, Jeremiah instinctively reached out to retrieve his lost hand. He opened his mouth to scream, but no sound came out. His mouth opened and closed like a fish gasping for air in the bottom of a boat while what was left of his arm spurted blood in all directions in a pulsating heartbeat rhythm.

Jeremiah watched his detached hand spiral down through the water. The graceful motion was interrupted by a large snapping turtle and two catfish that devoured first the fingers and then the much meatier palm, ripping the thumb away from the rest of the hand and then spitting it out into the bloody water. The thumb eventually hitchhiked its way to the water's edge, looking like a shriveled but positive thumbs-up review for a horror movie.

Skipper saw the rope go slack and circled back around to the now flailing Jeremiah. He assumed Jeremiah had simply let go of the tow bar. He punched the gas pedal when he saw Jeremiah's arm, minus one hand, spurting blood as he waved it frantically above his head.

By the time the boat reached him, Jeremiah's face was a grayish white with blue lips, as if all the blood that provided color and life was suddenly gone. Skipper pulled Jeremiah from the water and wrapped the bloody stump in the Hawaiian shirt he was wearing. He cut a piece of rope from the same rope that had just amputated the hand and made a tourniquet to stop the bleeding.

Jeremiah was still in shock as Skipper and his friends carried him from the boat, put him in a car, and took off for the hospital. One of them raced to the bookstore to tell Tammy and George.

The ER doctors admired the surgical precision of the cut. It was much cleaner than the jagged injuries from animal bites or power tools that usually came in, although ski accidents were not uncommon. Jeremiah's shoulder, however, required more extensive surgery.

"Altogether," the doctor told Jeremiah and his parents, "we're looking at two, maybe three weeks here with us."

"Here? In the hospital?" Jeremiah blinked in disbelief. He blinked again to hold back his tears.

"I'm afraid so," the doctor said. "It'll take four to six weeks for your arm to heal, and that's if we're lucky and there's no infection."

He tried to inject some humor into the situation. "I wouldn't want to drink the water in that lake." No one else laughed.

"That's for the arm," Tammy said. "What about his shoulder?"

The doctor nodded. "Well, that will be healing along with this other injury. He'll be ready to begin light physical therapy in about four, maybe six weeks. We'll just have to wait and see." The doctor picked up the end of Jeremiah's arm and examined the bandage. "We can start fitting the prosthesis in about three months, once the shoulder and everything here is healed up."

After the surgery, Jeremiah was placed in a semi-private room with no privacy. His roommate, Ed, was an older gentleman whose hacking, mucus-gurgling cough triggered Jeremiah's sympathetic gag reflex every time he heard it, which was often. Ed smoked Camel cigarettes between and sometimes during coughing fits. After his first smoke-filled, sleepless night, Jeremiah asked if he could be moved to another room.

"Well," the nurse drawled, "neither one of you is on oxygen, so it's safe. You'll be OK."

George and Tammy returned early the next morning. Tammy lifted the metal cover from Jeremiah's untouched breakfast plate. Jeremiah broke the three pieces of bacon and arranged them into a frowning face. He carefully dropped a tiny Tabasco sauce tear into the corner of one crispy eye.

"I'll take that bacon, if you don't want it," Ed said. George said nothing as he pulled the curtain shut. Jeremiah smiled for the first time since the accident.

"Thank you," he mouthed silently.

At Jeremiah's insistence, George left at 8:30 to open the store. Tammy would not budge. She was still sitting beside Jeremiah's bed when the nurse brought in lunch.

"You don't have to stay," Jeremiah told Tammy after he'd ignored his food for an hour. "It's not like my hand is going to grow back any faster if you're watching it."

He spoke from experience. He'd done nothing but stare at his "missing pieces" since he woke up after surgery.

George and Tammy unpacked the moving truck.

4

As much as he'd been dreading his parents' retirement and his instant promotion to store manager (which didn't feel like a promotion at all), Jeremiah hated being the reason his parents had to put their lives on hold. He knew, from conversations that went unfinished and the Oscars and Emmys on the mantle over the fireplace, that George and Tammy's lives were already very different from what they had hoped they would be. They didn't talk about it much, but Jeremiah had managed to piece a few things together over the years.

Retirement was not the first Malone family dream to be deferred. The bookstore itself, which George Malone liked to call their Second Act, was the result of a dream denied.

In 1954, when Jeremiah was not yet two, the Malones were successful Hollywood screenwriters with Oscars and Emmy Awards, both as a team and as individuals. They partied with movie stars, film directors, politicians, and college professors and enjoyed the kind of fame that happens when your words are spoken by people more beautiful than you.

Like many Hollywood writers, the Malones dreamed of directing their own movies. Their directorial debut, which they had also written, was to be a zombie apocalypse picture. For viewers astute enough to recognize the metaphor, the walking dead brain-eaters represented Cold War authoritarianism with zero tolerance for individuality or dissent. For those who didn't see the connection, it would have been a comedy.

"Too far-fetched?" George asked.

"I don't think so," Tammy said. "Besides, people aren't supposed to think that kind of thing could actually happen here. That's what makes it funny."

From what Jeremiah could piece together—because his parents were not entirely forthcoming—George and Tammy's Hollywood careers ended when someone less well-known and probably even less photogenic told the House Committee on Un-American Activities they were communists. The accusations escalated to Senator Joe McCarthy's anti-communist hearings. In its dogged pursuit of truth and riveting political theater, the Committee never revealed the identity of the informants or what evidence—if any—they offered as proof of the Malones' alleged Communist activity. Like creation itself, it was simply spoken into existence.

Proof was not a priority for the Committee on Un-American Activities. Nor were the First, Fourth, or Fifth Amendments to the Constitution.

George and Tammy were subpoenaed to testify before the House committee.

Their lawyers—which the Malones paid for entirely on their own, with no help from the Screen Writers Guild—told them the Committee, for all its intimidation and bluster, was essentially powerless. This was not a court. There was no judge or jury. Refusing to testify could lead to contempt of Congress, but nothing more. "A slap on the wrist," they said.

George and Tammy knew better. Ten screenwriters—a group that became known as "the Hollywood Ten"—refused to testify, were found to be in contempt of Congress, and all ten of them were sentenced to one year in prison. They were not punished for anything they had done, but for something they refused to do.

"I'm sure that detail will bring a lot of comfort while they're sitting in prison for twelve months," Tammy said as she and George were deciding what to do.

George and Tammy decided to try a different strategy. They would testify before the Committee, avoid the contempt charges, and get back to writing movies.

The Malones—George with his disheveled salt-and-pepper hair, round eyeglasses, and tweed jacket with leather patches on the elbows; Tammy, with her flowing Bohemian skirt and peasant blouse, looking every bit like the writer's muse, even though she could write circles around George most days—introduced themselves to the Committee.

"Are you now or have you ever been a member of the Communist Party of the United States?" bellowed the Senator.

"No," Tammy said.

"And you, Mr. Malone?"

"No," George said. "Not even close." He glanced at his attorney. All the lawyer could do was nod. Under Committee rules, lawyers were not allowed to speak to their clients during questioning.

George leaned closer to the array of microphones before him. "I would…."

The Senator interrupted him.

"Mr. Malone, we will ask the questions."

The Malones could have escaped the purge if they had been willing to provide the Committee with names of other supposed Communists among the Hollywood elite, preferably other writers or actors with greater name recognition than their own. They didn't even have to actually be Communists. Bonus points if the accused happened to be Jewish.

George had had enough. When asked to name names and go home a free man, George's reply was terse:

"With all due respect, Senator, go to hell."

For this, George was held in contempt of Congress. He was tried by a jury of his peers—if a screenwriter can truly have any peers in Washington, D.C.—convicted, and sentenced to three months in a minimum-security prison.

Tammy, who did not tell the Committee where to go, went home after she testified.

Prison was inconvenient, in the way that only steel toilets and thin mattresses can be, but the real punishment came from the movie studios themselves. What power the Committee lacked to punish those who did not cheerfully cooperate was made up for by the studios. Film makers were pressured by investors, advertisers, and other groups to "stop the red menace," even if, as it was in the case of George and Tammy, it wasn't all that red and wasn't especially menacing.

A group of studio executives announced they would not employ anyone who refused to cooperate in the investigations.

The Malones were blacklisted. Studios no longer accepted their scripts. People they thought were friends distanced themselves for fear of guilt by association. Even after George got out of prison, the Malones were still unhireable. They never worked in Hollywood again.

Jeremiah was too young to understand why Dad went away for three months. He couldn't understand why Mom stopped having friends over, why she stopped laughing, or why, once George was back home again, Mom and Dad no longer got dressed to go to work in the morning.

The Malones searched for ways to support themselves and their toddler son. Their search was turning from tiresome to desperate when Tammy saw an ad in one of the trade magazines for a bookstore for sale in a place called Clear Spring, Arkansas. A bookstore in the Ozark Mountains, she explained to George, would provide time to write and an opportunity to work with book publishers and local writers. They might even decide to start writing books. It was a small step towards getting their lives back. With enough time, she thought, they might be able to get back into writing movies or maybe a TV show, perhaps under a pseudonym.

The family packed up their belongings in a U-Haul and moved from California to Arkansas.

George and Tammy went from being Hollywood screenwriters to being Arkansas booksellers.

George even had business cards printed.

"George and Tammy Malone, Booksellers."

They did their best to blend in with their new surroundings, but their California license plates gave them away before they could even say hello. Word spread about the new people who bought the bookstore, along with speculation about how long the Left Coast Liberals would last in Clear Spring.

This perception was not helped by Tammy's reaction to her first sip of sweet tea at the Cozy Kitchen. She said something to George about sugar shock as she stirred the sugary sludge in the bottom of her glass. Jeremiah was already asking for a refill.

If the Malones were middle class in Hollywood, they were absolutely affluent in the mountain communities of rural Arkansas. The success of their movies and the relatively low cost of living compared to that of California meant they had plenty of money. Money from the sale of their California mansion was more than enough to pay cash for the bookstore and still have enough left to build a beautiful home in Clear Spring.

There was also enough money to update the inventory in their new bookstore. The previous owner, once he decided to leave, did not replace books as they were sold. Long, dusty gaps appeared on shelves. It wasn't long before the gaps took up more space than the books.

The less-popular books that remained were not bestsellers. They stood among the empty spaces, like orange cream truffles left in a box of chocolates after everyone takes their favorite piece. Some even had similar thumbprint indentations.

George vowed that there would never be gaps on his shelves.

Tammy Malone passed her love of reading along to her son. Jeremiah turned to books for answers, inspiration, comfort, and joy. George Malone handed down his anger at a government that would attack its own citizens over things they might have written or said or, in the case of their Hollywood careers, whispers that weren't even true.

"Why do you always order so many books?" Jeremiah asked as he was putting new books on the shelves shortly after they had bought the bookstore.

"So there's something for everyone," George said. "The man who isn't allowed to decide what he wants to read has no advantage over the man who can't read."

As he grew up with the bookstore, Jeremiah realized that most people had already decided what they wanted to read long before they came in. Maybe not the specific book, but the type of book, the subject, certain writers. While they had some regulars that Tammy described as "eclectic readers," very few of their customers were looking for books with new ideas.

5

Jeremiah's draft notice arrived about a month after the water ski accident, one week after he got out of the hospital, and several weeks before he was through with rehab. His arm was still in a sling, the end of his arm was still wrapped in bandages, and he was still trying to wrap his mind around losing a hand.

Skipper received his draft notice that same day. They both were told to report to the draft board in Little Rock in one week.

"I wish I'd been on the skis and you were driving the boat," Skipper said.

"Thanks, but it wasn't your fault," Jeremiah said. "You don't have to apologize."

"I wasn't," Skipper said. "I just wish I'd been the one on skis."

Jeremiah laughed. "At least you wouldn't be stuck in Clear Spring for the rest of your life."

"There is that."

They arrived at the draft board one week later. One draftee was on crutches, but stood on both feet when he thought no one was looking. Another complained loudly about his bone spurs.

The Army doctor smirked as he removed the bandages and inspected Jeremiah's arm. "Just last month, huh?" The doctor stamped "4-F" on his draft notice and handed it back to him.

"Congratulations," said the doctor. "I hope it was worth it. You could have just gone to Canada."

"What?" Jeremiah asked. "Why would I go to Canada?"

Skipper and both of his hands were declared fit for service and were sent on to the induction center. Jeremiah rode the bus home alone.

Jeremiah was fitted for his prosthetic hand about ten weeks after the accident, after the stump was healed and his shoulder had recovered from surgery enough to start physical therapy. Rather than wearing the hook-like device preferred by some, Jeremiah's prosthetic was in a fixed position. He could not move the individual fingers. The hand was made of shiny black plastic and covered with a black leather glove. With it, Jeremiah could push things around, carry packages with handles, and pick up a coffee mug as long as it was no more than half full.

Even by motherly standards, Tammy Malone took a special interest in her son's rehabilitation. With his mother as his personal occupational therapist, Jeremiah's physical rehabilitation proceeded faster than expected. He soon learned to do most tasks that ordinarily required two hands, at least the tasks that were important and practical. Carrying boxes or stacks of books with only one hand proved difficult at first, but Jeremiah and his mother learned to stack books on his right arm and hold the stack steady against his chest with his left hand. He adapted enough to play his guitar again, sort of, using a rubber band to hold the guitar pick on the end of his arm while he strummed along.

Jeremiah eventually learned to drive a car and how to cook his own meals with one hand. He adapted to wearing boots that he did not have to tie, so long as he could kick the boots off with his feet and one hand. He kept his room cleaner than George's place was when George and Tammy were dating. He could dress himself, including buttoning up shirts with only one hand when a pullover shirt just wouldn't do. To Tammy, this proved her son could do anything.

The psychological recovery was more difficult. Phantom pains in a hand that was no longer there reminded Jeremiah of what he had lost, along with his self-image, his plans for the future, and his ability to do even simple things without having to think about it. Reaching for something only to be reminded that it was still beyond his grasp. Hitting himself on the chin when he meant to cover a sneeze.

Tammy's faith in her son's rehabilitation convinced Jeremiah that he didn't have to do everything, just what needed to be done. Managing the family bookstore was still a realistic career. Jeremiah became slightly more optimistic about the future.

"It's all within reach," he told his parents, "as long as I'm not reaching with my right arm."

After eight months of relearning how to do almost everything, Jeremiah wanted to move out of the house he grew up in and into the small basement apartment beneath the electronics section of Clear Spring Books & Electronics.

"It'll be easier to watch the store," he explained to his parents.

"Watch the store." George cut a sharp side-eyed glance toward his son. "Is that what the kids are calling it these days?"

Finally living on his own, albeit in the basement apartment of his parents' bookstore, Jeremiah fully enjoyed and exploited the freedom of independent living. Being able to whisper "We should go back to my place" in a young woman's ear felt much more impressive than sneaking a potential overnight guest past George and Tammy and then hoping he could sneak her out of his parents' house before they woke up.

He had just said goodbye after one such sleepover and was getting dressed for work when Tammy knocked on his door.

"We need to talk," she said.

"Mom, I can explain." Jeremiah fumbled for words for a conversation he'd rehearsed many times in his head. "This was the first and only time that has ever happened," he lied. "We were watching TV and she fell asleep. I should have woke her up, but I just let her sleep there on the couch. That's all that happened. I promise."

Tammy wrinkled her eyes. She opened her mouth as if to ask a question. All she managed to say was, "Sit down." She sat on the bed and patted the mattress as a sign for Jeremiah to do the same.

"Skipper's mother just called." She took Jeremiah's hand, took a deep breath, and looked into her son's eyes.

She smiled only slightly as she gently brushed a piece of hair away from Jeremiah's face.

"Skipper is dead."

Jeremiah's heart twisted at the news. His mind replayed scenes of Skipper in his boat, pulling someone on skis, one hand on the steering wheel and the other holding a beer. Or anchored with a couple of fishing poles and a beer. Or just with a beer.

"He was killed in action, in Cambodia," Tammy explained, as if any explanation beyond saying he was in Cambodia was necessary. No one seemed to be able to explain why he or anyone else was there.

Skipper's body arrived in Clear Spring about a week later. Jeremiah was surprised to see an open casket at the viewing. Any injuries that might have caused Skipper's death were covered by his dress uniform and makeup. The obituary talked about Private First Class Edward Gilbert, but all the flower arrangements and cards said "Skipper."

"With a name like that, he should have been in the Navy," George observed, hoping to get at least a smile from Jeremiah.

Jeremiah gently touched the Bronze Star and Purple Heart medals on Skipper's uniform.

"He wasn't given a choice."

Skipper's family asked Jeremiah to serve as a pallbearer. Unlike the other pallbearers, who could lift with either hand, Jeremiah had to be sure to line up on the right side of the casket. He stood at the head of the flag-draped casket, beside the stars of the American flag.

The metal handle felt cold in his hand. Together, the six young men carried Skipper down the six front steps of the church, past the family, and on to the hearse that was parked in front of the church. Jeremiah tried not to look at the faces of Skipper's mom and dad as he walked past. Instead, he focused on the weight of the casket and the open door of the hearse. The ride to the cemetery was silent.

The graveside service was executed with full military honors and precision. Seven veterans, one from WWII, one who served in Korea, and five of whom looked like they could have fought in the Civil War, fired three rounds for the twenty-one-gun salute befitting a Private First Class in the Army. A bugler played taps somewhere in the distance. Jeremiah watched as the flag was ceremoniously folded into a precise triangle and handed to Skipper's mom. Mrs. Gilbert silently clutched the folded flag tight to her breast. She had no tears left to cry.

Jeremiah was surprised by how everything was different, but everything was the same after Skipper died. He didn't go to the lake again, but he still went to work, even if it seemed pointless. He still had dates, even if he didn't feel like saying much. In fact, it was during this period of reflective mourning that Jeremiah had his brief encounter with Mary Olson and her Marine boyfriend.

Skipper had been gone for three months when he died, enough time for Jeremiah to get used to him not being around. So why was he suddenly so lonely? His emotions ran from grief to guilt, both of which were almost too much to bear.

Jeremiah returned to the recruiter's office to volunteer. He argued that with his prosthesis, he could serve in a non-combat position, maybe work at a desk, or do something. Anything to get out of Clear Spring.

"Can you type 35 words per minute?" the recruiter asked.

"No." Although, to be fair, Jeremiah couldn't do that before the accident.

"Can you carry a five-gallon pot of boiling hot water from the stove to the sink?"

"No."

The Navy and the Air Force were the same. Beat down and defeated, he didn't even try for the Marines.

Instead of serving in combat, Jeremiah would service the lonely women left behind. And the best place to meet those lonely women was at church.

Tammy and George were just glad to know their son wouldn't die in a field in Cambodia, even if it had meant losing his right hand.

6

Skipper's death made Jeremiah rethink everything, including how he felt about books. Skipper already loved adventure stories like *Treasure Island* when they met in first grade, but he was not a great reader. Jeremiah was already reading books without pictures—big boy books, as he called them—long before he was enrolled in school. The boys would huddle together inside a small tent Tammy had set up in the back of the store while Jeremiah read and Skipper listened and both of them ate chocolate chip cookies. Later, when they were in high school, they used this same technique to study for tests.

Now, reading just reminded him of Skipper.

First-grade Jeremiah liked the books Skipper picked, even if they were not books he would have read for himself. He did not appreciate being forced to read beginning reader books in the first-grade classroom. "Look, Dick, look!" became Malone family code for saying something was obvious.

Every Friday, Miss Sanders, Jeremiah's first-grade teacher, would pick some lucky student's favorite book to read out loud to the class. Students usually brought books like *Clifford the Big Red Dog* or *One Fish, Two Fish, Red Fish, Blue Fish*. The student whose book was chosen got to sit beside Miss Sanders in the reading circle while the young teacher read. Some of these honored students, usually with Miss Sanders' help, even got to read portions of their book to the class! Others provided enthusiastic commentary while she read, usually describing what was happening in the illustrations or elaborating on the story in some way.

Jeremiah's favorite book was *Where the Wild Things Are*. He counted the days until it was his turn to bring his book to school and show it to Miss Sanders.

"I don't know, Jeremiah," Miss Sanders said as she flipped through the pages. "I don't think Max is a very good boy." Miss Sanders gave the book back to a very disappointed Jeremiah. "I'm afraid the other children might think it's OK to misbehave. Do you think you can find another book to share?"

Jeremiah tried not to cry as he put the book back in his cubby and returned to his seat. He didn't say much for the rest of the day.

As he was going to bed, Jeremiah asked his mom to read *Where The Wild Things Are* to him.

Tammy was puzzled. "You can read that book by yourself," she told him.

"I know," Jeremiah said. "I just want you to read it to me."

Tammy and Jeremiah curled up on his bed with the book. Jeremiah put his head on his mother's shoulder and snuggled in close. Silent tears rolled down the six-year-old's face as Tammy read. She stopped reading and quietly stroked Jeremiah's hair.

"What's wrong?"

Jeremiah sniffled and wiped his nose on the sleeve of his pajamas. "Mrs. Sanders wouldn't read my book in class. She said Max was naughty."

Tammy hugged Jeremiah even tighter and tried to hide her anger at an adult who would poison something her child loved.

"But what did Max learn?" she asked.

Jeremiah closed his eyes. Tammy felt his small shoulders shrug against her body.

Tammy closed the book and hugged her son.

"Max learned that being wild didn't make him happy," Tammy explained. "He learned that being loved meant more to him than being wild."

"His mom loved him," Jeremiah whispered.

"Yes, she did." Tammy turned Jeremiah around so he could see her face as she spoke. "Just like Daddy and I love you." She started reading again, but stopped to say one more thing.

"He also learned that even the Ruler of the Wild Things can always come back home, no matter how wild he might have been." Jeremiah snuggled in close while Tammy finished reading the book.

Later, as she was tucking Jeremiah in, Tammy asked him if he wanted her to talk to Miss Sanders about the book.

"No," Jeremiah said. "I'll just bring another book next time."

One month later, Jeremiah decided to take another favorite, *The Rabbits' Wedding*, to school. He was excited to show it to Miss Sanders and was sure she would read it.

When the time came for him to show her the book, Miss Sanders shook her head without even opening it.

"I'm sorry, Jeremiah," she said. "We can't read this book to the class."

Jeremiah put his hands on his hips and cocked his head to one side.

"Why not?" he demanded.

Miss Sanders pulled him in close and put her face on his level like she was sharing a secret she didn't want the other students to hear.

"Well," she said as she pointed to the rabbits on the cover. "This rabbit is white. And this rabbit is black." She paused and looked at Jeremiah.

"Do you see the problem?"

Jeremiah studied the book's cover and the drawing of two rabbits holding hands. He slowly shook his head.

"No," he said in all innocent sincerity. "I don't."

"Well." Miss Sanders cleared her throat and whispered in Jeremiah's ear.

"A white rabbit would not marry a black rabbit."

George and Tammy exploded when Jeremiah told them what Miss Sanders said. They visited the school and confronted the teacher during recess. Miss Sanders said the book violated district policy about the use of Black characters in children's books. She said she was simply doing her job.

"We're talking about rabbits," George said. "Rabbits. And even if they weren't rabbits, I still don't see the problem."

"I think we both know this story is not about rabbits, Mr. Malone."

"Oh. I see," George said. "Would it be OK if the black rabbit was gray? Brown, maybe? I suppose dapple is totally out of the question."

Miss Sanders raised one eyebrow and forced a twisted, tight-lipped smile. "We have to be careful about what we teach our children about these things. We don't want them to get any wrong ideas. Friends are fine, maybe, but not marriage."

George and Tammy went to the school's principal where they were told the same thing only in more legalistic language. "The district has strict policies about stories related to miscegenation and other crimes related to race. Mixed marriages are against the law in Arkansas."

George got up and walked out of the office.

"The law is wrong," Tammy said as she stood to leave. She stopped at the office door and looked back at the principal.

"And so are you."

Later that night, George and Tammy discussed their options.

"It's just one more thing he'll have to learn at home," Tammy said. She didn't know it at the time, but the list of things Jeremiah would have to learn at home would grow longer every year.

Rabbits or no rabbits, George was furious that a first grade teacher was promoting segregationist views in the classroom. He was infuriated that such views were school policy.

"We could homeschool," George said. "But what message will we send if we pull Jeremiah out of school now? People will think we agree with the racists." He gave a sarcastic smile. "But, hey! We'll fit right in."

Indeed, many white parents had started homeschooling because they did not want their children in class with Black kids. One of the local churches was rumored to be considering starting a private school "to prevent the mixing of the races." These parents agreed with and had voted for Alabama Governor and presidential candidate George Wallace, who famously said "Segregation now, segregation tomorrow, segregation forever."

George and Tammy decided to keep Jeremiah in school and to teach him that not everything a teacher said was true. "Sometimes teachers and even schools make mistakes," George told Jeremiah. "This was one of those times."

"I just wanted everyone to read about Max," Jeremiah said. "And I like rabbits."

"I think we can fix this," Tammy told him. That evening, Tammy ordered a dozen copies of *Where The Wild Things Are*. Jeremiah took them to school and quietly gave them to his friends when Miss Sanders wasn't looking. For Christmas, he gave them the blacklisted *Alice In Wonderland*.

Jeremiah's secret book club—and by extension, Jeremiah—became very popular. It wasn't long before kids who weren't in Jeremiah's class or who weren't even in first grade were asking for books. Jeremiah sold secret books from his parents' store to second graders, third graders, and even a few sixth-grade girls who told him he was cute.

The sixth-grade girls got their books for free.

Miss Sanders found out about Jeremiah's secret book club when one of Jeremiah's friends asked her to read *Wizard of Oz*. The classic story had been banned for its depiction of magic and for the unrealistic depiction of women in strong leadership roles. In what amounted to his friend becoming a confidential informant in exchange for a lesser sentence, the student confessed and told Miss Sanders that Jeremiah had given him the book.

Miss Sanders called Jeremiah's parents.

"I don't know if you're aware, but Jeremiah has been giving inappropriate books to his friends."

"I know," Tammy told her. "Would you like one?"

Once again, George and Tammy were called into the principal's office to answer for their son's behavior. George told the Principal the same thing he told the House Committee on Un-American Activities.

"With all due respect, go to hell."

The Malones went to Jeremiah's classroom and told Miss Sanders they would be taking their son home early that day. The ride home was silent as each of them thought, steamed, or grieved about what they had experienced.

"It's not fair," Jeremiah said from the back seat.

Tammy turned around to look at him as best she could in the station wagon's front seat.

"What's not fair?" she asked.

Jeremiah looked out the window and then back at her. His voice was soft. Not angry, not defiant, just soft. And sad.

"Those books deserve to be read."

7

George and Tammy built the "Books That Deserve To Be Read" display the following weekend. Jeremiah proudly donated his beloved copy of *Where the Wild Things Are* as the first book in the children's category.

Books That Deserve To Be Read was a collection of books banned or challenged in various places around the world, but mostly in schools and public libraries across the United States. It began as a modest table tucked away in the store's back corner with only a handful of books, some posterboard, and lettering that resembled an ambitious junior high class project. George soon realized that the table was not big enough to hold all the banned books. He added two wire racks to hold more. Then he put more wire racks on top of the table. Their small tabletop display grew into an impressive pyramiding tower of books. Local shoppers were happy to have choices of which Millicent Spate would not approve.

As word spread, Books That Deserve To Be Read became even more popular with visitors from out of town. And those visitors almost always bought several books.

As the months passed, George and Tammy talked about replacing the banned books display with traditional Christmas decorations for holiday shoppers. But the display was already so well-known and had sold so many books that they didn't want to remove it for something as temporary as a holiday, even if that holiday brought in more shoppers than any other time of year.

George and Tammy decided to make Books That Deserve To Be Read a permanent part of the store. They moved the table and wire racks to the front window so it could be seen from the street. Tammy worked on the display until it looked like something you might see in a bookstore in Hollywood, or at least in a Hollywood movie about a small town bookstore.

Books That Deserve To Be Read became the bookstore's visual centerpiece and its philosophical focus.

It wasn't long before people from all around the South were traveling to Clear Spring, Arkansas to see what was considered an honor roll of contested literary works. Newspapers in Little Rock, Memphis, and St. Louis recommended the bookstore specifically as a weekend destination trip, "something to do after you've seen the Dogwoods blooming." A book reviewer in New York called it "a shrine to free speech in the most unlikely place." A paper in Los Angeles, the same newspaper that reported on George and Tammy's testimony before the Un-American Activities Committee, wrote a Sunday feature article about "Once-Banned Writers Defend Banned Books."

Parents picked up *Charlotte's Web* or *The Giving Tree* and wondered why books they read and loved as children were banned.

The Diary of Anne Frank, Huckleberry Finn, and *To Kill a Mockingbird* were right there in plain sight for all to see, read, and be subverted.

Some residents of Clear Spring were happy to see a local business taking a brave stand on an important issue. Business owners appreciated the out-of-town shoppers that were drawn in by the bookstore and its increasingly famous display. The local restaurants and the hotel thrived because of the bookstore.

Other people in Clear Spring were not so happy. Complaints usually picked up between Vacation Bible School season and the start of the new school year. For perspective, George placed colorful satin bookmarks at some of the Bible's more egregious scriptures about incest, smashing the skulls of children, and other disturbing images, and read these verses to visitors who complained about having banned books so prominently displayed.

National press coverage inevitably mentioned how the Malones bought the bookstore after they were blacklisted in Hollywood, a fact that did not go unnoticed by the more xenophobic residents of Clear Spring. A growing and increasingly loud minority, led by a Millicent, believed a store that promoted banned books was just one more example of everything wrong with society. In Millicent's opinion, most of what was wrong with the country originated in California.

"For example," she would say when talking to her faithful, "look at the Malones."

In one of her more scathing Letters to the Editor of the local newspaper, Millicent—who, unlike Jeremiah, believed with all her heart that God *was* on her side—called the collection "an abomination that will bring a plague on our city, our state, and our nation unless we stop it now." These objections sometimes escalated to action, usually as a petition or a small protest in front of the bookstore and usually during political seasons or church revival meetings.

George and Tammy routinely received threats to their business and their lives. Bomb threats were not uncommon, even if they never proved to be true. But the blacklisted former screenwriters held firm. The display not only remained, it grew.

"This is not a store. It's a statement," George told Jeremiah as Millicent and her followers and their picket signs marched in a circle in front of the store.

"Without those books," George said, "we might as well close the bookstore."

"With those books, you might have to," Jeremiah said.

For the Malones, Books That Deserve To Be Read wasn't some gimmick designed to draw in customers. It had become a mission. It was about the fundamental right to free speech, a right he and Tammy were denied when their screenwriter careers were derailed. The First Amendment was as important to George and Tammy Malone as the Second Amendment was to the most gun-loving Arkansans.

The original display was mostly fiction. The exception was the very factual *Diary of Anne Frank*. That wasn't because of any specific decision to focus on fiction. George and Tammy simply could not imagine that people would want to ban actual facts.

They were wrong. Turns out, there were many facts that certain people wanted banned. Ignored. Forgotten.

And some stories were revised and retold by people who would have preferred to tell the facts but were not permitted to do so.

Mr. Crow, Clear Spring High School's only history teacher, kept his desk completely clear except for a framed picture of his wife and five children and a coffee mug that he nursed throughout the day. Student papers were kept in perfectly aligned, color-coded stacks on a table beside the desk, one stack for each of the six history classes he taught each day. Students gave their completed work to Mr. Crow, then he and only he would turn and place the papers in the appropriate stack.

Mary Waller, in an especially deep post-test stupor, forgot to give her midterm exam directly to Mr. Crow and simply placed it on top of the other third hour papers. Mr. Crow, who had been talking with a small group of students at his desk, stopped mid-sentence. He turned away from his conversation, picked up the entire stack of third hour papers, tapped them on the desk three times, rotated the stack ninety degrees and tapped it three times again, and then tapped it three more times after he'd rotated the stack back to its original upright position. He then carefully returned the stack to its rightful place on the table and placed his hand, palm down, on top of the stack before returning to the conversation.

Mr. Crow hated ragged edges. In his perfect world, everything sat on a square grid.

History helped Mr. Crow make sense of the chaos he saw all around him, smoothing the ragged edges of human behavior and making things line up straight. Seemingly random actions of individuals and nations took on new meanings when seen in the proper historical context. That context required facts. Mr. Crow tolerated historical inaccuracies about as well as he tolerated an uneven stack of papers.

The history curriculum required Mr. Crow to teach the Lost Cause narrative of the Civil War, a post-war Southern-friendly revision of history in which the war was about states' rights, not slavery. What rights the states specifically wanted—the right to own another human being—was mentioned only in passing. In the Lost Cause revisionist story, slavery was depicted as a benevolent institution in which compassionate slave owners provided free food and housing to laborers who sang while they worked in the fields. In this alternative version of American history—the basis for statues of Confederate heroes across the South—slave owners were not depicted as cruel masters, but as small business owners who treated their workers with collegial affection.

Mr. Crow knew this wasn't true. Pictures of hangings and scars from whips striking the backs of Black men were evidence of their physical abuse. The varied skin tones across the South were living evidence of the abuse of enslaved women.

This revisionist history sickened Mr. Crow. He agonized over every lie, every ragged untruth that he presented to his students as fact. But he also had a mortgage, a car payment, and five hungry children. When confronted with the choice between historical accuracy and economic survival, he chose to teach about the Lost Cause and the noble South and keep his job.

Mr. Crow lied and took a swig of Maalox. Another lie, another swig. He didn't even bother to pour it into a cup anymore; it was easier to drink straight from the bottle. He looked forward to teaching something less stressful, like the bombing of Hiroshima. At least he wouldn't have to lie about the atrocities.

The more perceptive students sensed Mr. Crow's conflict. When these students asked the right questions, which, in the eyes of the school were the *wrong* questions to be asking, Mr. Crow told them to see him after class. Then he wrote out a prescription on a prescription pad that he and George Malone created as a joke but had actually become quite useful.

"*The Strange Career of Jim Crow* is a good baseline antibiotic for this type of thing", Mr. Crow told students who knew something wasn't quite right with what was printed in the textbook. Crow also recommended *Black Reconstruction in America* by W. E. B. Du Bois if stronger treatment was required. As he would with any prescription, Mr. Crow warned students about sharing with other students. The Clear Spring School Board considered these books subversive and punished students who were caught reading them in class.

It wasn't long before several teachers had prescription pads of their own and were writing orders for books about science, world religions, and novels that were intentionally omitted from the school's required reading list.

But the most requested books of all were about human sexuality. Not salacious books about forbidden love, but factual books about basic human reproduction put in the most clinical terms possible.

Sex ed in Clear Spring was taught in seventh and eighth grade PE classes, after volleyball season (if you were a girl) and football season (if you were a boy) and before the start of basketball season, a period commonly known among the students as "Sex Week." The girls were taught by Mrs. Henderson, a former women's state shotput champion with a voice like a referee whistle whose primary motivation at this point was to hang on long enough to retire. The boys were taught by her husband and boys' wrestling coach Mr. Henderson, who shared his wife's belief that sex was a necessary evil, or at least it was when it was with Mrs. Henderson.

Sex Week always began with photographs from the Tuskegee untreated syphilis study with no explanation other than this is what happens to people who have sex before marriage. There was no mention of the ethical problems of intentionally withholding medical treatment for decades for the purpose of research. The graphic pictures were so shocking that students rarely noticed that all the men were Black. Students were told they were seeing pictures of what untreated syphilis does to the human body, which they were. They were not told that they were witnessing the effects of institutional racism.

Mr. and Mrs. Henderson must have coordinated with the school cooks because the cafeteria always served corndogs during Sex Week.

The Tuskegee pictures were the first day. On the second day, students were shown cartoon drawings of a happy sperm dressed in a tuxedo and a top hat carrying a bouquet of daisies to a smiling human egg with blonde hair in a flip hairdo and a wedding veil. The cartoons were on a plain white background. It was hard to tell if the sperm was swimming, walking, or flying through the air. The girls assumed the sperm was swimming. The boys knew it could be doing any of those three things.

The home economics teacher, a young woman named Miss Brooks who thought she would be teaching students to bake bread but ended up being an unofficial counselor to most of the seventh grade girls, was appalled. The problem was obvious: the lack of honest information about contraception, physical and emotional changes during puberty, and the "Just Say No" mentality of the Hendersons put students at risk.

The Malones gave Miss Brooks one of their emergency prescription pads. While Tammy was happy to provide any book that Miss Brooks or her students might request, she found that students were uncomfortable carrying around large or even normal sized books about human sexuality. She ordered small, easy to hide pamphlets from Planned Parenthood and the National Institutes of Health.

Miss Brooks lasted one semester at Clear Spring Junior High before she was asked to leave.

To George and Tammy, it felt all too familiar.

After Miss Brooks was fired, George and Tammy became less interested in writing books and movies and more concerned with fighting book bans. For the first time in a long time, they talked over dinner about what happened to them in Hollywood and what Senator Joseph McCarthy had done to them. This was all new to Jeremiah, who was too young when they moved to remember their pre-Arkansas life. The McCarthy hearings were not part of the regular history curriculum at Clear Spring.

Jeremiah was closing up the store alone one Thursday night when he heard something about the McCarthy hearings on all four of the TVs they had in the showroom. This was the first time he'd heard anyone other than his parents mention the name Joe McCarthy. He was glad to have official TV confirmation that they weren't making it up.

He grabbed a chair from behind the counter, turned off three of the TVs, and sat down to watch.

As Jeremiah watched the Special Report, he realized he had never really considered the national implications of what was a very personal tragedy for his parents. For the first time, he thought about what had been taken from his parents and their fellow writers: their careers, their homes, and, in a very real way, their lives. He wondered how much of George and Tammy's decision to move to Clear Spring instead of staying to fight for their careers was because of him. Would such a fight even have been possible to win?

The program concluded with a "If you'd like to know more…" segment that included a list of books.

"We have that book!" Jeremiah said as the list scrolled up the screen. He said it again when he recognized another title, *None Dare Call It Conspiracy*, by Gary Allen.

"Who was it that bought that?" Jeremiah whispered to himself.

The list concluded with *The Crucible*, by Arthur Miller.

"And I've read that one," Jeremiah said to no one. "I wonder why that was banned?"

The Crucible was not part of the recommended reading list for students at Clear Spring High School. Jeremiah saw it on the Books That Deserve To Be Read table the summer after eighth grade and decided to read it. For some reason, he never discussed the book with his parents. It just didn't come up.

Jeremiah wondered why *The Crucible* would be included on a list about McCarthy. Then he realized what he'd missed as an eighth grader. Both stories, fact and fiction, were about innocent people accused of things they didn't do. Both asked for false confessions and for the names of others. Both included a hero that refused to cooperate.

As a commercial for toilet paper played in the background, Jeremiah picked up *The Crucible* from the Books That Deserve To Be Read display. The publication date was 1953. Miller wasn't being prophetic; at the time, he might as well have been writing the evening news. Jeremiah smiled at how his younger self had missed such an obvious connection.

The program ended and Jeremiah turned off the TV. He put *The Crucible* back on the table. As he did, he noticed another book that was on the recommended reading list, *The Politician* by Robert Welch. *Jeremiah* took it home and started reading it that night.

The dense writing and convoluted conspiracy theories made *The Politician* difficult to read, but Jeremiah was determined to wade through the bog. His mouth dropped as he read praise for the infamous Senator Joe McCarthy and theories of global conspiracies.

"Why do we have *The Politician* on the display?" he asked George that Saturday.

"Because the John Birch Society was afraid they'd be sued if it was published," George explained. "That's the short answer. It wasn't officially banned like most of these. It was blocked by people who thought it was not in their best interest for it to be sold, even though they fundamentally agreed with what it said."

"That's why it was banned," Jeremiah said. "That's not why we have it on the display or why we're even selling it in our store." He walked to the table and picked up *None Dare Call It Conspiracy*. "This one too."

George was impressed. "You've read that, too?"

"No," Jeremiah admitted. "But it was on the list of books about McCarthy. I assume it's the same kind of thing."

George took *None Dare Call It Conspiracy* from Jeremiah's hand and set it back on the table.

"First, never criticize a book you haven't read for yourself. Secondly, you're exactly right. That writer is even more paranoid than McCarthy. And probably just as crazy."

"So why are we selling these books?" Jeremiah demanded.

"Why wouldn't we?" George asked.

"After everything that happened to you and Mom…" Jeremiah spoke in his strongest, you've-got-to-be-kidding-me voice. He looked to the ceiling, smiled and looked to the floor, and then put his hands on his hips and just shook his head.

"That's exactly why it is there," George said. "So people will see those ideas for what they are. Crazy. Paranoid. Wrong. People tend to forget those things. We can't let them forget."

Jeremiah tried to be nonchalant as he straightened the books on the table.

"Are we still planning on me becoming manager after I graduate and you retire?"

George looked puzzled, as if he was trying to connect *The Politician* to his family's future plans.

"Yes," he said. "That's the plan. The day after you turn eighteen."

"Then my first official act will be to get rid of that book."

"Are you planning on getting rid of every book you don't like?"

"Yes," Jeremiah smirked. "What's the point of owning a bookstore if I can't decide which books I want to sell?"

George handed the stack of conspiracy books back to Jeremiah.

"What's the point of fighting for free speech if you're going to ban books you don't like?"

8

Unknown to Tammy, Jeremiah's rehabilitation also included learning to use his fake hand to his romantic advantage. First, he slowly acclimated the target of his affection to the prosthesis, capitalizing on her natural curiosity while shying away from any specific explanations about how his injury happened. If asked, he would say, "I don't like to talk about it," maintaining both an air of mystery and the unspoken possibilities of heroism or, at the very least, tragedy. Even the women who knew how he lost his hand were intrigued. Once normalized, the private unveiling of his arm without the artificial hand created a sense of intimacy, like a secret you only shared with someone special.

If all else failed, there was the sympathy factor.

George chose to overlook his son's sexual indiscretions. To him, illicit romance was Jeremiah's consolation prize for losing a hand. God, or the Universe, or someone owed the kid that much. Tammy preferred to remain intentionally uninformed about her son's love life. Jeremiah gratefully granted her request.

By the time Jeremiah turned nineteen, George was ready to move on to retirement. He was convinced Jeremiah could manage the family business. Tammy reluctantly agreed. She did not want to leave Jeremiah, but she also could not deny that he was ready.

"A year ago, we were just glad you were alive," George said to Jeremiah. "You could have lost more than your hand in that lake.

Now, we are happy to turn the store over to you." He handed Jeremiah his own box of business cards.

"Jeremiah Malone, Bookseller."

George and Tammy left for Florida two days later. Jeremiah accepted his disappointing fate as the forever manager of Clear Spring Books & Electronics. He didn't feel like he had much of a choice.

But it wasn't a total loss. At age nineteen, Jeremiah's parents left him with a job that paid decently well and required minimal physical labor, and a home in which to live rent free. Best of all, there was no one in the area who might question him about his increasingly questionable life choices when it came to relationships. And while he'd made some dubious decisions in the past, especially regarding women, he intended to make many more mistakes in the future.

Jeremiah immediately moved out of the basement apartment at the store and back into his parents' house. Young women were impressed by his nice home and either didn't know or quickly forgot that the house and everything in it belonged to Jeremiah's parents. It was, in fact, one of the more upscale homes in Clear Spring, with décor and furnishings that reflected Tammy's West Coast taste more than anything in Arkansas.

Jeremiah's amorous affairs were assisted by religion's oldest allies, guilt and shame, both of which significantly reduced the likelihood of the blushing ladies of the church sharing stories about their romantic flings. It also helped that Jeremiah was good-looking.

With a classically handsome face, dark curly hair, and muscular build, Jeremiah looked as good in overalls as he did when he dressed up for church. He had mastered both the art of small talk and the skill of making eye contact during deeper conversations.

After only a few months of whirlwind romances and one-night stands, he became known as the kind of boy you date, but not the kind you marry. He also developed the reputation of being the kind of man women eventually leave. This was not an accident, but by design. Let her, not him, decide this relationship wasn't going anywhere. Let her get bored enough to look for something different. He could survive being left. He mourned the loss of his hand more than he grieved the loss of any relationship, with the possible exception of his friendship with Skipper. Seeing the expression on a woman's face when he told her it was over hurt more than any amputation. He'd rather be on the receiving end of that.

Jeremiah had been living on his own for almost a year when Susan Larch, a doe-eyed eighteen-year-old peroxide blonde, moved to town. Susan came from a military family and naturally assumed the missing hand was a war wound. She never asked Jeremiah how he lost his hand. Jeremiah met her before any of the women in her new church home could warn her about him, how he actually lost his hand, and how he used those circumstances to manipulate more than just their feelings.

One night, after planting a lingering, seductive, eyes-closed kiss on the scarred end of Jeremiah's bare stump, Susan asked him about the missing hand.

"I don't like to talk about it." Jeremiah pulled his arm back as if wounded and aimed his big blue eyes directly at Susan. Unlike his active serial fornication, this was a more passive sin of omission.

Also omitted on a particularly passionate Sunday afternoon was any form of contraception. Jeremiah may have been able to carry boxes and play guitar, but cellophane wrappers proved difficult to open with one hand, especially in the heat of passion. He watched helplessly as an excited, totally inexperienced, and increasingly frustrated Susan ripped the package open with her teeth and dramatically spat the cellophane corner from her mouth before closing her eyes and laying back on the bed, her hand and the open package raised high in victory. The sharp, serrated cellophane corner spun past Jeremiah's eyelashes and bounced off his right eye.

Susan interpreted Jeremiah's pained gasp as a sign that time was of the essence and threw caution to the floor, where it remained unfurled until morning.

Susan told Jeremiah she was pregnant eight weeks later. Then she told her parents, Colonel Howard Larch, US Army, retired, and Mrs. Larch.

"There is only one way to make this right," the Colonel conceded after he demanded to know how this happened, as if the basic mechanics of human reproduction had somehow changed in this particular case. The ambivalent couple were to be married the next weekend, in her parents' home, because getting married was what pregnant high school girls did in Arkansas in 1972.

Jeremiah convinced himself that he loved Susan. At the very least, he could learn to love her, just like he had learned to make do with only one hand. If she was going to have his child, he reasoned, the least he could do was to learn how to love her. Marriage wasn't that different from rehabilitation. He repeated this until he almost believed it. He wanted to sound convincing when he called his parents.

George and Tammy were thrilled when Jeremiah called to tell them he'd found "the one" and that he and Susan would be getting married. The excitement changed when Jeremiah told them they were going to be grandparents. They were still excited, but in a very different way.

"What were you thinking?" George growled. "I assumed you had enough sense to know how to prevent this kind of thing. Clearly, I was wrong."

Jeremiah resisted the temptation to describe how his eye injury disrupted his usual routine and accepted his father's comments in silence.

George lived in Clear Spring long enough to know how his unintended grandchild would be treated in a small Southern town. This might have worked in California. It was not going to work in

Clear Spring, Arkansas. He also knew that simply getting married before the baby arrived would not be enough.

"People will call him a bastard," George said.

That was enough for Jeremiah. "We won't be the first newlywed couple here to have a premature baby," Jeremiah reminded his father.

"Really?" George's sigh filled the silence on the line. "What part of this sounds like you didn't screw around and get a girl pregnant? I give this thing six months at the most."

Jeremiah reeled from his father's disappointment but would later admit the words were eerily prophetic.

"Your mother and I are perfectly happy here in Florida," George continued. "I do not want to come rescue you, especially since you created this problem. I don't know what you're going to do but I suggest you figure it out."

"I didn't ask for your help," Jeremiah snapped.

"No, you didn't" George said. "I just wanted you to know what our answer will be when you do."

Both men waited for the other to apologize, but neither one did.

Tammy broke the silence. "What do her parents think of this?" she asked.

"They want us to get married."

"Right away?"

"Her dad wanted us to get married this weekend but I told him I wanted to invite you and Dad to the wedding."

"Really," George said. "No doubt he was thrilled that his daughter had found true love. And so quickly. How long have you known this girl?"

Tammy ignored her husband. "We will be there, won't we George?"

George was silent.

"We will be there. Won't. We. George?"

"Yeah," George muttered. "We'll be there."

"It'll be nice," Tammy said after George hung up. "We can see the bookstore, maybe visit a few friends, and meet the mother of our grandchild!"

"Nice. Right." George pulled out the Clear Spring phone book they had brought with them when they moved. "We're going to need to get a hotel."

"Why?" Tammy asked. "We don't need a hotel. We can stay with Jeremiah."

"On his wedding night?" George reminded her. "But, hey, sounds like they've already had the honeymoon. No surprises there. Maybe we can sleep in the very bed in which our grandchild was conceived."

9

It was just after midnight on Friday morning when George and Tammy arrived at the Clear Spring Motor-In. George, usually a fan of clever business names, ignored the malapropism, which he attributed more to bad spelling than any real attempt at humor.

"Here's your key," the clerk said. He pointed to a building with large windows on the other side of the street. "And if you get hungry, Clear Spring's only twenty-four hour diner is right over there. Right where it says *EAT*."

"I know about the Cozy Kitchen," George said. "We used to live here." The overnight crowd usually consisted of State Troopers, truck drivers, and random local insomniacs who wanted to get out of the house.

After sixteen hours on the road, all George and Tammy wanted was sleep. They'd driven straight through because, as George said as he nodded and weaved for the last two hundred miles of the trip, "It's ridiculous to stop when we're this close." Food was one of the last things they wanted.

The absolute last thing they wanted was to see Millicent Spate sitting in a window booth at the Cozy Kitchen, talking to someone, and then waving at them from across the street. George acknowledged her wave with a head nod and nothing more. He felt Millicent's eyes following him as they took their suitcases out of the trunk and went to their room.

Tammy woke up the next morning excited to see her son. She was dressed and ready to go by the time George got out of the shower.

"We should go over there now. I'll fix him a good breakfast."

"Not sure that's a great idea," George said. "What if she's there?"

"Oh," Tammy said. "Jeremiah didn't say they were already living together."

"Clearly they have slept together," George reminded her. "Can we at least call first?"

Tammy glared at her husband and waited for Jeremiah to answer the phone. They agreed to skip breakfast and to meet at the store at 8:00.

"Told you," George said.

"You don't know that she was there," Tammy said.

"No, I don't. And you don't know that she wasn't."

George and Tammy arrived at the bookstore at 7:30. Jeremiah was still not there, so George used his key to get in. They were behind the counter, George reading the Little Rock newspaper he picked up at the motel and Tammy with a cup of coffee she'd made in the office, when Jeremiah walked in.

"You're late," George said. He smiled at his son. "Just like old times."

"Yeah," Jeremiah sighed. "Just like old times."

Jeremiah promised to introduce them to Susan later that morning. He was in the process of telling his parents what little he knew about his future wife when the bell on the door dinged.

They looked up to see Millicent walking toward the counter.

"I hear congratulations are in order," she said with way too much enthusiasm. "I understand you two just met? How romantic."

Jeremiah read his father's reaction. "I didn't tell her."

Millicent huffed. "There are no secrets in small towns."

"What can I do for you, Millicent?" George asked. "I don't suppose you want to read anything."

"I've missed you, too, George," she said. "And you, Tammy. It's just not the same without you. Your son here is smart enough but he doesn't really have your passion for the fight."

"Maybe he just has better things to do," George said. "Was there a reason you came by?"

"Not really," she said. "I saw you last night when you walked by the diner but you looked tired. I figured you'd be here so I thought I'd come by say hello." She looked at the Books That Deserve To Be Read display and then at Jeremiah.

"Still selling dirty books, I see."

"They're not dirty books," Tammy said. "They are books that have been banned. There's a big difference."

"Banned because they were dirty," Millicent said. "Or subversive, like your hippy friends in California. Or for some other perfectly legitimate reason. My point is that they don't belong in Clear Spring. They never did."

"Always nice to see you Millicent," George said with a forced smile. "Now, if you're not going to buy something, would you please leave."

"I've been thinking." Millicent scanned the room, with its rows of bookshelves, the books lining the walls, and the chairs in the readers' circle. "Someone who wanted to sell something worthwhile could really work with this."

"We already sell Bibles, if that's what you mean by worthwhile," George said proudly. "It's the best-selling of all the banned books."

"The first book to ever be banned," Jeremiah added.

Millicent ignored their comments and pointed to different parts of the store. "You could put Bibles there, commentaries over there, maybe even have a space for appropriate novels to replace that smut you sell. And I could have an entire section for people who homeschool."

She pointed to the electronics side of the store. "I could take that out and have church right in there."

"I'm sure," George said. "And you could have them walk through the gift shop as they come in and as they leave. Just like Cracker Barrel."

"I could." Millicent smiled as she considered the possibilities.

George looked around his store. "Of course, you'd have to drive out the demons. You know, to purify the place."

Tammy nodded in agreement with her husband. "And you'd better watch out for a guy in a robe turning over the tables and chasing you out."

"Not me," Millicent said. "I'm not the one who purifies." She picked up the Bible from the display but didn't open it. Her eyes closed as she recited a passage.

"For he will be like a refiner's fire…"

"I know," George interrupted. "Old Testament. Malachai, Chapter 3, verse 2." George tilted his head slightly and showed Millicent a flatline smile.

"I've read it, too."

10

Being married and pregnant changed everything in Susan's life. College, which had been her plan after high school, was no longer an option. Employers were reluctant to hire an inexperienced young woman who had only recently moved to town and who would be leaving the company once she had the baby, if she lasted that long. She was still new in town and didn't have many friends. The only people she had met were people at her church and they weren't being very friendly to a girl who got pregnant as soon as she moved to town.

Susan tried working at the bookstore, but she had not grown up dreaming of running a cash register and dusting book covers. She certainly did not know how to answer customer questions about the history or the importance of Books That Deserve To Be Read. She never thought about book bans and had no opinion on the matter. She was, in a word, bored. In three words, she was bored, lonely, and pregnant.

Dark circles formed under her eyes. Showering and changing clothes required too much effort. She stopped eating altogether and was losing weight, dangerous signs for a pregnant woman. Her mother started dropping by during the day to make sure she ate something.

Susan stopped going to the bookstore after her first trimester. After the second trimester, she moved back to her parents' house, so her mom could take care of her, and didn't return to Jeremiah's home for the rest of her pregnancy.

Jeremiah dropped by the Larches' house every night after work but was never invited to spend the night. Susan didn't feel right sleeping with him in her parents' home.

"Even though we're married?" he asked. "And you're already pregnant."

"I don't know," Susan said. "It just doesn't feel right. What if they hear us?"

"I'll try not to snore."

Susan came by the bookstore a few times before the baby was born. When she did, she sat on the couch, stared straight ahead, and said nothing until she got up to leave. Eventually she stopped coming altogether. Jeremiah called her at night, but they didn't say much to one another. The pregnancy really was the only thing they had in common.

When the time came, Susan's mom called Jeremiah to say they were on the way to the hospital to have the baby.

"Do you want to meet us there?" she asked.

Like most fathers-to-be in the 1970s, Jeremiah sat in the waiting room while the baby was delivered. Susan was already holding the baby when the nurses let the proud father come in.

They named the boy Zachary.

Susan's face beamed. "He has two hands!" She kissed each of Zachary's tiny fingers.

"I guess that means he's not mine," Jeremiah joked.

Susan pouted playfully.

"I know things have been weird," she told Jeremiah, "but it's going to be better now. We'll make it work." For the first time in a long time, she reached for Jeremiah's hand. In her post-delivery fog, she kissed the cold prosthesis instead.

Clear Spring was a small town of less than 10,000 people. With such a small population, Clear Spring Hospital didn't deliver many babies. The weekly list of birth announcements in the local Sunday newspaper was short and memorable. Zachary Allen Malone was the only baby on that Sunday's list.

Susan moved back in with Jeremiah. They put Zachary's crib in Jeremiah's old bedroom. Model airplanes still hung in the air, suspended from the ceiling with fishing line when Jeremiah was in junior high. A poster of Earth taken during one of the Apollo moon missions still hung on the wall.

"I'll take that stuff down and put up some baby stuff," Jeremiah said. "Maybe paint the walls a light blue. We'll put up pictures of circus animals. Maybe Snoopy and Charlie Brown. And I'll put a rocking chair over there."

Susan put Zachary in his crib and went back to bed without saying a word. She spent most of her days in bed, but she never really felt like she rested. When she did manage to try to comfort her son, nothing seemed to work. She stood by Zachary's bed and watched him cry, unable to console her child and exhausted from trying. This made her feel even more inadequate and more depressed.

She eventually stopped picking Zachary up and just waited for the sound to stop, which it rarely did. Jeremiah started closing the store at lunch, something he never did before, just so he could come home and check on Susan and the baby. At night, it was Jeremiah who got up to take care of Zachary and rock him back to sleep. In the mornings, the first and sometimes only person Zachary saw until lunch was Jeremiah.

Jeremiah found himself nodding off behind the counter at the store. Customers had to wake him up when they wanted to buy a book. He thought about putting a louder bell on the door but never got around to doing it.

Susan's father, Colonel Howard Larch, US Army, retired, learned about Jeremiah's reputation, about his injury, and about the stolen valor soon after Zachary was born. He relayed this information to his daughter, along with strong recommendations regarding what she should do next and what he would do if she didn't.

Jeremiah learned of the Colonel's plan when he came home from the bookstore and saw Susan's clothes in the backseat of her parents' car. He went inside and saw Colonel and Mrs. Larch sitting on his couch with Susan sitting between them, holding a sobbing, screaming Zachary on her shoulder. She simply stared straight ahead and had no expression on her face. Her eyes were red and very wet.

"You're finally here." The Colonel stood with military posture. He stared at Jeremiah while he addressed his daughter.

"Susan, give him the baby and let's go."

Susan slowly stood and handed Zachary to Jeremiah. Then she kissed her baby on the top of his head.

"Goodbye, little one," she said. She stroked Zachary's hair and sniffed back her tears. Jeremiah noticed a slight, sad smile, the kind of smile a mother might want her son to remember forever.

"What's going on?" Jeremiah asked as he swayed back and forth and tried to get Zachary to stop crying. The baby may not have understood the words, but he felt the pain in the room. Jeremiah also recognized the signs, but there was a slight twist. For the first time in his life, a woman was leaving him without him having to push her away.

"Why?" he asked, but the question was addressed more to himself than to anyone else in the room.

The Colonel stepped between Jeremiah and Susan.

"You lied to my daughter."

Jeremiah put Zachary on the couch and stood up to face Colonel Larch.

"You got her pregnant," Larch seethed. "You wrecked everything we wanted for her, everything we planned for her." The

Colonel punctuated his words with jabs to Jeremiah's chest. Jeremiah took a step back with each hit until he tripped over a chair and fell to the floor. He looked up at Col. Larch.

"You did this to her," the Colonel said.

"I will be a good husband," Jeremiah argued as he got up off the floor. "And I will be a good dad." He pleaded with Susan. "We can work through this."

"You want to be a good dad?" Colonel Larch clenched his teeth and dropped his volume by about half, switching from a bark to a much more menacing growl. "Then you should understand that I am being a good dad for Susan right now." His voice was only slightly less menacing when he turned to his daughter.

"This is best for everyone," the Colonel said flatly. "You two were going to split up sooner or later. We might as well do it before you're too attached to the baby." Jeremiah was unsure who the Colonel was trying to convince, himself or Susan. Mrs. Larch chewed on her lower lip.

"She is his mother!" Jeremiah screamed. "You can't act like he doesn't exist. Like he was never here."

"I can and we will," Colonel Larch barked in Jeremiah's face. He stepped closer.

"Do not push this."

Jeremiah remembered his physical confrontation with the Marine boyfriend and how that ended. He did not want Zachary to witness a similar beating, even if he wouldn't remember it. Just like he wasn't going to remember his mother. Jeremiah picked up his son and watched the Larches drive away.

Susan and her parents left Zachary, Jeremiah, and Clear Spring. At her father's insistence and while still in the midst of a major postpartum depression and probably more, Susan filed for divorce, a sinful (in the eyes of the church) but legal option her parents believed would allow her to move on with her life. On the paperwork, the lawyer wrote "misrepresentation and fraud" as the reason for the divorce.

As Colonel Larch said, it was what was best for everyone.

At an age when other young men were graduating from college or coming home in a casket, Jeremiah Malone became a single dad.

11

George once said, when Jeremiah was complaining about just wanting a normal life without activism, "Normal is what the average person can accomplish with little or no effort. Do you really want to be normal?"

Despite George's question—despite the boy not having a mother, a situation that Jeremiah knew was definitely *not* normal—Jeremiah was determined that his son's life would be as normal, beige, and vanilla as possible, at least until such time as Zachary could decide for himself which abnormalities he would choose to embrace.

Jeremiah marked the milestones of Zachary's first year—most of which were first reached while the boy was at the bookstore while Jeremiah worked—with the precision of a scientist: rolling over on his own at four months, sitting up at six months, first steps at eleven months. He recorded each achievement in a small photo album his mother gave him along with Polaroid evidence of the event. Every line was a reminder that life, in the larger sense, was moving forward, even if his own life seemed to be stuck in Clear Spring.

Despite Jeremiah's best efforts, Zachary cried nonstop after Susan left. "Be Mom" was the one thing Jeremiah could not do for his son. Jeremiah vacillated between helplessness, guilt, and fatigue. He blamed the fatigue on sleep deprivation. He blamed Zachary's crying on himself and his inadequacies as a father. The rest he blamed on sin.

On that weekend's phone call, Jeremiah told his parents how well the store was doing, how he'd decided to try a new book promotion that he thought would bring in more business, and how he'd even managed to sell two TVs. He said nothing about his workload as a parent.

Then, as they were about to hang up, Jeremiah casually dropped the news of his divorce.

"Ha!" The word exploded out of George's mouth like a sneeze. "I told…"

Jeremiah heard his mother snatch the phone from George and fumble with it before she spoke.

"You should try to work this out," she said once she had caught her breath. "A child needs two parents."

"Like a man needs two hands?" Jeremiah said. "I'll figure this out."

"I'm afraid it's not the same, Dear."

For the first time in his post-pubescent life, Jeremiah was not actively searching for romantic companionship. He loved Zachary, but his son, like his stump of an arm, was a living reminder that some actions actually had immediate and lifelong consequences. Sometimes, you get away with stuff; sometimes, you don't. The seemingly random nature of consequential justice brought little comfort to Jeremiah, especially when the life-changing consequence of his last relationship was sleeping in a crib in the next room.

But consequences require actions, and the newly divorced Jeremiah reasoned that the safest course of action for him was to not get any action at all.

Opinions about the town's most recent divorce broke down along the same lines as opinions about the Books That Deserve To Be Read display. Complete strangers felt entitled to weigh in on the scandal. Some respected the commitment of a single father to a son abandoned by his mother. Others felt vindicated and blamed the illicit pregnancy and failed marriage on banned books and their role in the death of family values.

It was months before Jeremiah thought about ever seeing anyone ever again. When he did, none of his former girlfriends returned his calls. Women he had never met crossed the street to avoid him on the sidewalk. Married women stopped coming into the store altogether, as did anyone who had a friend or relative in the military. Jeremiah told himself it didn't matter, but Zachary wasn't the only one crying himself to sleep at night.

Men he'd known for years weren't much better. Jeremiah's friends who had not been drafted, while impressed by his romantic conquests, were not the type of guys who read books or hung out in bookstores. Men who were not his friends did not want to risk the wrath of their wives or girlfriends. Soldiers who had returned from the war referred to him as "Jody" or "Lt. Douchebag."

For Millicent Spate, it was an obvious case of cause and effect. "What do you expect when you let your child grow up reading whatever he wants? Thinking whatever he wants."

She always paused for dramatic effect before her final burst.

"Doing whatever he wants."

Without intending to and with no action on his part, Jeremiah had attracted a new group of admirers. College-aged women and precocious high school girls began to stop by the bookstore, peeking over the tops of books and magazines they pretended to read, watching as Jeremiah played with Zachary, held Zachary, or was simply caught in the act of being a loving dad to his son.

Becky Pinkston, in her second year at Clear Spring Community College, was one of those young women.

"Isn't he adorable?" Becky asked her friend Maria. "I just want to eat him up."

Maria lowered the copy of *Tiger Beat* she was browsing only enough to expose her eyes. "Are you talking about the baby or the dad?"

Becky smiled. "Yes."

Maria put the magazine down and looked around the bookstore. "Is reading something without paying for it a form of shoplifting?"

"It is," Jeremiah answered from across the room. Becky and Maria jumped. They had not expected Jeremiah to hear them, much less to answer a rhetorical question.

"But Mr. Bookstore Owner," Becky cooed as she slowly approached Jeremiah. "I don't have any money. How will I ever pay you?"

"I'm sure we can work something out," Jeremiah offered. "But it will have to be tomorrow because I'm about to close and I don't want to wait on the police."

Becky raised her eyes to meet Jeremiah's.

"Or you could take me into custody tonight." She held out her hands in the handcuff position as she moved closer to Jeremiah. "You should probably frisk me."

Maria rolled her eyes. "Oh-kay. I'll be going now. Should I lock the door on my way out?"

"Please," Becky whispered in a breathy voice without taking her eyes off Jeremiah. Jeremiah wasn't sure if she was talking to him or to her friend.

Later that night, Becky snuggled as much as possible to a very distracted Jeremiah as he put Zachary to bed. The couple stumbled and groped their way down the hall to the master bedroom, crashing into walls along the way, pausing only to open the bedroom door before falling into bed.

His parents' bed. The bed in which, for all Jeremiah knew, he was probably conceived. Jeremiah's parents may not have been dead, but their ghosts were alive and well in that bedroom.

Young adult biology being what it is, Jeremiah pushed through the cognitive dissonance and proceeded toward their consensual goal.

Becky froze as her sweater fell to the floor.

"He's crying."

"He does that," Jeremiah whispered while nuzzling Becky's neck. "It's a game we play. Sometimes I cry and he ignores me."

Zachary's cries grew stronger and more insistent.

"Shouldn't you go check?" said a breathless, braless Becky.

Jeremiah raised his head to listen.

"That's the diaper cry," he said. "Gotta go."

Becky put on Jeremiah's shirt and followed him into Zachary's room.

"Does he cry like this all the time?" she asked. Any romantic notions about motherhood or even babies in general were drowning in the cries of the inconsolable child and the pungent smell of an especially dirty diaper.

"Couldn't you just give him some bourbon?" she suggested. "Cough syrup? Anything?"

The idea of drugging his son so he could have sex in his parents' bed was more than even Jeremiah's substantial libido could handle.

"I'm just going to rock him to sleep." Jeremiah put his son on his shoulder and had a seat. "He likes the rocking chair."

"I'm going to go." Becky walked back to the bedroom to put on her sweater and get her things. The front door slammed as she left.

"You didn't like her?" Jeremiah asked Zachary. "Remember these little interruptions when you're sixteen and I barge into your room when you have a girl in there."

Every romantic endeavor, on the increasingly rare occasions when such opportunities presented themselves, ended in a similar fashion. To Jeremiah, it was clear that if he was going to have any kind of social life, if he was ever going to be with a woman again, if he was going to find a mother for his son, he was going to need someone to watch Zachary.

Finally, on Zachary's first birthday, he admitted defeat in that week's phone call to his parents.

"Mom, Dad, could you please help me with this?"

"This is your job," George said. "We raised our kid. You see how well that turned out. Hopefully, you can do better."

12

Small towns have long memories. Zachary was up and running—around the house, around the store, into the street—before business at the bookstore fully recovered from the scandal.

"Seems like we're both getting on our feet at about the same time," Jeremiah told Zachary after he'd added up the monthly sales on a Wednesday evening. He kissed his son as he put him in his bed.

"That's a good thing."

The fourteen months since Zachary's arrival had been lean, but the store survived. At his insistence, Jeremiah had no real salary or paycheck. George and Tammy offered to pay a normal manager's salary, but Jeremiah wanted to "make it on his own." He rejected their help and lived solely on what the store brought in under his care. He paid himself what he needed for Zachary and what little money he required for his own needs. It seemed like he was always buying diapers. And pacifiers. Zachary was always losing his pacifier. On the rare good months, when the store had some money left over, he allowed himself a little extra for something exciting, like pizza one night instead of macaroni and cheese.

"If things don't get better soon," he told Zachary as he changed another diaper, "you're going to have to start sucking your thumb. Instead of baby food, you're going to be eating a lot of spaghetti." Zachary threw his pacifier across the room and laughed as it bounced beneath a chair. Jeremiah finished changing the diaper and watched as Zachary pulled himself up to a standing position in his crib.

"And I do not want to change spaghetti diapers until I have to."

Jeremiah's weekly business calls to his parents became more stressful as the weekly sales and expenses reports got worse.

"I hope you can turn this around soon," George told him. "We've got a lot invested in that place."

"George," Tammy said in the background. Jeremiah heard the sound of George's hand covering the phone. He could still hear Tammy's muffled voice.

"Couldn't we give him money, like a salary, until he gets through this?" she asked. She didn't think Jeremiah could hear her.

He did.

"No!" Jeremiah barked. Then there was a long silence.

"I can do this," he said in a more normal voice. "I don't need your money."

Several of the store's loyal customers—older women, mostly, who occasionally dragged their husbands along with them—belonged to a book club that met once a week in a circle of chairs in the center of the store. They discussed the book-of-the-month and, since the arrival of Zachary, took turns playing with the baby. Zachary enjoyed the company, even if he usually fell asleep when he was held by any of the more ample-bodied women.

And no woman had a more ample body or more gray hair than Ruthanna Jacobs.

Ruthanna never married or had children of her own, but she was a mother figure to almost every child in Clear Spring, including Jeremiah when he was a preschooler. When Ruthanna was younger, she ran a daycare/preschool in her home. Bad knees and chronic gout forced her to retire. When she sat, her body folded and creased like an under-stuffed beanbag chair.

"Miss Ruthy?" Jeremiah asked. "Would you, could you, please watch Zachary sometime for me?"

"I don't know, Jeremiah." She reached out as Jeremiah aimed the toddler at her and told him to go to Miss Ruthy. "But he sure is cute, isn't he?" Zachary ran toward Ruthanna with both hands raised high above his head and a wide smile consisting of four teeth.

"Yes, ma'am. I like to think so." It occurred to Jeremiah some humility might be in order. "Looks like his mom."

Ruthanna peeked around the baby's head at Jeremiah. Then she looked at Zachary. Then back at Jeremiah.

"Looks like you, is who he looks like." She looked back at the laughing child. "Lord help him. He already looks like his daddy." She spun Zachary around and sent him back to Jeremiah.

Ruthanna shook her head. "My knees are not what they used to be. I'm not sure I can chase him down with my cane." She smiled at Zachary and reached out her cane to hook him and pull him towards her. Zachary laughed and ran in for a hug.

"You could watch him here at the bookstore if you'd like," Jeremiah offered. "Think of all the books you could read."

"How would that be different than what I do now?" Ruthanna squinted her eyes and cocked her head to the side.

Despite her words, Jeremiah sensed a note of mercy in Ruthanna's voice. He was, after all, the son of her two best friends.

"If we do this, it'll be at my place," she said. "I still have a crib set up and everything's there." She groaned as she lifted Zachary and placed him on her lap. "What did you have in mind? Need a break during the day?"

"I was thinking more at night."

"I don't know if I want to watch your son while you're having a sleepover, young man."

"No, ma'am. Nothing like that." Jeremiah knew overnights were out for now. He would have to ease Ruthanna into this. Or learn how to entertain his more vocal guests without waking Zachary. Even on the best nights, Zachary was an extremely light sleeper. He didn't sleep through the night

"I'm going to see about taking some business classes at the community college," Jeremiah told her. "At night, after the store is closed." He wasn't sure why he felt compelled to explain to Ruthanna that his classes would not interfere with his job, but he did.

"I hear more women are going to college these days," Ruthanna said.

An involuntary smile appeared on Jeremiah's face. "I don't know about all that, Miss Ruthy. I'm just trying to better my situation for myself and my young son."

"Uh-huh." Ruthanna smirked and slowly shook her head. "Your young son. That's putting it on a little thick, don't you think? Even for you?"

"Could you please watch him?" Jeremiah pleaded. "I'll pay you. Just one or two nights a week. I'll know more when I've signed up for the class. They don't start until after Labor Day."

"You can't afford me," Ruthanna smiled.

"I'd figure something out."

Ruthanna looked Jeremiah up and down as if she was evaluating him for the first time. "If you were a young woman, I'd say you were looking for your M.R.S. degree. Then again, if you were a young woman, I suppose I would understand that. Is that what you're doing, Jeremiah? Are you looking for an M.R.S?"

Jeremiah's mouth involuntarily curled into a small, lopsided smile, a mix of embarrassment and amusement, like when he was younger and had just been caught stealing a homemade cookie that was cooling on Ruthanna's kitchen counter.

He quickly changed the subject.

"You went to college, right? What courses did you take?"

"Why?" Ruthanna asked. "You're suddenly interested in early childhood education?" Ruthanna waited for a reply but Jeremiah didn't say anything.

"I didn't think so," she said. "I wasn't either. I majored in philosophy with a minor in journalism."

"But you spent your life watching other people's kids." Jeremiah could not imagine Ruthanna as something other than a mother figure.

"I did," she said. "It was the 1920s. What else was a woman going to do with a philosophy degree? Why do you think I called the playroom 'Plato's Cave'?"

"I always thought you were saying 'Play-Doh'. 'Play-Doh's cave'."

"Well, you were still in preschool. I'll give you that one." She shook her head and smiled. She missed having babies around, in limited doses.

"OK. I'll watch him. But it will have to be at my place."

"Thank you!" Jeremiah hugged Ruthanna while she was still sitting down. Her automatic reflex was to put one hand on his shoulder and to pat him on the back with her other hand. She felt Jeremiah's emotional relief move like a wave through his body.

"I know," she whispered. "It'll be OK." She slowly rose from the chair. "Let me know which nights you're going to have class. I'll be sure to clear my calendar."

13

Jeremiah signed up for Business Law 101 because "I'm taking business classes at the college" sounded so much more impressive than saying he was taking Freshman English. The main thing was to get on campus. He smiled as he wrote out the twelve-dollar check for tuition.

There were only two empty chairs when Jeremiah arrived for class, both in the front row. There were no female students, just a bunch of guys with thick, black-framed glasses, pencils behind their ears, and pocket protectors. Jeremiah took the chair closest to the wall. It wasn't like he had a choice.

He sighed and reminded himself that he could meet women in the cafeteria or the library. Even if he didn't meet anyone, it felt good to be away from the store and not on alert for whatever Zachary might need. He loved Zachary in a way he had never loved anything or anyone, but he was looking forward to some socially acceptable breaks from parenting.

Despite having little choice in where he sat, the classroom felt remarkably free. No one here knew or cared that he had a child or under what circumstances. No one knew about the divorce. Or, if they knew, they weren't saying anything about it. As far as the class was concerned, Jeremiah Malone was just a slightly older guy taking business law.

Class was about to begin when a taller than average young woman wearing a dark, knee-length skirt below her crisply starched white blouse came to the door. She looked over the top of her own black-framed glasses to find an empty chair. Twenty-three geeks immediately sat up straight in their seats. Jeremiah's head was down, skimming the textbook's table of contents, so he missed her unintentionally dramatic entrance. He didn't notice her until her long black ponytail almost slapped him in the face as she turned to sit at the desk next to him.

Jeremiah waited for her to get seated before he spoke.

"Hi. I'm Jeremiah."

"I'm Theresa." She tapped a finger to her front teeth. "And you have spinach or something in your teeth."

While Theresa twisted around to put her purse over the back of her chair, Jeremiah discreetly rubbed his fingers across his teeth to make sure nothing was there.

Theresa fixed her purse, faced the front of the room, and said nothing for the rest of the class.

"I think we've met," Theresa said as she gathered her things after class. "Don't you work at the bookstore?"

"I'm the manager, but I don't think we've met." Jeremiah hoped she would be impressed that he managed the bookstore even if he couldn't recall meeting her before. He was willing to bet that none of the geeks had risen to the level of "store manager" yet.

"I thought so." Theresa nodded. Her voice slowed as if she was almost remembering some important detail. She pointed a finger at Jeremiah as her eyes narrowed. "And don't you have a kid or something?"

Jeremiah wasn't sure what the "or something" might mean in this context, perhaps a pet turtle or a small bird, but he confessed to having a child.

"A son. Zachary."

"Yeah." Theresa's laser gaze became even more intense before her expression relaxed into a slight smile.

"I don't know how you do it." She shook her head. Jeremiah thought he saw a shudder. "I am really not into kids. Not now. Probably not ever."

"Yeah, well..." Jeremiah's voice drifted off as he watched Theresa get up and walk away.

The semester continued, but despite his best efforts, Jeremiah was about to give up on the idea of meeting anyone at college. He tried to focus on his class instead.

On a rainy night in October Ruthanna called to say she wasn't feeling well and would not be able to watch Zachary while Jeremiah was in class that night. Jeremiah did the only thing he could think of: he packed the stroller in his car and took Zachary to class with him.

Zachary started crying before they entered the building. Once they were inside, Jeremiah gave him a sippy cup full of apple juice and kept pushing the stroller down the hall. They arrived in class a few minutes early.

"Couldn't get a sitter," he explained to a seemingly indifferent Theresa.

"Wow. I guess not. He's not going to smell up the room, is he?"

Zachary stared at Theresa, screamed, and started crying again.

"You hurt his feelings," Jeremiah joked.

"Feelings"? Theresa said. "He barely has thoughts, much less comprehension. They don't develop feelings until much later. In fact," she paused, "I've known people who never developed them at all. Some people are just lucky like that."

Twenty-three geeks glared at the inconsolable child. The anonymity Jeremiah enjoyed was replaced with harsh judgement and strong disapproval from his fellow students as his son screamed. Jeremiah apologized to the teacher and maneuvered the stroller toward the door. An anonymous male voice from the back of the class loudly asked if he needed a hand. Without turning around, Jeremiah raised his non-bendable prosthetic hand and sent a clear message usually expressed with a single finger.

Unsure of what to do next, Jeremiah stopped by the cafeteria. He was sitting at a table with Zachary, gently bouncing the stroller up and down, when he saw another stroller by the window and a tall redhead. She was looking the other way, facing the window. Jeremiah couldn't see her face. He only saw the face of a baby looking back at him and her mother tapping on her back, trying desperately to coax a burp from the child. At least Jeremiah assumed it was a baby girl. She had a pink bow in her fine, almost invisible baby hair.

Zachary laughed at the tremendous burp that came from this child. The woman hugged her baby like she'd won a trophy, which she might have had she been in a bar or if she was a junior high boy, and placed her back in the stroller.

Jeremiah took the mother's blushing red face as an opening. He picked up Zachary and approached the table.

"Hi. Mind if I sit down?" He bounced Zachary on his hip. "If we sit down?"

"Well," she said as her baby reached with both hands for another spoonful of strained butternut squash. Jeremiah did not wait for a more complete answer. "Well" was sufficient.

The young mother put down the spoon and looked up at her unexpected table guests.

"I'm Laura Summers. And you are?"

"Jeremiah Malone. And this is my son, Zachary."

Laura gestured toward the stroller. "And this is Grace." She glanced at the clock on the wall. "I should be in my accounting class right now, but Grace didn't seem to want to be there."

"I understand. Zachary insisted on skipping class tonight." Jeremiah noticed the absence of a wedding ring on Laura's left hand as she adjusted Grace's hat. He found himself wishing he'd taken accounting instead of business law.

They talked about what it was like to be in college when you have a child, what it was like to go to the grocery store with a child, what it was like to date with a child, and what life is generally like when you are completely responsible for the welfare of a small human being.

"I'm glad I have my mom to help," Laura confessed while mixing another spoonful of strained butternut squash with a scoop of peas. "I couldn't do this without her and Dad. They usually watch Grace when I'm here, but tonight they couldn't."

"Same here. I have a sitter who usually watches Zachary but she couldn't do it tonight."

Laura wiped some squash from Grace's face. "Your wife couldn't do it?"

There it was. A cut-to-the-chase truth detector disguised as a question.

"I'm divorced. Zachary's mother left soon after he was born."

The spoonful of butternut squash froze in mid-air. Laura showed a faint smile of condolence.

"I had no idea."

Jeremiah was always glad to meet someone who somehow had no knowledge of his life, but he didn't want to push his luck.

"What about you? What does Mr. Summers do?"

Laura looked inside the baby food jar and made a loud clanking noise as she scraped the glass for one last spoonful.

"There is no Mr. Summers." She scooped up some strained plums from another jar. "He died in Vietnam." She shrugged at Jeremiah's shocked reaction. Laura's voice reflected how tired she was of hearing condolences.

"It's the military; people get killed. Or hurt." She nodded toward Jeremiah's prosthesis. "I've seen those gloves before."

Jeremiah was tempted to let her observation stand. That strategy worked before. But that strategy also made him a single parent. An unfamiliar pain rose in Jeremiah's chest. That could have been his widowed wife sitting here without him. His baby without a father. Him dead in a war zone. Or in a training exercise. Did it really matter how it happened?

"I wasn't in the military," he said. He raised his arm and pointed to the prosthesis. "This was a water-skiing accident. I got a draft notice and RSVP'd like I was supposed to, but the Army told me to just stay home."

Laura looked at Jeremiah as she put the spoon back in the plums. "You were lucky."

He swallowed hard. "I'm sorry for your loss." Jeremiah hated how common that phrase had become.

"Thank you. I'm still mad at him." The widow looked straight at Jeremiah. "He wasn't even drafted. He volunteered."

It was a long few seconds before either of them spoke again. Laura started packing up her baby bag.

"I'd better get her home. It's way past bedtime."

"I don't usually do this," Jeremiah lied, "but can I get your phone number?"

"I'm not quite there yet," Laura said. "I'm sorry. But, I know where you work. Maybe I'll stop by and pick up a book."

Talking with Laura only made Jeremiah more aware of how alone he was. He called Susan later that night after he put Zachary to bed.

"She can't come to the phone," Colonel Larch said when Jeremiah asked if he could talk to the mother of his child.

"May I ask why?" Jeremiah asked.

"Because I'm not going to tell her you called." There was a click, and the call was over.

It took almost a week, but Laura and Grace came to the bookstore. Jeremiah was surprised. After so many disappointments, he did not expect her to actually show up.

Like most first-time visitors, Laura made a bee line for Books That Deserve To Be Read. She looked at the books on the rack and on the table before she picked up an unabridged leather-bound edition of *Canterbury Tales*.

"That one got me in trouble when I was a kid," Jeremiah approached the display and put down the books he had balanced on his right arm. "We were reading *The Knight's Tale* in some anthology in English class. It wasn't the entire book, just *The Knight's Tale* section. I liked it so my dad found that unabridged edition. I took it to school and got sent to the office for having a dirty book."

"I've heard *The Miller's Tale* is pretty naughty," Laura said.

"I think they preferred the term 'bawdy' in the Middle Ages," Jeremiah replied.

Laura's eyes grew wide and her jaw dropped. "And the wife of Bath? You took that to school?"

"Yes," Jeremiah confessed. "My father gave me an entire book of thirteenth-century Medieval smut when I was a child. That probably explains a lot." Jeremiah moved more copies of *The Scarlet Letter* from the Back-to-School display back to the Books That Deserve To Be Read section.

Laura brushed her fingers over the books on the table and scowled.

"Why do you have these out here, all featured and out in the open like this? I'm not sure I want my daughter reading some of these."

"Grace is already reading?" Jeremiah smiled. "That's impressive. She must be smart like her mother."

"No." Laura rolled her eyes. "But when she can read, I'm not sure I want her reading these books. Do you think these are appropriate for kids?"

"Not all of them, but not all of my customers are kids." He watched Laura as she picked up one book, put it down, and then picked up another.

"Have you actually read any of these?" Jeremiah asked.

Laura picked up the Bible. "I've read this one. Does that count? But not too many of these others. Maybe none of them." Laura's cheeks turned a slightly brighter shade of red. "But I trust the people who tell me they aren't good."

She slowly pivoted Grace's stroller away from the table to shield her daughter from the toxic aura of so many banned books in one place. Laura looked like she was about to leave but then suddenly veered toward the back of the store.

"What's over here?" Her red hair bobbed up and down above the rows of books as she pushed the stroller between shelves. The floating head stopped in the middle of the "Religion" section.

"Nice collection," she called out to Jeremiah. She smiled as she looked at the books on the shelves. Her expression changed as she moved past the seven-eighths of the aisle-long rack space devoted to Bibles, commentaries, and what were essentially Christian pop-psychology and self-help books and reached the sliver of the section that held a small collection of books from a few of the rest of the world's major religions. George and Tammy may not have been devout, but they knew what their community expected to find in a bookstore.

Laura smiled and waved goodbye to Jeremiah, gave Grace's stroller a slightly harder push, and left the building.

14

Jeremiah searched for Laura the next few times he went to class but could not find her on campus. He skipped a class and sat alone in the cafeteria where he first met her, hoping she would return. He wondered if his potential friend had dropped out of school.

"I don't think she's interested," he told Ruthanna one night as he dropped off Zachary. It had been almost a week since Laura's visit and her encounter with Jeremiah's banned books.

"From what you've told me," Ruthanna said, "I don't think she likes your taste in literature."

"I don't think she knows my taste in literature. We never got that far."

It was another week before Jeremiah saw Laura alone on campus. He was surprised when she called his name. She waved a piece of paper and power-walked towards him.

"You need to see this." Laura's hands trembled as she held out the glossy sheet. Jeremiah recognized the color immediately. Millicent's flyers and posters always used the same color—goldenrod. Not quite yellow, not quite orange. The color of overdue notices and detention slips. And, in Clear Creek, the color of a message from Millicent Spate.

"I'm not sure if I'm supposed to show it to you," Laura said, "but you need to see it. Millicent is doing this. She passed them out at church last Sunday. Gave them to everyone there. She's handing them out all over town."

"She's always handing out something," Jeremiah said. "If it's not about the bookstore, then it's about indecent swimwear at the swimming pool. Or evolution. Or the socialist plan to put recycling bins around town."

When she wasn't handing out goldenrod colored announcements, Millicent was writing Letters to the Editor pieces that George read aloud at breakfast. Millicent's "Dear Editor" pieces always included strong spiritual warnings about God's judgement on Western civilization in general and Clear Spring in particular unless they followed her advice and changed their ways.

"Dumbest woman on earth," George would say as he read.

Beads of sweat glistened on Laura's forehead as she handed the paper to Jeremiah. She closed her eyes, lifted her face to the heavens, and made sure she remembered to breathe before she spoke again.

"I haven't decided how I feel about your banned books," Laura said, "but it's not right to go behind someone's back like this. If Millicent has something to say, she should say it to you."

Jeremiah read the flyer. It wasn't hard. He could have read it from across the room and still have room to spare. Beneath the blazing red "PROTECT OUR CHILDREN!!!" headline was the time and date for an organizational meeting at the high school gym where they would discuss the dangers of inappropriate literature in the high school library and elsewhere in the community.

Jeremiah examined the flyer closely.

"Looks like *The Dixiecrat* printed this."

Laura agreed. "Millicent uses them for church bulletins and stuff. You know those yard sale signs that say 'I Found It' and 'You Can Find It Too!'? Those were all printed at *The Dixiecrat*.

"I never had it to lose," Jeremiah said. He handed the flyer back to Laura. "Whitely Parker probably loves this. I bet he did these for free."

Clear Spring's only newspaper was originally called *The Clear Spring Democrat*, although at the time, it was not necessary to include the word "Democrat" in the paper's name. That was assumed. No self-respecting Southern newspaper would identify as Republican for at least a hundred years after the Civil War.

That attitude and the name it inspired changed when the Democratic Party began to push for desegregation and civil rights in the mid-1940s. As a political party, the Dixiecrats lasted less than a year before they forgave Lincoln for his unprovoked attack on the South and folded into the Republican Party. Their influence, however, extended long after their demise.

The Dixiecrat party disbanded, but the newspaper kept the name, forever embedding the term and the ideology it represented in the local cultural zeitgeist.

The owner, editor, and head writer for *The Dixiecrat*, Whitely Parker, was a Clear Spring native who never left his hometown. Not for college, not for war, not for anything. He vigorously fought against ideas that threatened what he referred to as "traditional Clear Spring values," their way of life, and what he saw as the established Biblical hierarchy of races and genders.

The Malones and their books threatened those values.

The Books That Deserve To Be Read display had been the subject of several scathing *Dixiecrat* editorials over the years, all of which were more or less dismissed by the public with comments like, "Oh, that's just Whitely ."

To be fair, the good people of Clear Spring also thought the same of George Malone. "Oh, that's just George" was a popular sentiment when George voiced a public opinion at a PTA meeting or at City Council. Together, George and Whitely were Clear Springs' polar eccentrics, equally tolerated, equally dismissed, and equally respected as men who stood up for what they believed, even if no one else stood up with them.

The Dixiecrat blurred, if not completely erased, any lines between news and opinionated editorial content. Articles about the Civil Rights movement, anti-war protests, or anything Whitely Parker considered un-American were reported with a definite slant to the far right. When he wasn't attacking the Malones and their Books That Deserve To Be Read, Whitely's editorials highlighted the moral superiority and natural order of white supremacy. Whitely eventually expanded the scope of his editorials to include homophobia and antisemitism as well. That he could do so without losing any advertisers or subscribers was a testament to the loyal demographics of Clear Spring.

Clear Spring Books & Electronics never advertised in the local paper. "Why should I pay for an ad when he's going to mention us in his column anyway?" George would say. "His editorials are all the advertising we'll ever need."

George penned multiple Letters to The Editor about free speech and censorship over the years, not only in defense of his store but in defense of the First Amendment and what George considered intellectual integrity. *The Dixiecrat* never published any of them. For Whitely Parker, there was only one side to any issue, and that was the only side his newspaper would present, regardless of what may appear in any other newspaper.

"We don't need somebody from a big city like Little Rock telling us how to live up here," Whitely said.

"Something's wrong," George told Jeremiah when Jeremiah was in high school, "when a newspaper actively campaigns against free speech and the reporting of facts."

"Something's wrong when you think Little Rock is a big city," Tammy said on days when she missed Los Angeles.

Whitely Parker and his raging antisemitic, racist, homophobic editorials challenged George's belief in unrestricted free speech. As a reminder of his commitment to the First Amendment, George's desk held a small wooden plaque Jeremiah made for him in his junior high shop class. Burned into the plaque was the Evelyn Hall quote, "I disapprove of what you say, but I will defend to the death your right to say it," a quote usually attributed to Voltaire but which actually appeared first in Hall's biography of the French philosopher. George appreciated that kind of historical accuracy. Jeremiah Malone knew better than to put the wrong attribution on his father's plaque.

Even with his engraved motto to remind him, George could not imagine defending anything Whitely Parker might write or say. He wondered whether free speech should include the unchallenged freedom to be ignorant. To be hateful. Does it include the freedom to be so, so absolutely wrong? The part of George's brain that went to college understood that for free speech to exist, it must be extended to Whitely Parker just as it was to J. D. Salinger. The other part of his brain told him not to sell *The Dixiecrat* in his store. That side won, the side that told him not to sell the local newspaper, not because of George's feelings about censorship but because of his personal feelings about Whitely Parker.

Jeremiah remembered how his dad used *The Dixiecrat* as an example of a business not living up to its civic responsibilities. George often reiterated his belief in the obligations of small town businesses preceded by the word "the." *The* bank. *The* grocery store.

"It's in the name!" George would scream. "*The Dixiecrat* is *the* newspaper. Such a waste. A newspaper that doesn't report news. An opinion is one thing, but unsupported rants are no substitute for facts."

Millicent's group, the group responsible for the flyer in his hand, was calling themselves "Parents Who Deserve To Be Heard." It seemed clear who they wanted to hear them.

"I don't know why Millicent didn't bring this to me herself," Jeremiah said. "She usually isn't exactly timid about what she thinks." The flyer was aimed at the school and did not mention the bookstore, but Jeremiah understood the message. The name alone made their intentions clear. Besides, if someone wanted to ban books, they wouldn't stop with the school. They would come for the school first, then the library after that.

Jeremiah knew that if Millicent succeeded at the school, she would come for the bookstore. She and her people would come for him. They'd ask for new zoning laws and come up with new, ever-expanding definitions of obscenity. Whitely and his readers were already sensitive about stories that might offend descendants of former slave owners and other self-proclaimed patriots who waged war on the United States. Fortunately, as George used to remind

Jeremiah and Tammy, no one in city government liked to work with Millicent Spate.

Jeremiah hoped that was still the case.

"What are you going to do?" Laura asked.

"Nothing." Jeremiah handed the paper back to Laura and hoped he was right. "My parents dealt with Millicent or people like her all the time. They showed up at their meetings. They answered their questions. Nothing happened. She'll bang this drum for a while and a few people might even jump in with her parade. But watch. This will blow over. People know Millicent's crazy."

Laura looked surprised but relieved. "I thought I should tell you."

"Thank you. I appreciate you letting me know." Jeremiah smiled at Laura. "We should get together some time and do something besides talk about books."

Laura grinned, but slowly looked to the ground. "I'm busy right now. But, yeah. We should." Apparently, she meant some unspecified time in the future because she left before Jeremiah could pin down a date.

Jeremiah looked at the flyer again. He knew he did not want to go. But, he also knew that if he wanted to get to know Laura, this could be his chance.

15

The front door rattled as Ruthanna stormed into the bookstore. She slammed one of Millicent's flyers down on the counter.

"Have you seen this?"

Jeremiah glanced at the paper in Ruthanna's hand.

"Seen it," he said. He went back to straightening the cash in the cash register.

"What are you going to do?" Ruthanna was emphatic.

"Nothing."

He took the flyer from Ruthanna. "My parents wasted too much time dealing with people like Millicent Spate. Nothing ever happened. She's crazy."

"Nothing happened *because* your parents spent time dealing with people like Millicent Spate," Ruthanna said flatly. "They made it not happen. You don't know what the consequences might have been if they hadn't dealt with it."

"We're about to find out," Jeremiah told her. "They're not going to be at that meeting and neither am I."

It took two and a half years for the bookstore to return to full, pre-scandal sales numbers. Zachary was already saying complete sentences, including some short catch phrases from his favorite books. "Brown Bear, Brown Bear, what do you see?" had become a catch phrase as he ran around the bookstore.

Customers were buying books and newspapers again. Jeremiah was looking forward to doing more than just paying the bills. He fantasized about having actual discretionary income.

"This is not a good time for more bad publicity," he told Ruthanna.

Ruthanna stepped closer to Jeremiah, leaned on her cane, and looked into the eyes of the young man she helped raise.

"What do you stand for, Jeremiah?" Her eyes narrowed as she spoke. "Because this store stands for free speech, or at least it did when your parents were here. This store stands for the right to say things that might not be popular."

"It might be time to reconsider that," Jeremiah said. "I'm sorry, Miss Ruthy, but we won't stand for anything if we go out of business."

Jeremiah took two steps toward Ruthanna. He whispered so the customers wouldn't hear.

"The store's doing better, but I don't know if I can keep it going unless things improve a lot more. I may have to take another job and I don't know what I would do with the store if I did." He stepped back to a more conversational distance. "Maybe I rent the house, move back into the apartment. Or the other way around. I don't know."

He stopped.

"Or," he gulped, "it may be time to sell the bookstore."

Jeremiah had never mentioned selling his parents' store to anyone before. Saying it out loud and seeing Ruthanna's reaction suddenly made it very real. He hated the idea of losing the store and all it had come to mean to his parents and to Clear Spring. But from a purely business standpoint, selling the store looked smarter every month.

A third option, to quit and tell his parents to find another manager, felt like he'd be giving up the only job security he would probably ever have. Not to mention what it would do to his relationship with his parents. If he didn't manage the store, what would he do? He was, to himself and others, "the guy who ran the bookstore." Who was he if he wasn't a defender of free speech and bagger of books?

He didn't just fear losing the store. He feared losing his identity.

"Then I suggest you find a way to stay in business," Ruthanna advised. "Advertise. Put in a coffee shop and sell cookies. Something." The older lady took a seat in one of the book club chairs and motioned for Jeremiah to do the same.

Jeremiah hesitated. "Ruthy, there are customers in the store."

"Then sit where you can keep an eye on the counter."

Jeremiah knew Ruthanna would not take no for an answer. He took a seat in the book club circle where he could see the cash register.

"You know that poem about how "first they came for the Socialists and I didn't care because I wasn't a Socialist'?" Ruthanna asked. "Your father kept a copy of that behind the counter, if I remember right."

Jeremiah nodded his head. "It's on a little sign I made for him in shop class." His head moved back and forth as he recited the first few lines. "First they came for the socialists, and I did not speak out because I was not a Socialist. Then they came for the Jews, and I did not speak out because I was not a Jew."

Ruthanna held up a hand for him to stop. "You left out most of it, but that's the general idea. It ends with, 'And when they came for me there was no one left to speak for me'."

"It's not really a poem," Jeremiah said.

"You have a rather narrow definition of poetry." Ruthanna's glance cut like a sword. "I've thought about that piece a lot over the years, about what happens when no one speaks up and who might not be left to say anything when I need someone to speak up for me."

Her eyes tightened around the corners as she spoke. "It's important and it's true, but the man who wrote that, a Lutheran preacher named Niemöller, didn't go back far enough." Ruthanna leaned forward and put her hands on Jeremiah's arm. She looked deep into his soul and searched for whatever piece of his parents might reside there. She looked at Jeremiah with a laser focus.

"Before they came for anyone, they came for their books."

"They're not talking about condoning genocide," Jeremiah argued. "They just don't want their kids reading smut."

"They all say they want to get rid of smut," Ruthanna countered, "because how can you argue with that? That's like saying you want to cure cancer and work for world peace. But they keep changing what they mean by 'smut'."

"I have a customer." Jeremiah pointed to the counter and a woman with a large canvas book bag.

Ruthanna kept talking as she followed him behind the counter. "Today it's sex. Tomorrow, political content, or scientific facts they don't like. Black writers, women writers, any writer with a perspective different from their own? Gone. Then they're rewriting history to change some of the more embarrassing sins of our fathers. They'll recreate history in their own image, regardless of the facts."

"Will that be all, ma'am?" Jeremiah asked the puzzled lady with the bag. He wondered how much of Ruthanna's rant she heard.

"Yes, thank you." The woman picked up her book, smiled at Ruthanna, and headed quickly for the door.

"It's not just erasing history," Ruthanna continued as the door closed. "It's erasing people."

She sat down on the stool behind the counter. "It's deciding who gets to speak and who doesn't."

Jeremiah looked at Ruthanna while he pointed to the display that defined his bookstore. "And yet I am able to sell these books right here, in my store, in this town, with no serious interference from anyone other than the occasional flare-up from the crazy Millicent crowd. I don't see the problem."

"For now. But that might not always be the case." Ruthanna's voice grew more emphatic as she pointed to the display. "Things are changing, Jeremiah. It's happening slowly, but our 'live and let live' mindset is becoming 'I will tell you how you can live'."

"Maybe here in Clear Spring. I'll give you that," Jeremiah agreed. "I can't believe this is happening everywhere."

"It doesn't start everywhere. It starts in random places and spreads from there."

"It seems they're mostly concerned about sex," Jeremiah said. "Now that I'm a parent, I can almost understand that."

"We're not just talking about sex." Ruthanna pounded her cane on the floor. "If they can control what you read, then they can control what you think. Then they control what you believe. They will control what you do. Banning books is just the first step of the process."

"You're overreacting," Jeremiah told her. Then he smiled. "And you sound like Dad."

"I'll take that as a compliment." The never-married childcare provider paused as if she was considering carefully what she was about to say. Her voice dropped to a whisper.

"They're not just banning books, Jeremiah. They're targeting people," she said. "People to be deleted."

"We're talking books here," Jeremiah said. "You make it sound like people are going to be executed by the state."

"If you want to kill a person," Ruthanna explained, "you shoot them. If you want to kill a group of people, you simply stop acknowledging their existence."

Jeremiah smiled as a young mother came in carrying her toddler daughter. Jeremiah pointed to the playpen where Zachary was playing with his Winnie the Pooh bear.

"If you'd like, she's welcome to play with Zachary while you shop." He looked at Ruthanna and smiled.

"Eeyore could use a friend."

The young mother smiled at the idea of even a short break. "Emma, this is Zachary." She looked at Jeremiah. "Do you have *Curious George?*"

"One of Zachary's favorites." Jeremiah pointed to the back of the store. "Children's section. Over there."

Jeremiah looked back at Ruthanna and rolled his eyes. He spoke much more softly than before. "But they aren't killing people. I agree there is a problem, but nobody is saying they want to kill people."

"Look at what your parents went through," Ruthanna reminded him. "Look at what happened to their careers. To everything they worked for all those years. Are you telling me that wasn't an assassination?"

Ruthanna walked to the display and waved her hand over the table like a priest blessing a sacrament. "These are only the books we know about. How many more were killed before they could be published, shot down by editors or publishers or some other gatekeeper who didn't want to risk offending someone who probably wouldn't read the book anyway? How many were never written because the writer didn't feel safe writing that truth? And how many readers are afraid to buy those books or to be seen reading them? We're not just doing this to save books, Jeremiah. We're doing it to save people."

She sat down. "We do it to save ideas that need to be heard. We do this to give a face to people who don't have a voice. We do this because we are *the* bookstore."

Jeremiah rang up the mother's copy of *Curious George,* thanked her, and lifted her daughter out of the playpen. He waited for the door to close behind her before he spoke again.

He turned to Ruthanna.

"*We* don't have to worry about paying the bills. *I* do."

Ruthanna made her way to the door. She turned around before she opened it.

"Let me know when you figure it out."

Jeremiah watched her leave. He looked at the clock, turned the OPEN sign around, and locked the door. He picked up Zachary and spun him around in circles like the Dumbo ride at Disneyland.

The flying elephant in the room stopped when Jeremiah saw their reflection in the front window.

He looked older than he felt. He was too young to remember his father at this age, but he was beginning to see the resemblance in his own tired face. He didn't want to become his parents. He didn't mind selling books—he kind of liked it, actually—but he didn't want the fight. But he also didn't want to have to explain to Zachary someday why some book he wanted or, worse, needed to read wasn't around anymore or why he hadn't said anything when they came to take it away.

And maybe that was the problem. Not that he didn't know what to say, but that he was getting comfortable with not saying anything at all.

16

"I've been thinking about our conversation last night," Ruthanna said when she came back the next day. She'd brought cookies. Cookies meant that she wanted Jeremiah to listen carefully to what she had to say.

"The funny thing about this is that Millicent and your mother have a lot in common. Not so much your dad. He's an outlier with his commitment to absolute free speech. He honestly believes that everyone should be allowed to say or write whatever they please. He's probably one of the few free speech absolutists left, I suspect. But Millicent and Tammy are two sides of the same flag on some of this."

Jeremiah was incredulous. "Mom agreed with banning books?"

Ruthanna leaned back in her chair and put her cane across her lap.

"Your mother believes that certain books have the potential to do so much harm that they should not be passed around, much less read. Not many books, mind you. They have to do a lot to cross that line where she would say they shouldn't be here. But there were cases when your mom decided it would be irresponsible to sell certain books."

Ruthanna watched Jeremiah's face for any sign of recognition. "Sound familiar?"

"Sounds like Millicent, except for the part about having to do a lot to cross that line," Jeremiah admitted.

"Exactly." Ruthanna continued. "You don't see any copies of *Mein Kampf* on the banned books table, do you? That book wasn't banned by people like Millicent. It was your mother who believed that children, unstable adults and, for that matter, society and the world in general should be protected from those books and others like them."

Ruthanna lowered her head slightly as she looked at Jeremiah. "Again, does this sound familiar?"

"Sounds like Millicent," Jeremiah admitted.

"It does," Ruthanna said. Then she went on.

"Books That Deserve To Be Read confers a kind of credibility for these books. Some writers consider it an honor to be on that table, although it's an honor they would probably be glad to give up if it meant more people could read their books. Tammy does not want books she considers potentially harmful to benefit from the umbrella of that credibility. She did not want to be complicit in that."

"What about Dad?" Jeremiah asked.

"Your dad disagreed but he usually deferred to your mother on this one."

Ruthanna smiled and leaned back in her chair. "I know that Tammy and I are doing the socially-conscious liberal version of what we accuse Millicent of doing with her fundamentalism. We are both protecting our values. We are protecting people we consider vulnerable. And we would both ban, either officially or in practice, certain books we don't like, although I don't think Tammy would ever go as far with that as Millicent and her people would."

"What would she do that would be different?" Jeremiah asked. "A ban is a ban."

"Tammy would simply not have the book in her bookstore. She would let other bookstore owners decide whether they should sell a book like that. Ultimately, she would let readers decide whether they wanted to read the book. Millicent would have it removed from all bookstores and libraries everywhere. She wants to decide what people can and cannot read, even in private."

"What did Dad say when Mom wouldn't let him put a book on the table?"

"It wasn't easy for him." Ruthanna smiled slightly as she remembered her friends. "Your father is a free speech absolutist. He believes you should be free to say, print, and read whatever you want. You should be able to write a book about it. It should be available for people to read, if they decide they want to read it."

"Sounds like a good way to spread hate and misinformation," Jeremiah said.

"That is a risk. Your dad talked about what he called 'inoculation theory.' Instead of banning those books, he believes people should read them so they understand why those ideas are so dangerous or hurtful. Kind of a 'know thy enemy' type of thing. Your mother agrees with that, to a point. But she also believes that some books carry such a high potential for violence, or are so morally reprehensible, just so, so wrong, that instead of an inoculation, some people just get an infection."

Ruthanna smiled and shook her head as she remembered her friends.

"Let's just say that Tammy does not share your father's confidence in the critical thinking skills of her fellow humans."

Ruthanna picked up a copy of *Huckleberry Finn* from the table as an example. "Tammy did not want to sell this book. She said it was racist. George insisted until, well, you see it there on the table now.

"We actually don't sell many copies of that book," Jeremiah said. "Maybe one or two a year, if that. The rest of the time it sits here, like most of the rest of these." He took the book from Ruthanna and put it back on the table.

"I have to decide whether this is a bookstore or a museum."

17

One week later, against his better judgment and purely out of respect for Ruthanna, Jeremiah and Zachary edged their way through the door into a packed high school gym to see what the Parents Who Deserve To Be Heard had to say.

Theresa from Business Law 101 was sitting on the bottom row of the bleachers, desperately fanning herself with a hand fan provided by the Clear Spring Funeral Home. Her hair was twisted up off her neck, a concession to the Arkansas heat and humidity. She looked up as Jeremiah walked by.

"You brought your kid?" Theresa shook her head in disbelief and disapproval. "Why would you do that?"

"I couldn't find a sitter." He smiled with one side of his mouth. "You don't even have a kid. Why are you here?"

"Let's just say I'm a concerned citizen," Theresa said. She scrunched up her face and leaned slightly towards Jeremiah. She tapped a finger on one of her front teeth.

"You've got..." she started. Then she was interrupted by the sound of someone clearing their throat. Loudly.

"Oh," Theresa said. She nodded her head to the side without looking at the man with the loud sinus drainage problem. "And this is Malachai."

"Your brother?"

Theresa's eyes snapped in Jeremiah's direction.

"Oh, God, no," she said.

Jeremiah barely acknowledged the introduction before he turned back to Theresa. "I'm going to find a seat now."

Jeremiah hoisted Zachary higher on his hip and looked for two seats. He saw Laura sitting higher up in the bleachers and made his way to sit beside her, ignoring the looks, whispers, and pointing fingers as he and Zachary climbed through the crowd.

Laura leaned toward him.

"It's called a 'chignon'."

"What?" Jeremiah tried to get Zachary to sit in the bleachers.

"Her hair." Laura pointed to the back of Theresa's head. "That twist in her hair is called a chignon. You see them a lot at weddings." She looked at Jeremiah. "You were looking at her hair so I thought I would tell you what you were looking at."

Millicent stepped up to the microphone, told everyone to stand, and led the crowd in a fervent recitation of the Pledge of Allegiance, with extra emphasis on the "under God" clause.

"And now," Millicent said as a segue, "Jack Duncan, President of the Clear Spring School Board, will lead us in an opening prayer."

Jeremiah leaned into Laura's ear to whisper. "Why is the President of the School Board at a meeting like this?" Laura brushed him away without a sound.

"Dear Lord," Mr. Duncan began.

"Dear Lord," Jeremiah echoed with a very different inflection.

Mr. Duncan waited for the crowd to grow quiet enough for God to hear. "We want to thank you for these parents and community leaders. You have taught us that if we train up our children in the way that they should go, when they are older they will not depart from it. Thank you for your servant, Millicent Spate, and other people like her who are committed to doing that. In your name we pray."

And the people said, "Amen." Most of them. Some of them. A few of them.

Actually, opinions may vary on how many people said "Amen". To Jeremiah's ears, it became unanimous the moment Laura said it.

Millicent stepped up to the microphone. "Thank you, Mr. Duncan, for such an inspiring prayer." She took a dramatic pause and assessed the sizeable audience assembled before her.

"My friends and concerned citizens," Millicent began.

"Concerned citizens?" Jeremiah thought. *"Where did I just hear that?"*

Millicent continued. "We are meeting here tonight to talk about protecting our children from pornographic books in our schools." She held up a copy of *Are You There God? It's Me, Margaret* like a preacher holding a Bible. She waved the book for all to see.

"Our group found this and other filth in our school library."

The crowd gasped. Millicent smiled and emitted a snarky chuckle. Laura, who fought her own potential lust by sitting on her hands lest a rogue fingertip accidentally touch Jeremiah, sat up straighter to better see over the head of the man sitting in front of her.

Jeremiah noticed that Theresa was also sitting on her hands, staring at the gym floor, and moving her feet from side to side like a pair of windshield wipers.

"Don't worry," Millicent laughed. "Many of them have already been removed. You might say they've been checked out permanently."

Jeremiah turned to Laura. "What's she talking about?" he whispered.

Laura rolled her eyes as she turned to look at him. "Their kids check out these books and they just don't bring them back. Ever."

"Don't they have to pay for the book if they don't return it?" Jeremiah asked.

"That's the cost of war," Laura said with no expression.

"Sounds a lot like the cost of shoplifting,"

Millicent reached into her bag, pulled out Toni Morrison's *The Bluest Eye*, another banned book, and *Black Boy* by Richard Wright. She made sure the audience saw the covers before she put them down on the table beside her. She turned the bag upside down. Several books spilled out on the floor.

"These books do not belong in our school." Millicent's voice crescendoed to an exclamation point as she continued. "We are seeing more and more of this kind of thing. Books with explicit content, promoting rebellious behavior, and, worst of all..." Her voice dropped to a loud whisper for her most important point.

"Contradicting Biblical teachings."

The crowd gasped.

Jeremiah leaned toward Laura. "Wasn't that what she said about the Baptists before she left their church?" Laura pushed him away.

"We must stand against these books, these secular ideas." Millicent sounded like a preacher at a tent revival. "Our struggle is not against flesh and blood. This is a spiritual battle." She waited for the brief applause to stop before she continued.

Jeremiah saw Whitely Parker seated in the front row, taking notes in a small notebook, smiling and nodding his head up and down.

"We are a community of believers," Millicent preached. "Our school must remove books that do not reflect the values of our community."

"She's good," Jeremiah said. "Like, Joseph Goebbels good."

"Does that mean you're going to take down your display?" Laura asked.

"It means I wish she was not this good."

"I think she has a point," Laura said.

"Really?" Jeremiah whispered loudly enough for the people sitting in front of him to hear and turn around with a look of disapproval. He went back to whispering.

"You think the school should ban books?"

"Not every book," Laura whispered. "But some." She paused to hear what Millicent was saying.

"I'm sorry." Laura whispered beneath Millicent's speech. "There are some things I don't want my daughter to read."

"I get that," Jeremiah said. "But, when Grace is thirteen, will you stop her from reading *The Diary of Anne Frank?*

Laura grimaced as she closed her eyes.

"I don't know," she whispered. "I haven't read *Anne Frank.*"

At least Laura admitted she hadn't read them and didn't know whether she would let her daughter read them. That seemed fair. Jeremiah wondered how many parents in the gym that night had bothered to read the books on Millicent's list or if they simply wanted them banned because Millicent said so.

"Any questions?" Millicent asked with the confidence of someone who does not expect to be questioned.

Jeremiah leaned closer to Laura while the room waited for someone to respond. "Do you want Millicent Spate to decide what your child gets to read, even if you think it's a book that *should* be read? You should decide that. Not Millicent."

Laura crossed her arms and said nothing. Jeremiah looked around the silent room. Theresa was still staring at her feet. Other people were beginning to fidget in the uncomfortable silence. After a few seconds that seemed much longer, a big man who looked like he was old enough to have children in high school raised his hand.

"Yes, sir," Millicent said. Jeremiah saw Theresa looking back over her shoulder to see the stranger.

The big man did not stand up, but simply spoke from his seat.

"But isn't that what schools are supposed to do? To expose students to different perspectives?" the stranger said. "To teach some critical thinking skills so our kids can decide for themselves what is true and what isn't? Isn't that the point of..."

Millicent interrupted the question.

"I'm sorry," she addressed the man. "Could you please introduce yourself?"

The man remained seated.

"I'm Ethan Reynolds. And isn't part of the school's job..."

Millicent once again interrupted.

"Tell us where you work, Mr. Ethan Reynolds." Millicent had a talent for making something as simple as someone's name sound like a threat.

Millicent lifted her face as Ethan rose to his full six foot seven-inch height. He looked like a lumberjack, with his beard, his red plaid shirt, and shoulders broader than you would expect, even on such a tall man. Even with his loose-fitting shirt, it was clear that he was more muscular than most. His voice was deep and resonant, exactly what you would expect for a man of his build. He ignored Millicent's question and finished stating his question.

"Isn't part of the school's job to teach students how to determine what is true and what isn't?"

Millicent reached into her purse and pulled out a Bible. She slowly raised it over her head as she spoke. "*This* is what decides what is true and what isn't." A not-so-murmured whisper rippled across the crowd, punctuated by shouts of "Amen."

Jeremiah looked at Theresa in the front row. She was sitting on her hands staring at the ceiling while slowly rocking back and forth on the bleachers.

"Even the Bible is subject to interpretation," Ethan said, in a voice that matched Millicent's amplified volume but not her angry tone. "You can't claim to know what is true and what isn't."

The gym got very quiet.

The big man continued. "I just think parents are better equipped to decide what their children should and should not read than some committee full of church ladies."

The newcomer looked at the crowd seated around him and smiled. "No offense, ladies." Jeremiah smiled at the predominantly masculine laughter and feminine giggles as Ethan sat back down.

"None taken." Millicent forced a smile. "I'm proud to be one of those church ladies. But I can't imagine any parent would think these books are appropriate for children."

"Obviously some do," said a woman from another section of the bleachers. "Or that book you held up wouldn't have sold more than ten million copies already." She paused. "My daughter and I read *Are You There God?* together. There is nothing wrong with that book. I absolutely would let young girls read it. I would recommend it."

"And your name?" Millicent asked.

"Joan Campbell," she replied. "And before you ask, I work at the hospital. And what you're doing here is wrong."

Millicent closed her eyes and raised her hands to Heaven. "Straight is the path and narrow is the way and few there will be that find it." She looked at Joan. "Lord, be with this lost family." She stood there, her head raised and her eyes closed, as if she was waiting for God himself to respond. She lowered her head when he didn't.

"A group of us will be attending the next School Board meeting to talk about protecting our children," Millicent said. "We're putting together a list of books that we want removed from our schools. Please tell us if you know of any library books or textbooks that should be on that list." She looked out at the nodding heads. "And join us when we go to the School Board if you believe our school is no place for pornography, blasphemy, and books that teach our children to question authority."

Millicent looked back and forth across the audience, silently daring someone, anyone, to question her authority again.

Jeremiah stood up. He waited for the crowd to stop whispering before he spoke. There was no need to say his name. Most of them knew who he was.

"Excuse me." He caught himself checking to see if Theresa had turned around to see him. She had.

"This has all been very informative." Jeremiah handed Zachary to Laura, who initially hesitated but ultimately could not resist Zachary's outstretched hands, causing more whispers in the crowd. Once again, Jeremiah waited before he spoke.

"I just want to say that I have all of these books and more at the bookstore if anyone wants to read them and decide for yourselves."

"Get on the microphone!" someone yelled. "Millicent, give him the mic."

Jeremiah carefully made his way to the gym floor where an obviously angry Millicent slammed the microphone into his chest.

"Thank you," he said as Millicent walked away. "I was saying I have these books in my store if you want to read them and decide for yourself. I'll even throw in a fifty percent discount – half price off! – on anything on the Books That Deserve To Be Read table if you tell me you were at this meeting."

Millicent's face turned red and her eyes narrowed as she took the mic back. "Bless your heart, Mr. Malone. But I wouldn't take your dirty books even at half price."

"For you, Millicent, they're free," Jeremiah said loudly as he returned to his seat. He waited for the laughter to stop and then continued his thought.

"But you will have to turn in a book report on each book you take."

Someone in the crowd yelled, "I'll grade it!"

"If no one has anything more to say," Millicent announced, "then I adjourn this meeting. I hope to see all of you at the School Board meeting next Monday. Not this coming Monday, but the one after that."

Laura seemed much colder when she handed Zachary back to Jeremiah. She spoke without looking at him.

"You know what 'bless your heart' means in Southern church-speak, right?"

"I know," Jeremiah replied. "I wanted to tell her I'd be praying for her but I thought I'd be the bigger person."

18

The meeting ended and Jeremiah started getting Zachary ready to go. By the time he gathered Zachary's things, Laura was halfway to the gym floor. Jeremiah called her name, but she kept walking. He followed her outside, trying to keep sight of her auburn hair in the crowd, but kept getting further behind as he juggled Zachary on his arm. He was almost close enough to call Laura's name without attracting too much attention when he heard someone say his name.

"Mr. Malone!" the big man from the meeting boomed from across the street. "Mr. Malone. Could I talk to you?"

Jeremiah ignored the voice and kept walking, weaving his way through the crowd with Zachary riding along on his hip.

Ethan called out again. "Mr. Malone!"

Laura turned the corner and disappeared for the evening. Jeremiah smiled as best he could and slowly pivoted to face the approaching man.

"Aren't you the guy who spoke up at the meeting?" Jeremiah reached out with his left hand to shake Ethan's outstretched hand. "I appreciated that. Always nice to meet a kindred spirit."

Ethan nodded in the general direction of Laura. "I'm sorry. Was that Mrs. Malone?"

"No. She's a friend. A friend who apparently must be going."

"Sorry," Ethan said. "Didn't mean to block your shot."

"Not sure I ever had a shot. But I think I'm getting within range."

"Well, that's progress," Ethan said. "I'll be coming by your store to get my half-off discount!" The big man seemed friendly enough, despite being apparently oblivious to social cues. The two men chatted back and forth as they walked down Main Street toward the bookstore together. They saw the small crowd in front of the bookstore from about two blocks away.

"Looks like people are already taking you up on your offer."

Jeremiah picked up his pace. "I don't usually open the store at night but I may break that rule if all these people want some books." Zachary tried to run but his pudgy little boy legs could not keep up. Jeremiah reached down, picked up his son and carried him, running, the rest of the way.

The group dispersed quickly as Jeremiah got closer. They left behind several copies of *Are You There God?* with a few burn marks on the edges of the covers and pages, several discarded paper matches, and three half-empty cans of Pabst Blue Ribbon beer.

"I guess they couldn't get the pages to stay lit," Ethan said. "That's why we don't use beer as lighter fluid."

Jeremiah picked up the singed book. "And behold. They came with fire but the books did not burn." He looked at Ethan. "I wonder if Millicent would say this is a sign from God?"

Ethan noticed the "Property of Clear Spring High School" sticker on the spine of the book in his hand. He picked up another book and saw the same sticker. Five copies of the book were on the sidewalk, all from CSHS.

"This must be what Laura was talking about." Jeremiah picked up some of the larger pieces from the pile of books and ash. "She said they were checking books out of the library and intentionally not returning them." He laughed quietly. "This is an easy fix. I probably have twenty copies of this book. How many are there? Five copies? I'll give ten of them to the school tomorrow. Problem solved."

Ethan held the books while Jeremiah unlocked the door.

"Do you think Millicent had anything to do with this?"

"She didn't light the match," Jeremiah said. "And I don't think she drinks beer. But she's absolutely responsible. You are responsible for your wake."

"What is that?" Ethan wasn't familiar with the phrase. "Is that an Arkansas thing?"

"It's a lake thing." Jeremiah raised his prosthetic hand. "I learned the hard way."

Jeremiah unlocked the door to the bookstore and carried Zachary inside. Ethan followed close behind.

"I've got to see this forbidden books display I've heard so much about."

"There it is." Jeremiah pointed to the display as if Books That Deserve To Be Read could be missed. He took Zachary to the back room so the child could go to sleep.

"It's like the Tree of the Knowledge of Good and Evil," Ethan said when Jeremiah came back from putting Zachary to bed. "It is forbidden, and yet I want a taste."

He smiled.

"I guess that would make you the snake."

Jeremiah shook his head. He'd had enough religious imagery for one night.

"I haven't seen you around town before," Jeremiah said. "That's one thing about Clear Spring. New people tend to get noticed."

"I moved here about a month ago. I'm working on a book about music of the Ozarks, traditional instruments, the stories behind the songs, that kind of thing."

"Soon to be a *New York Times* best seller, no doubt," Jeremiah said.

"It's for my dissertation. I'm in a PhD program at University of Arkansas," Ethan explained. "What about you? You seemed as out of place at that clown show as I was but you seem to have been here a while."

"All my life," Jeremiah said. "And the way it's looking, I will probably die here. That wasn't the plan but that seems to be what is happening."

Ethan seemed to understand. "And you feel like someone else is making your plans for you? Made your plans for you?"

"Very much so." Jeremiah told Ethan about his parents being blacklisted, how they couldn't get work as writers after that, and how his mom saw an ad for a bookstore in some place they'd never heard of and they bought it.

"If you think I don't fit in, you should meet my parents."

Ethan's eyes grew wide as he connected the dots. "Your parents are George and Tammy Malone? *The* George and Tammy Malone?"

"I never heard them refer to themselves as 'the' anything, but yes. Those are my parents. How do you know them?"

"Are you kidding? They're famous among people who work with music, art, and literature that's not exactly mainstream. My thesis was about music of Black Americans. You'd be amazed how many songs by Black artists have been banned over the years. George and Tammy have written a lot of articles about that."

Jeremiah ignored the stranger's praise for his parents work against censorship. He'd heard it before.

"Banned for sexual content?"

"Some, but not always," Ethan explained. "And sometimes what they call sexual content is only an excuse for what the censors are really after, which is to stop music that might make people feel empowered or gives them a voice. Can't have people getting all worked up now, can we? Might start wanting equal treatment and stuff." The big lumberjack of a man looked around the store.

"Speaking of music, I'm surprised you don't sell records in here. Records take up a lot less room than TV sets."

"Yeah," Jeremiah agreed. "I don't know why Dad didn't think of that. I don't know why I didn't think of it. I should do that. Think of the trouble I could get into."

"Anyway," Ethan said. "Back to your parents. I was researching songs that had been banned from radio stations, like Sam Cooke's "A Change is Gonna Come" or Billie Holiday's "Strange Fruit", things like that, and the names George and Tammy Malone kept coming up."

The musicologist put his hand on Jeremiah's wrist and laughed. "I heard last week they were in New York protesting a local radio and record store ban on 'Lola' by The Kinks and 'Take a Walk On The Wild Side' by Lou Reed." He laughed. "Gotta love that."

"I had no idea," Jeremiah replied. "We're not talking that much these days. But that's their thing, fighting censorship. Fighting book bans." Jeremiah paused for a moment. "I knew they were protecting books. I didn't know about music or movies or anything else. I guess it's all the same, when you think about it. Freedom of expression. First Amendment stuff."

Ethan seemed skeptical. "Didn't your parents take you to these things when you were a kid?"

"No," Jeremiah said. "They left me with Ruthanna when they went out of town." He turned to his new friend. "She's a babysitter here in town. Once I got older, they left me to run the store. Honestly, I didn't pay that much attention to what they were doing. I was too busy being bullied at school because of my commie parents."

"Are your parents communists?"

"No," Jeremiah laughed. "Not even close. They're also not socialists, anarchists, hippies, or any of the other things I've heard them called over the years. They just happen to have different ideas about some things than most people around here."

Ethan stood up. "And you? Are you following in their steps? Preserving their legacy? All that?"

"Not intentionally," Jeremiah admitted. "Honestly, I don't know how I feel about book bans. I know how I am supposed to feel. What I've been taught to feel. I do what I've been told I'm supposed to do. And I agree with that, mostly, I guess. I do know that I don't feel as strongly about it as my parents do."

Ethan stroked his dark, full beard. "Then why did you say what you said at the gym?"

Jeremiah laughed a little. "I wasn't going to say anything, but I don't like bullies. And I guess I have a problem with authority figures, especially when they've done nothing to earn that authority. Millicent's entire argument is that those books are bad because she says they're bad. She would say that God says they are bad, but Millicent's god has a funny way of agreeing with everything Millicent says."

Ethan agreed. "She did seem rather confident."

"She's confident. I'll give her that," Jeremiah agreed. "But she's not smart enough to be an authority on anything. Someone needed to stand up to her. And, naturally, people expect me to do it because *I'm* the son of George and Tammy Malone. *I* run the bookstore with the Books That Deserve To Be Read display. We all have our characters that we play; our little roles in the community script. I guess that's mine, whether I want it or not."

"You don't sound like you're sure you want the part."

"My parents chose this," Jeremiah explained. "I mean, they didn't choose to get blacklisted, but they chose to come here. They chose to build this business and that display. They probably weren't thinking about it at the time, but they also chose how I would spend my life."

Jeremiah went to the back room to check on Zachary. He came out with the sleeping child resting on his shoulder.

"I don't mind their legacy", Jeremiah said. "I just wish I had been given a choice about my part of it."

Ethan nodded toward the sleeping child. "What legacy are you choosing for him?"

19

Jeremiah carried Zachary to work with him the next morning and wondered what new protest might be waiting for him when he arrived. Black marks from the previous night's aborted book burning were still on the sidewalk but there was no real damage. He wondered if the spontaneous combustion, so to speak, was inspired by Millicent or if it was part of a larger protest that he needed to learn more about.

He was in the children's section reading to Zachary when the bell on the door dinged. A corner mirror flashed a quick glimpse of someone moving from row to row but they disappeared before Jeremiah could tell who they were. He knew only enough to know it wasn't one of the regulars. Old people don't move like that.

"Maybe our book burners are back," he said to Zachary as they walked to the counter. His ears zeroed in on the sound of movement as he put Zachary in the playpen behind the counter and wondered how much longer Zachary would tolerate his imprisonment. He had no idea what he was going to do when Zachary outgrew the playpen and he was left with an extremely active little boy running around the store all the time.

Theresa's face rose up from behind the bookshelves like a grinning floating specter. Her grin broadened into a full smile that she tried to contain but could not. Jeremiah almost didn't recognize her face, so different was her expression than anything he'd seen in class or at last night's meeting. He smiled when she looked at him.

"You have some great books here!" Theresa yelled from the Comedy section. She disappeared behind another row of shelves. "I'm going to check out Mysteries."

Jeremiah stepped out from behind the counter.

"This is a surprise. I didn't expect to see you here."

"Why?" Theresa came around the end of a row in the Romance section. "I read. I just thought I'd come here and see this for myself. Maybe pick up one of your half-price books. She walked over to the Books That Deserve To Be Read display.

"So this is it?" She looked back at Jeremiah. "Satan's altar?"

Jeremiah nodded. "That's it. We'll be sacrificing a virgin at noon."

"I hear you're good at that," Theresa said.

She pointed to one of the books on the table. "I've read that!" And to another, and another. In all, Theresa had read ten books that Millicent Spate would have banned.

"You could have bought those here," Jeremiah joked.

"They may have come from here, for all I know. I get them from my friends. It's like a little book club." She got close enough to whisper in Jeremiah's ear. "And I found one of them in the bathroom at church!"

Jeremiah tried to think where he might have met or even seen Theresa besides class and the meeting last night. Clear Spring is not that big of a place. He had to know her from somewhere. He knew they hadn't been friends or even spoken to each other before this, but he could not stop thinking that he had seen her somewhere before.

"How is it that we never met?" he asked.

"I don't know," she said. "I think you were a senior when I was a freshman. That's probably part of it. That, and I suspect we didn't hang out with the same people." She cleared her throat and raised her chin.

"We're Baptists," she said.

Jeremiah nodded. "Church of Christ here."

"There's your answer," she said. They both laughed quietly.

Theresa's eyes grew wide as she looked around the store. Her smile brought out the dimples on her cheeks.

"I've never seen anything like this," she told Jeremiah. "I've lived in Clear Spring my entire life but I don't think I've ever been in here. I honestly did not know this existed."

"Not even when you were a kid?" Jeremiah asked.

"No." She turned to Jeremiah and tried to look very serious. "This is the store with the *sinful* books. Everybody in Clear Spring knows that."

Jeremiah ignored the sinful comment and stepped out from behind the counter.

"Are you saying you grew up in a house with no books?" Having grown up in a bookstore, Jeremiah could not imagine a life devoid of literature, information, or entertainment.

"No, not at all. We had plenty of books. And we went to bookstores. Just not like this one." Theresa kept looking around the store. "I have never seen this many books in one place before. And so many different kinds of books!"

"Really?" Jeremiah said. "This is not a big bookstore. Not really. Not like the big stores in Little Rock or Memphis."

Theresa gave a slight gasp and quickly turned to face Jeremiah. "And I don't think I've ever been in a bookstore that sold paperbacks with long-haired, bare-chested men on the covers. The kind of books women hide in their purses. And so many!"

Jeremiah nodded. "You should check out the Men's Health section."

Theresa laughed. She looked at the ceiling. Was she blushing?

"I can imagine."

Jeremiah wasn't sure what was behind this fascination with the bookstore. He decided to not ask and just accept it.

"I was surprised to see you at that meeting last night," he said after Theresa had looked at a few more books. "What did you think?"

"It was what I expected." She turned back to face Jeremiah. "Although..." She stretched out the word as she turned. "I did not expect you to be giving away door prizes for attendance."

"Neither did I, to be honest." Jeremiah shrugged. "It seemed like a good idea at the time. She ticked me off."

"I was impressed by how you stood up to her. Not many people do that." Theresa grinned as if she was hiding some secret. "Honestly. I was *very* impressed."

She did a quick physical and verbal pivot. "What else is here besides your dirty books?"

"These are banned books." Jeremiah pointed to the back of the store. "The dirty books are in the back corner, but I'm afraid you're going to be disappointed. Nothing with naked men. Let me know if you need anything."

He stepped outside to pick up the daily delivery of Little Rock newspapers and carried the bundles in. Then there were books to re-shelve in the children's section. More customers came in with questions about books from the night before. He even managed to sell several banned books from the display, enough that he put out more copies of some. The young bookstore manager tried not to think of how much money he was losing with his half-price offer. Fortunately, many people picked up other books that were not on sale while they were there.

After months of very few customers, it was good to see the store busy again. Jeremiah saw college students, retirees, and moms with small children. The same type of people as before and more of them.

He also saw Laura Summer, even if Laura was pretending she didn't see him as he walked toward her and the magazine rack.

"Can I help you?" Jeremiah asked.

"I wanted to explain about last night," she began. "I'm sorry I left so fast. I needed to get home to Grace."

"Sure, I get it. I needed to get Zachary to bed, too."

"I still think what you did to Mrs. Spate was rude. But there's something else I wanted to tell you and didn't get a chance to say." she began.

Laura's eyes suddenly grew very wide. She stopped mid-thought. She stepped to the side to better see what was behind Jeremiah.

"Theresa? What are you doing here?"

"Hi, Laura," Theresa said without getting out of her chair or looking up. She turned a page in the book she was reading. "How's it going?"

"You know each other?" Jeremiah asked.

"We do," they both said at the same time. Neither woman smiled.

"I'm..." Laura stopped and looked at her watch. "I'm sorry. I can't stay. I didn't realize what time it is. Mom is watching Grace and I told her I'd be home an hour ago. Nice to see both of you!"

Theresa said nothing as Laura walked away but her face begged for an explanation.

"She's a friend," Jeremiah explained. "I'm not sure it's even that, really."

Theresa laughed and kept flipping pages.

"Whatever you say."

Theresa stayed in the store, but it was noon before Jeremiah talked to her again. He was turning a corner to return some books. She was sitting on the floor in the Women's Interests, reading Sylvia Plath's *The Bell Jar.*

"Why are you hiding?" Jeremiah whispered.

"This book is amazing," she whispered back. "I've never read anything like this."

"Take it. Think of it as a gift." He went back to work and left Theresa to enjoy her new book.

"It's almost closing time," he told Theresa hours later. "Let me get Zachary and the three of us can go get something to eat."

"That sounds nice," Theresa said, "but I can't. I have to be somewhere tonight." She looked at her watch. "In fact, I should be somewhere now."

She took his hand. "Jeremiah," she stopped. "It is Jeremiah, isn't it?" she teased. "This has been a wonderful discovery. I didn't know something like this was so close to home. But now I must be going."

"Are you sure?"

"I am. But I will be back."

Jeremiah watched as she walked to the door and went outside. He kept watching through the window as she walked down the sidewalk.

As he watched her walk away, it was clear that Business Law 101 had been the right class to take.

20

Jeremiah wasn't alone for long before Ethan came in.

"Can you get a sitter for the kid?" Ethan asked before he reached the counter.

"I guess." Jeremiah took Zachary's hand. "And by the way, the kid's name is 'Zachary'."

Jeremiah looked at the cluttered front counter, the book club circle, and back in the children's area. He had not even begun to re-shelve books that people moved during the day. He still had to count the cash in the drawer.

"Why would I do this?" he asked.

"Because you need to get out of here and I might need a wingman."

"I can't speak to your need for a wingman, but you are right about me needing to get out of here."

The Clear Spring Annual Folk Music Festival featured some of the world's best dulcimer players, banjo players, fiddle players, guitarists, and folk singers performing traditional songs of the Ozarks. The population of Clear Spring temporarily tripled with tourists during the three-day weekend event. Restaurants, hotels, and local stores all benefited from the annual influx of people and their money. For some, this was the event that made it possible for them to stay in business for the rest of the year.

Ethan did not just have tickets. He had secured backstage passes so he could interview the artists.

The festival was like a musical time capsule. These were older, simpler songs that told stories that usually involved someone dying or being in love or dying because they were in love or some variation on the themes of love and death. Mountain music, especially when performed with a banjo and a washtub bass, sounds incredibly cheerful until you listen to the lyrics.

"Traditional music like this is kind of self-censoring," Ethan explained. "The words change as the culture changes. Verses are added or removed as performers see fit. People decide what they like and change what they don't. It's the same with all unwritten oral histories, but especially with music."

The band on stage was about to start another set so he stopped talking. They stopped to tune a guitar.

"It's not a bad thing that some of those lyrics were forgotten," Ethan said. "A lot of these old songs were pretty racist. And violent."

Jeremiah recognized the problem. His parents had these same conversations.

"Is it appropriate to ban a book because you don't like the culture that created it?" George would ask.

"I don't think it's inappropriate at all," Tammy would argue. "We have to recognize what those words mean today and all the cultural memories those books dredge up. We have to consider how those words hurt the people who hear them today."

Jeremiah stopped thinking about his parents when he realized Ethan was talking to him.

"There's kind of a Darwinian process that culls out the songs people don't like and keeps the ones they do," Ethan said.

Jeremiah was not convinced. "Just because people like something does not make it good. It does not make it right."

"No," Ethan agreed. "But it does keep it alive." He picked up a stray guitar pick that was lying on the ground, inspected it, and put it in his pocket. "I'm surprised you're even asking these questions, Mr. Save the Books. Preserving this music is no different than saving the books you want to protect. It's about deciding which voices get to be heard and which voices will be deleted. Next, they're deleting people and erasing histories."

Ethan looked at the stage and then turned to Jeremiah. "Here's the guy I came here to see."

Cleetus Bowman, a banjo player and a featured performer of the festival, was a lonely, wrinkled old man, a victim of old Southern conspiracy theories and an especially crackpot radio preacher with a heavy Eastern Oklahoma accent named Pastor Lawrence Kettle. Pastor Kettle hosted a radio show that broadcast from a cave somewhere beneath the Missouri boot heel from which he instructed his followers on, among other things, the finer points of survival during the upcoming race war. This holy war, according to him, was as inevitable as the return of Jesus. In case prayers were not enough, the good preacher also endorsed a local gun shop and some high-priced end-times survival gear, all conveniently available from his multiple sponsors.

For a love offering of only $10, Pastor Kettle would pray for you. For $10 more, he would send a handkerchief he used to wipe holy sweat from his anointed brow.

In Clear Spring, the good Pastor was even more popular than Millicent. At least half of Clear Spring tuned in every Sunday night, far more than attended Millicent's church services. And the half that didn't listen to him on the radio had to listen to their pastor-listening co-workers babble about it as if they were speaking in tongues for a week.

Cleetus often fell asleep while his headphones pumped Pastor Kettle directly into his brain. It was not unusual for him to be awakened in the night by dreams of Southern soldiers on horseback rising from beneath their Confederate States of America tombstones and flying through the air to avenge him and the rest of the faithful with the mighty sword of a reborn South.

Amen, praise God, and please pass the pancakes.

Naturally, Millicent Spate was also a big fan of Pastor Kettle and his sweaty forehead.

The musicologist, of course, was focused on the music and not on whatever tales emerged during any semi-psychotic breaks Cleetus may or may not experience while performing.

"Incredible talent," Ethan said after a blazing banjo song.

"You know he's crazy, right?" Jeremiah reminded him.

"He's passionate," Ethan said. Then Cleetus started talking again.

"And he's crazy," Ethan agreed. He smiled. "You can be both."

The three festival stages formed a triangle, with one point for traditional Ozark folk singers and musicians like Cleetus, one for bluegrass bands, and one for gospel groups. Tents offering food, traditional Ozark apple-head dolls, wooden toys, and other homemade items filled the space within the triangle and along the perimeter between the three venues. The air smelled of barbeque, roasted ears of corn, tanning lotion, and mosquito repellant.

Within that center, holding an ear of corn and wiping butter from her chin with the back of her bare hand, her eyes closed in salt and peppered happiness, strolled Theresa.

"I'll be back," Jeremiah told Ethan. "Or I'll find you later."

Theresa appeared to be in no particular hurry as she walked across the festival grounds. Jeremiah bought two bottles of off-brand coke and was by her side in less than two minutes, all while watching Theresa enjoy a giant ear of corn.

"Want something to drink?" Jeremiah juggled the two bottles between his fingers as he offered one to Theresa.

"Need a hand?" she asked. Theresa immediately gasped and put her hand over her mouth. Her face flashed a bright red.

"I am so sorry. I did not mean..."

Jeremiah smiled and again offered her something to drink. "Don't worry. That's not the first time I've heard that."

Theresa regained her composure and smiled. She shoved her free hand into the pocket of her jeans in search of something other than her fingers to wipe the butter from her face. She found nothing. Jeremiah handed her a napkin he'd picked up in case he sneezed.

"What are you doing here?" she asked.

Jeremiah tapped one of his front teeth. "You've got something..."

"Do I?" Theresa blushed as she covered her mouth with her hand and discreetly rubbed a finger across her front teeth.

"I do not."

"Actually, yes you do," Jeremiah raised his prosthesis toward Theresa's face. "Some pepper or something. Let me get it for you."

She slapped his hand away. "You are NOT putting your fingers into my mouth."

"Plastic fingers, I remind you."

"I know about you," she said. "You and your little harem at the Church of Christ."

Jeremiah gave a slight smile. "Harem is a bit of a stretch."

"I don't know," she teased. "I hear you were a regular King Solomon. Not the wisdom part. The part about all the wives and concubines. It was mostly concubines, wasn't it? Is there a third category?"

"Mostly concubines if that's the word you're choosing. I think of them as women who happened to enjoy my company, even if it was only for a moment."

Theresa raised her eyebrows. Jeremiah hoped he could change the subject in the time it took her to finish her drink.

"I'm surprised to see you here," he said.

"My mom comes here every year so I tag along. I've been doing this since I was a kid. I never listen to this stuff at home, but I like coming here. And the music is good, if you're into this kind of thing."

She turned to Jeremiah. "Is there even such a thing as bad live music? I mean, even if it's not great, it's still live. People are creating something in real time. There's an energy there. I love that."

"We came here, too," Jeremiah said. "My parents used to set up a table and sell books. I could have rented a space this year but I didn't."

"Banned books?" Theresa asked.

Jeremiah laughed. "No. This is not the crowd for that. Mostly histories. Some song books. They liked to use events like this to promote books by local authors." Jeremiah tried to remember the last time there were any local authors from Clear Spring. It had been a while.

Ethan must have gone to the food booths because he was carrying what looked like a turkey drumstick. Jeremiah realized that for a drumstick to look that big in Ethan's oversized hand, it must have been from an emu. Maybe an ostrich. Ethan noticed Jeremiah and waved to him between bites.

"Why aren't you doing that today?" Theresa asked.

"What?" Jeremiah's attention snapped back to Theresa. "You mean selling books? Because I'm the only person working at the store and I didn't get around to doing it." He didn't want to say he was cutting costs by not hiring any extra help to work while he was gone and not paying for a booth.

They moved closer to the stage and sat on the ground close to one another. On another edge of the triangle, Jeremiah noticed Millicent walking through the crowd with a clipboard and a pencil with an American flag attached to the eraser.

"She's gathering signatures on her stupid petition," Theresa explained. "It's part of what she was doing at her meeting the other night."

"You're probably right," Jeremiah said, "but how do you know that?"

"Because she's my mother."

21

Jeremiah's jaw dropped. "You're kidding."

"Why would I kid about something like that?" Theresa allowed herself a slight smile. "Actually, I have lied about that," she said. "A lot. But I usually lie and say she's not my mom."

Jeremiah looked at Theresa. "There is a certain family resemblance. Around the eyes."

"It ends there."

Theresa Spate had spent a lifetime sitting in public meetings from Little Rock to Memphis but mostly in Clear Spring, watching her mother accuse and intimidate people with complaints about school curriculum, the sale of alcohol, and all manner of social degradation.

"I was brought up as an observer," Theresa said. "With the clear expectation that someday I will be the one speaking."

Books allowed Theresa to endure the boredom of hearing the same arguments over and over again as she sat in churches, auditoriums, and gymnasiums where her mother was speaking. While Millicent railed against obscenity and blasphemy in all their subtle and not-so-subtle forms, Theresa sat on the front row and read books from her mother's approved reading list. Or, if she was feeling especially daring, she read forbidden books wrapped in the covers of approved books.

Reading opened new worlds to Theresa and challenged her with ideas and perspectives very different from what she heard at home. Books made her realize she was not the only person who felt certain ways, or believed certain things, or who had experienced whatever she was going through at the time. Books made her feel like she was not alone.

In the end, books made her realize that her mother was wrong about banning books.

Not everything Theresa read was forbidden. There were certain books that Millicent made sure her daughter read. By age ten, Theresa had gone through the entire King James Bible three times. She read novelized versions of popular Bible stories, stories by C.S. Lewis, and other books deemed safe or appropriately informative by her mother. She studied books refuting evolution, the age of the planet, and almost every scientific theory that did not include scripture references in the footnotes.

Theresa was expected to do well in school, but not at the expense of her religious indoctrination.

Her mother stressed that no matter what a textbook might say about a subject, the Bible was the ultimate authority in all matters. Hard questions about slavery or genocide or why a benevolent God would allow natural disasters like tornados to kill people, were explained as "God's will." Disease and suffering were caused by sin, if not personally—which was usually the case—then through the original sin of Adam and Eve.

Millicent often reminded her daughter that not everything she heard at school was true, a sentiment which, ironically, she shared with George and Tammy Malone but for entirely different reasons and from very different perspectives.

"Couldn't you just homeschool?" Jeremiah asked.

Theresa half-laughed. "Mom always said we were called to be a light to the world," Theresa explained. "Apparently you can't be a good light if you stay at home." She looked at Jeremiah.

"This little light of mine...", she sang, while she waved her finger like a candle.

Jeremiah sang along with her. "I'mma gonna let it shine...".

Their fingers bumped into one another, fingertip to fingertip, and Jeremiah playfully hooked his finger around hers as they sang. Jeremiah hoped Theresa had not noticed him blushing as he pulled his hand away.

"Got it," Jeremiah said.

By junior high, Theresa had worked up the courage and the necessary skills to sneak forbidden books she got from her friends into her bedroom and read them with a flashlight under her blanket. She'd read *Are You There God? It's Me Margaret* that way, along with several other favorites. Her friends understood life with Millicent was not easy and provided Theresa with whatever books she wanted to read.

Whitely Parker of *The Dixiecrat* attended many of those same events, both as a reporter and as a supporter—some would say disciple—of Millicent. Persistent rumors implied that their relationship went deeper and was not necessarily purely pure. Theresa's stomach turned a little at the idea of any such relationship.

Whitely's son, Malachai, was the same age as Theresa. Malachai was homeschooled, although he spent his mornings folding newspapers and placing them in newsstands around Clear Spring. Then he got on his bicycle and threw newspapers on the front porches of most of the homes in Clear Spring.

His only socialization, outside of church, happened when he accompanied his father to events where Millicent was speaking. Consequently, Theresa was one of his few friends, or the closest thing the boy had to a friend. Malachai always hoped it would become something more.

For Theresa, the forced proximity to Malachai only made her want him to leave.

When Theresa was in high school, while attending a meeting about whether girls should be allowed to wear blue jeans and the appropriate length of skirts, Malachai sat down next to Theresa. She looked up from the book she was reading only long enough to see it was Malachai who had disturbed her. Then she went back to reading her religiously-safe, Millicent-approved book.

"You read a lot," Malachai observed.

Theresa did not look up and kept on reading. "Nothing gets by you, does it?"

While Theresa read, Malachai slowly reached behind her for her backpack, grabbed it, and carried it out of the gym as casually as possible while looking over his shoulder to make sure Theresa was watching. Theresa was under strict orders not to move or to do anything that would call attention to herself or distract from her mother's important work. That was the rule. Violations for drawing attention to herself during a meeting were rapid, severe, and very public.

Malachai carried the backpack into the hallway where he stood out of sight of Millicent but where Theresa could see him when she turned her head.

Theresa resisted the urge to run to the hallway to retrieve her backpack as long as she could. She waited until her mother was on the opposite side of the stage, then made a fast but silent exit from the gym when Malachai opened the backpack.

"I saw what's in your bag," Malachai told her in a sing-song voice.

"You sound like a little girl," Theresa replied. "Are you a little girl, Malachai?"

"And I'm going to tell your mom," he continued.

From her vantage point in the hallway, Theresa watched Millicent make her way back to center stage. Theresa recognized the beginning of the end of her mother's usual speech. She was sure her mother had noticed she was gone by now.

"Give me the bag," Theresa demanded.

Malachai opened the backpack. "Kind of weird for a girl to be using a backpack." He looked at Theresa. "But you're kind of a weird girl so I guess it's OK." He pulled out a well-worn paperback copy of *Coffee, Tea, or Me? The uninhibited memoirs of two airline stewardesses*, a current best seller the mother of a friend of Theresa's had checked out from the library. Theresa's friend had taken the book from the drawer of her mother's nightstand—her mother assumed she'd lost it but was too embarrassed to ask her husband or anyone in the house if they had seen it—and started passing it around among her friends.

"What's this?" Malachai grinned as he flipped the pages.

"It's a book," Theresa said. "Why don't you take it out and read it? Here, let me show you the good parts." She opened the book to one of the many dog-eared sections and handed it to the wide-eyed boy who had taken her backpack. "Here." She winked at Malachai, sending his already elevated blood pressure and his propensity for stammering even higher. "You'll like this."

Malachai read one page and then another, his mouth and his eyes growing wider with each paragraph.

"Isn't that something?" Theresa pointed to a passage in the middle of the book and watched as Malachai pointed to each word as he read.

Malachai instinctively flinched when Theresa touched the page he was reading.

"It's OK." She looked at Malachai and grinned. "Look at this."

Theresa turned to another even more salacious part of the story. It wasn't long before Malachai was flipping from one thumb-stained section to the next.

While Malachai was engrossed in the steamy prose, Theresa slowly retrieved her backpack and re-entered the gym in time to hear her mother tell everyone to stand up for the closing prayer. Theresa took her seat while her mother prayed and everyone had their eyes closed. Millicent was winding up her monologue for God and was about to ask him to bless the troops overseas when a military-grade voice boomed from the hallway.

"What is this?"

Instead of bowing his head silently in prayer, Whitely had walked to the side of the gym for one last picture of the crowd. He had just put down his camera when he saw Malachai sitting in the hallway, his head moving side to side as his eyes tracked the words across the pages, licking his thumb to turn each page as he read, turning back and forth between pages. Malachai was flipping to the next turned down page when Whitely slapped the book from his hand and picked it up from the floor.

"What is this book?"

Whitely could be heard across the gymnasium and into the parking lot. By this time, people were leaving the gym, including Theresa, who filed past the father-son scene as it played out in the hallway—along with her mother and a hundred other people. The last thing Theresa heard before she got into her mother's car—the last thing any of them heard as they left the building—was Whitely barking at Malachai, asking him if he had any idea what was going to happen to him when they got home.

Theresa smiled but kept her head down to hide her silent laughter.

"Malachai's in trouble," Millicent said. She turned to her daughter.

"I'd better not find out that was your book."

"You won't," Theresa assured her.

And she didn't. Malachai may have threatened Theresa, but he loved her too much to get her in trouble. Her crime, like his affection for her, would remain an unspoken secret. He took her punishment as a demonstration of his devotion to her. He hoped she would see it his way.

Millicent never knew. Theresa never cared.

After that, Theresa avoided Malachai as much as possible. Sometimes it was not possible at all, like at her mother's meeting in the gym when she'd been forced to introduce Malachai to Jeremiah.

Theresa didn't know if Malachai was at the music festival that day but she knew Whitely would be covering it for the paper. She made a mental note to avoid the father and the son. She imagined the headline: "Daughter of Local Obscenity Fighter Found With Purveyor of Raunchy Books." Theresa was not a journalist, but she knew nothing sells newspapers like a scandal. What bigger Clear Spring small town scandal could there be than for the daughter of Millicent Spate to be sharing dirty books with the son of George Malone?

"I can understand being dragged to these things when you were a kid," Jeremiah said, "but why are you here now? Do you really want to spend your days doing this?"

"Today, I am here for the music," Theresa told him. "And this ear of corn. You don't see me walking around with a clipboard."

She stood up. "I don't know. More out of a sense of duty than anything else, I guess. Obligation. That, and I live in her house so it's easier to just do this and avoid the argument."

"I could ask you why you were at the gym the other night," Theresa told Jeremiah. "But I already know. It's what people like us do. We carry the torch of the family legacy. Family honor. All that."

She paused before speaking again. "It's what we were raised to do, regardless of what we might think of it. You'll probably do the same thing to your kid."

Jeremiah hoped he wouldn't do that to Zachary but he understood what Theresa was saying.

"I guess we all want to leave something behind," he said.

Theresa looked straight ahead and then turned back to Jeremiah.

"A legacy can be a heavy thing to carry," she said. "Especially when you're carrying it with only one hand."

22

Theresa was waiting outside the bookstore when Jeremiah and Zachary arrived the next morning.

"We don't open for another hour," Jeremiah told her.

"That's too bad." She stepped closer to him and pretended to be confrontational but with a smile. "Because I need to speak to a manager now."

Jeremiah held Zachary up to the doorknob and watched patiently while Zachary carefully worked the key into the keyhole. With Jeremiah's help, he eventually unlocked the door. Triumphant, Zachary gave the key to his dad and ran inside.

"Come on in. I'll see if I can find a manager."

The store was exactly as Jeremiah left it when Ethan dragged him to the music festival the night before, although, in retrospect, Jeremiah could not complain. The cash register drawer was closed with the money still in it, something Jeremiah never did. Freshly unboxed books were spread across the counter waiting to be catalogued and shelved. A half-empty coffee mug sat beside them. More mugs sat on the tables in the book club circle.

Theresa surveyed the scene. "You must have really needed to get to that concert."

"I really need to hire some help," Jeremiah admitted. "And Ethan was kind of pushy." He smiled at Theresa. "But I'm glad I went."

Jeremiah looked around the countertop and then at the rest of the cluttered store. It wasn't like him to leave the store in this condition. George and Tammy believed every morning should look like opening day, ready to impress customers and sell books. This looked like it was the end of a busy and understaffed shift, which is exactly what it was when Ethan offered Jeremiah a chance to get away.

Theresa watched Jeremiah hang empty coffee mugs on each of his prosthetic fingers and carry them back to the sink in the break room.

"You're not looking for a job, are you?" he asked.

"Not really," she said, "but I'll put this stuff away."

"I'm serious." Jeremiah stepped out from behind the counter. "You love books. You're smart. I could use the help. What do you think?"

"I can't."

"I'll even throw in free rent in the basement apartment," Jeremiah offered.

"That would make conversations with my mother so much more interesting," Theresa said. "Me living with you in a basement."

"That's not what I said."

"But that is what she will hear."

The offer was tempting, but Theresa knew she could not accept. Explaining Jeremiah to Millicent would be hard enough.

Telling Millicent she was moving into Jeremiah's apartment, even if he wasn't going to live there, was more than she wanted to face.

"I can't," Theresa said. She seemed to be prioritizing what needed to be done in the store. "I'll start on the children's section."

They were still straightening up the store when Ethan walked in. He helped himself to a cup of coffee from the coffeepot in the book club circle and took a seat.

"Quite the happening last night, wasn't it?" he said. "I told you that you needed to get out." Ethan took a long drink from his mug. "Have you thought about how you're going to handle the crazy lady? I saw her there last night with her petition."

Jeremiah flinched. He looked to see if Theresa had heard what Ethan had said about her mother. She was still working in the children's section. Jeremiah decided to hedge his bets just in case.

"I'm not sure if she's crazy or just misguided," he said, loudly enough for Theresa to hear.

"She's crazy," Theresa said while she was still several feet away. "Flat out crazy." She stopped and looked at Ethan. "She's also my mom, for better or for worse. Mostly worse."

Ethan shot a look at Jeremiah. "You could have mentioned that."

Jeremiah threw up his hands. "I didn't know until last night."

"Which kind of surprised me, that you didn't know," Theresa said to Jeremiah. "Once I thought about it, I remembered seeing you at some of those meetings when your parents would argue with my mother. I assumed you knew." She smiled. "But then I realized you didn't remember me."

"Well, you were doing your best to not be noticed," Jeremiah said. "And you succeeded."

Theresa grinned. "I saw the girls you dated in high school. I wasn't even on your radar."

Ethan sat in the book club circle. "Tell me more. Inquiring minds want to know."

"More about Jeremiah in high school or more about my mother?"

Ethan laughed. "I can guess what Jeremiah was like in high school. Tell me about growing up with Millicent. What was that even like?"

"There's not much more to tell," Theresa said. She smiled and shrugged her shoulders. "She's my mother. She believes certain types of books should not be read, especially not at school and especially not by children, although she also thinks someone needs to screen books for adults, too. Mainly she believes she should be the one who decides which books are appropriate and which are not. Welcome to my world."

Theresa looked at the Books That Deserve To Be Read table.

"If you really want to understand Millicent," Theresa said, "you should read the books she's read."

"I've read the Bible," Jeremiah said. "Cover to cover, even all the 'begats'."

Theresa laughed. "That's a start, but it doesn't end there. There's this one." She picked up *None Dare Call It Conspiracy* and tucked it under her arm. She reached for *The Politician*. "And this one." She looked at the assortment of books on the table. "There were others, but I don't see them here. Does that mean they must not have been banned?"

"Seriously?" Jeremiah took *Conspiracy* and laughed. "I wanted to get rid of this book years ago but Dad wouldn't let me. I told him I was going to throw this out when I became manager."

"What happened?" Ethan asked. "And why did you want to throw it out?"

"I put it in a box in the office the day after they left for Florida," Jeremiah said. "I was going to throw it out. To be honest, I forgot about it." Jeremiah mimed the movements of putting the book on his desk as he tried to remember what he'd done.

"And I left it there," he said. Then he smiled. "And Dad must have put it back on the table when they were here for the wedding."

"And now you need to read it." Ethan laughed. "Oh, the irony. It's the whole 'know your enemy' thing."

"Thank you, Sun Tzu," Jeremiah said.

"Although…". Ethan dragged out the last syllable as he picked up the book and looked at the front and back covers. "I don't think this was officially banned, not by law anyway. It was more like nobody would carry it in their bookstore. So, a kind of unofficial ban. A publisher ban. A book industry ban."

"That's what we do," Jeremiah said. "We carry the books no one else wants to touch." He took the book from Ethan and flipped through the pages. He looked at Theresa.

"I hope your mom didn't buy this from us."

"No way." Theresa laughed. "She would never buy a book from you. There are stores that have entire sections of this kind of stuff. Until I came in here, I thought every bookstore was like that."

Jeremiah smiled. That explained Theresa's reaction the first time she came to the store.

"I take it you do not share these beliefs?" Ethan said.

"I was raised with those beliefs," Theresa said. "Some of them are valid. But lately I've been thinking about what all that means. I don't like my mother telling me what I can read, and she's my mother. I can't imagine her treating other people's kids that way, much less doing that to an adult. I'm not sure some random person should have the authority to decide what someone else or someone else's child can read. At the very least, there should be a committee or something."

"Your mother would say she has a committee," Ethan countered.

"But they all think the same thing," Theresa said. "Her committee might as well be one person. Usually you have to attend a family reunion in Mississippi to find that kind of inbreeding."

Coffee spewed out of Jeremiah's mouth, spraying hot liquid on everything in its path. Ethan, who was putting his mug back on the table, froze mid-reach and looked at Theresa until he could no longer hold back the laughter. All the laughing made Zachary laugh. Seeing Zachary laugh made Theresa laugh.

"Intellectually, I mean." Theresa added over the laughter. "Intellectual inbreeding."

"Thank you for clarifying that," Jeremiah said.

Ethan stopped laughing and smiled. "Sorry. You were saying?"

"I was saying that I am reconsidering my role in my mother's crusade. Her ministry, as she calls it. Her campaign." Theresa sat down in a chair. "Although I don't really have a role other than to sit in the audience. But you're right. She is crazy."

"Crazy or not," Ethan said, "she knows how to organize. She knows how to motivate people to act. She's very good at this."

"Thank you for saying that," Theresa said. "People are always saying she's stupid or whatever. They don't think I hear it, but I do. She's not stupid. She's just a control freak. She's actually very smart and she knows exactly what she's doing."

"That's what I said," Jeremiah agreed. "And she's been doing this a while. She knows what works."

"We have to know just as much," Ethan said. "And we don't have much time to catch up." He raised a finger to his lips as if to think and then pointed to Jeremiah.

"If only we knew someone, maybe two people, a married couple, maybe, with experience with this kind of thing." The big man stood up. "Someone, I don't know, someone with a national reputation, a global reputation as free speech advocates." Ethan's deep voice became more intense. "Someone respected as published experts in the field. Imagine knowing people like that. People with experience. People with a voice. A following."

Jeremiah would not yield. "We are not calling my parents about this. Dad is still asking if he needs to come back and take care of the store. He'd be here tomorrow if he heard about this."

"My mother would love that," Theresa said. "She talked about your parents all the time when they lived here.

"Why?" Jeremiah asked.

"Because you can't be a hero without a villain," Theresa said. "She would love to feel like she beat the evil George and Tammy Malone."

"Could she?" Jeremiah asked. "Could she get a book ban past my parents?"

"I don't know," Theresa answered. "But, to be honest, I don't think she would have tried this if your parents were here. Sorry. There were other things, too, if that helps. I know she was waiting for the right people to get on the School Board. That's why she worked for those campaigns."

"Your School Board president seems to be on her side," Ethan said.

"He goes to our church." Theresa faced Jeremiah. "Mom's church," she clarified, in case there was any confusion. "But, yeah, she probably would have been at least a little less bold about it if she had known she was going to have to fight George and Tammy."

"We need to have a meeting of our own," Jeremiah said. "We may not be as alone on this as we think. That crowd the other night was pretty one-sided, but there has to be more people out there who think like we do. If nothing else, we could at least let those people know they are not all alone."

Theresa agreed. "That's a big thing for her, to make people feel like they are alone. Like they are the only ones who disagree with her, as if everyone agrees with her about whatever it is she's fighting. She's been doing this for so long I think she actually believes that."

Jeremiah picked up a calendar from the wire rack that held calendars, maps, and notebooks. "The School Board meets on the second Monday of the month. We have just over two weeks to get this done. Millicent is going to show up with a crowd of people. We need to do the same."

"We're going to need to advertise," Ethan said. "What about the local newspaper?"

"*The Dixiecrat?*" Jeremiah laughed again. "I don't see that happening. And we'll need someone to print any flyers or other papers we might need. I don't think Whitely is going to help us on that."

"I don't know," Theresa said. "Whitely is a businessman. In my experience, he's an 'anything for a buck' kind of guy."

"Seriously? He hates my parents. Dad never advertised with him."

"That doesn't mean Whitely wouldn't have run their ad," Theresa said. "I'm telling you, the guy would sell his mother for the right price."

Jeremiah gave a dismissive wave. "Honestly, I'd rather not have *The Dixiecrat* involved in this. Too much history between him and my parents." He turned to Ethan. "I've read exactly one edition of *The Dixiecrat,* when Whitely ran an op-ed about the display. I haven't picked up one since. I'd rather not give any money to Whitely Parker."

"Fine," Ethan said. "Ask Ruthanna what to do when she gets here."

23

"Call your parents," Ruthanna said as soon as she came in.

"No," Jeremiah told her. "We can do this."

Ruthanna shook her head. "You're so stubborn. You really are just like your father."

"If I am just like my father, then tell me what my father would do about this problem."

"Looks like you're already getting some advice." The former babysitter looked at Theresa. "I must say this is a surprise, to see you here." Theresa was one of the few people her age in Clear Spring who had not grown up with Ruthanna as a babysitter. Ruthanna knew her only from seeing her with her mother when Millicent was protesting something. It was not a good impression.

"I've had a change of heart," Theresa said.

Jeremiah turned to Ruthanna. "Where do we begin? Should we have a meeting of our own? We could use the gym like Millicent did."

"If you have a meeting," Ruthanna began, "what's to stop Millicent from turning it into her own platform?" She grinned and tapped Jeremiah on the shin with her cane. "Like you did when she had her meeting in the gym?"

Instead of hosting their own meeting, Ruthanna suggested a whisper campaign starting with the women in the book club. "If we tell the book club, they'll tell other people. Word will get around. And if we printed some flyers and handed them out to people who come in the bookstore, those will get around. They'll show up to support us without us showing Millicent what we're going to say beforehand. Kind of an unexpected show of strength."

Ethan liked the idea. "If we don't do a meeting, Millicent has no warning."

"An ambush," Ethan said.

"This is good," Theresa said. "Mom and her friends like to disrupt other people's meetings. They can take over before you know it. You can avoid all of that. Instead of hosting a community meeting to explain why book bans were wrong, they decided to dedicate their time to preparing what they would say to the School Board.

"So it will be the three of us," Ruthanna said. She turned to Theresa. "Unless you want to speak."

Theresa shook her head.

"I can't. Not now," she said. "And I may sit with my mother for this just to avoid the fight. Please don't feel like I'm a spy or something."

Ruthanna raised an eyebrow but said nothing. She knew Theresa wouldn't have to say anything if she didn't want to. Simply sitting with them instead of sitting beside Millicent would send a huge message to the School Board and everyone else in the room. But, while Theresa might be comfortable talking about her mother within the safety of the bookstore, Ruthanna knew they could not expect her to suddenly and publicly defy Millicent. The personal consequences would simply be too great.

Ruthanna knew Jeremiah had a lot to lose as well, including possibly the store. It was hard to say which of them, Theresa or Jeremiah, stood to lose the most.

Their impromptu meeting was interrupted when customers started coming through the door. Jeremiah took his place behind the counter. He told everyone about the upcoming vote and their plan to fight the bans. "It would be great if you could be there," he said as he handed people their books.

Ethan helped three older ladies who wanted half-priced books from the Books That Deserve To Be Read display, answering their questions about why certain books were banned, knowledge he never expected to use outside of an academic setting. Ruthanna noticed a mother and her small child who seemed to be looking for something in the children's section. She limped over to help them. Theresa checked to see if a book a customer had ordered last week had arrived.

"Have you been doing all this by yourself this whole time?" Ethan asked Jeremiah during a lull in traffic in the store. "Helping customers, stocking shelves, and everything?"

"I have," Jeremiah said. "And, honestly, I am getting tired of doing it."

"I could use a part-time job," Ethan said. "I still have to work on my dissertation, but a little extra income wouldn't hurt. I worked in a bookstore when I was a kid, so I know a little about it."

"Honestly, I already asked Theresa if she wanted a job." Jeremiah looked across the room at Theresa. "But she didn't seem interested."

Ethan stepped behind the counter. "I am interested."

"The store still isn't making much money," Jeremiah explained. "I'm covering expenses, but that's about it. Not much left over for me to live on." Jeremiah paused. "How about I pay you by letting you live in the apartment downstairs and you only work part time?"

"Works for me. When do I start?"

Jeremiah shook Ethan's hand. "Right now would be good."

"Great!" Ethan lifted three unopened boxes of books at once, sat the stack gently on the counter, and then unstacked them so they could be opened. Jeremiah was impressed, even if Ethan did have two hands.

Jeremiah and Ruthanna huddled behind the counter while Ethan worked on the books. Ruthanna pointed out that the School Board limited the time for guest speakers to three minutes each. Speakers had to be approved a week in advance to be on the agenda. Board members, of course, could speak for as long as they wanted. They also had the advantage of speaking last. The President of the

School Board, Jack Duncan, had the final word before any vote was taken. He might not win every vote, but he had a definite advantage built into every agenda. Jeremiah already knew how Duncan was going to vote. This was the same man who led the opening prayer at Millicent's rally.

"I want to do something," Theresa said. "Let's do this. I'll stay here at the counter while the three of you work on what you're going to say at the meeting. If I have any questions, I'll be sure to ask."

"Works for me," Jeremiah said.

Ruthanna wasn't so sure.

"What happens if Millicent hears you're working here?" she asked. "Correction. *When* Millicent hears you're working here?"

"That is a good question." Jeremiah turned to Theresa. "What would Millicent say if she knew you were here?"

Theresa gave a heavy sigh. "You're right," she said. "I should probably be going."

Jeremiah turned to Ruthanna as the door closed behind Theresa.

"You didn't have to run her off," he said. "I mean, I didn't expect her to stay, but, still…"

"You need to be careful with that one," Ruthanna interrupted. "I understand your new friend is rebelling against her mother. Or standing up to her. Whatever. More power to her. But she is still Millicent's daughter. She was brought up with certain values, just like you. And when it comes down to it, she will act on those values just like you are acting on yours. It's practically an instinct."

"I don't know," Jeremiah said. "I like her. She's got guts."

"Really?" Ruthanna said. "Her guts were the first thing you noticed?"

Jeremiah felt his face flush.

"I'm not just talking about protecting yourself," Ruthanna told him. "Think about her. Think about how Millicent is going to react to all of this. Do you want to put her at risk of all that? Be careful, for her sake and yours."

Jeremiah stayed at the counter while Ethan and Ruthanna sat in the reading circle and got to work. With their academic backgrounds, they were naturals at making logical, persuasive arguments with just enough of an emotional pull to make it work. They seemed to have enough ideas for the three of them and then some, certainly more than one person could say in the allotted three minutes per speaker time limit. He could always use their extras if he couldn't come up with something.

Jeremiah wondered how an adult like Theresa could be controlled by her mother as if she was still a child. Even though he lived at home with his parents until he was nineteen, he'd been more or less independent since he was in high school. Unlike Theresa, he'd been free to choose what he wanted to read since he first started reading. There were some books and magazines that made his parents roll their eyes and tell him he could be making better choices, but nothing was forbidden so long as George or Tammy deemed it age appropriate, a category that got larger as Jeremiah got older.

This same parental freedom and his sense of personal independence allowed Jeremiah to move into the basement apartment when he was eighteen. Theresa was still living at home at twenty. As for differences in how parents treat sons and daughters, Jeremiah knew several women Theresa's age or younger who were living on their own or with a roommate. The number was higher if you included women who went to college and lived in a dorm. It soared if you included women who got married so they could move out of their parents' house. Jeremiah wasn't sure where marriage fell on the continuum of independent living.

It slowly dawned on Jeremiah that moving out of your parents' house, something he once considered the ultimate sign of adult independence, was one thing. Breaking away from your parents' beliefs is completely different. Independent thought required more effort and much more courage than simply dragging some furniture from one place to another. He might have a house and a child, but Theresa was engaged in a battle for freedom that he never fought. Not like the kind of fight Theresa faced if she was going to be truly on her own.

Jeremiah flinched when he remembered how his dad reacted when Zachary was born. How would his parents respond if he walked away from the bookstore or failed to address a challenge like Millicent Spate?

More immediately, he wondered how the others were going to react when they realized he did not know what to say.

He decided to change that.

24

Jeremiah put Zachary down for his nap in the back room, asked Ethan to watch the store, and left. He carefully considered what he was about to do and the motivations behind it. Was he just looking for something new? Was he asserting his independence? How would he feel after he did it?

What would his parents say?

He decided none of that mattered. Some things just have to be done.

He went to the grocery store and spent thirty-five cents on the latest edition of *The Dixiecrat*, something he'd promised himself he would never do. He considered grabbing something to eat and reading the newspaper while having a cup of coffee at the diner but he didn't want to be seen reading *The Dixiecrat* in public. He took the paper back to the bookstore.

Whitely Parker did not disappoint. There, on the front page above the fold, was Whitely's story about Millicent's meeting, complete with a description of Jeremiah's "typical liberal knee jerk reaction" of trying to influence public opinion "by giving things away for free."

"Listen to this," he called to Ethan. Then he read.

"Mr. Malone, local bookseller, mocked the proceedings and instead used them to promote his place of business," the news story said. *"His brazen grandstanding and his announcement of a half-price sale on the same banned books*

Mrs. Spate wants to keep out of the reach of children was a slap in the face to everyone who shares our community's concern for our schools and our kids."

"Dad was right," Jeremiah said. "Why should we pay for advertising when Whitely gives it to us for free?"

"I don't recall you slapping anyone," Ethan said. "I must have missed that."

"It was right after the grandstanding. Try to keep up."

Whitely made no mention of Ethan or the mysterious Joan Campbell and their questions about Millicent's allegations. If *The Dixiecrat* was to be believed, everyone there agreed with Millicent. Everyone, that is, except for Jeremiah.

"Mr. Malone, who comes from California, ultimately contributed nothing of value to the discussion."

"We moved here when I was two," Jeremiah said. "I'm not sure if that qualifies me as a Californian."

Jeremiah knew the details about his birth did not matter. Towns like Clear Spring don't consider you "from there" unless your family has lived there for at least two generations and has a street named after them. George and Tammy Malone were outsiders. So was their son. The fact that Jeremiah had no memory of having lived anywhere else made no difference.

Jeremiah looked at Ruthanna. "I never read this paper. Does Whitely always write like this?"

Ruthanna took the paper from Jeremiah and started reading.

"This is actually pretty mild," she said. "I have some old *Dixiecrats* at home. I'll bring them in so you can get the full Whitely Parker experience."

Unlike George, who enjoyed tossing *The Dixiecrat* in the trash along with coffee grounds, egg shells, and the occasional banana peel, Ruthanna kept especially offensive copies for future reference. She often referred to some of Whitely's more vicious editorials when she needed to explain an extreme right wing position. And Whitely had many extremist positions on a variety of topics from which to choose.

"I'm going home," she announced shortly after lunch. "But I'll bring some old *Dixiecrats* with me when I come by tomorrow," Ruthanna said. "Try to write something for the presentation."

Ruthanna had only been gone a few minutes when Jeremiah heard the bell ding again. He looked up to greet the next customer.

Standing before him was Millicent Spate.

"Surprised to see you here," he said. "Are you here for the half-priced books?"

"It's been a while." Millicent looked around the store. "How do you like managing your own Den of Inequity?"

"Is there something I can help you with?" Jeremiah asked.

"I'm here to make you an offer," Millicent said as she stepped up to the counter. "Your parents worked hard to build this business. I never agreed with them, but I respect what they have built here."

"But..." Jeremiah said.

"But nothing." Millicent tore off a piece of tape from the tape dispenser on the counter, formed it into a loop, and rolled it between her fingers and thumb. "Here's my offer: If you let me have this one, then I will leave your business alone."

"This one?" Jeremiah asked. "This one what?"

"The School Board," Millicent said. "If you don't go to the School Board meeting and just let me make my case so they can pass the proposal, I will leave you and your store alone. For now."

"Leave my business alone?" Jeremiah laughed. "What are you? Mafia? Klan? What is that even supposed to mean?"

Millicent ignored the laughter.

"It means exactly what it sounds like. I will leave you alone. I know you're going to the meeting. It's what your parents would have done and after the other night, I expect no less from you. You're going to go and you're going to oppose my plan. And you'll probably bring some friends with you."

"That's the general idea," Jeremiah said.

Millicent rolled the tape into a ball and leaned over the counter to toss it in the trash. "I'm saying that if you don't do that, if you don't go to the School Board, then I will leave your bookstore alone. I will tell my people to leave you alone."

"And if I go to the meeting? If we explain to the School Board why what you're doing is wrong?" Jeremiah was taken aback by the pure audacity of what Millicent was saying.

"Then I can't promise that your store will be left alone. People will protest. I will have so many people marching back and forth on your sidewalk that you won't be able to open the door. It doesn't matter how far they drive from out of town, people will walk away without ever stepping inside."

"That sounds like a threat." Jeremiah thought about a pool hall that opened up when he was in high school. He and Skipper became regular customers, along with a lot of other Clear Spring kids. The way Millicent preached about the immoral implications of playing pool, you would have thought she was auditioning for the part of Professor Harold Hill in The Music Man. The pool hall didn't last six months after that.

Millicent smiled. "I'm glad we understand one another." She stopped at the door before she left. "Have a great day. I'll see you at the School Board meeting. Or maybe not. Up to you."

Jeremiah was still thinking about what Millicent said when Ruthanna came back with the promised copies of *The Dixiecrat* for him to review. She opened one to the editorial and handed it to Jeremiah.

"Here," she said. "Read this. Classic Whitely."

"*While we sympathize with the widows and children who are growing up without fathers, we cannot encourage the idea of the single-mother household,*" Whitely had written. "*By accepting the idea that a woman does not need a man to have a family, we are condoning premarital sex, divorce, and other promiscuous behavior. Men who encourage this kind of behavior or who take advantage of the permissive sexual attitudes it promotes are unwittingly planting the seeds of their own destruction and the loss of any husbandly authority they may wish to have when they eventually want to start families of their own.*"

"Another good reason to avoid wars," Ruthanna said. "But I digress."

"I'm still trying to figure out what 'husbandly authority' is supposed to mean." Jeremiah scanned the editorial, then slipped into a Southern preacher drawl:

"If we want God to bless our country, we must discourage the glamorization of single-mother families, lest children grow up thinking that's an acceptable structure."

Jeremiah stared at the editorial's closing line again. The real fear wasn't broken homes—it was broken roles.

Whitely wrote a lot about family values, by which he meant the value of a traditional mom, dad, and however many kids they might have. But this definition of family was changing, even within small towns like Clear Spring. The war created too many single-mother households to be ignored. Were they not families? These women, mostly young widows like Laura, were bravely showing how a single mother could, in fact, raise a child. How long would it be before other women, women who never married, looked at them and decided they did not need a man to have a family, either?

And wasn't that what men like Whitely Parker really feared? That they would be rendered unimportant or, even worse, unnecessary? To be, for all practical purposes, impotent?

Ruthanna stabbed at the newspaper with her finger. "They want to decide what is and what isn't a family. Doesn't Zachary deserve to read about a family that looks like his family? Once he realizes he does not have a mom, will he really need a library or a story he might read in class to remind him of that?"

"We can't eliminate all the books about kids with two parents just because some children might not have a mom," Jeremiah said. "That's not realistic. It's not even healthy."

"We don't have to," Ruthanna said. "But we shouldn't eliminate books about kids who don't, either. This is not an either-or situation. There is room for more than one type of family in schoolbooks."

Jeremiah thought about the bookstore's inventory. He had two titles in the store about being a single mom, a self-help book and one semi-poetic anthology, as well as children's book about a child raised by a single mom. While much of that applied to him and Zachary, he had yet to see a book about being a single dad or one featuring a family with a single male parent. Zachary had never seen a book with a family that looked like his.

It wasn't that Jeremiah was intentionally not ordering books about single parents. The books he had were all that were available from his suppliers on the topic of single parenting, a topic closer to Jeremiah's heart than he ever thought it would be. While not an official ban, the result was the same. Books about single parents were banned by publishers and bookstores, just like they unofficially banned the McCarthy books.

Whitely wanted to take this unofficial ban a step further with policies that would ensure that no child with a single parent ever saw or read about a family that looked like theirs. To Whitely, if a group of people living in the same home didn't include a mom, a dad, and at least one child then it wasn't a family and should not be represented in a book or in class.

"Whitely is worried about normalizing single-mother households," Jeremiah said.

"Trust me," Ruthanna said, "the children of single parents feel abnormal enough already."

What Ruthanna said about children seeing themselves in children's books and the realization of his own bookstore's limited supply of books for single-parent families made Jeremiah wonder whether other bookstores, bigger bookstores, faced the same problem.

Jeremiah had been running the store on muscle memory since before George and Tammy left. Sell a book, replace it with the same book. Order something new only if it looks like the type of thing someone from Clear Spring would buy. He hadn't thought about the types of books he *wasn't* ordering. Books with different types of characters or different kinds of stories. Books about different kinds of families or from different perspectives.

He realized, if he was being honest, that he was engaged in a kind of passive censorship of his own, not by actively banning books but by unintentionally not making certain kinds of books available for his customers.

He had no market research or business stats, but he suspected he was not alone. Small town bookstores like Clear Spring Books & Electronics tend to reflect the interests and tastes of their owners and their local markets. George and Tammy had a wide array of interests, but they, like everyone else, were products of their time. The preferred things familiar. Now there were new people with new circumstances. And those new people deserved new books.

Jeremiah sensed his tastes were changing, and not just his taste in books. He was no longer as interested in the Mary Olsons and Becky Pinkstons of the world, friendly and abundant though they might be. He was looking for something—*someone*—less generic, less interchangeable. Someone who understood who he was and what his life was like *now*, after the divorce. After becoming a parent. Someone who, like him, was trying to be a responsible adult, whatever that meant.

Once again, he wondered about his options. Then he called Theresa.

"We need to go to Little Rock," he told Theresa on the phone. "You and me."

"Why do I need to go to Little Rock?" Theresa asked.

Jeremiah froze. He tried to remember the last time he'd had to give someone a reason to spend time with him. By the time he was inviting her back to his house, the "why" was understood and usually already in progress. At least that's how it was before Zachary was born and he had a more active social life.

All he could do was smile. He had no words. Theresa did not wait for an answer.

"When?" she asked

"Does this afternoon work?"

"Some of us are still taking classes," she teased.

"Hey. I didn't quit," Jeremiah said. "I've just missed a couple of times." He looked at his watch. "It's about three hours there, then three back, plus whatever we decide to do in the big city. Would tomorrow be better? Leave around eight and spend the day? I can pick you up at your house, if you'll tell me where that is."

"You picking me up might not be the best idea," Theresa reminded him. "Why don't we just meet at the bookstore?"

"Works for me."

"Mr. Malone, that almost sounds like you're asking me out on a date."

"I'll be leaving Zachary with Ruthanna, so I guess I am."

25

"You drive a station wagon?" Theresa did an exaggerated eye roll and smiled.

"Another hand-me-down from my parents," Jeremiah said. "They got it so they could carry boxes of books. I got it because Dad got a Corvette." He stopped and corrected himself for Theresa's benefit. "*When* Dad got the Corvette. Mom called it his midlife crisis car." Jeremiah lifted Zachary's car seat out of the front passenger seat and put it in the back of the red Ford Country Squire.

Theresa ran her fingers along the side of the station wagon. "Nice faux wood. I bet this was a chick magnet in high school."

"Actually," Jeremiah smiled, "these seats all fold down." He casually flipped the middle seat down flat. "See? Nothing but front seats and a nice big space to, er, carry things. Or whatever."

"It is important to have room to carry things." Theresa looked at him over the top of the vehicle. "Or whatever." She looked inside the car. "Is that why the blanket's back there? To cover the things you carry?"

"That's for Zachary."

"Zachary. Right."

Jeremiah opened the door for Theresa. He was opening the driver's door when he realized his checkbook was behind the checkout counter.

"I'll be right back."

Jeremiah ran inside and had just come out of the bookstore when he saw Laura coming around the corner.

"Hi." She clasped her hands and gave an awkward smile. "We never had a chance to talk."

"I didn't realize we needed to talk." Jeremiah pointed to the station wagon. "But I'm about to go somewhere. I can't talk right now."

"Are you going to the School Board meeting next week?" Laura asked.

Theresa opened the passenger door and got out of the station wagon. She made sure to slam the car door hard enough to get Laura's attention.

"Mind if I run inside?" she asked Jeremiah as she walked by. "I'll be real quick." She looked at Laura.

"Hi, Laura." She gave an artificial smile. "I'm surprised to see you here."

"Me too," Laura said. "Surprised to see you here, I mean." Laura blew a strand of red hair away from her face and looked to the sky.

Theresa turned to Jeremiah. "I'll be right back." She ran to the bookstore and quickly went inside.

Laura moved one step closer to Jeremiah.

"I didn't know you two were friends."

"We took a class together. She likes books," he said. "That's about it. How do you know her?"

"I've been going to her mother's church." Laura leaned into Jeremiah's ear. "And the three of us are supposed to be doing something together this weekend." She stumbled over her words as if she had said too much. "Millicent, Theresa, and me, I mean." She was flustered, and it showed.

She turned and looked at the spot where Theresa had been standing.

"Us."

Laura closed her eyes, took a breath, and tried again. "Millicent wants Theresa to go with us to this church retreat Pastor Kettle is having. It's a big deal. Lots of people will be there. I came here to pick her up so we could ride up together. We talked about it but I guess Theresa forgot."

Laura looked at the bookstore and then back to Jeremiah. It was obvious that she wanted to change the subject.

"Remember how I told you about Millicent's meeting at the gym?"

Jeremiah nodded. Laura continued.

"I did that because I think that no matter what side you're on, it should be a fair fight. I hadn't known Millicent very long when that happened. I understand her better now and I understand what she's doing. And, to be honest, I agree with her, mostly."

She looked at Jeremiah with a tight-lipped smile. "But I also like you. More than I should, probably." She stepped closer to Jeremiah. "And because I like you, I thought I should tell you something."

Jeremiah nodded. "OK."

Laura leaned close to Jeremiah's ear. She spoke softly.

"Millicent isn't just going after the school," she told him. "She's coming after you. She wants to close your bookstore."

Jeremiah remembered Millicent's threat but decided not to share that with Laura. Still, he was glad that Millicent couldn't see his face while she was whispering in his ear.

"How would she even do that?" he asked.

Laura shook her head. "I don't know. Zoning laws? A boycott? Something. I don't know the details, but I've heard her talking about it with Pastor Kettle. They're going to talk about it some more this weekend. They want to put you out of business."

"You said you agree with Millicent. Why are you telling me this?"

Laura looked back at the bookstore. "I'm not sure. It just doesn't feel right not to. I may be going to her church, but I'm not sure I agree with everything she says. Some of it just seems wrong." Laura paused for a moment. "And...If we're being honest, I was hoping to get to know you better, but now I see I may have missed that opportunity."

"Theresa and I are just friends," Jeremiah said, regretting that it was mostly true. "She doesn't like kids and she hasn't done or said anything about feeling anything for me."

"Whatever you say," Laura told him. "I swear, sometimes you guys are just blind."

"Please don't," Jeremiah said.

"Don't worry." Laura patted the back of his hand and then held it. "Your secret is safe with me. I'm not going to tell Millicent about you and Theresa."

Theresa came through the bookstore door as if on cue. Laura tried to intercept her while she was still on the sidewalk, but Theresa did not stop. She just looked at Laura, held up a hand, and shook her head. Laura watched Theresa slam the heavy station wagon door shut. Then she walked away.

Jeremiah was still thinking about what Laura said about the retreat with Theresa's mother and the good Pastor Kettle as he slipped behind the steering wheel.

"I know this is kind of spontaneous," he said. "Are you sure this works for you? Do you have anything else going on?"

"Nothing," Theresa said. "There is nowhere else I want to be."

Jeremiah decided not to ask about what Laura had told him. He turned the key to start the station wagon. The starter clicked a few times before the engine made a grinding noise and then slowly came to life.

Theresa was fascinated with the knob on the steering wheel. "Is that how you drive? How you steer?"

"Yeah. The whole hand-over-hand thing wasn't working for me."

Theresa allowed herself to laugh. "I guess not. Sorry. It's just that..."

"It's just that you forget I only have one hand?" he asked. He was actually glad to hear her say that. "So do I, until I need the other hand. Then I remember. But then I think about when I had two hands and I would be doing something and wishing I had a third hand. We're just never satisfied."

Theresa laughed and rubbed her hands together. "Where are we going?"

"I thought we could go to Little Rock and go to a real bookstore," he said. "Or we could get crazy and drive to Memphis."

Theresa pointed back to Jeremiah's bookstore. "You have a real bookstore."

"Yes I do." He smiled. "I mean a bigger bookstore, with more books, and more types of books, and other things I don't have here."

"And why don't you have those?"

"I'm not sure. My parents set all that up, decided which books we would stock, which suppliers we would use. I went with what they had." He pulled the station wagon into the street. "I just want to see what other guys are doing with their stores."

Jeremiah looked at the gas gauge and remembered the wagon's impressive 12 mpg mileage. "We're going to have to get some gas before we go too far." He turned to Theresa. "Where to? Little Rock or Memphis?"

"Memphis is a half hour more, so not much difference." She looked at Jeremiah. "You decide."

"Let's keep it in state," Jeremiah said.

The Ozarks are not very tall as mountain ranges go. But the roads are still steep, with plenty of twists and blind turns along the way. A canopy of old-growth forests of oak, hickory, and pine shaded the highway as they headed south toward Calico Rock and on to Little Rock. Dogwoods grew beneath the taller hardwoods, using what little sunlight that made it through the filter of trees overhead.

"Your blanket in the back made me think of my dad," Theresa said.

"It must be a good memory." He looked at his passenger. "You're smiling." He wondered why he hadn't seen the elusive Mr. Spate at any of Millicent's events.

"Yeah, for the most part. You know how Clear Spring is a dry county? We're not supposed to buy or sell alcohol here."

"Right." Jeremiah was very familiar with Clear Spring's dry county status. "Apparently that was a big shock to my parents when they came here from California. I heard about that a lot. Their friends would send them bottles in the mail. Wine for Mom, Bourbon for Dad."

"OK. Same idea. Slightly different execution." Theresa continued. "My dad would run up to Missouri, buy enough alcohol for all of his buddies, and then sell it to them out of our house."

The car swerved to the edge of the road as Jeremiah laughed. He regained his composure and his control of the car as quickly as he could while driving with one hand.

"Your dad was a bootlegger?"

"He was," she laughed. "My job was to sit in the back of the El Camino and make sure the tarp didn't blow off on the way home." She looked out at the forest going by. "I was like eight years old the last time we did that."

"That's crazy." Jeremiah laughed at the idea. "What did Millicent say about all this?"

"She didn't like it."

"Is that why I never see him at any of her events?"

"No." Theresa shook her head. "He died when I was eight. DUI."

"I had no idea." He turned to Theresa. "I'm glad you weren't in the car."

"He wasn't driving," Theresa explained as if she'd told the story more times than she wanted to remember. "He wasn't even drunk. He got hit by someone who was."

Travis Spate was enjoying the peaceful bliss of an evening walk in the snow—without the mellowing effects of alcohol—when he was struck by the blade of a snowplow driven by Joe Bob Walker, an employee of Clear Spring County who did not expect to be working that night and was enjoying his holiday cheer in liquid form with more than the usual amount of cheerfulness.

Joe Bob was called in to clear the roads when the ice and snow started piling up. He did not tell his boss he'd been drinking.

Travis was crossing the street when the blade of the snowplow hit him. Joe Bob didn't stop until he had gone over the curb, across the sidewalk, and hit a tree in front of the *Dixiecrat* building. He was still sleeping in the cab when Whitely noticed the yellow snowplow the next morning. Joe Bob's thermos of hot rum punch was on the seat beside him.

Joe Bob told the police that he thought the bump he felt before crashing into the curb was just a rock or something on the street. Maybe a pothole or some snow that had piled up. Travis Spate was spread down the street like so much chunky peanut butter on frozen toast, depriving Theresa of a father and interrupting the flow of alcohol to the citizens of Clear Spring County.

Theresa looked out the passenger window as they drove down the same street. "It was back there," she said. "We drove past it."

Jeremiah noticed the lump in Theresa's throat. She turned to look at him.

"That was when Mom really got into what she's doing now," Theresa continued. "It wasn't like she had to get a job. They'll be paying her every month for the next twenty-five years. She never told me the exact amount or any of the details about the settlement. I was just eight years old. What did I know? She just said it was God's way of preparing us for a bigger plan."

"I'm sorry," Jeremiah said. "I did not know that."

"She said the money would take care of me, too," Theresa said, "but I'm sure that would disappear if I ever did something she didn't like."

It was a few long moments before either of them spoke again.

"That's my story," Theresa said after a few silent miles. "Now, tell me how you became a single parent."

"I was stupid," Jeremiah admitted. "And Susan was struggling with some things." He told Theresa about his relationship with his ex-wife and how she suffered during and after her pregnancy.

Jeremiah looked in the mirror and then at the winding road in front of him. "She thought I lost my hand in Vietnam. I didn't tell her that's how it happened, but I didn't tell her the truth either. I just didn't say anything."

"You don't come off as the military type," Theresa said.

"Maybe you don't remember, but most of the guys they sent to Vietnam were not the military type," Jeremiah reminded her. "At least they weren't before they left."

"You also don't seem like the type to get married."

"I wasn't back then, that's for sure." He looked at Theresa. "But I wanted to try, you know? Do the right thing and all that." He turned back to look at the road before him. "What's funny is her parents insisted we get married as soon as they found out Susan was pregnant. I mean, that was when they thought I was a war hero, so I guess there is that."

"There is that," Theresa agreed.

"But they were just as fast, or her dad was just as fast, to make her get divorced when they found out I was just a regular guy."

"A regular guy who lied to their daughter," Theresa reminded him.

"I guess. I mean, I didn't lie. I just didn't tell the truth."

"Same thing." Her voice went to a slightly higher, more encouraging register. "But, I've seen you with Zachary. You're a good dad. That says a lot."

"I thought you didn't like kids."

"I don't," she said. "But, I can tell the difference between good parents and bad parents. You are a good dad. You love your kid. Not every parent does that."

They drove on until they reached Mountain Home and stopped to get some gas. The attendant started pumping the gas while Jeremiah and Theresa talked in the car. Once the tank was full, Jeremiah paid him and reached over the steering wheel to turn the key. The car clicked and sputtered like it had before. The sputters got progressively slower. Soon there were no sputters at all.

"It's the starter," Jeremiah said. "Great."

"I can check that for you." The attendant pulled a shop rag out of his pocket and wiped his hands with it. "Open the hood and I'll have a look."

"It's the battery," Theresa whispered to Jeremiah. "The starter is probably fine. The battery is dead."

The attendant was already looking under the hood. "They don't make those starters easy to get to," he said.

Theresa got out of the car and stood beside Jeremiah. "It's not the starter," she said softly in Jeremiah's ear. "Tell him to check the battery."

Jeremiah ignored her while he and the attendant, who was apparently also the mechanic, stared at the dead V-8 engine.

"Starters aren't cheap. The mechanic wiped his hands on a red shop rag as he spoke. "I can get one. I'll have to figure out how much it'll be with parts and labor."

Both men went back to looking beneath the station wagon's hood.

"It's not the starter," Theresa said loudly enough to be heard inside the gas station. "It's the battery."

The two men froze beneath the hood and then slowly backed away so they could stand up.

"How do you know?" Jeremiah asked.

"Because I know cars. And I know this is what happens when a battery is old and isn't holding a charge anymore."

"It could be both, Ma'am," said the mechanic with more than a touch of condescension. "Sometimes these things fall like dominos. I'll know more once I have it on the rack and can look at it."

"I'm telling you it's the battery," Theresa insisted. She turned to Jeremiah. "This guy wants to sell you a starter because he makes more money installing starters than he does putting in a battery."

The mechanic side-eyed Theresa from beneath the hood. He stood up slowly. "We need to put it on the rack," he insisted. "Help me push it over there."

As the men got in position to push the heavy station wagon, Theresa looked under the hood, saw what kind of battery the wagon had, and made a straight line for the garage. She came back with a new car battery in her hands.

"We'll test it right here." She put the battery on the ground near the engine. "Get me some jumper cables."

The mechanic wiped his hands again while Jeremiah retrieved a pair of jumper cables from the back of the station wagon and attached them to the dead battery. Theresa took the other ends of the cables and touched them together.

"No spark." She turned to the attendant. "It's dead." She put the cables close to the attendant's face and slapped them together several times. There were no sparks.

She turned to Jeremiah.

"How old is this battery?"

"I don't know. Six, seven years?"

"Wow," said Theresa. "They don't usually last that long." She attached the cables to the new battery that was sitting on the ground.

"Try it now."

The engine started on the first try.

"OK. Turn it off." Theresa disconnected the cables from both batteries and returned the cables to Jeremiah.

"Got a wrench?" she asked. The mechanic stomped back to the garage to retrieve the tool.

"I wasn't asking you," Theresa announced as he walked away. She turned to Jeremiah. "Please tell me you have a toolbox with you and then get me a wrench or a pair of pliers or something so I can replace this battery before Farmer Joe here tears your engine apart."

Jeremiah found a small set of pliers in the glove compartment and handed them to Theresa.

"Seriously? You're that guy?"

"What guy?"

"The guy who uses pliers instead of a wrench. Wow."

Theresa worked quickly. She already had the battery loose when the attendant returned with a battery wrench.

"Already got it," she told him.

"I told you it wasn't the starter," Theresa said as she removed the dead battery from the station wagon. Jeremiah picked up the new battery and placed it where the old battery had been. Theresa made the connections.

"Get in," she told him.

Jeremiah got in and turned the key. The station wagon immediately came to life. Theresa closed the hood while Jeremiah was still behind the wheel. Then she put both hands on the closed hood, leaned forward, and winked at Jeremiah.

All Jeremiah could do was smile. The black grease smudge just below her right eye looked sexier than any makeup he'd seen.

"What do I owe you?" he asked the mechanic when he'd gotten out of the station wagon.

"Well, let's see." His eyes rolled upward and slightly to the right. "With parts and labor..."

"Labor?" Theresa repeated. "Seriously?"

The mechanic rolled his eyes. "It's $16," he said. "The battery is $16."

"Just out of curiosity," Theresa said. "How much would a starter cost?"

"About $30 new," said the mechanic. "A little less if I got it from the junk yard."

"And labor?"

"About the same." He avoided Theresa's glare by looking down at the hood when he spoke.

"Will there be anything else, Ma'am?"

"No," Theresa said. "You want anything else, Jeremiah?"

"I'm good."

26

"Where did you learn about cars?"

"I told you. My dad was a bootlegger. Bootleggers know cars. I could have changed the oil and given you a tune-up if you'd needed it." She smiled at Jeremiah. "I wouldn't even charge you for labor."

The road got wider, and the forest grew thinner as they approached Little Rock.

"I thought we'd go to the bookstore in the mall," Jeremiah said. "We could grab lunch there and do whatever else you might want to do without driving all over town."

Crosswalk Mall, as it was known, was shaped like a cross. Jeremiah and Theresa window-shopped their way past a jewelry store, two shoe stores, a very upscale store for women, and a walk-in haircut place that—unlike the hair salons in Clear Spring—did not require making an appointment a week in advance.

The Corner Bookstore sat at the intersection of the mall's two corridors, The Promenade and The Boardwalk. Customers entered the store through the open front along either walkway. Unlike most of the stores in the mall, The Corner Bookstore occupied two floors. An ornate winding staircase in the center of the store connected the two levels. Less energetic shoppers used the escalators at the back of the store as a shortcut to get to stores on the mall's second level.

Theresa had never seen so many books in one place. The walls of both levels were lined with books from floor to ceiling. On both of the store's two floors, bookshelves were arranged to form small reading areas with lamps, couches, and small tables with ashtrays. A man smoked a pipe as he sat in a leather chair and read.

"Sir Walter Raleigh." Theresa closed her eyes and smiled as she breathed in the scent. "Cherry. My dad smoked that."

Theresa grew more excited with every step. "It's like a sanctuary," she said. "A sanctuary for books."

Jeremiah's assessment was less spiritual. "It's the ultimate setup for impulse shopping. They can't go anywhere in the mall without passing by the bookstore. And half of them will walk through the bookstore on their way to another store on the other level even if they didn't come here to buy a book."

"I wonder how many sales he makes from those walk-throughs," Theresa said.

"More than we do. We barely get people to come in off the sidewalk."

Jeremiah was right about there being more books and more different kinds of books than he had in Clear Spring. He was surprised to see books of essays or newspaper columns by writers he recognized from his dad's habit of reading most of the major newspapers in the country. It had not occurred to him that newspaper columns could appear somewhere other than a newspaper or that these columns could be put together in a kind of "greatest hits" format for favorite writers.

He noticed other books in subgenres he had not thought merited an entire section. Sci-Fi was separate from Fantasy. The Religion section faced the equally well-stocked Philosophy section and included books from Buddhist, Hindu, Wiccan, and other faiths alongside Christianity. There was a section for philosophically inclined Atheists, books that Jeremiah had never seen in a bookstore anywhere in Arkansas. Jeremiah assumed this was a reflection of religious diversity among the faculty and students of the nearby university, a diversity missing in the Clear Spring community and consequently missing from Clear Spring Books & Electronics.

Theresa made her way to "Women's Literature" only to find it was dominated by bodice ripper romance novels and books about the joys of motherhood with the Cookbook section close at hand.

"You have most of these," she whispered to Jeremiah in Literary Fiction. "They have more copies but that's because they have more space."

"Yeah. There are some things we don't carry, but I'm kind of proud of how well we've kept up." He looked around at the large overhead signs marking where each section was.

"I want to look at the kid books." Jeremiah headed for the large sign that said "Story Time". He spent several minutes looking at books for different ages before he realized that, like his own bookstore, The Corner Bookstore did not carry any books about kids who had no mother. There were no blended families, no families with parents whose relationships might not be recognized by the state. If these books were to be believed, all children lived happily ever after with Mom and Dad. And a dog. Maybe a cat.

"This is disappointing," he told Theresa.

"There was something I wanted to pick up," Theresa said. She took Jeremiah's hand and led him to the Corner Bookstore's much smaller version of Books That Deserve To Be Read.

"*Peyton Place.*" She picked up the book and showed it to Jeremiah. "Why don't you have this one in your store?"

"I do. Or I did. It was on the display, banned for fornication, incest, adultery, and abortion, if I remember right." He paused as if he was taking a mental inventory of the Books That Deserve To Be Read. "Maybe it sold. We don't get a lot of requests for that one. Why do you want it?"

"My dad liked to watch it when it was on TV. Mom never let me watch it with him. I just want to see what it's about."

"It's about the scandalous secrets of a small town," Jeremiah said. "Sound familiar? If it's not there then I should order some replacement copies."

"Then I should buy them from you."

"Why?" Jeremiah asked. "Get it while you're here. Think of it as a souvenir. A reminder of the first time you went to a big bookstore." Jeremiah picked up the book and handed it to Theresa.

"Merry early Christmas," he said.

"A very early Christmas," Theresa said. "But thank you."

Theresa smiled and carried her souvenir banned books to the checkout counter. The cashier, a man about the same age as Jeremiah's parents, rang up the book while Jeremiah got out his checkbook.

"I'll need to see an ID if you're going to write a check, please," the cashier said as he put Theresa's book in a bag. According to the slightly diagonal nametag hanging above his pocket protector, "Randy" was also the store manager.

Jeremiah placed his driver's license on the counter. The man picked it up, looked at it, and then looked at Jeremiah. He took his glasses from his pocket protector and looked at the license again to make sure.

"You're Jeremiah Malone?"

"I am."

The cashier/manager smiled and extended his right hand for a handshake. "I'm Randy Liles," he said. Jeremiah responded by extending his left hand.

"Oh. I'm sorry." Randy did an awkward juggle to switch hands. "Habit." He greeted Jeremiah with an enthusiastic lefthanded handshake.

"We've actually met several years ago," Randy put his glasses back in his shirt pocket. "Or, I should say, I met your parents. You spent the entire time they were here in the comic book section if I recall."

Randy stepped back as if he was admiring a statue. "That was what? Ten? Twelve years ago? And now you're all grown up. How are George and Tammy?"

"They are retired. I'm running the bookstore now."

"Really? How do you like it?"

Jeremiah hesitated. "Most days are OK."

Randy laughed. "You're honest, like your folks. Are they still doing the banned books thing?"

"Yes, but they're in Florida now." Jeremiah paused. "Which is kind of a problem because now we have people in Clear Spring trying to get some books banned from the school. I'm not sure how to handle that."

"We had that same problem here a few years ago," Randy said. "Some lady from out of town seemed to be the one pushing it. But we got lucky. George and Tammy helped us deal with her, but we also have a lot of students at the school whose parents teach at the university. They got together with a couple of the TV stations and shut all that down before it could take hold."

"Were you involved in that?" Jeremiah asked.

"A little," Randy said. "But the parents and the people from the university did most of it. I just kind of watched and hoped they didn't come after me."

"That's where I am," Jeremiah said. "Hoping they don't come for me."

"You're doing more than watching." Theresa interjected. "He and some of his friends are going to the School Board meeting about it." She turned to Jeremiah. "Give yourself some credit. You're doing a lot more than just watching."

"I'm trying to keep my store open," Jeremiah said. "It's like you said, first they'll come for the school. Then they'll come for me."

Randy agreed. "That's not quite Niemöller, but you're right about what will happen. They won't stop once they think they've won with the school." The bookstore manager placed the shopping bag in Theresa's outstretched hands while he talked to Jeremiah. "I would love to visit with you about all this. Let me get someone up here to watch the counter so we can talk."

The manager summoned a nametag called "Estelle" to the counter.

Theresa handed the bag to Jeremiah. "Would you hold this for me? I want to walk around and see what else is here."

"Sure."

Theresa's eyes sparkled almost as much as her smile. She squeezed Jeremiah's hand.

"Thank you. I won't be long."

"Let's go back to my office," Randy said after Theresa left. "We can talk there."

The office was cluttered with paperwork, books, unfinished bottles of Coke, and the litter box for the store cat. Randy removed a stack of books from a leather swivel chair and told Jeremiah to have a seat.

Jeremiah explained what he, Ruthanna, and Ethan planned to do, about their split presentation, and how they were quietly spreading the word that people should be there.

"What about your friend out there? She seems to like books."

Jeremiah hesitated before he spoke. "She's got some other things going on right now."

"Shy?"

Jeremiah's face broke with a single-note laugh. "No." He shook his head. "She's not shy."

"OK, but you're going to need everybody you can get," Randy warned as he picked up the phone but hung up before he dialed. "You can bet that the other side will have plenty of people. What they lack in logic they make up for with volume. That's how they win. Pure volume. They act like they're the majority even when they're outnumbered."

Jeremiah smirked. "Perception is reality."

"That's what they'd like us to believe," Randy said. "Look, small bookstores like yours are on the way out, I'm afraid. Your store is famous, but my guess is you're not making much money. How would you like to make more money without as many hassles?"

Randy continued before Jeremiah could answer. "The Corner Bookstore is going to be opening at least three new locations next year. With your experience and reputation, you could manage one of them."

"I don't know," Jeremiah said. "For all its problems, Clear Spring Books is our bookstore. My bookstore."

Randy wrote down some numbers and slid the piece of paper across the desk to Jeremiah.

"That would be your starting salary," Randy told him.

Jeremiah gulped at the figure. It was almost double what he'd brought home for all the previous year.

"You would be managing a new store in Memphis," Randy said. "We haven't even finished building it yet. But when it is finished, it's going to need a manager. It could use a manager right now, honestly, to help us get things ordered and ready to go."

Jeremiah stared at the paper. This would mean leaving his bookstore and leaving Clear Spring, both of which he would have done without hesitation only a short time before. It would also mean leaving Theresa.

"I'll have to think about it," he told Randy. "No offense, but I'm not a fan of how big chains are killing small local bookstores.

Stores like ours have character. We have a history. We serve our communities. There are people there who depend on us."

"All valid points," Randy said. He pointed to the scrap of paper in Jeremiah's hand. "Does that strong community relationship pay what I'm offering you?"

"Not even close." Jeremiah smiled and put the scrap of paper in his pocket.

"It's up to you," Randy said. "You'll know when you're ready." Randy talked to Jeremiah as he searched for another scrap of paper. "Back to your original problem. The best thing the Little Rock parents did was to get the local TV stations involved." He jotted down the name of the producer for Channel 12 News.

"I'll call him and tell him you're coming," Randy said. "His name is Joe Monroe. Talk to him."

27

Joe Monroe was big and balding and was tucking his shirt into the stretched waistband of his polyester pants when his secretary led Jeremiah and Theresa into his office. The station manager motioned for them to have a seat. Then he hiked up his pants and sat down in an over-sized office chair beneath the taxidermized head of a very large elk with an exceptionally large set of antlers and a blank stare. A rifle rested on hooks below the trophy, presumably the same rifle that was used to kill the creature.

"I told Randy I'd see you because he's a friend of mine," the big man said. "Or he has been. We haven't seen each other in a while." Monroe pointed a finger at Jeremiah. "Randy's told me about your parents, but I only met them once and we didn't have much of a chance to talk."

Monroe picked up a pencil and slowly tapped it on the wooden top of the metal desk.

"So, that's what I was thinking when Randy called," he continued. "But, I thought more about it while you were driving over here. I don't think we're going to be able to cover your School Board meeting."

Jeremiah pulled his chair a little closer to the desk.

"Why not?"

The news producer blocked out words on an imaginary marquee.

"*Church group seeks to ban books*." He looked at Jeremiah. "It's not exactly breaking news."

"If you knew you weren't going to cover it," Jeremiah asked, "then why didn't you tell him over the phone?"

"You never know. I thought there might be something more. But if there was something more, you would have lead with that when you came in." Monroe looked at Theresa and then at Jeremiah.

"Is there more?"

"Millicent will be there," Theresa said. "Millicent Spate."

"Millicent Spate?" The newsman laced his fingers together and smiled as he leaned back in his chair. It was a moment before he said anything. Theresa hoped he didn't recognize her.

"That makes it only slightly more interesting." Monroe noticed Jeremiah's puzzled reaction to what Theresa said. He turned to Jeremiah.

"Looks like your girlfriend here knows more than you," he teased.

"We're not..." Jeremiah and Theresa looked at each other and then back to Monroe. "She's not..." he stammered.

"We're colleagues, Mr. Monroe," Theresa said flatly.

"Co-workers. Nothing more," Jeremiah agreed, but he couldn't help smiling at Theresa when he said it.

Theresa had a much better poker face. "And that's a stretch."

Monroe held up his hands. "Whatever you say."

The big man crossed his arms on top of his desk and leaned forward to speak to Jeremiah. "Since you don't seem to know, Millicent Spate helped a group here in Little Rock that was against evolution. She didn't think about how many of those students have parents who teach at the university, including one of the School Board members." He chuckled as he put his pencil down on the desk. "Not a friendly crowd for Millicent, but she hung in there."

"The Board voted seven to zero against her," Theresa said.

Monroe smiled. "Like I said, she hung in there."

"There's a rumor she's running for office," Theresa teased.

"Millicent Spate?" Monroe rocked his leather-clad executive chair slowly back and forth. "State office? I could see that. What would she run for? House District 37?"

Theresa smiled slightly. "It's just a rumor. But she will be at this School Board meeting and she is acting like a candidate." Theresa relaxed and leaned back in her chair, satisfied that she had successfully threaded the needle between telling the truth – Millicent was rumored to have political ambitions, even if she never said so herself – and saying what she needed to say to make Monroe want to cover the School Board meeting.

More importantly, it was clear Monroe did not know who Theresa was. It had been a little over a year since the Little Rock

School Board meeting. Theresa had been there, seated in her usual place at the end of the front row with her usual book with her usual head down posture, wishing she could disappear and praying she wouldn't be noticed.

"Finally," she thought, *"being invisible is paying off."*

"A rumor isn't enough," Monroe said after thinking things over. "And neither is this School Board meeting you want me to cover. Unless Millicent is running for office and that office is much bigger than the Clear Spring City Council, there is nothing here that anyone outside of Clear Spring would care about. This is a local story at best. Whitely Parker will cover it."

"This is more than a local story." Jeremiah realized he was almost shouting and lowered his volume before going on. "My parents have fought this kind of thing all over the country. You just said they tried it in Little Rock last year."

"They did," Monroe agreed. "And it failed. That's why no one cares. People don't care unless it's happening to them."

Jeremiah sat up. "Still. *The Dixiecrat?* Really? You know what kind of coverage that will be," he said. "You should have seen what he wrote about me after they had their big organizational meeting."

"I did." Monroe seemed quite amused. "I thought it was a very well-written piece. Excellent journalism."

"It was an editorial," Jeremiah argued. "He ran an editorial as a front page news story. Above the fold. That's all he writes. Editorials."

Monroe chuckled. "Nobody outside of Clear Spring thinks of *The Dixiecrat* as news. It's pure entertainment." He laughed softly. "And, say what you will, Whitely Parker is entertaining." He picked up a copy of *The Dixiecrat* from a stack of newspapers on his desk. "I have yesterday's edition right here."

The *Dixiecrat* headline said "Liberal Judges Destroying America!" To Jeremiah, it might as well have said, "Local Bookstore Closed." It wasn't that hard to imagine.

Monroe put the newspaper back on his desk. "I understand where Randy is coming from on this. But what Millicent is saying makes a lot of sense. I'm afraid somewhere in their battle for free expression, Randy and some of my more liberal friends have lost their way and veered too far to the left."

"Just so I understand," Jeremiah began, "you're OK with Millicent telling other parents what books their children will and will not be allowed to read. What if other parents don't agree with Millicent? Shouldn't the parent decide what's best for their child?"

"Unfortunately, parents don't always know what is best for their children," Monroe said. "I appreciate people like Millicent who are willing to protect children from parents who refuse to control what their kids are reading. Or doing."

Jeremiah pointed to the elk with the rifle and the dead eyes.

"There is no minimum age to have a gun in this state," Jeremiah said. "We've got ten-year-olds running around with shotguns and rifles. All perfectly legal."

"Second Amendment." Monroe nodded. "And your point is?"

"You let parents decide when their kid is ready for a gun," Jeremiah told him. "But you want Millicent to decide which books other people's kids will be allowed to read? What about the First Amendment? Is a book more dangerous than a rifle?"

Monroe rose from his chair with his fingertips still touching his desk. The elk stared straight ahead over his left shoulder.

"Millicent is doing the Lord's work out there in Clear Spring," the newsman said. "But no one outside of Clear Spring cares."

28

"Ready to head home?"

The station wagon sprang to life without a single stutter. The TV station may have been a disappointment but at least his car was working again. Jeremiah and Theresa looked at each other and smiled.

"Are we giving up on news coverage?" Theresa asked. "There are other TV stations. Radio."

Jeremiah shrugged his shoulders. "We'll figure it out. What do you want to do for lunch?"

"My dad used to take us to this place that makes great sopapillas," she offered. "We could go there."

The restaurant was dark except for small lights dotting the ceiling. Jeremiah wasn't sure what effect the designers were going for, either nighttime stars or fireflies. He wondered if they were originally stars but years of thick cigarette smoke turned them into amber colored fireflies.

Their waiter lit the candle on their table before he handed them the menu.

"I don't need a menu," Theresa said. "I'm not even going to have a meal. I'm going straight to the sopapillas."

"And I'll have the tacos," Jeremiah said. The waiter politely disappeared.

"That's a pretty simple order," Theresa said.

"I'm a pretty simple guy."

Theresa didn't think of Jeremiah as simple. He seemed fairly complex to her.

"Dad always got a Sangria when we came here," Theresa said. Then she smiled. "Mom hated him drinking in public."

"Did he smuggle Sangria, too?" Jeremiah asked.

"Never," Theresa said. "He wanted his friends to think he only drank bourbon."

The waiter returned with their food. It tasted just as delicious as Theresa remembered.

"I have to admit, I have a soft spot for fried things dipped in honey," she confessed as she wiped honey from her chin. "These are great. You should try one."

Jeremiah considered leaning across the table and biting off a chunk of the sopapilla she was waving in front of him but decided against it. He took one from the basket and bit off a corner.

"These are good!" he said between bites.

"They're better when you put honey in them," Theresa said. "Like this."

Jeremiah tilted the opened corner of his sopapilla toward Theresa so she could pour honey in and then watched as she licked the sticky syrup from her hand one finger at a time.

"See?" she said between licks. "I told you they were good!" She raised the little Mexican flag that was on their table. Jeremiah smiled at her and lowered the flag to its original position. Theresa gently moved his hand away from the flag.

"They'll bring you more if you raise the flag," she said.

"What if it's at half-mast?"

Theresa tried not to laugh. "No, it has to be all the way up. Otherwise they'll think you're in mourning and they'll just leave you alone."

As they drove back to Clear Spring, Theresa found herself looking at Jeremiah more than she was looking at the scenery. She wondered – to the extent she had to wonder, she was pretty sure she already knew – what her mother would say if she knew her daughter had spent the day with the notorious Jeremiah Malone, seducer of women, divorced single father, defender and purveyor of dirty books. Even worse, this was the man who challenged Millicent in public and refused to back down. That alone made him attractive in Theresa's eyes. But there were other things Theresa could not define.

"I have to ask," Jeremiah began. "Is Millicent actually thinking of running for office of some kind?"

"I said there were rumors she might run." She settled back into her seat and looked straight ahead. "There are always rumors."

"The scary thing is she might win," Jeremiah sighed and then bit his lower lip. "She and her band of merry book burners." He looked at his passenger. "I'm sorry. Sometimes I forget she's your mother."

Theresa looked out the side window.

"I wish I could forget." She turned to look at Jeremiah again. Theresa was trying not to be obvious, but looking away from Jeremiah wasn't easy. She found herself glancing his way to see if he was looking in her direction. Of course she'd noticed his appearance before. Who didn't? With his hair, his face, and his build it wasn't surprising he had the reputation he did. He was, by any definition, a good-looking guy.

But there was more. There was maturity in Jeremiah she had not expected to find in a man known for the immature way he treated women.

"This was a good day, even if the TV station was disappointing," Jeremiah said.

"It was," Theresa agreed. "Have you thought any more about what you're going to tell the School Board?"

"I have thought a lot about how much I don't know what to say," he said. "We're going to work on that tomorrow, Ruthanna, Ethan, and me. I'm hoping I'll get something from them." He turned to Theresa. "How do you explain something when you're not sure why you believe it? I mean, I believe in free speech. I just don't know how to say why."

"I've been thinking about that same question," Theresa said.

"About books?"

"No," she said. "Just about life in general. Right now, I'd settle for being able to explain that to myself."

Theresa hoped the warmth spreading across her cheeks wasn't visibly red. For her, the day with Jeremiah raised more questions than it answered and not just about books. She was hoping to have those questions and many others answered before morning. She raised the armrest that separated the station wagon's bucket seats and turned her body toward Jeremiah.

"You're opening the neutral zone," he said.

"I'm what?"

"Opening the neutral zone," Jeremiah repeated. "That's what my dad used to say to my mom when she put the armrest up like that. It's a Star Trek reference." He cocked his head to one side as if he was considering a Great Question.

"Think they'll ever have phones like they do in Star Trek?" he asked. "Phones you can carry around with you? Imagine how convenient that would be to be able to call people like that."

"It never really crossed my mind," Theresa said. The thought of her mother being able to call her anytime from anywhere when she was in any location made her shudder, especially since she was supposed to be at the retreat with her mother and definitely not with Jeremiah. She wondered if Millicent had seen Laura and what Laura might have said.

"Answering machines are bad enough," she said.

Jeremiah wondered where this might be going. He pushed his hair away from his face to see what would happen. As he expected,

Theresa did the same thing, apparently without thinking about it. Then she reached over and gently touched his hair.

"It was about to fall back in your face."

Jeremiah recognized what was happening even if Theresa didn't. His relationship with Susan had started much this same way.

Theresa's romantic experience was limited to church hayrides on which blankets may or may not have been allowed, depending on which adults were chaperoning, and other church-related activities. She was not allowed to attend high school dances, was not allowed go out with boys unless it was in a group, and, even as she approached her twenty-first birthday, would certainly not have been permitted to have a man in her bedroom in her mother's house, should she ever muster the courage to invite one in. Sneaking in a book to read beneath the covers was one thing. Hiding a man between those same covers was unthinkable.

Or it had been until she met Jeremiah.

And, while she no longer shared her mother's religious fervor, she was still a good Baptist girl at heart. Jesus would know even if her mother didn't. There was no hiding from that.

These were feelings and sensations Theresa had not experienced before, feelings her girlfriends had told her to expect and her mother had warned her to avoid. She wasn't sure what to do.

Not the least of these feelings was fear; fear of the unknown, fear of rejection, and, if her mother was to be believed, fear of eternal damnation in a lake of fire should she decide to act on her new emotions. She was thrilled and terrified, her trademark confidence shaken by something she could not identify, much less explain. She found herself wrestling with unfamiliar feelings, a mixture of longing that was undeniably physical but so much more than the mere lust her mother preached so adamantly against. Theresa knew how to walk away from purely physical feelings. She'd been doing that for years. She did not know how to walk away from whatever this was.

Equally frightening was the possibility of Jeremiah taking her to his house. He was, after all, infamous for taking women home, even if Theresa had seen no firsthand evidence of his reputed womanizing. She wanted to dismiss it all as rumor.

"How well do you know Laura?" she asked, seemingly out of nowhere.

Jeremiah involuntarily tightened his grip on the steering wheel. "I met her in the cafeteria, on campus. She had her daughter with her. We talked about what it was like to have kids." He looked at Theresa. "And that is how well I know Laura. That, and she agrees with your mother about books."

Theresa believed him. Maybe Jeremiah wasn't as much of a bad boy as everyone said. But he was divorced, something that in itself was a scandal. And he had a son. Zachary was a very real reminder not only of Jeremiah's past but of the potential consequences should she follow through on these new feelings.

At the same time, she was alive in ways she had not been before, as if something deep and primal had been awakened and was demanding to be fed regardless of the consequences.

She looked at Jeremiah and wondered if he was thinking the same thing. She was sure his thoughts would be much more graphic, with details drawn from personal experiences she had only read about in books hidden beneath her blankets. Her curiosity turned to fear, a kind of inexperience-based performance anxiety and the fear of being compared to other women Jeremiah had known. She didn't know how many women that might be, but she knew it was more than a few. She decided it was best not to ask.

Despite these feelings, Theresa allowed herself to imagine the possibilities and to make a plan should she decide to act on her feelings. Zachary was with Ruthanna. They could go to Jeremiah's house or the bookstore and then into the apartment if she wanted to look less obvious. Or, if Jeremiah preferred, they could have her house to themselves. Millicent was spending the night at the retreat, although Theresa knew from experience that Millicent could come home and walk into her bedroom at any moment without so much as a knock on the door.

Thoughts of her mother brought an involuntary shudder that made Jeremiah ask if she was OK.

"I'm fine," she said. "It's been a good day."

Theresa knew Millicent had expected her to go to the retreat and was probably wondering where she was, if Laura hadn't told her already. There were probably at least a dozen messages on the answering machine by now. Depending on what Laura said, Millicent could be waiting at the front door when she got home. The thought of her mother finding her with Jeremiah was almost enough to kill every emotion she might have other than fear.

Almost, but not quite.

Even with the threat of Millicent hanging over her head, Theresa's curiosity and desire were still stronger than any doubts or fears she may have had. She didn't know how to communicate those feelings to Jeremiah without sounding desperate.

Her thoughts were again interrupted by the sound of Jeremiah's voice.

"I said," he laughed, "did you drive to the store or should I drop you off at your house?"

"What?"

"When we get back." He turned to look at her and smiled as he spoke. "Should I take you to your house or did you drive to the store?"

"Take me to my house," Theresa said. She instinctively reached out to touch his hand and realized it was the prosthetic right hand. She pushed back his shirt sleeve and touched his bare arm with her fingertips.

"Mom's not there," she said.

Jeremiah had a twisted smile.

"I would love that," he said, "but I can't. Ruthanna is expecting me. Then I need to spend some time with Zachary before I get him ready for bed." He looked at Theresa and smiled.

What is wrong with you? Jeremiah asked himself. They were driving through a forest. In a station wagon with fold down seats. With a blanket. And plenty of places to pull off the road and disappear.

He found himself counting how many times he'd been in this same situation in high school. Same station wagon. Same forest.

"I could help get him ready for bed," Theresa offered.

"That involves giving him a bath and putting the sheets in the dryer on his bed." He turned to Theresa. "I'm not sure you're ready for that level of domesticity."

"Maybe not," Theresa said, as she withdrew her hand. She added rejection to the list of emotions she was experiencing for the first time. She was already familiar with embarrassment from being seen in public with her mother. According to Millicent, men were ready to jump at the hint of the possibility of sex. If Millicent was wrong about that, then what else was she wrong about?

She wondered if there was something wrong with her.

"But I would love that. Yes, I would," Jeremiah whispered, just loud enough for Theresa to hear. He shook his head and turned back to Theresa. "But I can't. Really. This was the first time I've been away from Zachary for this long. I don't want to push it with him or with Ruthanna."

"That's sweet how you think of your son like that," Theresa said. She shifted in her seat, using the movement as an excuse to "accidentally" touch Jeremiah's arm. "You're a good dad."

The sun had just set by the time they got back to Clear Spring. Jeremiah parked the car and walked Theresa to the front door of her house.

He pointed to the El Camino parked in the driveway. "Is that the car?"

"It is."

"I've seen that car around town," he said. "I just never noticed who was driving it."

"Sometimes we miss things that are right in front of us," she said.

"We do that. Sometimes." He stepped closer.

Theresa felt the electricity as Jeremiah's fingers softly touched her arm and then moved to her cheek. His fingertips, calloused from playing guitar, felt rough and gentle at the same time. The steadiness of his hand was a sharp contrast to the trembling she was experiencing inside.

Her eyes closed as she leaned into him. Their lips met in a soft, tentative kiss. Theresa had read about kisses like this, but this, even with the hesitation, was so much more than what the books had described. She withdrew, inhaled deeply, and then leaned in for another, deeper kiss as Jeremiah pulled her closer .

They pulled away slightly, leaving only their foreheads touching and her hands on his shoulders.

"Like I said," she whispered, "sometimes you don't see the things that are right in front of you." She stepped back and smiled.

"Are you sure you can't come in?"

"I would love to," Jeremiah admitted. "But I can't. I told Ruthanna I wouldn't be late." He squeezed her hand. "I am trying to be a responsible adult, remember?"

"Responsibility is overrated," Theresa said. "But I'll let you figure that out for yourself."

Theresa stood on the front porch as Jeremiah walked back to his car. Once he was gone, she went inside the empty house. The light on the answering machine showed three messages, but those could wait. The only person who would have called would have been Millicent. She would already be angry. A little more time wasn't going to make a difference.

Theresa sat down in the living room and started reading *Pride and Prejudice*. Somehow Mr. Darcy was no longer enough, at least not tonight. Her thoughts drifted to more proactive leading men.

The phone rang. Theresa's reflex was to reach for it but she caught herself mid-reach. *That can wait,* she thought.

Theresa walked to her room, laid across the bed, and reached to the floor for her backpack. She thought about Jeremiah as she struggled to open the nylon zipper with only one hand. Then she snuggled back beneath the covers and opened the copy of *Sex and the Single Girl* she'd picked up in Little Rock when Jeremiah wasn't looking.

Jeremiah sat in his car in the driveway and took advantage of his time alone, when he wasn't being a dad, when he wasn't defending books, when he wasn't even with Theresa. Solitude was a rare and increasingly precious thing for him.

It took only a few minutes for him to start feeling guilty about just sitting there doing nothing. He pulled into the street and headed for the bookstore. He was sure Ethan and Ruthanna had locked up and done everything else on the store-closing checklist, but he thought he should check anyway.

The store was silent in the way that things can only be silent at night. He stepped behind the counter and looked in the cash register. He'd told Ethan not to worry about making the night deposit or even counting the money. Jeremiah picked up a stack of twenties and started counting.

He stopped counting at $180 in twenties. He never made it to the tens.

No matter how much he tried to ignore it, he couldn't stop thinking about The Corner Bookstore and Randy's offer to make him the manager of the new store in Memphis.

He closed the cash register drawer, took a seat in the reading circle, and surveyed his kingdom. Or his prison. Some days it was hard to tell. Every shelf, every display—every book—had some engrained memory, rubbed in over the years, polished by his parents and him until it glowed.

He thought about the tent in the children's section where he'd read to Skipper while they ate Ruthanna's chocolate chip cookies. The talks that he and his mother had in the quasi-living room setting of the reading circle and the comments George made from behind the counter. The unspoken things that said so much.

He remembered the first time he saw Theresa smile. She was standing in the Poetry section, her head barely visible behind the row of bookshelves.

It hit him, not like a brick, but more like a blanket. The store had never been just a business. It had been a lifeboat for his parents. A refuge for Ruthanna. It had become, he hoped, a sanctuary for Theresa.

And, if he was being honest, a burden for him.

But, as he sat in the soft light of the lamp behind the counter, it felt like home.

Because it was.

29

The phone in Theresa's house rang again a few minutes after 9:00. She wanted to ignore it but decided she might as well get it over with, whoever it might be.

"Hello?"

"I thought you were coming to Pastor Kettle's retreat with Laura," Millicent growled before Theresa had completed the word. "I thought you were rooming with me. Was I mistaken?"

Theresa heard the forced smile over the phone line. Laura, her newest acolyte, was probably in the room with her. She could be in the room for all Theresa knew. Theresa shuddered at the thought of what Laura might have already told her about their encounter at the bookstore.

"I decided not to go this year," Theresa explained. "I had some things I needed to do today so I did them."

"And why didn't you call me back?"

"I knew you'd be busy all day. I didn't think you'd be in your room." She was glad Millicent hadn't asked for details about the unspecified "things" that prevented her from going to the three-day retreat.

"I'm sorry," Theresa lied. Of all the feelings she had about missing her mother's phone calls, regret was not one of them. "I should have called and left a message at the hotel or at the church or something. I thought I'd wait until you were free and call you then."

She thought about what Jeremiah said about Star Trek and whether portable phones might exist someday. She was glad they didn't.

"Well, I'm free now," Millicent snapped. "Where were you all day and why didn't you come up here with Laura like you were supposed to?"

Theresa wasn't in the habit of lying to her mother. She had long since rationalized—or realized, depending on her mood and when she might be asked—that sneaking books into her room and reading them beneath the covers wasn't really lying. Not really. Disobedient, perhaps, but not a lie. Definitely a violation of the whole "children obey your parents" commandment Millicent loved to quote, but not an outright lie. Millicent never specifically asked if Theresa was reading forbidden books with a flashlight beneath her covers. In fact, she never specifically told her daughter she could not read books beneath the covers in bed.

Besides, if over a decade of legalistic religious fervor had taught Theresa anything, it was how to parse words. Since she was no longer a child, Theresa decided any Biblical verse addressed to "children" did not apply to her.

Millicent, of course, chose to interpret "children" to mean "offspring regardless of age."

"You may not be a child, but you will *always* be *my* child," she told Theresa on her daughter's sixteenth birthday. Theresa heard those words as the promise of a loving lifelong mother-daughter relationship, the kind of bond you never outgrow and can always come home to, no matter what. Millicent certainly implied that was the case.

As Millicent became more dogmatic and Theresa matured into an adult with thoughts, dreams, and conflicting values of her own, the "obey your parents" verse had taken on the tone of a commandment subject to Millicent's singular interpretation. When talking with her friends, Theresa often referred to her mother as "She Who Would Be Obeyed."

Over the phone, Theresa could hear Millicent's controlled breathing, something that she only did when she was trying not to explode.

"I had class and some other things to do." Theresa reminded herself to remain calm. "That's why I didn't go today. And I won't be coming up tomorrow or on Sunday." She waited for Millicent to erupt but heard only more deep breathing, a sure sign that her mother was not alone.

Theresa decided to make her stand.

"But, even though I have things to do," Theresa told her mother, "I don't want to be there. I'm going to stay home." For Theresa, three days of Kettle's fire and brimstone preaching about the evils of this world would be anything but a retreat.

Plus, there was a high probability that Malachai would be there with his dad.

Another a long pause.

"Theresa..." Millicent's voice changed to a much softer tone. Theresa could almost hear her mother smiling. "I want to ask you something and I want you to give me an honest answer. I'll love you no matter what. You'll be my child forever."

"No mother. I am not pregnant." The words exploded from Theresa's mouth before Millicent had time to start the all-too-familiar question. "Not now, not in the past, and with how my life is going, probably not at any time in the future. I am going to hang up now. Goodnight."

She'd lied, of course. Not about being pregnant—of course she wasn't pregnant, that was physically impossible—but about how there was no chance of pregnancy happening in the foreseeable future. Maybe not tomorrow or not even next year. But, for the first time in her life, the idea seemed like a realistic possibility for a life she might choose.

It was the same kind of realization she'd experienced on her seventeenth birthday, when she did the math and realized how old her then thirty-four-year-old mother was when she was born. Which meant her father, Travis, would have just turned twenty-three at the time. It wasn't technically illegal—the age of consent in Arkansas was sixteen—but it was definitely creepy. As the older Millicent would say, "There should be a sin against that." Theresa was fairly sure there already was.

It also explained something her mother said after a handsome, silver fox deacon of the church seemed a pay her a little too much attention after a Sunday evening service. She remembered being furious when Millicent rudely interrupted their conversation.

"Men go after girls because they can't handle women," Millicent told her. "Never forget that."

It was one of the few things Millicent said that in Theresa's experience with unmarried youth ministers and a few other men of the church turned out to be absolutely true.

Theresa was no longer a high school girl. For the first time in her life, Theresa was realistically thinking about all the risks and implications of an adult romantic relationship. Risks she was becoming more willing to take each day.

She went to the kitchen to get a Coke. The flashing red light of the answering machine still mocked her, demanding that the messages be heard. She would have to hear them, eventually.

Theresa hit "play".

Millicent's first message was from early that afternoon, before Laura drove up to the retreat.

"Please bring extra blankets when you and Laura come up," a cheerful Millicent said on the machine. "See you later!"

Millicent's second message was much less cheerful but more annoyed than angry.

"Laura is here," Millicent growled on the recording. "Where are you? She said she went by the house to pick you up and you were not there. Call me!"

Theresa closed her eyes and took a deep breath. At least it didn't seem like Laura told Millicent about seeing her with Jeremiah. There was no way Millicent would have let that go without saying something.

Theresa clicked the button for the third message. She heard heavy, labored breathing, as if the caller had been running hard before making the call.

"I saw you with him," said the panting male voice. "I know what you did."

The voice may have been muffled beneath heavy breathing, but there was no mistaking it. The caller was Malachai Parker.

"End of message," said the machine.

Theresa slowly lowered herself into one of the dining room chairs. Malachai must have called soon after she got home from Little Rock, probably after he saw her outside with Jeremiah. Theresa wasn't sure what Malachai might have seen or why he would leave such a threatening message. She imagined the headline in tomorrow's *Dixiecrat*: "Romeo and Juliet at the Bookstore."

Theresa picked up the phone to call Millicent but stopped before she made the call.

She called Jeremiah instead.

"Are you OK?" Jeremiah asked after Theresa told him what happened. "You should come over here. I'll come get you."

Theresa knew what would happen if she went to Jeremiah's house. As much as she wanted that to happen, she didn't want it to happen tonight. She wanted to spend the night with Jeremiah because they wanted to be together, not because she was afraid and running away from something.

"I'll be fine tonight," she said. "He wouldn't have called if he was going to do anything stupid."

"You mean anything more stupid than calling to tell you he's been spying on you?" Jeremiah asked.

Theresa ignored his comment. "But he will talk to my mother. That's OK, but I would like for her to hear it from me first before she reads about it in the *Dixiecrat*."

"I'll come over."

"No," she said. "Don't. You have Zachary and the meeting to get ready for and everything else to think about. I'll be fine. Malachai is just weird. I've known him a long time. He won't come back. And, if he does, he won't break in. Malachai is strange but he wouldn't hurt me. I'll call you if there's a problem."

"You can call me even if there's not a problem," Jeremiah said. "Are you sure you don't want me to come over? I could sit outside in the station wagon. I'll bring coffee. It'll be like a stakeout."

It was good to hear Theresa laugh a little, even if she was nervous. "That's very chivalrous of you, but I'll be OK."

Theresa had just gone to sleep when the phone rang. She made her way to the kitchen to answer it.

"It would mean a lot to me if you would come up here," Millicent said over the phone. It almost sounded like an apology. Theresa did not respond so Millicent continued. "You don't have to. But it would mean a lot to me."

Theresa looked at the clock. She could be there by midnight. She would have to deal with Millicent but she would not have to worry about Malachai, at least not while she was there.

The Pastor Lawrence Kettle Christian Radio Network Church Camp, its private runway for the private Pastoral Plane, its full-service garage for Pastor's growing collection of classic automobiles, and the pastor's private spa were originally a large convention center in the Missouri Ozarks. The property and its subsequent renovations and maintenance were paid for by contributions from the radio flock. The Pastor's private residence, a sprawling, antebellum plantation-style mansion, occupied the northeastern corner of the property. It sat behind a high wall with a guarded gate.

Most campers stayed in a dormitory-style hotel on the property. Other lodging was available for followers with different levels of commitment. In exchange for their tax-deductible love offering of $10,000 or more, donors were given a timeshare condo to use during camp meetings and for two additional non-camp weeks each year. The condos were on the opposite diagonal corner of the 250-acre property, as far as possible from the gated mansion. Only very special guests were invited to the mansion.

As one of the Sanctified Select, Millicent was part owner of a premium timeshare condo, guaranteed for her exclusive use during Pastor Kettle's retreats and for four additional weeks each year.

The retreat, like the Clear Spring music festival, had been a constant in Theresa's life since her dad died. As the daughter of Millicent Spate, she enjoyed a certain celebrity status at camp that she never experienced in high school, where she was the weird girl who never cut her hair and had to beg her friends for books she wasn't allowed to read. In a world where she felt like The Other, church camp was one place where she didn't have to explain or apologize for her beliefs, as long as she had the same beliefs as everyone else there.

I could use some comfort tonight, Theresa thought. And while she would have preferred to have been comforted by Jeremiah, church camp promised far fewer complications and much less potential guilt than spending the night with a divorced single dad.

Theresa packed up her things, got in the El Camino, and headed north to Missouri.

30

The next morning, Theresa stepped out of Millicent's condo and into the familiar scent of pine, cedar, and the perpetually damp soil of the Ozarks. It felt as comforting as she remembered. The morning fog blocked the view of the tall sloping roof of the former convention hall turned sanctuary, but she didn't have to see it to know how to get there. The asphalt path would take her when she was ready to go.

She just wasn't sure when she would be ready to go.

"Theresa! I didn't hear you come in last night!" Millicent stepped outside and hugged her daughter in a tight embrace. "Laura isn't really ready yet," Millicent said as she took a step back. "Let's get some breakfast and talk, just mother and daughter. Me and you."

Laura might not have been ready, but she was certainly *awake*. "Up and about," as Millicent would say. She sat at the kitchen table, carefully folding the three-fold goldenrod handouts that Millicent would use at her session that afternoon.

Millicent noticed that Theresa had noticed.

"Laura's been a huge help." She turned towards Laura who was licking her fingers and making sharp creases in the pamphlets. "Thank you, dear." Laura smiled and said nothing.

"Such a servant's heart," Millicent said.

Laura smiled, but her eyes showed no sense of joy.

"I just like being of use."

Straight may be the biblical path, but the camp walkways were full of twists and turns through the heavily wooded campus. Small wooden benches engraved with the names of Prophetic Elect status donors offered rest for the weary. It was a path designed more for contemplative thought than it was for efficient movement from place to place.

They headed down the winding path to the dining hall. Theresa wanted to tell Millicent about the treasures at Jeremiah's bookstore. She wanted to tell her about the incredible books in the bookstore in Little Rock, about how many types of books were there, and about the sheer volume of books on the dark wooden shelves.

She wanted to tell her mother how she felt when she was with Jeremiah, but she realized she didn't know what words to say.

Instead, they talked about the morning air and the smell of trees. No questions were asked, and no answers were given about why Theresa had not come up with Laura.

As they walked past the sanctuary, Theresa was reminded of what Pastor Kettle's retreat meant to her mother and how much it had meant to her as a child. But she also remembered the restrictions required to be holy.

It was in this sanctuary that Millicent publicly committed her life to removing ungodly books from schools, public libraries, and eventually the rest of the world. This was Millicent's mission, called by God, confirmed by Pastor Kettle, and supported with prayers if not funding by the Lawrence Kettle Christian Radio Network. A modern day female Gideon, Millicent was called to destroy these altars to a literary Baal.

They had just walked past the sanctuary when Theresa decided to wade into the unspoken topic of their conversation.

"I went to Jeremiah Malone's bookstore," she said.

Millicent closed her eyes and tried not to react. "And what did you think?"

Theresa knew she had to be honest, but not so honest that Millicent might feel the need to scream. Or to immediately drop to her knees and pray.

"There are a lot of books."

"Yes, there are," Millicent agreed. "But not all of them deserve to be read." She glanced at her daughter. "There are a lot of books in the Christian bookstores, too."

"Yes, there are," Theresa agreed. "But not nearly as many. And I've read most of them." She turned to Millicent. "Have you been in there? It's amazing. And so many different types of books. I've never seen anything like it." Theresa realized she was conflating her experience at The Corner Bookstore with the time she'd spent at Jeremiah's store, but it didn't matter. She was sure that Millicent had not been inside either place.

Millicent held up her hand to stop Theresa. "Are you still planning on speaking at the School Board meeting? I reserved a time for you. It would be helpful if you could speak."

"Why would that be helpful?"

"Because you're young," Millicent said matter-of-factly. "You're closer in age to the high school students. Without you, we just look like a bunch of cranky old people. With you we don't look so old."

"Even though I'm your daughter and would basically be saying the same things you say? That's not much diversity."

"Unity beats diversity every time," Millicent said. "We are united."

"I'll be there," Theresa said. "Wouldn't miss it."

Laura met them in the dining hall. Between bites of biscuits and gravy, she told Millicent that Curtis, the church piano player, called to say he could not be at church tomorrow. Curtis played piano every Sunday and filled in for Millicent on the rare occasions when Millicent couldn't be at church. Unlike Millicent, Curtis did not enjoy preaching. It was easier for him to open the church song book and, as Curtis would say, "let the Spirit lead us." Conveniently, the Spirit usually led Curtis to have an opening prayer followed by singing for the entire hour. At the end, when he felt led, he would ask someone to say the closing prayer and go home.

"I could go back to open the doors," Theresa offered. "I'll go back tonight."

"You just got here." Millicent turned to Laura and smiled. "Laura can go back."

Laura quickly wiped sausage gravy from her lips and swallowed the biscuit she'd just put in her mouth.

"Sure. I can go back." Laura pulled away from the table and sat back in her chair. She glanced at her watch as she crossed her arms across her chest. She turned back to Millicent and tried not to sound sullen. "Are we going to the morning service?"

Music from The Blessed Campers, the official praise team of the Christian Radio Network Church Camp, could be heard coming from the sanctuary. Theresa, Millicent, and Laura entered and took their seats on the second pew, surrounded by familiar faces. Pastor Kettle welcomed everyone to the service with a special welcome to "those who could not be with us yesterday but were able to make it today."

"He's talking about you." Millicent smiled and squeezed Theresa's hand.

Pastor Kettle spoke of unwavering faith, "knowing that you know you know," as he called it. Theresa wasn't sure what she knew, but she was beginning to understand that she didn't know enough about a lot of things.

Theresa thought about another sanctuary. There were thousands of books in The Corner Bookstore, books that promised ideas, wisdom, adventure, and comfort. Books that talked about things she was feeling, things she experienced every day. Books that provided answers that she wished she'd had when she was younger. Books that provided explanations for what she was feeling now.

Theresa was torn between what she'd been taught and what she was now discovering. She compared her lack of enthusiasm with the passion of Laura's newfound faith, trying to remember the last time she felt that way about church. She realized the last time she'd experienced that kind of excitement was when she first stepped inside Jeremiah's bookstore.

"This is Laura's first time here," Theresa explained as they walked back to the condo. "She should stay for all three days. I can go back." Laura tried to contain her excitement, but Theresa could tell that she'd said the right thing. She hoped that it was enough to keep Laura from saying anything about Jeremiah after she left.

Theresa wasn't on the road long before the rain began. The windshield wipers could barely keep up with the downfall.

Inside the car, Theresa rubbed her eyes with the heels of both hands and wondered why she was crying.

31

Theresa woke up in her own bed to the sound of the phone ringing.

"Hello?"

"Good morning," Millicent said over the phone. "Did you get the same storm we had?"

"It rained. That's all I know." Theresa flipped the light switch, but the room stayed dark. "Looks like the power's out. Nobody's going to church when it's like this."

"You should open the church anyway," Millicent said. "Storms are when some people need the church the most." She sounded very confident that people would still show up. "Open the windows and let some sunlight in. I'm sure the lights will be on soon. I'll be home tonight. I want to talk to Pastor Kettle about the School Board meeting."

"Is he going to the meeting?" Theresa asked.

"I would love that," Millicent said. "Someone of his stature? Can you imagine?" She laughed. "But he can't. I told him not to worry because we've got this. I've—we've, you and me—have been doing this for years. We've got this."

Millicent paused but Theresa said nothing.

"Still there?" Millicent asked.

"Yes."

"Are you still planning on going to the School Board meeting tomorrow night?" Millicent asked. "Or are you going to decide not to do that, too?"

"Wouldn't miss it," Theresa said.

"Good." Millicent's smile was audible. "That makes me feel better."

Theresa drove the El Camino to church and unlocked the doors. The power was still out, but the stained glass windows let in enough sunlight to move around the dim sanctuary without bumping into too many things. The light danced with the shadows of the trees on the walls and the plain wooden pews. She listened to the wind blowing outside and wondered if a tornado was imminent.

Theresa sat alone in her usual spot at the end of the second pew. The first row was always left empty for those who felt the need to ask for prayer. Theresa doubted that would be the case today, but she didn't feel comfortable sitting on the front row. This was her unofficial officially assigned seat, even if she was the only person in the room.

Christianity, Theresa had been told, was about love. That was the theory. In practice, the Christianity Theresa knew was about consequences. For all its philosophy, Christianity, as presented to Theresa, was incredibly Newtonian: For every action, there was an opposite and usually negative reaction. Reactions ranged from negligible to extreme, from simple guilt to eternal damnation in Hell for those who fell completely off the path.

And everything eventually came back to sin.

According to Millicent, Theresa's father died from the sin of alcohol. That Travis was not drinking at the time of his death was irrelevant. Alcohol was part of his life, therefore it made sense that it would be the cause of his death, in whatever unusual manner that may be. There was no ironic poetic justice; only Divine retribution. And while she missed her husband, Millicent accepted the court settlement and Travis' life insurance payout as God's reward for her own faithful living.

Theresa looked at the large wooden cross hanging behind the pulpit and wondered about the consequences of the numerous sins she was considering. Sins that did not require action. Merely having the thought was enough.

She was not alone. Everyone was thinking about the consequences of what they were about to do, whether they believed in sin or not.

Ruthanna's thoughts were accompanied by crescendos of thunder, heavy rain, and strong gusts of wind that must have blown down a power line somewhere. The soft glow of a candle illuminated the desk where the former philosophy major-turned-babysitter worked. Ruthanna half read and half recited the handwritten pages out loud.

As a woman who chose not to marry at a time when women faced serious social and financial consequences for remaining single, Ruthanna felt there was always a certain distance between her and most of the people in Clear Spring. People were polite. They certainly trusted her or they would not have asked her to watch and teach their children. But she was single in a world designed for couples.

She was "the Other."

Strange. Different.

Queer.

That sense of otherness and isolation drew her to George and Tammy—and them to her—when the Malones first arrived in Clear Spring. For the Malones, Ruthanna was a reminder of friends and colleagues they knew when they lived in California.

George and Tammy did not make Ruthanna feel othered. They made her feel like a friend.

A clap of thunder sounded like a nearby explosion. Ruthanna looked out the window and watched the rotating clouds and looked for signs of a tornado.

Her thoughts turned to a shy, quiet girl named Stephanie that she knew in high school. Ruthanna was convinced that Stephanie would still be alive if she hadn't been othered her entire life, first by kids at school, then by her family, and then by the community. Unlike Ruthanna, who enjoyed wearing dresses and other traditionally feminine attire, Stephanie preferred leather work boots and flannel shirts that made her a target for verbal and physical abuse.

Ruthanna picked up the picture of the two of them that she kept on her dresser. They were both happy, both smiling. Stephanie didn't smile often, especially towards the end, but when she did, she smiled with her entire body.

Stephanie was born in Clear Spring. She died an outsider looking in. Worse, despite spending so much time together, Stephanie died before Ruthanna felt confident enough with her own sexuality to tell Stephanie she loved her.

"This is why people need access to books," she said out loud to the empty room.

Ruthanna wiped her eyes at the thought of explaining what happened to Stephanie to the School Board. Two members of the Board—President Duncan, who was about Ruthanna's age, and the retired teacher Mr. Gallop—were old enough to remember Stephanie. The others never knew her.

Ruby: A Novel by Rosa Guy was one of the books challenged by Millicent and her Parents Who Deserve To Be Heard. She wondered how much her and Stephanie's lives would have changed if they had read the love story of Ruby and Daphne or something like it when they were in high school. She wondered what Stephanie's life would have been like if she'd known there were other people who felt like her and somehow managed to be loved.

Ruthanna was not so naïve as to believe books alone could have saved her friend. But if she learned anything from her years of reading to children, it was that people need to see themselves in the books they read. That was her motivation for working so hard against book bans. She knew those stories made a way for a child or an adult to feel like they're not a freak. That they could be the hero of their own story, on their own terms. Books gave people permission to accept themselves even if they were not accepted by others.

Books were also a way for people outside of a community to look through someone else's eyes. To understand what someone else is going through and to develop some sense of empathy. A little empathy and understanding could have made Stephanie feel less isolated and more accepted, perhaps even loved.

Ruthanna leaned back in her chair and let the tears run down her face. She wasn't only speaking for the school or for Jeremiah. Tomorrow night, she would be speaking for all the Stephanies who needed her to do for them what she couldn't do for the woman she loved.

The storm grew more intense as it moved closer to Clear Spring. A bolt of lightning hit a transformer down the street. The explosion could be heard all over town, even in the basement apartment of the bookstore.

Ethan listened on his battery-operated radio for storm updates while he worked on his own three-minute segment. As an outsider, he knew his only hope at credibility was to be seen as an expert witness, but he needed to be more than just someone from out of town with a briefcase. He needed a local angle if he was going to connect with his audience.

"As George Malone said," Ethan read from his notes by candlelight, "'the freedom to read is pointless unless you are free to choose what you read'." Like the Malones, Ethan saw the freedom to read as one of the foundations of democracy, the bedrock upon which America was built.

"There's a reason why the First Amendment is first," he continued. "To the men who wrote the Constitution, freedom of speech was just as important as freedom of religion."

A loud blast on the radio signaled a tornado warning.

"Good thing I live in a basement," Ethan said to himself. He went back to writing.

"This proposal removes that freedom. It removes the right of parents to decide what is best for their child and replaces it with someone else's rules." He stood and began to pace as he read his words. "Don't be misled. As a parent, you have the absolute right to tell your child what they will and will not be allowed to read. You make the rules for your children until they are ready to decide for themselves."

Ethan stopped, leaned into a pretend microphone, and looked out at a make believe audience. "But you do not have the right to impose your rules on other people's children."

He sat back down and wrote.

" I can never meet Benjamin Franklin, but I can read his private thoughts in his autobiography—an autobiography that groups have been constantly censoring or trying to ban since it was published in the seventeen hundreds." He looked to the ceiling for inspiration and then wrote again. "I will never meet Anne Frank, but I know about her life because I have read her diary. It always amazed me how the people who object to that book on sexual grounds usually happen to be the same people who question the truth of the Holocaust."

The town's tornado siren began to wail. Ethan knew he should take cover. Instead, he walked up the stairs, stepped outside, and watched the storm from beneath the awning of the bookstore.

About a mile down that same street and around a corner, Jeremiah carried a frightened Zachary to the basement of his home. It was Zachary's first time in the basement. Jeremiah showed his son how the battery-powered light came on even though the power was out.

"Let's camp out here," he said.

Jeremiah and Zachary came upstairs once the tornado siren stopped. He put Zachary to bed and tried to stop thinking about Theresa long enough to focus on the presentation he was supposed to be writing. He knew banning books was wrong. More and more, he found himself leaning toward his father's free speech absolutism when the topic came up. But he still didn't know and certainly could not articulate why he felt that way. Some books might be inappropriate, but who gets to decide that? And what are the consequences of that decision, for people, communities, or, for that matter, society in general?

His dad taught him that you didn't really know something until you could explain it in a single sentence. Not the details, necessarily, but the idea. The thought.

For Jeremiah, the only single-sentence explanation that came to mind was "Because it's wrong." The harsh reality was that on that level, he was no different from Millicent. Maybe worse. At least Millicent could explain *why* she believed what she did, even if she was wrong.

Jeremiah picked up his pencil. He looked for a notebook or something to write on, but couldn't find anything. He seemed to remember a Big Chief tablet he'd tucked beneath his bed when he was in first or second grade. He wasn't sure.

He was surprised it was still there.

32

A line of the concerned, the curious, and the cold greeted Jeremiah when he opened the bookstore Monday morning. Everyone wanted to see the potentially banned books one last time and maybe buy a few for themselves. The Board had mentioned only a few specific books that would be challenged, followed by an ominous "and others", a footnote that sent a chill down the spines of readers.

Ethan asked whether Jeremiah's offer of half-off for all banned books was still in effect.

"Yeah," Jeremiah said, "but I think we should limit it to two books per customer."

The little information that had leaked out about the proposal seemed to say that the Board and Millicent wanted broad bans on categories of books, regardless of content. "They might decide to ban all fantasy novels," Ruthanna said. "Or ban Young Adult books like *The Outsiders* because they don't want to encourage smoking and drinking."

"But most of the high school smokes and drinks," Jeremiah said. "Or they did when I went there."

"It's easier to ban a book than it is to change a behavior," Ethan said. "Book bans require no effort and they make it look like you're doing something about the problem, even if you're not."

"They say they want to get rid of books about sex," Jeremiah said, "but it seems like there's more to it than that."

"Let's be honest," Ethan said. "They want to ban books that feature Blacks, women, gay people, or anyone else who doesn't look and think like them. They want to remind people that no matter what the law might say, no matter what might happen in the rest of the world, they are still in control here."

Another rumor was that Millicent wanted to automatically remove any book that any parent reported as inappropriate before any hearing or discussion about the book took place. Since no one bothered to define what was "inappropriate", any book could be removed for almost any reason. A parent simply had to object. The burden would then be on the teacher or the school to show why the book should be reinstated.

It reminded Jeremiah of the stories his parents told him about the McCarthy hearings. You didn't have to be an actual communist to be accused of communism. It was enough simply to be named. If someone said you were a communist, you were treated as a communist. If someone said a book should be banned, it would be banned. It was a "shoot first and don't bother to ask questions" policy.

Hanging over all this was Millicent's commitment to banning anything that might be construed as part of the "anti-God agenda of the bleeding hearts on the Left."

But as the day wound down and Jeremiah locked up the store, there was only one thing on his mind.

"Where's Theresa?"

School Board President Jack Duncan moved the meeting to the gym to accommodate the anticipated crowd. Board members were seated on the stage at one end of the basketball court. Two hundred chairs were on the floor. An aisle down the middle made it easier for people to negotiate the rows that spanned the width of the gym. A single microphone on a silver mic stand stood between the chairs and the stage, right below the basketball hoop. Printed copies of the agenda with the proposal printed in a dramatic black box on the back of the page could be picked up at the door, courtesy of *The Dixiecrat*.

"I'm surprised it's not printed on goldenrod," Jeremiah said.

"Separation of church and state," Ethan said. "How quaint."

The chairs on the floor were full. People were already sitting in the bleachers when Jeremiah, Zachary, Ethan, and Ruthanna arrived. They stopped by the front of the stage to ask the Board Secretary, Mrs. Irvin, one last time if they were on the agenda and would actually be allowed to speak. Ruthanna knew that President Duncan liked to accidentally forget to put dissenting views on the agenda and then claim they must not have requested to speak. She was not going to let him get away with that tonight.

Board member Brent Bates watched the group check in. He looked at Jeremiah and smiled.

"Thanks for coming," Bates said.

"Wouldn't miss it," said Jeremiah.

As promised, seats had been reserved for them on the front row, including a seat for Zachary. They took their seats. Jeremiah put Zachary on his lap so there would be an empty chair for Theresa, should she decide to show up. Should she decide to sit with them.

Millicent sat on the other side of the gym, on the front row with Laura at her right hand and an empty chair, presumably also for Theresa, to her left.

Maybe that's why she's not here, he thought. He couldn't blame her. He turned to Ethan.

"So, is she skipping the meeting because of her mother or because of me?"

Ethan smiled at him. "Don't be so narcissistic. She's not here because she's not here."

"That's very Zen of you, my friend."

Ethan patted Jeremiah on the leg. "Yes, Grasshopper." He nodded his head and pointed to a man talking to Millicent as he squatted next to her chair.

"Who is that?" Ethan asked.

Jeremiah leaned forward for a better look across the center aisle. Then he stood and quickly sat back down.

"That's Joe Monroe," Jeremiah said. "He's with Channel 9 in Little Rock." Jeremiah and Ethan looked around the gym and saw a

TV camera on a tripod in the back between the rows. "Theresa and I met him when we went to Little Rock." Jeremiah watched the newsman laughing with Millicent.

"I'm not sure why he's here. He told us this wasn't news."

"Maybe he's just here because he wants to see what happens," Ethan said. "Or maybe he's just doing some old fashioned journalism."

Jeremiah shook his head. "I think he has a thing for Millicent."

President Duncan gaveled the meeting to order, led the Pledge of Allegiance, then offered an opening prayer that was oddly reminiscent of the opening prayer he delivered at Millicent's meeting two weeks before. The prayer was followed by reminders that all comments were to remain civil and that regardless of the outcome, the decision of the Board was final.

"Each speaker will have three minutes to make their presentation," Duncan explained. "I will put the time up on the scoreboard so everyone can watch the clock. You are to stop speaking when you hear the buzzer." He looked around the room.

"The Board recognizes Millicent Spate."

Millicent stepped to the microphone and addressed the Board. "We are asking you." She paused for dramatic effect. "No, we demand that you stop the liberal agenda from poisoning our children's minds," she began. "And I would remind you that this started when the Supreme Court took prayer out of schools. It has gone on for far too long."

Millicent launched into the same presentation she'd given at her own meeting. She reiterated her accusations that filth and other inappropriate books permeated the school library and classrooms. She looked past the audience and straight at the TV camera as she ramped up to her conclusion. The cameraman obliged, picked up a second camera from the floor, and walked up the aisle for a closer shot.

"The books in our school should reflect the shared values of our community, including our shared religious values," Millicent said to the camera. She closed her eyes and slowly raised her hand to the "hallelujah" position. "God has told us to think on that which is true, that which is noble, whatever is pure, whatever is lovely, whatever is admirable. We are to think on whatever is right, as defined by your word, oh Lord."

She opened her eyes as her hand came down. "There are books in our school right now that are not true, are not noble, and certainly are not pure, not from God's perspective. In fact, they are pure filth."

Without warning, she spun and looked directly at Jeremiah and Ruthanna. The camera followed her direction and turned to the front row where they were seated.

"Some would have us believe that smut is admirable or lovely. That defiance is the same as wisdom. But I assure you, there is nothing admirable or wise about being outside the will of God."

The scoreboard buzzer signaled that Millicent's time was up.

"At least no one said 'Amen'," Ethan whispered.

"I was waiting for an altar call," Jeremiah said quietly. "Or a collection plate."

"Is there anyone else here to speak in support of this proposal?" President Duncan asked.

"We had one other," Millicent said, "but she's not here right now. I'm not sure where she is." She smiled at the man with the gavel. She stepped forward, put her hands on the stage, and looked up at Duncan.

"Jack, we're waiting on Theresa," Millicent explained. "I'm sure she'll be here soon. She'll be speaking in favor of our proposal. Would it be OK if she speaks when she comes in?"

Ruthanna shot a concerned look toward Jeremiah.

"In favor?" Ruthanna mouthed silently. Jeremiah formed a polite smile but said nothing.

"You're talking about your daughter?" Duncan asked. Millicent nodded.

Duncan looked up and down the table at his fellow Board members. No one seemed to disagree.

"We'll give her until the end of this part of the meeting," Duncan said. "But once we move on, we are not coming back to this."

As Millicent was returning to her seat, President Duncan stood up. "Just out of curiosity," he said, "how many people in the audience agree with Mrs. Spate?"

Jeremiah watched as about a third of the crowd raised their hand. A male voice said, "Amen!".

"That's not as many as I thought it would be," Ethan said as he looked around the room. "I thought it would be unanimous."

"No," Jeremiah said beneath the buzz in the room. "That's about right. Not everyone agrees with Millicent. She just has the advantage of having the loud people on her side."

"Our job," Ruthanna said to Ethan, "is to let people know they are not alone. Remember that."

President Duncan banged his gavel and called the meeting back to order.

"We will now hear from those who oppose. Remember, each speaker has only three minutes to speak."

Ethan approached the microphone with the confident stride of a college instructor who was accustomed to speaking in crowded lecture halls. He took the microphone from the stand, introduced himself to the Board, and explained that he had followed the careers of George and Tammy Malone and their fight against book bans for years.

"I am a historian," he explained, "specifically about music. Ordinarily, I would be talking about music history. But music, literature, and history are closely connected. An assault on one inevitably leads to an attack on the other two."

"Wait," Duncan interrupted, "you're not from around here?"

"I am not," Ethan said. "But I've lived here for about six months because of my work. And, like I said, I am very familiar with George and Tammy Malone's work on this topic. I was asked to speak about the effects of banning books."

Bates looked at Duncan. "I say we let him speak. What do you have to lose?"

"Three minutes of time," Duncan said.

"And you've just wasted at least that much arguing about whether he should speak," Bates said.

Duncan scowled at his fellow Board member. "Fine. Let him speak."

Ethan turned away from the stage to face the audience.

"Book bans are used to silence opposing views, to control what people can and cannot know, and to erase embarrassing truths from our past. In short, book bans are used when groups are afraid of ideas other than their own or when one group wants to control another."

He looked at Millicent.

"But why would anyone who is confident in their beliefs be afraid of an honest examination of those beliefs?"

He turned to the Board seated on the stage. "Schools have banned *The Autobiography of Malcolm X* because it talks about Black pride, Jim Crow, and other things that make some people uncomfortable. Biographies of Martin Luther King, Jr., Harriet Tubman, and other historic figures have been banned for no reason other than they might make white students feel uncomfortable."

He paused. "Actually, they make the parents of white students uncomfortable. The kids seem to be okay with it."

Ethan watched the audience and wondered if he'd made a mistake. The cameraman put the camera on the floor and started packing up the tripod.

"And that's OK", he added. "History should make you feel uncomfortable sometimes. The Holocaust should make you feel uncomfortable. Slavery should make you feel uncomfortable. And I promise you that learning about slavery isn't nearly as uncomfortable as being a slave."

"We should not fear books that make us feel uncomfortable," he told the crowd. "And we should be very uncomfortable with books and people who reject honest discussions about history."

Ethan looked at the scoreboard. He had just under one minute left.

"It's not always about race. A county in California banned Steinbeck's *The Grapes of Wrath* from their public library. They said it would cause farm workers to demand better working conditions and better pay."

Ethan turned away from the audience to address the Board directly.

"This proposal seeks to remove the right of parents to decide what their child can read. If this proposal is adopted, your child will only be allowed to read books that have been approved by Millicent Spate."

President Duncan pounded his gavel as gasps from the crowd morphed into quiet laughter. "I would remind the speakers not to make personal attacks."

"I apologize." Ethan turned to Millicent. "And I apologize to Mrs. Spate." He turned to face the audience again.

"There are already policies about age-appropriate books. This policy removes the right of parents to decide what is right for their child. No one has the right to tell a parent what their child can and cannot read."

It was a buzzer beater. Ethan just hoped it scored.

Ruthanna's hands trembled as she gathered the pages of her speech and approached the microphone. She looked at the audience and saw the smiles on the faces of adults she'd cared for as children.

Then she faced the School Board and wondered if they would still be smiling after they heard what she had to say.

She cleared her throat before she spoke.

"In case anyone doesn't know, I am Ruthanna Jacobs." The audience chuckled at the idea that Ruthanna would have to introduce herself. She'd babysat most of them when they were younger and their kids when they had them.

Ruthanna cleared her throat and began.

"I want to talk about my friend, Stephanie." With tears in her voice, Ruthanna told the story of a happy child who became increasingly less happy as she grew older until she reached the point where sadness and grief were all she had left.

"Had Stephanie known that she was not alone, she might still be with us. Had she, as a junior high or high school student, been able to read about the struggles of others like her and how they not only survived but flourished under other circumstances, she might be speaking at this meeting instead of me. But she didn't have that. And she can't speak here today."

Ruthanna turned to the audience.

"Not every student is a star football player, a cute cheerleader, or even a nerdy kid who solves mysteries, but you wouldn't know that from most of the books in the fiction section of our school library. Students need to read about heroes who look like them, heroes who face the same problems they face. They need books that offer the hope of acceptance, not condemnation for being different."

Ruthanna wiped tears from the corners of both eyes. "Stephanie had none of that. If anything, the books Stephanie was forced to read in her classes only reinforced the idea—for her and for other students—that she was different. That she did not deserve to be loved."

She stopped talking, closed her eyes, and took a deep breath.

"She was wrong," Ruthanna said softly. An audible gasp went through the gym. Ruthanna ignored it.

One by one, Ruthanna looked each Board member in the face. "It is impossible for us to know how different our students may be from one another. Some differences are obvious, but others aren't. All of our students, regardless of whatever those differences may be, need to see themselves and their values reflected in the books they read. When we take those books away, we are taking away a part of who they are. When we do that consistently, we make those students disappear."

Ruthanna glanced at the scoreboard clock and then at the audience. "Your children deserve to see themselves in the books in their school library and in their classrooms. That includes kids who struggle, kids who are different, and kids who are like Stephanie."

The buzzer sounded. It seemed much louder than it did for basketball games. Jeremiah stood as Ruthanna took her seat.

"I am Jeremiah Malone," he began. He paused when he heard the unmistakable sound of the gym door opening, followed by the hard rhythmic clicks of high heels on a gym floor.

Millicent Spate saw Jeremiah's face and jumped to her feet without even looking at the door.

"Mr. President," Millicent announced, "our other speaker has arrived."

Everyone turned in their seats to watch a very confident and professional looking Theresa Spate marching up the center aisle, with her head held high and her hair cut in a dramatic chin-length bob, wearing a classic navy blue skirt suit with a crisp white, buttoned up silk blouse beneath her jacket.

Millicent's jaw dropped as her daughter walked to the front of the room. The two women looked at each other for a moment as Theresa stood between the two front rows. Millicent regained her composure and patted the empty seat next to her. She motioned for Theresa to sit down.

Theresa looked straight ahead at the stage.

President Duncan leaned into his microphone. "Mr. Malone, you were promised the last word. You may either speak now or you may wait until Miss Tate has finished."

"I yield my time," Jeremiah said, quoting one of the few lines he remembered from watching the Watergate hearings on slow days at the store.

Jeremiah returned to his seat and placed Zachary on his lap.

Theresa stepped up to the microphone. She removed it from the stand and turned to address the audience.

Then she froze. It was the same feeling she had the first time she stood on the edge of the high dive on "Women Only" night at the pool. That ended with a gut-busting belly flop. She hoped this wouldn't be the same.

"I am Theresa Spate," she began. "And I want to talk about books."

The room buzzed. President Duncan hammered the gavel several times before the room was quiet. The cameraman quickly unpacked his gear and put the portable unit on his shoulder.

"Go ahead, Miss Spate," Duncan said.

"When I was growing up," Theresa began, "my mother decided which books I could read and which books were off limits. There were a lot of books that I was not allowed to read. Was not supposed to read." Theresa inhaled deeply, looked up to the ceiling, and went back to reading her prepared notes. "There still are, to be honest."

"Of course," she said with a smile, "I read them anyway." She held the smile while the audience chuckled. Years of watching her mother's performance art sermons were paying off. "My friends gave them to me. Or I bought them when Mom wasn't looking. When you want something bad enough, you find a way to get it."

President Duncan pounded his gavel over the laughter in the room.

"I hid beneath the blankets in my room to read at night," Theresa continued once the room was quiet. "I read *Are You There, God?*, *The Diary of Anne Frank*, and most of the other books that were so important to me that way. I read at school where no one could see me. I read at church. I read wherever I could."

She looked directly at Jack Duncan.

"Books, including the Bible, helped me through some of the hardest times of my life, like the death of my father. But books also helped me understand what was happening to my body and my emotions in junior high. Books let me know that even though I felt alone, I wasn't. Other people had been through what I was going through. Other people had mothers like mine.

She turned to the audience. "More importantly, books showed me the possibilities for people who did not give up. They inspired me, they taught me, they shaped who I am. Books made me think. Books, more than anything else, made me, me."

Theresa's hands shook but her voice was steady as she moved like a televangelist across a stage. "My mother tried to control every book I read. In reality, that control only forced me into hiding and turned me into a liar."

She addressed the School Board seated on the stage.

"If you adopt this proposal, you will be imposing that same rule on our schools. It would almost certainly have the same result. It would turn our children into liars and would prevent them from having healthy conversations about what they had read. Because of that, I encourage you to reject this ban on books and to work toward a more reasonable and responsible book policy for Clear Spring Schools."

Theresa looked at her mother. Millicent had her head bowed, her eyes closed, and her hands clasped in prayer. The cameraman moved in for a closeup on Millicent praying before swinging toward her daughter.

"Mom, I love you. But you are wrong about this." The silence in the room underscored what Theresa said.

She turned to the Board. "Thank you for letting me speak." She took a seat in the empty chair between Jeremiah and Ruthanna. The room held a stunned silence for almost a minute.

Duncan looked at Jeremiah. "Mr. Malone, I believe you were about to speak."

Jeremiah knew nothing he could say would carry the weight of Theresa's courageous statement. It was Theresa's voice he wanted the board members to remember when they voted.

"I think Theresa has said all there is to say," he said.

Half the room applauded as they rose to their feet. The other half glared at the back of Theresa's head and her freshly cut hair.

33

President Duncan pounded his gavel. "Come to order! Be seated!" He hammered the tabletop three more times before the room was quiet.

"Before we vote," Duncan said, "did any board members wish to speak?"

No one raised their hand.

Duncan exhaled directly into the microphone, an unintended reminder of the howling winds in Sunday night's tornado.

"Then I want to say something."

The School Board President cleared his throat and began. "Mr. Malone," he said. "It's interesting that you chose not to speak, yet you are obviously concerned. Do you understand that we are talking about books in the school library? This board has no control over what you sell in your bookstore. In fact, I would argue that there has never been a true book ban in the United States. People can still buy these same books at your bookstore. Nothing we do here tonight will affect that."

Ethan nodded his head as Jeremiah whispered something in his ear.

"Mr. Malone?" Duncan asked as if he'd caught students whispering in class. "Is there something you'd like to share?"

Jeremiah stepped up to the microphone.

"First, that's not true. What you do tonight will have a direct effect on this community. That's the goal here. Let's not kid ourselves about that. Secondly, weren't libraries, including school libraries, started for the purpose of providing books for people who could not afford them?"

He turned to the audience. "Benjamin Franklin said our libraries have made our farmers as intelligent as gentlemen from other countries. That's why libraries are free." He turned back to face Duncan. "Are you saying that knowledge and serious philosophical reflection should be limited only to those who can afford it? If that's the case, then why do we even have public schools?"

"Still," Duncan said, "it's not like we're burning books in the town square. Why just last week, I picked up..." His voice trailed off before he finished the sentence.

"Just last week you picked up a *Playboy* at my gas station," yelled a voice from about midcourt.

Mrs. Irvin looked at Duncan in disgust as the embarrassed Board President tried to gavel the meeting back to order. "I wanted to read the Hunter Thompson interview," he tried to explain.

"Really?" laughed Bates. "You read the interviews?"

Duncan pounded his gavel like he was working on a roof until the room got quiet.

"My point, Mr. Malone, is that books are never truly banned in the United States of America. We might remove them from schools, but those same books are still available if people want to read them. They're still in your bookstore."

"Have you never heard of books that were banned in Boston?" Jeremiah said. "For a long time—and not that long ago—the City of Boston forbid stores to sell or even to display certain books."

He turned to the audience and spoke loudly enough that he didn't need to use the microphone.

"We're not talking *Playboy* or *The Joy of Sex*. They banned *The Sun Also Rises, Grapes of Wrath, Elmer Gantry*, and dozens of other classic books that challenged people born with money or industries with political power. Books that talk about the inconvenient facts of real life. Not just from the schools and public libraries, but from bookstores just like mine."

"But," Duncan attempted to interject.

"But nothing," Jeremiah insisted. "Booksellers were arrested, prosecuted, and penalized over books that we now consider classics. Readers were arrested for buying them or having them in their possession. Please don't tell us that books have never been banned in America, Mr. Duncan. That's simply not true."

Mr. Duncan clearly wanted to move on. "Thank you, Mr. Malone."

Jeremiah turned to return to his seat but did a quick pivot.

"They did it so much that 'Banned in Boston' became a badge of honor for writers." He remembered what Ruthanna had told him. "Much like Books That Deserve To Be Read is today."

"That's enough, Mr. Malone."

Ethan shook Jeremiah's hand as he returned to his seat. "Nice job with the Franklin quote," he said. "That almost sounded like something I would say."

"It was something you said," Jeremiah admitted.

"Mr. Reynolds," Duncan began, turning his attention and his gaze to Ethan, "you stated that no one has the right to tell parents what their children can or cannot read."

Duncan paused and looked at Millicent before turning back to smirk at Ethan. There was a gleam in his eyes.

"But as a School Board, it is not only our right, it is our responsibility to do *exactly* that. It is our job to decide what is and what is not appropriate for students."

Duncan looked up and down the table at his fellow School Board members, daring them to refute the logic of what he'd said or what he was about to say. His voice became stronger with more than a tinge of suppressed frustration. "Emotions aside, it is our job to ensure that every book in Clear Spring Schools meets certain educational standards and that every book, from textbooks all the way to novels, magazines, and other reading material, is appropriate for students and reflects the values of this community."

Board member Brent Bates shook his head as he raised his hand. He did not wait for President Duncan to recognize him from the chair.

"I understand what you're saying, Jack." Bates spoke with a calm but steady voice. "I would remind you that we don't all share the same values. There's five different churches in this town, all proclaiming to be Christian, and each with its own view of what is right and what is wrong. And there are people who don't go to church at all. Those people pay taxes, too. We need to think about the entire community and not just the loudest voices." The youngest board member looked at Duncan and aimed his comments directly at him. "This school serves all of the families of Clear Spring, not just a few."

Duncan clenched his jaw and closed his eyes as if he was about to reply but decided against it lest he open another embarrassing personal revelation. He took a deep breath.

"Thank you," Duncan said as he looked down at the table. "Any other comments?"

The silence was unanimous.

"In accordance with the rules," Duncan explained, "the Board President can only vote in case of a tie. If need be, I will be voting last." He turned to Bates. "On the question of regulating books, Mr. Bates, what say you?"

Bates shook his head.

"No." He leaned back, folded his arms across his chest, and looked straight ahead.

Ruthanna turned to Jeremiah and the others. "We expected Bates to vote no," she reminded them. "I'm glad he went first."

Duncan did not look up as he made a note on his copy of the agenda. "Mr. Foster, what say you?"

Mr. Foster turned to Bates. "Yes," he hissed. "Absolutely. For the children."

"A simple yes or no will do," Duncan said. He smiled as he recorded Foster's vote. He turned to his left.

"Mrs. Irvin?"

Mrs. Irvin looked at Duncan.

"No," she said softly. "I vote no." There was a slight but audible gasp from the crowd. Duncan ignored it.

"Mr. Gallop? What say you?"

All eyes turned to the retired teacher and longest serving School Board member.

Gallop cleared his throat before he spoke. He looked directly at Theresa.

"I came here tonight believing I knew how I would vote," Gallop said. "And I was ready to vote that way for much of this meeting. What I have heard this evening changed my mind." He looked at Duncan.

"Sorry, Jack. I vote No."

Duncan's chin dropped to his chest. He put one elbow on the table and covered his eyes. He slowly dragged his hand down his face as if wiping away any expression he might have had. He cleared his throat again and raised his head.

"The vote being three to one, the President will not be voting," he said. "The resolution does not pass." Duncan immediately pounded his gavel. It was clear that he wanted to move on.

"The next item on the agenda is the school lunch menu…"

Millicent launched out of her chair. She shot a narrow-eyed glance at her daughter, then at Jeremiah, and then walked quickly down the basketball court and out of the gym. Laura followed, dragging Grace behind her.

"We won!" Jeremiah turned to Theresa. "We actually won."

Duncan pounded his gavel again.

"Order, please."

Ruthanna gathered her things. "We won this time," she whispered. But she could not help smiling. The group quietly left the gym as President Duncan gaveled the Board back into session. Ruthanna gently put her hand on Theresa's arm as the doors closed behind them.

"What you did tonight was incredibly brave," the older woman told Theresa once they reached the hallway. "Let me know if you need a place to stay tonight or if you need anything. I have empty rooms with beds already in them. They're twin mattresses, but you'll fit just fine."

"Thanks." Theresa watched the door as it closed behind Laura. "I probably should have spent my money on a hotel room instead of going to Little Rock and getting this suit." She tried to smile. "Or this haircut."

Jeremiah smiled at Theresa. "I like the hair," he whispered. "And there's always the basement apartment at the store. It's got a bed and everything. I'll just kick Ethan out and you can move in."

34

They walked down the street until they reached Zachary's favorite diner, the one with the word *"EAT"* painted in large red letters on the front window, along with tempera paint artwork of a fried drumstick and a slice of pie.

Whatever was on the window, the sign above the door insisted the name was "The Cozy Kitchen." Zachary liked to eat there because they had frog legs and red checkered tablecloths. Jeremiah always pointed out the giant *"EAT"* and read the word out loud for Zachary like some kind of early reading lesson.

For all Zachary knew, EAT was the name of the restaurant and was always written in all caps.

The Cozy Kitchen was almost empty when they walked in. They slid into a booth—ever the blocker, Zachary placed himself between Jeremiah and Theresa—and talked excitedly about the meeting. They were trying to guess what Millicent might try next. She couldn't approach the school for another year.

"She's not through," Ruthanna reminded them. "She'll go to the City Council next. Or the library board."

Theresa said nothing but tilted her head just enough to get Ruthanna to look over her shoulder at someone sitting behind her.

Millicent sat alone in her usual corner booth beside the window, sipping her coffee without looking at the cup, glancing at her watch and then looking through the window again.

Theresa recognized the pose. "She's planning something. Either that, or she's waiting on someone," Theresa whispered as she watched her mother's face. "My mother never drinks coffee unless she's planning something or waiting for someone. She's usually doing both at the same time."

Without Millicent so much as acknowledging their existence, they watched as Millicent took one of the goldenrod flyers from her purse. She smirked as she looked it over. Then she wadded it up and sat it on the table beside the discarded packages of non-dairy creamer.

"Do you think she knew we'd stop here?" Jeremiah asked.

"I don't know," Ethan said. "It's close. It's between the school and your store. Maybe she's just hungry. It's not like there's a lot of fine dining choices in Clear Spring." He reached for a frog leg from Zachary's plate. "May I? I've always wanted to try this."

"Sure," Zachary said. "It's OK. It's not Kermit."

Ethan studied the small fried drumstick from all sides and pondered the courage of the first person to think that the hind legs of a giant frog might be a good thing to eat and what that first man—he was certain it had to be a man—had to do to answer that question. How hungry was this guy?

"We didn't win tonight," Ruthanna said once everyone had had a few more bites. "This is a delay, at best."

"I don't know," Jeremiah ventured. "Maybe we just won. Period."

"There will be a next time," Theresa said quietly. She took a sip of sweet tea and nodded her head towards Millicent. "She did not expect to lose. Duncan did not expect to lose. They are not going to give up. If anything, they're going to come back harder. Maybe not through the School Board, but they're going to try again."

"If they didn't expect to lose," Ethan said as he wiped his hands, "then I wonder who changed whose mind?" The question was clearly rhetorical.

He looked at Theresa and grinned.

Ethan raised his glass. "To Theresa!"

"To Theresa!" They all said too loudly as their glasses clanked together. Jeremiah couldn't help noticing that Millicent was ignoring their celebration.

Jeremiah was splashing hot sauce on his crawdad etouffee when a firetruck rushed by the front window with full lights and sirens. Right behind the firetruck was the sheriff and two patrol cars. It looked like a high-speed version of the annual Festival of Lights Christmas parade.

He quickly turned away from the window to see Millicent's reaction. She was getting out of her chair, but the expression on her face was unchanged. She put a dollar on the table, took one last sip of coffee, and headed for the door. Jeremiah felt a blast of cold air when the diner door opened. He watched Millicent walk confidently past the window and towards the school, the opposite direction of the bookstore.

"I wonder what's going on," Ethan said

"I am surprised Laura or someone else wasn't with her," Ruthanna said. "She must have wanted to be alone."

"So, back to the meeting," Jeremiah said, as he tried to signal that he'd thought enough about Millicent for one night. He counted off Board members with his fingers. "We knew Bates was going to be with us. And Gallop said he changed his vote. I wish I knew where Irvin was before tonight, how she felt going into the meeting."

Ruthanna smiled. "I have to admit I'm surprised she went with us."

"Ethan! Watch!" Two of Zachary's frog legs, one in each greasy hand, were performing Rockette-style kicks like some kind of disembodied amphibious chorus line.

Ethan turned back to Ruthanna. "People like Jack Duncan don't make a motion to vote unless they think they are going to win. And they like convincing victories. My guess is Irvin was a surprise to everyone."

While Ethan and Ruthanna playfully argued about what might have changed Mrs. Irvin's mind—sound reasoning, peer pressure, or the realization that future historians would refer to her for a cautionary tale of a vote that could have made a difference, Jeremiah quietly put his hand on Theresa's shoulder and spoke softly for only her to hear.

"You did this."

Theresa leaned her head towards his. "No. This was a team effort."

"Well," Jeremiah said. "I'm glad you're on the team."

She smiled. "So am I."

And then there was silence. Not like a vacuum. They were surrounded by people talking, clanging plates, and the sound of a firetruck going by. But for Theresa and Jeremiah, there was a long, profound, and very comfortable silence. A silence that spoke volumes.

Somewhere in the distance Ethan was laughing. He cupped his hands around his mouth like a megaphone.

"Theresa! Theresa!"

"Sorry," she said. "You were saying?"

"I was wondering," Ethan said, "if you were late because you were late, or was it so you could make a dramatic entrance?"

Jeremiah laughed. "Very dramatic."

"I could have done without the drama." Theresa blushed. "Honestly, I was late because I couldn't find shoes in the mall to go with this suit. I ended up going to another shoe store somewhere in downtown Little Rock. Your friend at the Corner Bookstore recommended it."

Another fire engine rolled past, its siren blaring and bells clanging.

"I need to go home," Theresa said. "Mom is going to want to talk about this. And I need to talk to her."

"Are you sure you want to do that?" Jeremiah asked. "You could always stay at my place." He caught himself and thought he should elaborate. "In the apartment, I mean. You could spend the night at the apartment. You could just move in there."

"Ethan lives there," she reminded him.

Jeremiah grinned. "For now." He looked at Ethan. "I'm sure he'll understand." Ethan took a drink and looked at Jeremiah over the top of the glass.

"Sure." Ethan smirked. "Kick me to the curb and you get the girl. I see how it is."

"We've talked about that," Theresa reminded Jeremiah. "Besides, that seems rather cowardly, doesn't it? I'm pretty sure I know what's going to happen when I get home, but I want to explain to her why I did this and hope she understands."

The Channel 9 van zoomed by, its amber lights flashing as if it was an emergency vehicle. As it passed the window, Theresa saw Malachai casually walking in the opposite direction. The same direction that Millicent went when she left the diner.

"Was Malachai at that meeting?" Theresa asked softly.

"I didn't see him." Jeremiah wiped some ketchup from Zachary's face.

Theresa's mouth dropped as she grabbed Jeremiah's arm. "We need to get to your store! Now!"

Jeremiah looked around for the waitress so he could get his check. Ruthanna recognized the look on Theresa's face.

"Now!" Ruthanna felt the urgency of Theresa's words. "I'll get this. You get to the bookstore. I'll take Zachary home with me. Now go!"

Jeremiah, Theresa, and Ethan jumped out of their chairs, knocking two of them over, and ran out of the diner. Swirling streams of water ran down the sloped street. They ran upstream as quickly as they could on the slippery surface.

Jeremiah tripped as he turned the corner and fell face first in the running water. He grabbed his knee and winced. When he opened his eyes, Clear Spring Books & Electronics was in flames.

35

Ethan lifted Jeremiah to his feet and helped him limp toward the burning bookstore. They made their way through the fire hoses and pools of water to the middle of the street where Theresa stood watching. Clusters of other people watched as the building burned.

The bookstore refused to surrender quietly. Mixed in with the crackles and random loud pops of the campfire from Hell was the sound of wooden beams breaking as they gave in to the heat. Burned bookshelves snapped in two, creating avalanches of books that crashed to the floor. The fire itself roared as it sucked up oxygen and hissed in angry protest to the high pressure water that was attacking it.

A fireman with a walkie-talkie told Jeremiah they would have to move to the other side of the street.

"But this…" Jeremiah blinked and shook his head at the scene before him. He pointed to the store with his prosthetic hand. "This is my bookstore."

"I know," said the fireman, "and we're doing everything we can. But you need to get out of the way before you get hurt." He looked at the growing crowd.

"All of you, move." The fireman pushed people back until everyone was standing on the other side of the street.

Everyone moved except Whitely Parker and Joe Monroe. The two newsmen stayed in the middle of the street, Whitely with his notepad and pencil and Joe with some kind of small tape recorder he spoke into while his cameraman sat up a tripod. They saw Jeremiah and raced to reach him first.

Whitely won.

"Do you think this is related to the School Board meeting earlier this evening?" His pencil was poised to document Jeremiah's reactions. "Is this about your dirty books?"

Whitely may have won the race, but Joe Monroe was not going to miss Jeremiah's response. He shoved the cameraman in between Jeremiah and Whitely.

"What?" Jeremiah said. "Get that thing out of my face. I don't even know what happened yet."

Whitely knocked the cameraman to the ground and then stepped over him.

"Do you think this might have been a bomb?"

"A bomb? What…" Jeremiah closed his eyes and took a deep breath and immediately started coughing. He managed to say, "Who said anything about a bomb?" between coughing fits.

Jeremiah was still coughing as he walked away but the newsmen was undeterred. He followed Jeremiah until Ethan stepped in front of them and held up his hand.

"You need to leave Jeremiah alone," the big man growled quietly. "Talk to one of the firemen or something, but you need to let Jeremiah do what he needs to do."

"And who are you?" Whitely asked.

Ethan folded his arms across his massive chest, which was about eye-level for Whitely, and looked down at the reporter.

"I am the man who is going to make sure you leave Jeremiah alone."

The crowd got bored and began to leave as the flames died down.

"You can go in now, if you'd like," the fireman said.

A lake of steaming gray sludge covered the floor of the bookstore. The books that weren't burned were soaked, waterlogged beyond recovery. Jeremiah, Theresa, and Ethan watched as firemen checked the smoldering ashes for hot spots and any obvious clues that might explain how the fire started. After a few minutes, the fireman with the walkie-talkie walked over to them.

"The front window was already broken when we got here," the fireman explained. "We didn't see any evidence of an explosion. The simplest explanation is that someone broke the front window with a rock or a brick or something, entered the building, and set fire to that big rack of books you had in there. A bonfire, basically. The fire spread out from there."

The fireman bit his lower lip. "Is there any reason why someone would specifically target that rack of books?"

Jeremiah looked at what remained of the Books That Deserve To Be Read. "That was kind of the centerpiece of the store. It was a display of books that had been banned."

"Ohhhh." The fireman nodded his head. "I've heard about this. I didn't realize you kept it up all the time." He looked at the building. "Once they lit that, it looks like they squirted something, probably lighter fluid, around the place so the fire would spread."

The fireman turned back to Jeremiah. "We'll have to do a full investigation," he said, "but that's what it looks like for now. We'll need to know where all of you were for the last hour or so."

Jeremiah suppressed his anger at the implication.

"That's easy. We were at the School Board meeting and then we got something to eat."

The two newsmen stood at a distance while they noted Jeremiah's response. Ethan positioned himself between them and Jeremiah.

"And people saw you there?" the fireman asked.

"The entire town saw us at the Board meeting," Ethan said sharply. "And there were people at the diner. The waitress. Some other customers." He pointed to the burning building. "We did not do this. We're not the people who burn books. But we did see Malachai Parker walking away in the other direction."

"You saw Malachai walking away from the fire?"

"We saw him through the window of The Cozy Kitchen. He was walking towards the school."

Whitely walked away at the mention of Malachai as a suspect.

"Whitely's kid?" the fireman asked. "OK. We'll check it out. Is there anyone else who might have done this?"

Theresa, Ethan, and Jeremiah looked at each other. They were about to provide a solid alibi for the most obvious suspect.

"Millicent Spate," Jeremiah said, "But she was at the meeting with us. She got to the diner before we did. The fire engines were on their way before she left."

Ruthanna and Zachary eventually made their way down the street and around the corner. Zachary let go of Ruthanna's hand and ran to his dad.

"What happened?" Zachary asked.

Jeremiah kneeled down beside his son and put his arm around the boy's shoulders. He looked up at Ruthanna and then back to his son.

"The store caught fire. That's all we know right now."

The fireman with the walkie-talkie walked up again. He took a knee in front of Zachary and motioned to another fireman to get something from the firetruck.

"Everything's going to be OK," the fireman said. The other fireman brought a child-sized fire helmet from the truck and placed it ceremoniously on Zachary's head. Then he handed him a teddy bear with the same helmet and a firefighter's jacket.

"Nobody's hurt," he said. "This can all be rebuilt. It's just stuff."

The adults knew the fireman was speaking as much for their benefit as he was trying to comfort Zachary. They also knew this was about more than "just stuff."

Ruthanna put a hand on Zachary's shoulder. "OK. We saw it like you wanted to. Now, why don't you and I go to my house while your dad takes care of this? He can come get you when he's done here."

"Right," Jeremiah said. "You can go with Miss Ruthy while I take care of this. You can sleep there and I'll pick you up later."

"I want to sleep in my bed," Zachary said. Jeremiah saw the tears in his son's eyes and looked to Ruthanna for help.

"Then we'll go to your house and wait there," Ruthanna told him. "Is your bed big enough for me?"

"No." Zachary looked puzzled as to why Ruthanna would even say something so crazy.

"Then I'll sleep on the couch," she said. "Or maybe your dad's big chair. I think I'd like that."

"You said you were at the School Board meeting," the fireman began. "Do you think the fire might have something to do with that?"

"I don't know what else it could be," Jeremiah said. "Someone tried to set some books on fire in front of the store after her last meeting."

"Her? Who is her?"

"Millicent Spate. But she didn't set that fire. And she couldn't have set this one."

The fireman looked puzzled. "Why didn't you report that?"

"It wasn't that big of a deal," Jeremiah explained. "There were a few singed books on the sidewalk. They couldn't really get a fire going."

"The call came from the phone inside the store," the fireman said. "Honestly, I assumed you were the one who reported it."

"Wasn't me," Jeremiah said. "We were all at the school. Why would someone who just started a fire hang around to call 911?" He looked at Theresa and then at the fireman.

"Do you know who made the call?" Jeremiah asked.

"They did not give their name," the fireman said. "Dispatch didn't say whether it was a man or a woman on the phone. The police will start looking at that tomorrow after they've looked at your building. I'm sure they'll want to talk to whoever made the call."

"Maybe they changed their mind after they started the fire," Theresa said.

"There's no telling." The fireman nodded toward the building and the rising mixture of smoke and steam. "You had a lot of fuel in there. We were able to stop the fire before it burned all the bookshelves, but the books that are left are soaked. And everything in here is going to smell like smoke."

He turned to Jeremiah. "It was a hot fire."

"451 degrees," Jeremiah said quietly.

An involuntary smile formed on the fireman's face. "Yeah. Fahrenheit 451," he said.

"What about the other part of the store?" Ethan asked. "The TVs? The apartment?"

"Same story," said the fireman. "We saved what we could, but there's water everywhere."

"My dissertation," Ethan whispered the word like a prayer. He closed his eyes. "All that work."

"Did you have copies?" Jeremiah asked.

Ethan physically shook as he buried his face in his hands. "That was my dad's typewriter."

Jeremiah, Theresa, and Ethan sat down on the grass across the street from the store, devastated. In light of the fire—in the literal *light* of the fire—their victory at the School Board meeting seemed too long ago to remember.

Theresa silently reached for Jeremiah's hand. They sat on the grass together, holding hands, not saying anything, and watched the firemen roll up their hoses and put everything back on the firetrucks. Then they watched the firetrucks roll away. Then they watched the police put crime scene tape across the front of the building.

"We'll be back in the morning," a policeman told them. "I know you want to see what happened, but don't go in there without us. We don't want to disturb any evidence."

"Wouldn't any evidence have been burned by now?" Jeremiah asked.

"There is always evidence with something like this," the officer said. "I know you want to get in there, but wait for us to clear it."

"I left my car parked at the school," Ethan told Jeremiah as the officer left. "I'm going to go get it and then get a room at a hotel or something."

"You can stay at my place," Jeremiah offered.

"Thanks," Ethan said. "Right now I just want to be alone so I can figure out what to do next." He paused to consider his options. "This is going to take more than one night. I'll just go to the hotel where I stayed when I first came here. They rent by the week. I'll see you guys in the morning."

The smell of smoke and burned paper hung in the air as Jeremiah and Theresa sat in the grass across the street and looked at the charred storefront. The broken window, the bookstore's initial injury, framed a much different picture than it had when they left to go to the School Board meeting just a few hours before. In the dark with just the light of the street lights, the Books That Deserve To Be Read display was a black wire skeleton standing in the middle of a pile of ash.

"I hate this." Jeremiah sniffled and tried not to cry in front of Theresa. "I really, really hate this. For my parents. For Ethan."

"I hate it for you." Theresa handed him a Kleenex from her purse.

"But…" Jeremiah said after several minutes had passed. "This might not be all bad." He took a deep breath and tried to smile as he turned to Theresa. "I mean, OK, it's obviously not good. But I've been wanting to do something different. Something on my own. Something besides books."

"What would you do?"

"I have no idea. I haven't thought about it a lot. I didn't feel like I had a choice. But this… this changes everything."

"What about the special obligation for businesses that start with the word 'the'?" Theresa asked.

"Well, someone set *the* bookstore on fire," Jeremiah said. "After we just had a fight about banning books at *the* school. I would think that would kind of end any obligation a business might have, with or without a *the* in the name."

"Hard to argue with that." Theresa squeezed Jeremiah's hand. "I'm parked over by the school. I need to go get some things. Pretty sure Millicent won't want me to sleep at her house tonight."

"She's still your mother," Jeremiah said.

"Yes," Theresa said. "No matter what happens, she will always be my mother. Unfortunately."

They walked around the corner, past the Cozy Kitchen, and on to the school where Theresa had parked. The El Camino sat alone in the school parking lot.

"Do you think Malachai set the fire?" Jeremiah asked once they were in the El Camino and headed for his house. "He looked like he was running away from it when we saw him."

"Except," Theresa said, "I don't see Malachai having second thoughts and reporting it after he set it."

"That part doesn't make sense," he said. "Why would you set a fire and then call it in?"

"Maybe it was those kids that burned those books that night," she said.

"Hopefully somebody saw something," Jeremiah said. The car stopped. A goodbye hug in the car turned into an intense goodnight kiss at Jeremiah's front door.

"I can't go in," Theresa said. "I need to get some clothes that don't smell like smoke."

"Is that your nice way of telling me I smell like smoke?" Jeremiah asked.

"I'm sure we both do," Theresa said. "We won't know how much until we get out of these clothes and take a shower."

Jeremiah walked Theresa down his driveway to her El Camino. "Call me and let me know how it goes when you get home.

And if you need a place to stay, you can always stay here. I promise to be a complete gentleman."

Theresa smiled for the first time that night. "You wouldn't take advantage of my emotional vulnerability?"

Jeremiah grinned. "There was a time." He paused. "But, no. This is different. I promise to behave."

"That's good," Theresa said, "but I'm not sure I would."

36

The kitchen light was on when Theresa pulled into her driveway. Millicent's driveway. At Millicent's house.

She knew she would have to talk to Millicent, but all she could think of was how much she wanted to take a shower. Theresa grimaced as she slowly pushed the door open and then closed it behind her, as if her pained expression would somehow reduce the sound of opening and closing the latch.

Ice cubes clanked in an empty glass in the kitchen. Theresa froze just outside the open kitchen door to hear what her mother was saying, careful not to be seen. It was a one-sided conversation, even by Millicent standards, with several seconds of silence between exclamations. It didn't have the cadence of a phone call but there were no other voices to be heard.

"It's humiliating," Millicent said. "If I can't manage my own house, how am I supposed to manage a congregation? What are my people going to think?"

Theresa peeked inside the kitchen. Millicent had her back to the door and could not see her. Sitting at the other side of the table was Laura, her head tilted downwards with her arms across her chest. She looked pale.

Theresa tiptoed up the stairs and quietly closed the bathroom door. She wondered if turning on the water for a shower might give her away, but she couldn't stand the smell of smoke on her clothes and in what was left of her hair. She had to wash herself clean.

Water sputtered as Theresa pulled the knob that changed the water from the tub faucet to the shower nozzle. She was sure the clank in the water pipes would give her away, but there was nothing she could do about that now. She locked the bathroom door just in case.

Theresa closed her eyes as the water hit her face, ran down her chest, and over the rest of her body. The hot water felt good on her skin.

Theresa squirted some shampoo into her hand and massaged it into her scalp. Her hair felt much lighter. Not thinner, just not as heavy. Black and gray rivulets of ash swirled around before going down the drain. Turning around, she felt the hot water running down her bare back for the first time in years. It was a new and pleasant sensation.

The smoke, ash, dirt, and sweat were washing away but the weight in her chest remained. She knew speaking to the School Board was the right thing to do, not just for the books but also for herself and other women like her. But that knowledge did not change her feelings of guilt or her sense of loss for having done it.

Once she felt fully cleansed, she pushed down the knob that directed the water to the shower head, creating another loud clank in the water pipes. She turned the water from the showerhead to the main faucet and closed the bathtub drain. She watched the clean water cover her feet. Then she slid down into the tub until she was fully immersed.

She stayed until the water started to get cold then she stood up and reached for a towel. Her hair felt much lighter than it usually did when it was wet. She wasn't sure what it was going to do, she only hoped she could recreate the look she had last night.

The fresh honeysuckle fragrance of her hair and hands only intensified the smell of smoke when she picked up her dress from the bathroom floor. She put on a robe and went to her bedroom to change and to pack her suitcase. The smell of smoke would permeate everything in the suitcase, but the alternative was to either stay until it was clean or to leave the dress and everything it stood for in her mother's house.

Once she was dressed, Theresa summoned her courage and walked to the kitchen, suitcase in hand. The smell of charred wood, like the sound of Millicent's voice, grew more pungent with each step.

Theresa stopped just outside the kitchen door before her mother could see her.

"I worked so hard to get them elected," Millicent was saying. "Especially Irvin. And then they do this."

Theresa took a deep breath, and looked around the corner at the back of her mother's head.

Across the table from Millicent, and now face to face with Theresa, sat a very pale Laura. Her hands were still shaking. Her eyes grew even wider when she saw Theresa.

Millicent saw the reaction in Laura's face and turned to see Theresa standing in the kitchen door, suitcase in hand.

"Why are you here?" Millicent asked.

Even more color drained from Laura's face as she stood up. She smelled like smoke.

"You saw the fire?" Theresa asked.

"I walked by when it was burning," she mumbled without turning around.

"Smells like you did more than just walk by." Theresa told her. "Smells like you stayed and watched it burn." She stepped in front of Laura.

"Or did you go inside to use the phone?"

Laura froze in place and said nothing. Theresa's fists were clenched and her eyes were slightly squinted. She was ready to fight. She didn't speak as much as she growled.

"Get out of here before they have to arrest me."

Millicent stayed in her chair. She waited for Laura to leave before she spoke.

"Why are you here?"

"I thought we should talk."

Millicent took a sip of sweet tea and nodded toward Theresa's suitcase. "You don't need a suitcase to talk."

"I wasn't sure how the conversation was going to end."

"I think you know how this ends." Millicent sat back in her chair and swirled the ice around in her glass. "But, just out of curiosity, how did you think it was going to end when you stabbed me in the back like that?"

"I also said I love you. Did you hear that part?"

"You said, 'I love you, but'." Millicent took a long drink of tea. "And now you're running away. Is that how you deal with things now?"

"I don't think you call it 'running away' when someone is almost twenty-one years old."

"What do you call it?"

"Moving out."

"And your sudden independence wouldn't have anything to do with your birthday coming up? The trust f..." Millicent captured the final word before she finished it. It wasn't soon enough.

"Trust fund?" Theresa asked. "Were you about to say trust fund?" She knew her mother received a settlement from the county, but this was the first she'd heard of a trust fund for her. Millicent never mentioned it.

"There is a trust fund from your father's accident," Millicent said. "It's separate from the settlement that I got. You got some of the money when you turned eighteen."

Theresa's eyes narrowed. "I don't recall getting any money when I turned eighteen."

"I am still the trustee. I determine how the money is dispersed. And to be honest, I didn't trust you yet so I just left it in a savings account. Now, I see my instincts were correct. You'll get more when you turn twenty-one and the rest when you turn twenty-five. It was part of the settlement. I didn't tell you because I wanted you to learn how to work for a living. I didn't want you to think life was that easy."

Theresa heard her suitcase hit the floor before Millicent finished her sentence. Heat started rising in her chest and moved up her neck and into her face. Her hands clenched as her eyes closed.

"How much..." Theresa held up her hand as a signal to stop. "No. Don't tell me. I don't want to know. This isn't about that."

Millicent looked at her daughter. "I did what I thought was best for you." She sat up straight in her chair. "Do you think this has been easy for me?"

Theresa sat down in the chair formerly occupied by Laura.

"I grew up without a father," she growled. "Do you think I care about a trust fund?"

Theresa's eyes narrowed as she tried to control her rage. "The only man—the only *person*—who ever put me first. The only one who cared about what I thought. Who wasn't constantly telling me that I was a disappointment to him, God, and everyone else." She swallowed hard but she could not get the anger out of her mouth.

"My life was never going to be easy," she growled through clenched teeth. "Money was not going to change that."

Millicent stood up and stepped toward her daughter. "I know. If we could just talk..."

"Talk? When did you and I ever talk, Mom? You talk, I listen. That's how it's always been. That's how it is with every conversation you have with anyone except Pastor Kettle. You sure listen to him."

Theresa picked up her suitcase and made her way to the front door.

"Where are you going?"

"I don't know," she said without turning around. "Anywhere but here."

37

Ruthanna was snoring in the recliner when Jeremiah got home. The TV was dark and silent, a clear indication that this was no accidental nap. Down the hall, Zachary was asleep in his bed. Jeremiah decided to let them both sleep while he took a shower and got rid of the smoke and ash that seemed to cover every inch of him.

Ruthanna yawned and rubbed her eyes as a freshly scrubbed Jeremiah came back into the room. It took all of her strength, but she pulled the lever on the recliner to return the chair to its upright position.

"Zachary had a bath before I put him to bed. He was a little scared about the fire but I told him you were going to be OK. Have you called your parents?"

"Not yet. I was going to wait until morning," Jeremiah told her. "They're already in bed by now." Jeremiah's hesitation to deliver the bad news pushed against his fear that George would hear about the fire from someone else before he called. The absolute worst scenario would be if they got the news from Whitely Parker. Jeremiah imagined what kind of editorializing that message would include. Whitely would have them believing that Jeremiah lit the match.

Jeremiah was dialing the last digit of his parents' Florida phone number when they heard a knock at the door. The door opened as he hung up the phone.

"Anybody home?" Theresa asked.

"Oh," Ruthanna said as she struggled to get out of the chair. "I'll let you two talk."

"You don't have to leave," Theresa said. "I wanted to ask you a favor anyway. Could I please spend the night at your house?"

Ruthanna did not hesitate. "Of course. But I am going to go home. It's been a long day." She held out her arms so Jeremiah could help her out of the recliner.

"Call your parents tonight," Ruthanna reminded Jeremiah. "You do not want them to hear about this from someone else first. You really don't want them to hear about this from Whitely Parker."

Jeremiah took Theresa's hand as Ruthanna was leaving.

"I was thinking," he said, "that you could stay here."

Theresa shook her head, smiled, and then bit down on her lower lip.

"I can't," she said. "I just can't. Not right now." Theresa saw the word "why" forming on Jeremiah's lips. Either that, or he was preparing for an extremely awkward kiss. Theresa kissed him before he could say the word. Despite her lack of experience with such things, her kiss was simultaneously passionate and comforting, a definite goodnight kiss but with a promise of things to come—if Jeremiah would be patient. She withdrew, put her hand flat on his chest, and pushed his hair out of his face so she could look into his eyes.

"Thank you."

"For what?" Jeremiah asked. "For messing up your life?"

"For giving me the push I needed." She put her hand on the back of his neck and pressed against him. He instinctively pulled her closer.

"Sure you don't want to stay?" he whispered in her ear.

"Oh, I want to stay." She looked at Jeremiah's face and smiled. "Which is why I shouldn't. I know me. If I sleep with you tonight, I'll always wonder if I did it because I loved you or because I was mad at my mother." She kissed Jeremiah again and then pulled away. "I would prefer to not have any questions." She looked over Jeremiah's shoulder at the clock above the fireplace. "Besides, Ruthanna is expecting me."

Jeremiah stood in the door and watched Theresa's El Camino drive away. It was almost midnight in Florida. He knew his parents would be sound asleep by now. He remembered his previous bad news phone calls, when he told them about Susan being pregnant and then when he called again to tell them about the divorce. He cringed at the thought of how George would react when he found out his bookstore was destroyed in a fire.

Still, Ruthanna was right. George and Tammy needed to hear about the store from him, before anyone else called to let them know or, worse, before Whitely Parker or Joe Monroe tracked them down. He wasn't sure how they might do that, but Jeremiah had great faith in the phone company's 411 information operators.

He started dialing the phone but stopped and hung up before he finished. For the first time that day, he was alone. Losing the bookstore felt a lot like losing a close childhood friend. He'd grown up with that store. He may have had questions about his future, but that didn't change how he felt about the store.

He wiped his eyes, his fingers pausing at the bridge of his nose while his eyes were not yet open. He blinked back the tears he couldn't wipe away.

It was almost one o'clock in Florida before he called his parents. Tammy picked up the phone on the third ring.

"Hello?" she whispered.

"Hi, Mom. It's me."

There were some muffled sounds, some whispers. Jeremiah imagined it was Tammy sitting up in her bed.

"Is everything OK?"

"We're fine. Could you hold the phone so you and Dad can hear me at the same time?" Tammy woke up George and huddled close with the phone.

"Is everything OK?" Tammy asked.

"We're fine," Jeremiah said, again. He still wasn't sure how to begin the conversation. His hesitation only made Tammy more anxious.

"Is Zachary OK?" Tammy's voice shook.

"We're all OK," Jeremiah said.

"Does this have anything to do with Millicent and the School Board meeting?" George mumbled.

That caught Jeremiah off guard. He temporarily forgot about the fire as his mind went back to what happened with the School Board just a few short hours ago. He fumbled his words.

"How did you know about the meeting?"

"Randy Liles called a few days ago and told us what was going on. He said you and some friend of yours came by his store and that Millicent was causing trouble again. From what Randy said, it sounded like you knew what you were doing," George said.

"Apparently I didn't," Jeremiah said.

"What do you mean?" George asked. "Did the School Board go with Millicent and start banning books?"

"No," Jeremiah said. He felt his mouth turning up into a smile. "Millicent lost," he said with pride. "The Board voted against her proposal."

"Then you knew what you were doing. Good job. And good night." Jeremiah could hear George smiling over the phone.

Jeremiah took a deep breath. "And then they burned down the bookstore."

"What?!" Jeremiah heard his dad grab the phone.

"What happened?" More sounds of George and Tammy wrestling with the phone so they could both hear.

"There was a fire at the store tonight, after the School Board meeting" Jeremiah said. "We weren't there when it started. I won't really know how bad it is until morning, but it doesn't look good. The Books That Deserve To Be Read display is gone. I'm not sure how many other books we lost."

"But you're OK," Tammy said. "Zachary's OK? How's Zachary taking it?"

"He's fine. He's already sleeping. Ruthanna watched him while I tried to find out what happened. She seemed to think he's OK. A little shook up, but OK."

"I don't know what you could have done," Tammy said. "That is not your fault."

Jeremiah could hear George talking loudly in the background. "I guess Millicent finally got what she's wanted."

"We don't know who set the fire," Jeremiah said. "It probably wasn't Millicent. She was at the School Board meeting with us. We left before she did. I don't think she had time to do it."

George snatched the phone from Tammy's hand. "Doesn't matter," he insisted. "This is on Millicent. You are responsible for your wake."

Jeremiah hadn't thought about that line since he'd lost his hand at the lake.

"When you start something, when you say something, you are responsible for where it goes," George said. "You are responsible for any damage your words may cause. It doesn't matter who struck the match. Millicent set this in motion, even if she wasn't there when the fire was lit. The fire would not have happened without Millicent."

"You're not upset?" Jeremiah asked.

"Oh no. I'm mad as hell," George said. "I'm just not mad at you."

"This is actually the second time this has happened, sort of", Jeremiah said. "Someone tried to burn some books in front of the store after Millicent's first meeting in the gym. I didn't think it was a big deal so I didn't tell you."

"I know," George said. "Ruthanna told us. But I don't know what you could have done besides what you did. I didn't call because it sounded like you had it under control. You can't be everywhere."

"So you knew about the first meeting?"

"Yeah. Ruthanna called and asked if we wanted to be there. I told her I wanted to wait and see what you would do."

Jeremiah heard George softly chuckle. It was the first real laughter he'd heard since they were at the diner.

"Nice touch with the half off sale, by the way. I would have done the same thing."

Tammy took the phone from her husband. "We're just glad you and Zachary are OK. We'll figure out what to do in the morning. Try to get some sleep."

Once again, Jeremiah heard the sound of his parents wrestling for the phone.

"Jeremiah?" his mother said. "Still there?"

"Right here."

"Hey." Tammy was almost whispering, as if she didn't want George to hear. "Randy said you had a young lady with you when you visited his store. Is this a new friend?"

Jeremiah felt his face blush. Once again, he was back in middle school.

"She's a friend."

"Does this friend have a name?"

"I'm surprised Ruthanna didn't tell you," Jeremiah said.

"Ruthanna isn't trying to tattle, Jeremiah. She just thought we needed to know what was happening with Millicent. She meant well."

George rolled toward Tammy so he could hear.

"Theresa," Jeremiah said. "Her name is Theresa."

Tammy looked at George and smiled.

"And does Theresa have a last name?"

"Spate, Mom. Her name is Theresa Spate."

The other end of the phone went silent.

George rolled over and stared at the ceiling. Tammy put her head on his shoulder.

"Oh, my," Tammy said after a moment. She tried to remain calm. She put her hand over her husband's mouth before he could say anything. "Well, your father's tired. You'll have to fill me in tomorrow."

"So our son is seeing Millicent Spate's daughter?" George said as soon as Tammy hung up the phone. "Did I hear that correctly?"

"They're probably just friends," Tammy said. "I wouldn't read too much into that." She quickly changed the subject. "We'll have to call the insurance company tomorrow and let them know about the fire."

"Sounds like we need to call Ruthanna and find out what's going on with our son before we have another grandchild." He shook his head. "Millicent's daughter. My God."

Tammy sat up in bed and looked at George. Her wide laughing smile made it difficult for her to speak.

"Do you think Millicent knows?"

George laughed. "I don't know, but I would love to see her face when she finds out."

Tammy snuggled up to her husband's back and kissed his shoulder. "We could go for a visit." Then she quickly added, "To check on the store. Not to spy on our son's love life."

George rolled over and squeezed Tammy's shoulders, pulling her tight to him.

"Our son stopped Millicent Spate," he said proudly. "I'll take that as a win." He laughed softly. "We have insurance on the store. We'll be fine," George said. "He'll be fine." He rolled over to sleep on his side. "We're all going to be fine. I'll call the insurance people in the morning."

Back in Clear Spring, Jeremiah pulled the blanket up around him and looked at the empty side of the bed where he'd hoped Theresa would be spending the night. He wasn't even sure why he wanted her there. He just wished she was.

38

Jeremiah woke up the next morning from what he hoped was a bad dream. A quick sniff of the smoky clothes on the floor reminded him that it wasn't.

He flipped the switch in the kitchen. The light blinked once, then flared and went dark with a soft pop. Burned out.

"Of course," Jeremiah smirked.

Zachary was on the couch watching cartoons, his legs tucked under him like he was trying to disappear into the cushions.

"Mind if I change this?" Jeremiah asked.

Zachary didn't blink. "No," he said, and quickly added, "What's for breakfast?"

Jeremiah opened the kitchen curtains to compensate for the burned out light bulb. Then he switched channels to watch the news.

"Things got heated at a School Board meeting in Clear Spring last night," the perky blonde host of Good Morning, Arkansas read with entirely too wide of a smile. "Channel 9's News Director Joe Monroe was there."

Jeremiah finished pouring the milk and turned up the TV.

"Thanks, Julia," Joe said. He was standing in front of Clear Spring High School, the dark parking lot illuminated by what looked like the headlights of a parked car. He glanced at the small notepad in his hand and then back to the camera before he spoke.

"What should have been a routine School Board meeting in Clear Spring in rural Northern Arkansas was disrupted last night when free speech extremists forced the School Board to reject a modest proposal designed to remove inappropriate books from the school library and classrooms."

Jeremiah's phone rang. It was Ethan.

"Are you watching this?" he asked. Jeremiah could hear the TV in the background. Joe Monroe was asking Jack Duncan what happened.

"Well," said the School Board President, "three of our Board members were persuaded or, more likely, intimidated, by these free speech extremists."

"I guess we're extremists now," Ethan said over the phone.

"Guess so," Jeremiah said.

"I'll be right over," Ethan told Jeremiah.

Jeremiah had just hung up the phone when it rang again.

"Are you watching Channel 9?" Theresa asked. "Did you see that?"

"Yeah," Jeremiah said. "What about Ruthanna? Did she…"

"She did," Theresa answered before Jeremiah finished the question. "She told me to call you." Theresa started to say something else but stopped.

"What?" Jeremiah said.

"I started to ask if you wanted to meet at the bookstore," Theresa explained, "but that's not really an option, is it?"

"Funny how Mr. Monroe left that out of his report," Jeremiah said. "Sure. Come on over."

Ethan handed the latest edition of *The Dixiecrat* to Jeremiah when he opened the door. Channel 9 may not have thought a fire in a small town bookstore was news, but Whitely Parker thought it deserved a banner headline. "BANNED BOOKS BURNED!!!" spanned the entire front page. Below the headline was a picture of the burning building, a police officer, and both of Clear Spring's firetrucks. Another headline, "School Board Caves to Extremist Pressure," appeared below the fold in the right-hand column. Both stories were continued on Page 5, right below the obituaries.

Whitely's editorial appeared in its usual center spot on Page 3, above the Letters to the Editor. Jeremiah had just started reading it when the doorbell rang. Zachary ran to answer it.

"Did I miss anything?" Theresa asked once she'd made it to the kitchen.

"Jeremiah's about to do a dramatic reading," Ethan said.

Jeremiah cleared his throat in the most exaggerated way possible and began:

According to initial reports from the police and the fire department, last night's fire at Clear Spring Books & Electronics appears to have been the work of an arsonist. This was not, as some have speculated, an act of God, although one could be forgiven for assuming God had seen enough.

Ethan pointed to the page. "I thought that line was an especially nice touch. Good job, Whitely."

Jeremiah continued.

While The Dixiecrat cannot condone the destruction of private property, we recognize that actions have consequences. It seems that for the Malone family, the proverbial chickens have come home to roost.

"Well," Jeremiah pointed to the line he'd just read, "if we're critiquing Whitely's writing, that's kind of cliché."

For more than two decades, the Malones have trafficked in books that not only don't deserve to be read, but which harm the very soul of our community and our nation. These are books that theologians, elected officials, and everyday regular Americans have determined are unfit to be read. And yet the Malones insist on promoting and selling these banned books.

As a newspaper, The Dixiecrat understands the importance of the First Amendment. Americans have a fundamental right to free speech. But, as Supreme Court Justice Oliver Wendell Holmes famously wrote, one cannot shout fire in a crowded theater—especially when one stands to profit from doing so.

The Malones shout "racism!" where none exists. They shout "science!" while promoting theories that contradict sound Biblical teachings.

They shout "value all families!" while undermining traditional family values and the natural order of society. They do this not to improve the lives of others but to profit from the sale of banned books.

Jeremiah shook his head. "The store hasn't made a profit since Zachary was born."

"Really?" Ethan asked. "How have you kept it open?"

"It hasn't been easy," Jeremiah admitted. "Mom and Dad get residuals from their scripts. They live on that. It really helped when they started showing movies on TV." He looked back to Ethan. "They're making a fortune from HBO."

"And you?" Ethan asked.

"I don't have a salary. I pay the bills and pay myself from what's left."

"Your parents didn't offer to help?" Ethan asked. "Not even with Zachary here?"

"They did. I told them we were fine," Jeremiah explained. "The store was in good shape when they left. I didn't want to be reminded that I screwed this up."

"So you really can't afford to hire help." Theresa smiled. "And I just thought you were cheap."

Jeremiah handed the paper to Ethan. "You can read the rest."

"I already did."

Theresa snatched the paper from Jeremiah's hand. She paced back and forth and gestured with one hand as she read.

In the name of free speech, the Malones have encouraged promiscuity, deviant behavior, and all manner of immorality while promoting their immoral anti-American agenda. They do so with impunity and smug arrogance, believing,

She stopped pacing and read the next line.

Given such circumstances, what is an ordinary American to do?

"Burn the bookstore down, apparently," Jeremiah said. "Can you believe this?"

"I guess," Theresa said. She went back to reading.

School Board members who refuse to stand up to the Malones should be recalled and replaced with citizens who will take seriously their obligation to protect Clear Spring's children from such filth. Petitions for recall elections for Bates, Irvin, and Gallop have already been printed. Volunteers are gathering signatures. If you see it, sign it.

The Dixiecrat is proud to endorse all three recall campaigns.

They all sat in silence and wondered how many Clear Springs agreed.

After a long minute, Jeremiah called to ask Ruthanna if she could watch Zachary while he went to what used to be the bookstore. He looked at Theresa and Ethan as he waited for Ruthanna to answer the phone.

"Want to go with me?" They dropped Zachary at Ruthanna's and headed for the bookstore.

39

Theresa spotted the crowd in front of the bookstore from three blocks away, an angry, churning gumbo of bodies and signs garnished with bright yellow sprigs of crime scene tape. White posterboard signs bobbed up and down as people marched in front of the store. Some carried signs; some carried other things that Jeremiah couldn't make out.

Ethan moved into the street to get a better view of the scrawled messages.

"Wait," Jeremiah said. "Before we wade into this, we should probably figure out whose side they're on." He looked at Ethan. "Are those bricks? Is this a riot?"

"Too many different sizes to be bricks. Too colorful." Ethan looked back to Jeremiah.

"Books, maybe?"

"Who brings a book to a protest?"

Another less enthusiastic group stood on the grass across the street from the store. They looked confused and dejected, as if they'd come for breakfast but had just been told it would be at least an hour before they could be seated. A few of them almost looked interested in what was happening across the street, but their movements were nothing like the animated crowd in front of the store. Three policemen formed a strategic triangle between the two groups while a fourth officer guarded what was left of the front door of the bookstore and causally chatted with some of the marchers.

Jeremiah pointed to the smaller group. "I'm guessing those people are with us."

"If they are, then they—we—are really outnumbered," Ethan said. They moved closer to the group of dejected people on the grass. Two of them stood as he approached.

"Hey," Jeremiah called. "What's going on?"

"That's her!" Suddenly people were shouting and pointing at Theresa.

"Traitor!"

The lethargic group that had been sitting on the grass sprang to life. The group was moving towards them and specifically towards Theresa when one man charged ahead. Ethan moved instinctively, intercepting the would-be assailant with a spearing tackle that would have been at least a 15-yard penalty if he was still playing football for the University of Arkansas. Another man ran to help his friend but froze when Ethan stood up, both fists still clenched.

"Everything OK?" Officer Belmont asked as he stepped over the man lying on the ground.

"Yeah." The would-be assailant managed to get back on his knees. He looked up at Ethan's flared nostrils. "I just tripped."

Ethan smiled, helped the man up, and brushed some dirt from his shoulder. He pointed to the small but gawking crowd. "Ya'll take care, OK?"

Jeremiah looked at the crowd in front of the store. "So those are our people? We've got the big crowd?"

"They're waving books," Theresa said. She turned to Jeremiah and Ethan. "Those people in the street. They're waving books."

She was right. While some of the more creative supporters carried signs with phrases like "Millicent Doesn't Speak for Us!" and "Demand Freedom", and another that said "Burn Grass, Not Books!", others chose to carry books as a show of support for Jeremiah and the bookstore.

People ranging from Ruthanna's age down to high school or possibly junior high school students were there. And not just random individuals. There were complete families, with moms and dads carrying a sign in one hand and pushing a stroller or carrying a baby with the other. A very authoritarian looking miniature dachshund strained against his leash.

"They've been here since before sunrise," Officer Belmont told Jeremiah.

Ethan pointed to the other group. "And them?"

"They showed up about half an hour ago. Said they were waiting for Millicent."

"Did she tell them to meet her here?" Theresa asked.

"I asked but none of them seemed to have talked to her. I think they just assumed she would be here. Now she's not, and they're not sure what to do. They're kind of outnumbered."

"Any fights?"

Officer Belmont looked at Ethan. "Not till you showed up. Nice tackle, by the way."

"Sorry," Ethan said. "Reflex."

Jeremiah turned to his friends.

"Should we go talk to them?"

"I think you'd better," Theresa said. "You need to say something."

"You're the hero," Jeremiah reminded her. "You should be the one to speak."

"No thanks," Theresa said. "And I'm not the hero."

The crowd cheered as Jeremiah, Theresa, and Ethan approached.

"Good morning," Jeremiah said as loudly as he could. A couple of high school boys put a large plastic ice chest in front of him.

Jeremiah stepped up on to the ice chest.

"Thank you," he began.

"Thank you for supporting our kids!" someone yelled from the crowd.

"Thank you for supporting free speech!" yelled another. The crowd cheered in agreement.

"Thanks for stopping Millicent!" The crowd roared.

"Sorry about your bookstore!"

Jeremiah laughed a little at the sentiment. "Thanks." Jeremiah looked at the bookstore behind him, blinked his eyes, and told himself not to cry. He whispered in Theresa's ear.

"Focus on the good, right?"

"For now," Theresa said.

"I don't know what to say," Jeremiah told the crowd. He looked back over his shoulder at the charred remains of the bookstore and swallowed hard. "But, as you can see, the fight is not over."

"We'll help you rebuild!" someone called out from the crowd, which prompted another round of cheering. "We've all got books that deserve to be read!"

Jeremiah looked closer at the books people had in their hands. The familiar covers looked like friends in the crowd. He didn't know if he could recreate the entire Books That Deserve To Be Read display from what he saw before him, but it would be close.

"Thank you," Jeremiah said. Tears rolled down his face all the way to his smile.

A young woman called out from somewhere in the middle of the group.

"Theresa, we love you!"

Jeremiah turned to Theresa. "You've got a fan."

"She used to bring me books," Theresa explained.

Jeremiah helped Theresa step up beside him on the ice chest. The crowd applauded in appreciation.

"I love you, too," Theresa mouthed. She reached down and took Jeremiah's hand.

"When will the store be open again?" someone shouted.

Jeremiah looked over his shoulder at the burned building behind him and had his first laugh of the morning. "Probably not today. We have a lot of things to do before that can happen. But, thank you all for showing up. It means a lot." He clapped his hands together and looked around.

"I have to do some things," he told the crowd. "So, if you'll excuse me, I'm going to get to work."

Officer Belmont walked over to Jeremiah as he helped Theresa step down from the ice chest.

"Want us to send them home?" he asked.

"I don't care," Jeremiah said. "But we need to get in the store."

Ethan held up the crime scene tape so Theresa and Jeremiah could walk underneath it. They stepped over the burned and broken door and went inside.

Officer Belmont pointed to the skeleton of the Books That Deserve To Be Read display. "You can see where it started here and then spread out like spokes on a wheel. The arsonist stood here with the fire and squirted lighter fluid around the room for as far as it would reach."

The store was dark except for the sunlight coming through the broken window and the front door. Jeremiah reached for the flashlight he kept under the counter but the melted switch would not move. As he put the flashlight down, he saw the "First they came for the socialists" sign he'd made for his father. It was burned around the edges but he could still read the words.

The familiar smells of books new and old were gone. There was no coffee smell, none of the scented candles that he burned on the counter to cover the smell of cigarettes from customers who smoked. In their place was the acrid smell of burned paper, melted plastic, and the toxic fumes of fried electrical components. Gray pools of water and ash covered the soaked carpet. Jeremiah couldn't tell if the sick feeling in his stomach was from the overwhelming smell or from being hit with the reality of what had happened.

The walls were soft and mushy, with holes where the sheetrock had fallen off in chunks from its own weight. The plaster had turned to mud. Exposed studs and electrical wiring made the room look naked. The carpet squished beneath their feet.

"I'm going to check downstairs," Ethan said. "I'll let you know what I find."

"This is still a crime scene," Officer Belmont told him. He called for another officer to go with Ethan.

"Everything in here is evidence, so don't touch anything," Officer Belmont reminded Jeremiah. "And watch where you step. The fire investigator may want to come back for another look when the light is better."

Jeremiah turned to Officer Belmont. "Our insurance papers, inventory records, all of that is in a safe in the office. I need to get that."

"I'll go with you." Officer Belmont shined his flashlight so Jeremiah could make his way to the office door.

Standing alone in what had been the book club circle, Theresa wondered if the fight was worth it. She'd probably lost her mother and her home, if not permanently then at least for the foreseeable future.

Jeremiah had lost his store. Ethan had probably lost two years' worth of work on his dissertation. *"For what?"* she asked herself. *"So people can have access to books that they probably won't even read?"* She felt a reflexive urge to apologize, but to whom? And for what? She could not shake the feeling that somehow all of this was her fault, that she was the one to blame. That this happened because of her sin.

The flames stopped before they reached the office. Inside, the sheetrock walls were blistered from the heat and full of holes from the water. The door to the closet was open.

Inside the closet, sitting in a small puddle on the linoleum floor, was the gray steel safe.

Officer Belmont stopped Jeremiah before he opened the safe. "It would be better if we could take that to the station with us."

"It's bolted to the floor," Jeremiah told him. "We'd have to open it to remove the bolts."

"Great." Belmont pulled a small camera from a holder on his belt. "Then I'll need to get a picture of that before you open it and some more pictures of what's inside."

"Then I can take what I need?" Jeremiah asked.

"Sure. Once I have it on the list."

Jeremiah turned the combination for the lock in the light of Belmont's flashlight. Inside the safe was the bookstore checkbook and the business ledgers where George and Tammy, and later Jeremiah, had recorded every sale and expense since the store opened. There was another book for inventory.

"Been meaning to update that," Jeremiah said. "Guess it's too late now, huh?" He pulled out each item and placed it on a shelf inside the closet for Belmont to take pictures.

"There it is," Jeremiah said. He reached into the safe and pulled out a small gray box with its own lock.

"Insurance, the deed, stuff like that." Jeremiah looked up at Belmont. "This is what I was looking for."

"Where's the key to that box?" Belmont asked.

"At my house," Jeremiah said.

"You should take that other stuff, too," Belmont told him. "Take anything that's important in case you need it. We can't guarantee someone won't want a souvenir."

Jeremiah saw Theresa and a very happy Ethan standing near the remains of the counter. Ethan held up a large leather satchel. The leather was burned and there were dark spots from sitting in water, but the contents was unharmed.

"It's all here!" he said. "My dissertation lives!"

Jeremiah stood at the counter and took one last look at the place where he'd grown up. This wasn't just his store. For as long as he could remember, this had been his home. He took his first steps here, in life and in business. Zachary took his first steps here. He looked across the rows of bookshelves and remembered Theresa's excitement when she came in for the first time. He thought about the nights spent working on the books, rearranging things, working to keep the store open. All that was gone now. All of that was, in the end, for nothing.

Jeremiah walked towards the door. Theresa and Ethan followed him outside.

"I'm going to have to find a new job," Ethan said.

Jeremiah nodded his head. "Me too."

"What do you mean?" Theresa asked. "Your job is here."

Jeremiah looked back at the bookstore as they walked away. "Not really. Not anymore. Look at this."

"I know this is bad," Theresa said, "but you can't just leave." She stopped walking. "What about all those people? What about protecting books?"

Jeremiah turned to face her. "I've had one job offer already. Even if I hadn't, why would I stick around here? You saw what happened to the store. I'm tired of being where I am not wanted."

"But you are wanted!" Theresa was passionate. "Did you not just see those people? They are looking to you to get them through this."

"You two look like you want to be alone," Ethan said. "I'm going to go back to the hotel and look over my stuff. I hope I was smart enough to put everything in this satchel."

Theresa stepped closer to Jeremiah. "They came here this morning for you because of you. For you. They need you."

Jeremiah desperately wanted to turn the conversation away from the crowd and the community. He jumped at the chance.

"They don't need me," he argued. "Dad will handle the insurance stuff. He's probably already made a dozen phone calls by now. And it's not like they need the income. They're making a fortune in residuals from their movies on TV. And now there's HBO…"

"I'm not talking about your parents," Theresa interrupted. She pointed to the crowd still in front of the bookstore. "*They* need you. You see what they're up against, not just in the school but in this town. Probably in this entire state. They don't want to be erased. They don't want to watch while other people are erased. They're willing to stand up and fight, but they need someone to show them how."

"Which Ruthanna, Ethan, or you can do," Jeremiah said.

"And what are you going to do, Jeremiah?" Theresa asked, her hands on her hips. "You're always talking about how you want to get out of here, how you don't want to spend your life in a bookstore in Clear Spring. But look where you're talking about going! You're leaving here to go sell books somewhere else. Another store that wouldn't even be yours."

"With emphasis on the word *sell*," Jeremiah said. "Not defend, not protect, and not constantly wonder if today will be the day that someone burns down my store. Yes, I would like to do something different, maybe go back to school. Maybe open a store that sells individual gloves. I don't know. But I don't have that luxury right now. Right now, I need a job. I have a son who eats so much yogurt that I should buy a cow. I have a chance to make more money than I would ever make here. I just hope they haven't already hired somebody else."

Jeremiah wanted desperately to steer the conversation away from the topic of him staying in Clear Spring. He touched Theresa's hand.

"Why don't you come with me? I could use you at the new bookstore. Zachary loves you."

Theresa did not answer. She quietly withdrew her hand from Jeremiah's touch without looking away from his eyes.

"And you?" she said finally. "Do you love me, Jeremiah?"

Jeremiah blinked. He swallowed. It was a fair question, one that he had asked himself. He was sure the answer was "yes", but he didn't know how to say it. He wanted to say it, but love was one of a dozen emotions swirling around in his brain. He hoped his eyes would say it for him. Unfortunately, he blinked.

All he could think of was the fire's aftermath, his parents, and his overwhelming desire to be anywhere other than Clear Spring.

"Now is not the time to have this conversation," he said.

Theresa froze; her mouth open; her eyes, unbelieving.

"I think we just did."

Theresa's words hung in the air like smoke from the bookstore fire. And then, like the smoke, the words were gone. Only the ashes remained.

40

For the first two weeks that Jeremiah was gone from Clear Spring, Ruthanna let copies of *The Dixiecrat* pile up on her front porch, Ethan sorted through the pages of his dissertation, and Theresa began the difficult process of starting her life over with only the items she could fit in the back of her El Camino.

It hadn't been easy, but Theresa managed to avoid Jeremiah while he was still in town. Jeremiah dropped the business law class so he could take the job in Memphis. It seemed like a waste of tuition to her, but she knew he didn't want to hang around. He wasn't simply going to Memphis. He was leaving Clear Spring.

"I could use you at the new bookstore," he'd said.

"Zachary loves you," he'd said.

The conversation looped in Theresa's head like an earworm that would not let go. Captain & Tennille singing "Love Will Keep Us Together", with that relentless synthesized bass line and ridiculously toothy smile that you could hear in the vocals, right along with the irony. There was nothing Theresa could do to make it stop. Telling herself not to think about it only made her think about it more.

True, she hadn't said "I love you" either. Not in so many words. She'd publicly challenged her mother and declared that Millicent was wrong in front God, the School Board, and everybody. She'd changed her appearance with new clothes and a drastic haircut and turned her entire life totally upside down. She'd put everything on the line and lost most of it. Maybe that wasn't enough for Jeremiah to get the message.

Were men really that dense?

"Do you love me, Jeremiah?"

"Now is not the time to have this conversation."

He was supposed to say "yes", to which she would reply "I love you, too", they hug, end of scene. But he missed his line and her cue never came.

She'd spent that first night at Ruthanna's, but she couldn't stay there forever. She wanted a place of her own, with her furniture and a place for her books. She started looking for an apartment the next day. Fortunately, Clear Spring seemed to have an ample supply of places where people used to live.

Theresa spent the first night in her new apartment sleeping on the floor because there was nowhere else to sleep. Millicent wouldn't let her take her bed or any other furniture when she left. She said she'd paid for it and she was going to keep it. Theresa did manage to snag her red beanbag chair and her blue lava lamp, but only after she reminded Millicent that she bought those with money she'd made babysitting for some couples at the church. Otherwise, the apartment was unfurnished.

Theresa pulled her knees to her chest and wrapped her arms around her legs. She smiled because it reminded her of how they sat during tornado drills when she was in school.

"You know why they move us all to the hallway for this, right?" she'd said to one of her classmates. Then the punchline:

"It makes it easier to find the bodies."

She remembered the horrified expression on the boy's face. "I guess that wasn't the time for that conversation," she said to the lava lamp.

She wondered if this is just how breaking up felt. If this was it, then it was much less dramatic than she had been led to believe. There was no shouting. No one stormed angrily out of the room. Just the slow realization that there was nothing left to say.

She'd rented this apartment because it had a big closet that made a nice showcase for her new dress. The dress cost over half a month's rent, something she did not know when she bought it since she wasn't paying rent at the time. It deserved a closet with some space. It also had a bookcase. Not a big one—just a few shelves, really—but it was built in. Permanent, unlike most of the books that had walked through her life. It would make a nice trophy case for the books she'd been hiding under her bed and in the bottom of her sock drawer.

Theresa was surprised Millicent didn't say something as she carried her last suitcase to the El Camino. She just sat at the kitchen table and watched her daughter leave.

The few books she'd managed to smuggle out would turn the apartment into a home once she had them properly displayed in the bookcase. For now, they remained in the suitcase.

Tammy retrieved Ruthanna's newspapers when she came by after she and George got back to town.

"I'm fine," Ruthanna told Tammy, "but you should check on Theresa. "She's lost more than I have."

"So I guess Millicent knows about her and Jeremiah?" She smiled. Ruthanna looked surprised. "He told me on the phone," Tammy explained. "Is that it?"

Ruthanna nodded her head. "No, but I'm sure that didn't help. You should have seen Theresa. She stood there in front of the School Board, in front of the entire town practically, and told her mother she was wrong about banning books."

Tammy gulped. "I hope she didn't say it like that."

"Her exact words were, 'Mom, I love you. But you are wrong about this'." Ruthanna's face beamed with an almost maternal pride. "I have never witnessed anything that brave. And for that, she was kicked out of her house that same night. She ended up sleeping here after that."

They talked a little more, about Florida, about George, about what Tammy and George had been doing since they left Clear Spring, the book rallies, the library board meetings.

"Jeremiah told me." She when she saw tears forming in Ruthanna's eyes. She was trying to decide if the tears were from pain, pride, or exhaustion. She laid her hand gently on top of Ruthanna's.

"Jeremiah told me what you did at the meeting. He said that if it wasn't for you, the Board would have voted the other way."

"I said a few things," Ruthanna said. "But the real credit goes to Theresa, honestly. More than any of us." A smile slowly formed on Ruthanna's face. "You should have seen her, Tammy. It was incredible. She'd even cut her hair and bought new clothes for the occasion."

"She cut her hair!" Tammy's jaw dropped. She covered her open mouth with her hand. "I thought that was a no-no in Millicent land."

"It is. Or it was," Ruthanna said. "But that's how serious Theresa was about this." Ruthanna continued. "She's serious about books. I thought she was serious about Jeremiah. He seemed serious about her. Or he did, before he left and she stayed here."

They talked a little longer. Ruthanna was polite, but it was clear she just wanted to be alone. Tammy hugged her friend as she said goodbye. "Call me if you need anything. Please."

"Thanks." She gave a tight, forced smile. "I'll be fine."

Ruthanna wasn't the only person working her way through the stages of grief at that moment. As Ethan dug through the satchel that held his dissertation, he realized that while the leather bag had protected some of his work, other chapters were missing. He grabbed a flashlight and ran to the bookstore, hoping to find the missing pieces. He'd been working on Chapter Two (his voluminous review of all previous research regarding traditional Ozark music) and Chapter Four (the results of his own research) on his desk.

He must have left them there. In the open. Unprotected.

He carefully stepped over the crime scene tape and went inside.

The crucial chapters had been soaked by the building's automatic sprinklers and then scattered by a fireman's hose. The result was some granular, PhD-level paper mâché goop that would have to be scraped off the floors, walls, and everything in the room with a putty knife. Or just bulldozed with the rest of the building.

All of it would have to be re-researched and rewritten.

None of it could be reread.

Ethan slammed his fist against the charred desktop. He'd come to Clear Spring to interview traditional Ozark musicians and gather oral histories. He'd gotten sidetracked with this book banning mess and, at least in retrospect, had probably spent too much time on that and not enough time interviewing people like Cleetus Bowman. All his interview notes were gone. His meticulous review of previous research, was completely gone. Eighteen months' worth of work for nothing. He'd have to go back to Little Rock and start over. He wondered if he'd have to pay tuition for three more semesters.

Reeling from the loss, he made his way to the only other person in Clear Spring who could possibly understand.

"Two chapters," Ethan told Ruthanna. "Literature review and my findings. Basically the meat of the dissertation." He blinked back tears, still in disbelief. "Two years of interviews, transcripts, analysis. All of it. Just gone."

"Do you at least have the bibliography?" Ruthanna asked. "Some notes? Something so you don't have to start from scratch?"

"That's all there," he said. "Lists of books, and songs, and people. But the living context, everything that makes that research matter, is gone. Without those stories, these are just old songs."

Ruthanna nodded. "You were preserving voices, making sure they were heard and remembered."

"Yes," he said. "I wanted to save as many of those stories as possible. Now, someone else will decide who gets to be heard and what will be remembered." He sighed. "And what we will be encouraged to forget."

If Millicent was celebrating the fire or mourning the loss of her daughter, she was doing so in private. What should have been a victory—the fiery destruction of Sodom, as it were—was undercut by the School Board's decision not to ban any books. The very books destroyed by the bookstore fire were still available at the school. Her followers, disappointed by her absence from the demonstration after the fire, awaited her instructions. Two weeks later, they were still waiting. They were not alone.

No one in Clear Spring had seen her since the night of the fire.

Millicent's absence was noticed first by the waitresses at the Cozy Kitchen, then by Whitely, and finally by her flock when she didn't show up for church on Sunday. Curtis played piano, and the people sang for most of the service. Millicent was mentioned only in prayers and whispers.

She did, however, have time to write another of her signature Letter To The Editor pieces for *The Dixiecrat*.

To the Editor,

The School Board's decision to keep inappropriate books in our public schools is deeply disappointing to those of us who care about children. While I respect the democratic process, I cannot remain silent as the voices of concerned parents are again muzzled under the guise of so-called free speech. The decision reeks of the kind of Marxist tyranny that has become all too common in America today.

Moral decay rarely arrives all at once. It seeps in, like a cavity in a bad tooth, disguised as tolerance and progress while silently destroying everything it touches.

Those who applaud this decision no doubt feel they have won. But make no mistake:

We are not finished.

We will not be silenced.

We will not rest until this threat and everything that contributes to it have been removed.

"It's as if the fire never happened," Theresa said when she read it. "There was no arson. It was just a happy tourist."

41

Four weeks after the fire, Malachai Parker walked into the police station and confessed.

Malachai expected shackles and handcuffs. Maybe a SWAT team surrounding him, barking orders for him to put his hands behind his head. He'd worn clothes that he wouldn't mind trading for an orange prison jumpsuit. He'd stopped at The Cozy Kitchen for his last meal as a free man. He expected to be in jail on Thanksgiving, so he ordered turkey.

The waitress put down her pencil.

"Honey, it's not even Halloween yet. We won't have turkey until Thanksgiving," she said. "You can come back then."

"Yeah… Probably not."

Disappointed but not deterred, Malachai ordered fried chicken, mashed potatoes with white gravy, and green beans cooked with bacon. He savored every bite as only a condemned man can. He had a hot fudge sundae for dessert.

Then he walked to the police station.

"I did it," he told the woman at the front desk as he approached her desk. "I burned down the bookstore."

"You don't say," said the guard, a woman named Lydia who looked like she'd lost her share of bar fights but probably had an overall winning record. Rumor was she'd bitten off a man's nose.

She looked Malachai up and down.

"Have a seat over there and someone will be right with you."

"I really did it," Malachai argued.

"I believe you," Lydia told him. "Just have a seat and someone will be there soon."

Malachai's mouth dropped open in disbelief.

"Aren't you going to put me in handcuffs?"

"No."

"What if I run?"

Lydia took off her glasses and looked at Malachai.

"Then I'll shoot you. Now, go have a seat."

Officer Belmont glanced at Malachai as he strode into the room with two Coke bottles. He gave one to Lydia and sat the other one on the counter. He pulled a bag of peanuts out of his pocket.

"Want some?"

Lydia smiled. "No."

"Suit yourself." He took a sip and then poured the peanuts into the Coke bottle. "This is lunch. It's been that kind of day." Officer Belmont leaned on the counter. "And how are you doing?"

"You've got one more," Lydia said. She nodded towards the couch. "Says he started the fire at the bookstore." Belmont stayed at the counter but turned his head to see Malachai sitting in a chair near the window.

"Really?" He took another long drink of peanut infused Coca-Cola. "Well, let's see what he has to say."

Malachai held his head high as Officer Belmont escorted him into a plain room with green tile walls, a table, and two folding chairs.

"Lydia said you've got something to tell me."

"I did it," Malachai insisted. "I set the fire at the bookstore." He held out his hands to be cuffed.

"Whoa, slow down, Pyro," Belmont insisted. "First, you…"

Malachai interrupted. "I know. I have the right to remain silent. I know. Anything I say can and will be used against me in a court of law. Got it." He closed his eyes and once again held out his hands for handcuffs.

Belmont put his hand on Malachai's and slowly lowered them so he could see his face. "Actually, I was going to tell you that should probably call an attorney."

"I don't need a lawyer," Malachai said. "I'm just going to confess. I can't take the guilt."

Belmont started again. "You have the right…"

Malachai interrupted again. "To an attorney. If I cannot afford an attorney, one will be provided for me."

"Are you kidding me?" Belmont said.

"I watch the cop shows. I know my rights."

"I still have to read you your rights."

Belmont repeated the Miranda rights that Malachai had already recited.

"Now, do you understand these rights as I have explained them to you?"

"I think I've shown that I do." Malachai rolled his eyes and smirked.

"Yeah," Belmont said. "Keep smirking like that. You'll be the most popular guy in prison."

Belmont took out his notebook and a pencil. "Let's get started." He looked at Malachai.

"Did you do this on your own or was someone else involved?"

"I was all alone. This was me. Nobody else helped or did anything."

"OK. So, you set the fire. What did you do next?"

"I ran," Malachai said.

"Immediately or did you stick around?"

"I lit the match, threw it on the books, and ran."

"OK," Belmont said. "You ran. Did you do anything else?"

"No. I just ran home as fast as I could."

"Did you use anything else?"

"What do you mean?" Malachai had not expected to be questioned. He was confessing. Wasn't that enough?

"Malachai, focus." Belmont leaned slightly forward in his chair. "Did you use anything else when you started the fire? Lighter fluid? Gasoline? A flamethrower?"

Malachai gulped and wiped his hand across his face. "None of that. I just broke the window and tossed in the match."

"That's a big fire for one match, Malachai."

"I used a book of matches. I threw the whole thing in."

Belmont stuck out his lower lip, nodded his head a few times, and wrote "matches" in his notebook.

"Did you tell anyone about this?"

"No. That's why I came in today. The guilt was killing me."

"And that's why you came in. Guilt." Belmont leaned his chair back, rocked a few times, and then set the front legs back on the floor.

"I have to tell you, it's kind of unusual for someone to just walk in and confess to a crime. I mean, you're right. Guilt can be a powerful motivator. But it's usually not powerful enough to make someone want to go to jail.

"I did it," Malachai repeated.

"So you say," Belmont answered. "And I don't doubt that. I just want to know why. For my own sake, you know? Curiosity. What makes a man do something like that?"

"I just didn't want anyone else to get hurt."

Belmont nodded. "Anyone in particular that you didn't want to get hurt?"

Malachai looked down at his feet. Then he looked at the ceiling.

"She didn't mean for it to go this far."

"She? Who is this 'she', Malachai? A friend? A girlfriend?"

Malachai blinked and looked at the door.

"I don't have a girlfriend." He sniffed and looked back to Belmont. "I did it. I set the bookstore on fire."

"Know what I think? I think you did it…"

"I told you I did it already."

"I know," Belmont said. "Let me finish. I think you did it to impress some young lady." The police officer put his elbows on the table and leaned towards Malachai. "But who? I've seen you with Laura Summers. Both of you go to Millicent's church. Was it her?"

Malachai said nothing.

"Or someone else." Belmont continued. "You seem to like Theresa Spate. Did you do it to impress her?"

Belmont looked at Malachai. Clearly, his 'good cop' routine was not working. Time to change gears.

"You know she doesn't like you, right? I mean, seriously, Malachai. She hangs out with Jeremiah all the time. I hear they're quite an item."

Malachai smirked at the idea but said nothing.

"Anything else you want to tell me?" Belmont asked. "Did you go into the store?"

"Why are you asking me that?"

Belmont put down his pencil. "Because if you did, then we'll add breaking and entering to the arson charge. There may also be a separate vandalism charge for breaking the window. Take anything when you left? Because that would be stealing. These things add up."

Belmont paused as he watched Malachai's eyes dilate. "You might end up with four or five charges for the same crime."

Belmont leaned his chair back on two legs and slowly shook his head. "You're looking at a *lot* of time here."

Malachai's face turned the color of milk that was turning into yogurt in a cereal bowl in the kitchen sink. "No. I did not go inside. I broke the window and tossed in the match. The book of matches. That's it. That's how it happened."

"If you say so," Belmont said. "Well, let's get you booked into one of our luxury accommodations. Stand up."

Belmont put Malachai in handcuffs and took him through the booking process. Then he led him to the drunk tank.

"Good thing it's early in the day," Belmont told him. "Enjoy your private room while you can."

He went back to Lydia at the front desk.

"So," she said. "Case closed?"

"He didn't do it." Belmont looked back over his shoulder as if Malachai was somewhere behind him. "I don't know why he's saying he did it or who he's trying to protect, but he didn't light that fire."

Lydia looked up from behind the desk and raised a single eyebrow.

"So why'd you put him in there?"

Belmont laughed. "He knows who did do it. With the proper encouragement, he might decide to share. Besides, it's not like I'm holding him against his will. The man came in here asking for it. I'm just fulfilling his request."

42

The Corner Bookstore smelled like new beginnings; like carpet glue, fresh paint, and shrink-wrap on books. The smell of sawdust and cleaning supplies. The top note of this fragrant chord was the smell of books: fresh cut paper, glue, and the occasional leather binding. It was a much more appealing scent than the acrid fumes of burned paper and melted plastic that Jeremiah would forever associate with his final days sifting through the ashes in Clear Spring. The smell filled the new store like the aroma of barbeque and hickory smoke that permeated the air and concrete of Memphis.

Jeremiah's first task as Manager was to make sure the new Corner Bookstore in Riverside Mall was set up and ready for its grand opening. After a month of hiring and training ten employees, opening boxes, stocking shelves, and doing other pre-opening managerial things, Jeremiah knew the new bookstore was ready to greet the public. He just wasn't sure if he was.

The mall would open in one hour. Jeremiah came in an hour early because it seemed like a managerial thing to do. That, and he was required to come in one hour before the store opened. The other employees, eager bibliophiles who had not yet realized that most of their time would be spent explaining the company's return policy and not in excited conversations about their favorite literary works, would clock in at 8:30. Together, they had managed to get the store ready to open on the Monday before Thanksgiving, just in time for the Christmas rush. The Assistant Manager, Tamika Jones, built a beautiful Christmas display in the front of the store just for the occasion.

Memphis stretched and yawned around him, an attractive but aloof potential lover that he'd like to get to know but probably wouldn't. Between working at the store and taking care of Zachary, he hadn't had time to do much exploring. In a city of almost a million people, his ten employees were the only souls Jeremiah knew. Eleven, if you counted Patricia, the niece of Randy Liles, the man who got Jeremiah his new job.

Randy recommended Patricia as a babysitter for Zachary. She seemed nice enough, not Ruthanna levels of inherent grandmotherly comfort but kind and bubbly as only young and over-caffeinated preschool teachers can be. Jeremiah looked around. The house seemed safe. The environment felt stimulating, with bright primary colors and child-sized furniture.

Almost as important as demeanor and childproofing was affordability. Jeremiah was making more money, but he was still adapting to paying for things he wasn't in the habit of paying for, like childcare and rent. Best of all, Patricia said she didn't mind working late. Tamika would eventually be closing the store at nights, but once the store opened and until Jeremiah was convinced things were running smoothly, he was working twelve-hour days. At least.

Theresa still wasn't returning his calls.

He inspected a bookshelf and straightened some books that didn't need to be straightened. He glanced at the clock.

8:15.

Jeremiah had grown accustomed to window-shoppers and mall-walkers peering into the store through the rectangle frames of the garage door-style security gate. He was used to it, but he still felt like an exhibit in a human zoo. *Homo bibliophilus,* perhaps. He raised the gate about three-quarters of the way so he could see the mall without the metal frames, creating a Schrödinger state of readiness in which the store was both open and closed at the same time.

The second floor gate could wait until the official opening at 9:00, when Tamika would be at her post. Tamika's job, when she wasn't stocking shelves or learning how to make night deposits, had been to make the corporate Corner Bookstore feel less like a corporate chain and more like a cozy, family owned local bookstore. She'd arranged several faux living room sets with wing-back chairs and end tables with an assortment of random lamps and ashtrays. It reminded Jeremiah of a furniture show room. He resisted the urge to put price tags on the furniture, although if someone asked, he would have been willing to sell it for the right price. Theresa convinced three local artists and a sculptor to let her place their art in these sets. Jeremiah had the idea of selling the pieces on consignment. The artists thought it was a good idea.

Jeremiah was putting out the daily newspapers, *The New York Times*, *Wall Street Journal,* and others that had been somehow magically shipped in overnight, when a short man in a blue blazer and khakis walked confidently into the store. He walked like he owned the place; which he did.

"Opening early?" he asked.

"No," Jeremiah said. "We won't open until nine. I just wanted to see how the store looked without the gate." Jeremiah walked out from behind the counter to escort the stranger out of the store. "Guess I should close that door before people start coming in."

"Thomas McKay," the man said as he stuck out his hand. "I don't think we've met since Randy hired you. I've heard good things." Clearly Mr. McKay had not heard that Jeremiah had a prosthetic hand. He reached out for a handshake and looked momentarily disoriented when Jeremiah reached back with his left hand. Jeremiah had long since learned that he preferred the confusion over the look that came over someone's face when they realized they were clasping a prosthesis. McKay made the adjustment to his left hand almost without missing a beat.

"I'm looking forward to you doing good things for us here in Memphis."

"Thomas McKay," Jeremiah repeated. "How do I know that name?"

"I sign your paychecks," he said. "Not personally. They use a rubber stamp for that. But that's probably where you saw my name. I'm impressed that you could make out the signature."

Jeremiah smiled. "Nice to meet you. Welcome to my store. Your store. The store."

"I like to think of it as the community's bookstore," Mr. McKay said. "That's what we're about. Community values. Family values."

Jeremiah felt an involuntary twitch at the "community values" pledge, somewhere between a nervous tic and a full-on convulsion. Community values burned down his bookstore in Clear Spring. He already knew that family values were more about which families were valued and which weren't.

"I'll get to the point," Mr. McKay said. "I know that banned books were a big part of your business in Clear Spring. They certainly brought a lot of customers into your store. I have nothing but respect for your parents. How are they dealing with the fire? The protests?"

"They seem to…"

"You're in a mall now," McKay interrupted. "Your neighbors won't appreciate picket signs and protesters. They don't even like it when you put a sign outside your door. Mall management doesn't want their mall burned down. This is why we don't do banned books here."

"No argument there," Jeremiah said. "So no display?"

"No banned books display," McKay echoed back. "You can make other displays like that Christmas display you have over there. But no special table for banned books. And every book in this store will be approved by me." McKay's head tilted forward slightly. His eyes narrowed.

"And no banned books on any front displays." McKay was adamant. "No matter what the display is about."

Jeremiah nodded his head to show he understood. Then he stopped.

"So, no *Grapes of Wrath* on a front display on the Fourth of July?"

McKay gave a tight-lipped nod.

"Now, where exactly is that line that separates the front from the back?"

McKay smiled, but it was clear he did not share his store manager's amusement. "Good book, but not on a front display. Maybe on an end cap or small table towards the rear of the store, but not in the front." He ran a fingertip along the counter, looked at it, and smiled. "Exceptions create problems," he said. "It's easier if there is just one rule that applies across the board." He walked to a small table near the front counter and did a similar fingertip inspection.

"This is all in the employee handbook," McKay said. "Section 8: Shelving and Displaying Books."

Jeremiah nodded and smiled. He'd read the handbook, sort of. A more accurate description would be to say he'd skimmed most of the chapter headings over coffee one morning and then sat it aside. He must have missed the part about displaying books.

"Are there books that you won't approve?" Jeremiah asked, remembering what Ruthanna said about his mother's belief that some books should not be sold.

"Again, in the handbook," McKay told him. "But the short answer is, 'not many.' I don't like the idea of censorship— stupid stuff, terrible stuff—but we need to appeal to as many customers as possible." McKay ran a finger along the edge of a bookshelf near the door, looked at the dust on his fingertip, and smiled.

"You're going to want to dust in here before you open."

"No banned book displays is fine with me," Jeremiah said, ignoring the dust. He'd put up a couple of displays—books on cardboard shelves without much decoration or description—but had not built anything about banned books. He silently breathed a sigh of relief at the news that he would not have to make that decision. He remembered Theresa's prediction, that he was only going to end up doing the same thing somewhere else, and smiled. She was only halfway right. He was still selling books, but he was no longer responsible for protecting free speech. No protests, no meetings, and no one threatening his business or his life.

Tamika walked through the door at 8:25, followed quickly by two more employees, Darnel and Stacy.

"Go ahead and clock in," Jeremiah told them. "Big day today!"

Tamika turned to Jeremiah before she went up the stairs. She smiled and lightly touched his arm.

"You look nervous. You okay?"

And because he didn't want to lie, he said, "Maybe."

Being okay would have required Theresa.

43

For all her fundamental faults, Millicent Spate was not a liar. She was many things—a joyless prig, a perpetual scowler, someone who smiled with the same strained tension as if she was squeezing a zit on her face—but she was not, at least not intentionally, a liar. When she was wrong, it was because she believed it. When she said *Are You There God, It's Me, Margaret* was pornographic, she honestly believed that a book about a girl asking God if she could just have her first period and get it over with already was genuinely pornographic. She was a misinformer, an unreliable source, an error that refused to be corrected. She was not, in the strictest sense, a liar.

She hadn't lied about the fire, but only because no one had asked her the right questions. When Officer Belmont came to her house and asked if she started the fire, she could honestly say she had not. Belmont took out his pencil and noted her response in his notebook.

His "Do you know who did?" follow-up was nothing that couldn't be handled with a little nuance and finesse. "I wasn't there" was technically true. And no one came to Millicent and told her they did it. Laura dropped by the night of the fire but she didn't say anything. She not only didn't say anything about the fire, she didn't say anything at all. She just sat there, like a pale, smoke-wilted daisy shaking in the wind, and listened while Millicent ranted about how Theresa had betrayed her. Laura noticed but did not point out to

Millicent that she referred to Theresa only as "Theresa" or "that girl" and never as her daughter. Then "that girl" came in and Laura left. She never *said* she started the fire.

Millicent had her theories, which she was fairly sure were accurate, insomuch as Millicent *always* thought her theories were accurate, but they were still only theories. She was not willing to risk sending an innocent person to jail because she had a theory. Especially when that innocent person might be someone she cared about.

"Did you know it was going to happen?" Belmont asked.

"I know that God punishes sin," Millicent said, "so I guess I knew something was going to happen sooner or later. But, no. I did not know the time or manner of that punishment until it happened."

Belmont wrote something in his notebook. "What if I told you that someone came in and confessed?"

"On their own?" Millicent asked.

"All on their own." Belmont tapped his pencil on his knee. "Out of the blue. Surprised us. We weren't expecting anyone to confess to something like this. We didn't even have any real leads."

"Then, if you've got the arsonist, why are you here?" Millicent asked.

"Because I don't believe him," Belmont said. "I don't know if he's doing it to be chivalrous or because he feels like he owes someone something. Maybe he just wants to see his name in the paper. Who knows?

Millicent gave a knowing nod. "I might be able to help if you told me who it is."

"I can't talk about an ongoing investigation like that," Belmont said.

He paused to watch Millicent's reaction, but she sat in Sphynx-like silence and did not flinch. So he continued.

"I would hate to see this guy go to prison for something he didn't do, even if he was dumb enough to take the fall. I know that you would hate that, too. But I can't turn him loose because, if I do, people will say that we have an admitted arsonist, someone who turned himself in, running around and the police let him go. Then, if there's another fire, they'll think we didn't do our job the first time. And they'd be right, but for the wrong reason."

Belmont leaned back in his chair. "Do you see the problem?"

Millicent folded her arms across her chest. "So you would rather do this guy an injustice than tarnish the reputation of the Clear Spring police?"

"Something like that, yeah." Belmont put his hands on the table. "It wasn't like we forced the confession. I'd be glad to play the tape of the interrogation if this went to trial. I did everything I could to get this kid to shut up. But I would rather put the right person in jail. And I think you know who that is."

"I told you," Millicent said slowly. "I did not see who set the fire."

Belmont stood up to leave. "You might want to tell the person you didn't see that someone else will be going to jail for their crime. See how they feel about that." He stood up to leave.

Millicent's eyes narrowed as if she was weighing the information. "They might be glad that they're not going to jail."

"They might," Belmont said. "But something tells me that if they're one of your people, the guilt will eventually get to them and they'll speak up. I don't think they want this guy to burn for their sins."

"They could be executed for this?" Millicent asked.

"Just a figure of speech, Millicent. But they will go to prison if no one else comes forward." Belmont stood up to go. He smiled as he reached out to shake Millicent's hand.

"If they're as honest as you, they'll want to do the right thing. They might just need you to encourage them to take that first step."

44

Jeremiah didn't know what to expect on the Monday of the week of Thanksgiving when The Corner Bookstore officially opened for business.

In the Ozarks where he grew up, school was out for the entire Thanksgiving week, not because Clear Springers appreciated turkey and cranberry sauce—with ridges, thank you, as God intended—more than other Americans, but because that Monday traditionally coincided with the first day of deer season. If school had not let out, every man and boy tall enough to hoist a rifle to his shoulder would have been absent, along with several of the girls and most of the male teachers.

Most Clear Spring moms and daughters spent those deer hunting days satisfying their own primal hunter-gatherer urges by shopping. It was a good week to be a bookstore.

Memphis schools didn't let students out for deer season. Their Thanksgiving break began on Wednesday. The mall would be closed for the Thursday holiday, which meant that Monday, Tuesday, and Wednesday were dress rehearsals for Black Friday and the Christmas season.

At precisely nine o'clock, Jeremiah rolled the gates on both levels all the way up and wondered what kind of hunters would be coming to his store today.

McKay's visit before the store opened was an unexpected wrinkle. Jeremiah had been expecting Randy Liles—the man had offered him a job; it made sense that Randy would drop by on opening day. Thomas McKay was a surprise. That the owner of the now-three store chain chose to stay and observe was a shock. He'd never really had a boss before, certainly not one who owned multiple stores, so he didn't know what to expect. Jeremiah watched McKay inspect shelves for inappropriate or miscategorized books, critique Tamika's displays while people were looking at them, and interrupt customers who were reading books in one of Tamika's living room sets by asking if they needed help finding anything.

McKay picked up a copy of *Slaughterhouse-Five* from a display near the register—a display Tamika had topped off with a big sign that said "Perennials"—and motioned for Jeremiah, who was checking out a customer at the time. Jeremiah hurriedly gave the woman her change, bagged her books, and said thank you just as McKay was calling his name.

"This one." McKay tapped a finger on the cover. "This one always causes problems. War books are generally okay, but this one is just weird. Vonnegut's weird." His mouth formed a twisted smile as he glanced at the back cover and shook his head. "Modern writers are just weird. Can't anyone just tell a good story anymore?"

"Weird sells," Jeremiah said. "Besides, that's going to be a classic. People will be reading this a hundred years from now."

McKay put the book back in its rightful place on the shelf. "Just watch it. If we get any complaints, I'll ask you to pull it."

Jeremiah interpreted McKay's statement as "If we get any complaints *today, while I am in the store, I'll ask you to pull it.*" When McKay wasn't there, Jeremiah planned to tell any complaining customers "thank you" and then ignore the complaint.

"I'll take care of it," Jeremiah said.

"And another thing," McKay began. Jeremiah flinched. In his experience, "another things" were rarely good news.

McKay led Jeremiah behind the counter as if it was a very public private office. He looked around to make sure no one could hear, then he looked at Jeremiah and leaned in close.

"I noticed you hired a Black assistant manager," he said in a conspiratorial whisper.

"Her name is Tamika Jones," Jeremiah told him.

McKay scowled at the interruption. "Right. Tamika." McKay repeated her name one separated, over-enunciated syllable at a time. "Anyway, that's fine, if that's what you choose to do, but you're going to need another employee—a white employee—to work on the same floor with her. Ideally, you want at least one white employee and one Black employee on each floor at all times. Same with behind the counter. We don't want people getting the wrong impression."

Jeremiah was beginning to understand what the wrong impression might be. "I was thinking more of a boy-girl thing, in case a woman is uncomfortable asking for books about health, or sex, or maybe even a romance novel. Some of these church ladies are funny about that. Or a man might be more comfortable buying certain books from another man."

McKay vetoed the idea with a dismissive shake of his head.

"That might work in Clear Spring. You're in Memphis now. You're going to have a more, shall we say, *diverse* clientele." It was an assumption, and Jeremiah knew it. The guy had never been to Clear Spring and probably couldn't find it on a map. Jeremiah had just met Mr. McKay but he could already tell that his new boss didn't wait until he had all the information before he reached a conclusion.

However, in this case, he had to admit that the assumption was correct. Jeremiah hated when that happened. But Memphis was more diverse than Clear Spring in virtually any way you defined the term.

"Honestly, I didn't think about that when I hired her," Jeremiah said. He cringed at the sound of his own words. He sounded way too much like someone saying, "I don't see race," which he had come to understand meant that race was usually the *first* thing people who say things like that notice. He was just glad that such a qualified person was willing to work sixty-plus hours a week for what they were paying her.

Jeremiah put on his best diplomatic face and voice. "She has a great résumé, good people skills, and she's smart."

"You got all that from a job interview?" McKay asked.

"I got all that from working with her and having lunch with her every day for the past six weeks."

"Still," McKay said, "I would feel better if we kept at least a one-to-one ratio on this. It just works better for everyone involved." He smiled awkwardly. "It's just good business."

Jeremiah wasn't convinced that quiet segregation was any better than quiet censorship, but he didn't know how to respond other than to acknowledge McKay's not-so-subtle request. He and Darnel would work the lower level while Tamika and Stacy worked the upper level. Men who wanted dirty magazines would just have to face a woman when they pointed to the sealed plain black plastic wrappers behind the counter. They always pointed. No one ever said *"And I'd like this month's Playboy, please"* out loud.

Jeremiah told McKay he'd figure out where to put the other part-time employees once he knew more about traffic in the store. McKay told him to do what he thought was best, although, based on their conversation, Jeremiah was pretty sure that he and McKay might not agree on what was best.

McKay hung around the store until noon, running a fingertip along the edges of random shelves and either smiling or grimacing at the results. He had more rules for Jeremiah before he left.

"Do not schedule more than one of them for breaks or for lunch at a time," McKay said. "You don't want people congregating in the breakroom."

As he looked over McKay's shoulder, Jeremiah saw Tamika descending the staircase from the upper level. She paused on the landing between the two levels when McKay turned around to see what Jeremiah was looking at.

"Thomas McKay, meet Tamika Jones," Jeremiah said. "Our Assistant Manager."

McKay smiled and nodded as Tamika finished coming down the stairs. "Nice to meet you. Welcome to The Corner Bookstore family."

"Thank you." She looked at Jeremiah. "We forgot to schedule a lunch time for Darnel and Stacy. When do you want them to go to lunch?"

"Ladies first," Jeremiah said. "Tell Stacy to take her lunch now. Darnel can go when she's finished."

McKay's eyes followed Tamika up the stairs.

"You're going to want to talk to her about her hair," he said. "We need a more professional look."

Jeremiah hadn't noticed anything unprofessional about Tamika's hair. It was thick and tied into two big Afro puffs. She wore square black-rimmed glasses like the ones worn by Black women he'd seen on TV or in the newspapers. He was no expert on women's hair, but to him, Tamika looked fashionable. And Professional.

McKay read the expression on Jeremiah's face but misinterpreted its meaning. Jeremiah was wondering what could possibly be wrong about Tamika's hair. McKay thought the new manager was wondering why something about hair and appearance wasn't in the handbook.

"There are some things I can't put in the handbook. I'm sure you understand. I trust you will enforce them anyway."

Jeremiah expected McKay to come back after lunch, but he never did. Jeremiah wasn't sure if this was a good or a bad thing. If this was a test, had he passed or failed?

Later that day, during a lull in traffic, Jeremiah broke one of McKay's rules and left the lower level in Darnel's care and journeyed upstairs to visit his assistant manager.

"OK, I'm new here, so maybe I don't know, but here's what McKay told me." Jeremiah recounted for Tamika the conversation about racial ratios in the store.

"He said this was for the comfort of everyone involved?" Tamika asked.

"That's what he said. Among other things," Jeremiah said. "Do all the stores in Memphis do this kind of thing?" He'd heard about racial tension in the city. He wasn't sure how those tensions played out in the workplace.

"Not really," Tamika said. "Most of them avoid the whole thing and just don't hire Black folks. Certainly not in management."

"Yeah," Jeremiah said slowly. "I kind of picked up on that when I was talking to McKay."

"But that's not why he wants a white person on each floor," Tamika said. "First, he's worried about shoplifting. He figures people are less likely to steal something if there's a white guy following them around the store. But he also wants a white guy up there so I don't 'accidentally' slip a book into a bag for someone without them paying for it. Or so I don't take any books back to my place without paying for them."

"Seriously?" Jeremiah's eyes narrowed as he shook his head. "He hires employees to watch other employees?"

"Happens to Black folks all the time," Tamika told him. She rolled her eyes and shook her head.

"Welcome to Memphis, Jeremiah. You've got a lot to learn."

Jeremiah was becoming more aware of how much he had to learn every day, like learning what it was like to pay someone to watch Zachary while he was at work. It wasn't just the cost, although writing that check every week had taken some getting used to. The bigger adjustment was having to consider Patricia's schedule when he needed to work late, a problem that would only get worse now that the store was open.

The family-values Corner Bookstore had a strict "no children in the workplace" policy, including for those committed managers who worked after hours. An assistant manager in Little Rock was using the children's reading area as her son's personal playpen while she did payroll in the back office on Sunday mornings. The child, a precocious five-year-old, reshelved all the books in alphabetical order according to the first letter in the last word of the title. Using this logic, darling Timmy put *Horton Hears a Who* next to *Whistle for Willie*, while *Snow White and the Seven Dwarfs* ended up next to *Alexander and the Terrible, Horrible, No Good, Very Bad Day* and so on. Then, because Timmy was only five and getting bored, he put *Curious George* next to *Green Eggs and Ham*.

McKay ordered the manager to "straighten out this mess." When it wasn't straightened out by the end of the day, he fired her. The resulting rule was added to Chapter 10: "Workplace Expectations."

If he was going to put in late hours for work, he was going to need someone to put in late hours for Zachary. He needed a Ruthanna in his life. In more ways than one.

Unfortunately, the only Ruthanna he knew lived back in Clear Spring.

This was one decision that he could put off until after the new year, after the Christmas rush, after he was more settled in. Tamika recommended a preschool/daycare place that catered specifically to the needs of single parents, with evening hours that went late into the night and a more educational environment, as opposed to Zachary watching TV at Patricia's all day, something that Jeremiah never really liked. Jeremiah took Zachary and visited the preschool on one of his rare days off. It wasn't Ruthanna, but it seemed to be as close to Ruthanna as he was going to find in Memphis.

That night, Jeremiah ate delivered pizza and tried to process McKay's written and unwritten rules. Neither of the two restaurants in Clear Spring delivered food. They grumbled when you asked for something to go. Garibaldi's was a little pizza place near Memphis State, which was near the small, two-bedroom home that Jeremiah was renting. The campus area had sandwich shops, a grocery store, and other businesses—all within walking distance of his house. It was one of the more walkable parts of the city. It reminded him of Clear Spring that way, except there was a lot more traffic.

But the best part of the city was the fact that no one knew him. He was just a guy in a bookstore, with no family history, no one trying to burn down his business, and no ghosts of book bans past expecting him to live up to anything.

He was also the new manager of a new store at retail's busiest time of the year. He didn't have the energy to think about banned books or what might be happening in Clear Spring.

45

Under Arkansas law, Malachai could be held for 72 hours without being charged with a crime. Not that anyone wanted to hold Malachai. The prosecutor, Buford Atkins, was reluctant to file criminal charges without any evidence that Malachai actually did it. Buford didn't need *all* the evidence, but he needed something. A fingerprint. A witness. Something. They couldn't just take the boy's word for it.

"What's the plan, Officer Belmont?" Buford asked. "You can't just hold him forever and hope that the real arsonist will suddenly feel guilty and come forward. That's illegal. And it probably wouldn't happen anyway."

Belmont had thought the threat of extended jail time would make Malachai more helpful. At least he'd planted some seeds, to borrow a familiar Millicent phrase. Hopefully they would take root soon. He was also counting on Malachai's dad. *The Dixiecrat* covered the fire with the gloating tone of someone who enjoyed watching the bookstore burn, with multiple articles and Whitely's uniquely scathing editorials. Belmont wondered how Whitely would report his son's confession. Or if he would even mention it at all.

Nobody believed Malachai started the fire, although Malachai seemed to be working on convincing himself that it was true. It was also clear, at least to Belmont, that Millicent didn't strike the match, at least not physically. But something didn't smell right. Millicent's statement that she "did not see who set the fire", while probably technically true, didn't mean that she didn't know who did. It also didn't mean she wasn't behind it.

"The woman could have been a lawyer," Belmont told Buford.

"Funny how that phrase is rarely used as a compliment," Buford replied.

With just over 60 hours left before they would have to release Malachai, Belmont decided to drop by Whitely's house.

"I'm afraid I've got some bad news, Whit. Your boy's confessed to starting that bookstore fire."

Whitely's face turned a whiter shade of pasty.

"He came in and confessed right before lunch," Belmont explained. "Shame, too. I was looking forward to the fried chicken special at the Kitchen and I ended up having to talk to him."

Whitely tried not to react but his dilated pupils gave him away.

"Is that so? Did he say who was with him?"

"Said he did it all by himself."

Whitely laughed. "Well, that's a lie. That boy never did anything all by himself in his life."

"Is that so?" Belmont said. "Whitely, you need to know what Malachai is looking at if this is true. And, if it's not true—if Malachai is doing this to cover for a friend or whatever—then you need to know what he's looking at if he doesn't tell us what happened and he goes to jail."

"You want me to talk to him?"

"I would if it was my boy," Belmont said. He turned to go but then turned back around. "You also might want to talk with Millicent Spate. See what she knows."

Millicent was sitting on her front porch when Whitely pulled into the driveway.

"I suppose you want to interview me about the fire."

"What makes you think that?"

"Belmont was by here earlier," she said. "I figure he went to you to tell you he had a confession."

"Did he tell you who made the confession?" Whitely asked.

"No. Said he couldn't talk about an ongoing investigation like that."

Whitely smiled. For the first time in his life, he knew something Millicent didn't know. He wasn't sure what to do with that information, but it felt good.

"He said it was my boy, Millicent. He said Malachai came in and confessed."

Whitely watched Millicent's eyes first seemed to look deep within and then move slowly from side to side, as if she was searching for an answer but found none. She was somewhere between confusion and disbelief. Her lips parted only slightly, as if about to ask a question but then realizing she didn't know what to ask. She grasped for words but found none.

"I'm sorry to hear that," she said softly. It was almost a whisper. "Real sorry, Whitely."

"Do you know who did it, Millicent?"

Millicent looked at her friend. Whitely was no longer a newsman or even someone in her flock. He was a father asking her to help his son.

"I didn't see anything, Whitely. I wasn't there."

"Stop!" Whitely closed his eyes and took a long, deep breath. "We both know that you didn't have to be there to know who did this. Now, who was it?"

"Whitely, I'm sorry." She stopped while she could still tell herself she wasn't lying.

She blinked back the tears. Something in her posture softened, more from resignation than relaxation.

"But if I hear anything, I promise to tell you first."

Millicent waited for the sound of Whitely's truck to fade in the distance. Then she got in her car and drove to Laura's house. She hadn't seen Laura since she'd left the School Board meeting. She just hoped she was at home.

Laura's mother answered the door with her granddaughter Grace.

"Jean, I need to talk to Laura," was all she said.

"I'll get her."

"Is she in her room?" Millicent asked as she brushed past Jean. "I'll just go on back there."

There was no response when Millicent knocked on the bedroom door. She waited a moment and knocked again.

"Laura, dear. Are you in there?"

The door opened. Laura's face was drained except for the deep, dark circles beneath her eyes. The eyes themselves were red. Her hair was stringy and unwashed, much like the bathrobe that she clutched to keep closed.

Millicent sat on the bed beside her.

"Honey, we need to talk."

"It wasn't right, Millicent," she said softly. "The way they forced the Board to vote that way. I had to do something."

Millicent hugged her. "I know. But Malachai told the police he did it."

"What?" Laura seemed genuinely surprised by the news. "Why would he do that?"

"I don't know," Millicent admitted. "Can you think of a reason?"

"We'd talked about it," Laura said. "But we were just joking around. We talked about a lot of things that might happen to that bookstore. A tornado. Maybe an earthquake. A flood." She smiled and did a single fist pump. "Real wrath of God kind of stuff."

"And fire?" Millicent asked. "Did you talk about a fire at the bookstore?"

"We did." Laura's chest rose as her eyes closed and fell as she opened them.

Millicent took Laura's hands in hers.

"And did you talk about lighting the fire?"

Laura nodded. Then she sat on the bed. "We talked about it, but we weren't going to do anything. And then, when I saw what they did to you at that meeting, how they ignored what you've been trying to warn them about. How Theresa humiliated you." She turned to face Millicent.

"I knew it wasn't what God wanted."

Millicent put her arm around Laura.

"So what did you do?"

"I did what I thought was right. What I thought you would want," Laura told her. "I set the building on fire. But I called 911 right away. I thought they'd put it out before it got out of control."

There was a long silence.

"Does Malachai know you did it?"

Laura rubbed her eyes. "I didn't tell him. He didn't see me. But we've been talking about stuff like that for a long time. It was kind of a joke." She looked at Millicent.

"He had to know something," Laura said.

"Listen," Millicent said in a very deliberate voice, as if she was giving instructions on how to defuse a bomb and every detail was the difference between life and death. "You can't tell anyone what you just told me. Malachai made his choice. And, honestly, without any evidence, they'll have to let him go. They'll write it off as one more crazy stunt, like that time Whitely caught him reading Theresa's book."

Laura allowed herself a slight laugh while she wiped away a tear.

"You knew about that?"

"Of course I knew about that," Millicent said. "Theresa's not as slick as she thinks she is. And that's just the way Malachai is. Poor boy. He's always been that way with you girls."

They looked at each other and smiled.

Millicent took Laura's hand again. She stroked it a few times, as if she was petting a nervous cat in the vet's office.

"Malachai's going to be okay," she said. "But you won't be, not if anyone finds out you did this." Millicent could see Laura's instinct for self-preservation was eroding beneath the weight of wanting to protect Malachai.

"You need to let the police figure this out on their own. They'll investigate and they'll realize Malachai didn't do it. Then they'll turn him loose."

She paused to make sure Laura was following her.

"But." Millicent spoke as if she was warning Laura of imminent danger ahead. " If you tell the police that Malachai is lying, then he'll be in trouble for that. They won't just let him go. They'll charge him with obstructing justice and interfering with an investigation. And lying to the police."

Laura looked confused. "You want me to lie?"

"To protect Malachai, yes," Millicent told her. "Besides, you're not lying. You're just not saying anything." She stood up. "It's in the Constitution. The Fifth Amendment. You have the right to remain silent."

That night, Laura replayed the scene as she laid in bed not sleeping. She did not share Millicent's confidence that Malachai would eventually be set free if she said nothing.

You shall know the truth and the truth will set you free.

Millicent was asking her to erase that truth. To let Malachai repeat the lie until the lie became the truth. Millicent wanted the truth removed from the record, as if it was some book she wanted to ban.

The next morning, Laura went to the police station. She told Lydia she had something to tell Officer Belmont. Lydia called Belmont who then took her to the interrogation room. Even though it meant going somewhat out of their way, Belmont made sure that he and Laura walked by the drunk tank where Malachai was being held.

Out of the corner of his eye, Malachai saw Laura enter the hallway. He went to that side of the drunk tank and watched as she walked in his direction. He stood as she passed, his hands gripping the bars of the cell, his face pressed between them. She said his name as she walked by.

"Don't talk to him," Belmont said. "Look straight ahead."

"Millicent must have told her to tell the truth," Malachai whispered to himself. "Millicent did this to protect me."

He watched Laura go down the hall until he couldn't see her anymore.

"Thank you, Millicent."

Belmont told Laura to sit.

"You have the right to remain silent…"

Laura was shocked by how quickly things moved after that. Once Belmont was convinced this wasn't another false confession, he escorted Laura to his patrol car and then drove her to the bookstore.

"Walk me through what happened," he said.

Laura told Belmont how she'd taken a big rock from across the street and smashed it through the window. It took several tries, and she was afraid she'd get caught, but the glass eventually cracked and then broke.

Belmont wrote in his notebook.

Laura pointed to what looked like a pile of ash or burned wood just inside the store.

"There," she said. "That's the rock."

She showed Belmont the scratch on her arm from where the shattered glass cut her as she stepped through the broken window. She explained how she squeezed the bottle of lighter fluid that she'd picked up at the drug store until it was empty.

And then she lit the match. There was only one.

Finally, she told Belmont how she called 911 from the phone on the counter to report the fire.

"I'm sure they record those calls, don't they?" Laura asked softly. "You can check. That's my voice on the call."

Belmont put Laura back in his patrol car and drove back to the police station. He put her in handcuffs and escorted her to the cell they used for female prisoners. Malachai was still standing with his hands on the cell bars when she and Belmont walked past.

Then he unlocked the drunk tank door. Lydia gave Malachai's clothes back to him and told him to go home.

"You'll need to change clothes," Lydia told him. "Bring me the jumpsuit when you're done."

Clear Spring's most recently freed man started walking home. But first, he wanted to tell his parents the good news. His mother hugged him when he walked through their door.

"Did you decide you didn't want to be in jail?" Whitely teased. "Confessing to a crime you didn't commit. Why would you do something like that?"

"I don't know." Malachai laughed. "It seemed like the right thing to do. I'm just glad Millicent was able to get Laura to tell the truth. They weren't going to let me take it back."

"Recant," Whitely said.

"No, we can't," Malachai replied. Whitely started to correct him, but stopped. Why bother?

Whitely thought about what happened. Millicent talked Laura into telling the truth. Had she also talked Laura into setting the fire?

The next day's *Dixiecrat* featured a bold headline in a font Whitely usually reserved for moon landings, Presidential elections, or when the Governor rejected especially onerous liberal legislation.

"ARSON CONFESSION!!!"

Whitely reported that Laura voluntarily confessed to the police. There was no mention of Malachai. But tucked away in the fourth paragraph was this:

"Laura Summers is part of a group led by local activist Millicent Spate. The group, Parents Who Deserve To Be Heard, says it is committed to removing inappropriate books from schools and public libraries. Mrs. Summers accompanied Spate to the School Board meeting in which Spate spoke about the alleged dangers of these books. Witnesses say that Spate was seen talking to Summers during the meeting. These witnesses also report that Summers left the meeting immediately after the Board rejected Spate's proposal.

Spate has declined to comment on the matter.

"She declined to comment because I didn't ask her," Whitely said to himself as he typed the last line. "You don't get credit for cleaning up a mess when you're the one who created it."

46

Theresa's new apartment was filling up, first with a bed, then with a kitchen table and two chairs, then a couch to sit and read on. In her living room. No more reading in bed unless she wanted to and certainly no more reading under the blankets.

She still wasn't sure how she felt about the trust fund bomb Millicent dropped in their last conversation. She hadn't told anyone, not even Jeremiah. She wasn't sure if she even wanted the money. The whole thing felt too much like she was profiting from her father's death. She'd withdrawn just enough money to pay the deposit on the apartment and a few things she needed, like the bed. The rest could wait.

She was excited about filling the built-in bookcase with what she was now calling her "trophy books," not to impress any unexpected visitors who might drop by, but because the familiar titles made her happy. She managed to sneak a few favorites into her suitcase as she was leaving, secret books that she'd hidden from Millicent over the years. She would have to buy other under-the-covers favorites later, not to read, but to make her smile when she saw them out in the open on a shelf.

Ironically, the first book she put on the top shelf was the Bible, not because she planned on reading it every night or, honestly, ever again, but because it reminded her of home and growing up. She hadn't lost her faith in God. Only in her mother.

On the top shelf, next to and currently leaning on the Bible, was *The Bell Jar*, a gift from Jeremiah from the first time she visited his bookstore. On the middle shelf was *Are You There God, It's Me Margaret*, one of the first of Theresa's "secret books" that she kept after reading it. Like the title character, *Margaret* sat alone on the bookshelf, waiting for someone, preferably a book and not a potted fern, to come along beside her and tell her everything was going to be okay. *I Know Why The Caged Bird Sings* sat uncaged but alone on the bottom shelf. She looked inside and found where she'd highlighted in pink marker, "There is no greater agony than bearing an untold story inside you."

Theresa was ready to live her story. She was still deciding how.

Her book list was almost complete. She thought about going to the bookstore to buy more of her favorites, but that wasn't an option now that the bookstore was gone. She considered driving to Memphis for a shopping trip at new The Corner Bookstore. Jeremiah would be there. Maybe they could talk.

Or maybe not.

Maybe later.

Maybe she should go to Little Rock instead. At first, she wasn't as interested in acquiring new books as she was in filling her bookcase with old favorites. But that was starting to change.

"The problem with trophy books," she said to herself as she read down the list, "is that they've already been read." She knew people—her mother, for one—who bought books and never read them. Decorations. They might as well set out wax fruit and a plastic fern. Theresa smirked at the thought and allowed herself, for a moment, to feel slightly superior.

Theresa had no problem reading a book more than once, but she wanted something new to christen her new home. The idea of casually leaving books out around the apartment felt very "grown up." She couldn't wait to go to whatever store she wished to visit, buy whatever books she wanted to buy, and carry them proudly through the mall without even putting it in the bag. Then she would come home and casually toss it on her kitchen table and not care who saw it.

Even if there wasn't anyone there to see it.

"Or I could just go to the library," she thought, although library books were, by definition, borrowed books. Books she would have to return. It felt a little too familiar. She wanted a more permanent relationship with the written word.

Still, a book from the library would give her something to read until she had time to drive to Little Rock, or, maybe, to Memphis. She wondered if Jeremiah's store was open for business yet or if they were still setting things up. Maybe he'd give her a preview.

The Clear Spring Public Library was in the basement of the Courthouse, along with the boiler room, an abandoned cafeteria, and the janitor's storage room. It smelled like old paper, coffee, and something Theresa couldn't quite identify, possibly Lemon Pledge.

It felt like a chapel in the catacombs.

"Let me know if you can't find what you're looking for," a voice called from behind the circulation desk.

"Just looking around," Theresa said. "I'm really not sure what I'm looking for."

The woman behind the desk looked up. She smiled and walked around the counter. Her red tee-shirt said, "I READ BANNED BOOKS."

"You're the one that spoke at the School Board meeting!" she said.

"That was me," she admitted.

"I'm MaryElla Bryant," the librarian said. "Nice to meet you. You're all our patrons have been talking about for the past three weeks."

"I'm afraid to ask what they're saying," Theresa said.

MaryElla laughed as she walked back to her place behind the checkout desk. "Nothing but good things. I was at that meeting. If anyone had anything bad to say, I wouldn't let them say it here. We don't do book bans."

Theresa pointed to MaryElla's shirt. "I see."

MaryElla closed the book she had on the counter. "You wouldn't happen to be looking for a job, would you?"

"Not really," Theresa said, "but I might be talked into it."

"One of the girls just had a baby," MaryElla explained. "She's going to take some time off to be a mom. I could use some help until she gets back. You're not going to get rich. It pays minimum wage and the position is only part-time, but you'll have all the books and all the quiet you could ever want."

Theresa blinked. For a second, she wasn't sure she'd heard right.

Me?

"I—yeah," she said. She felt a little flustered by the surprise. "I would like that. When do I start?"

MaryElla smiled. "What are you doing right now?"

Theresa beamed. Her first job offer. And it wasn't, like it was at the meetings and the protests, because she was Millicent's daughter. It was because of something *she'd* done; because *she'd* stood up for something she believed in.

Theresa felt at home working in the library, surrounded by books, talking to people who liked books, reading books to children on Saturday mornings. Yes, there were actual tasks that she was expected to perform. It was a real job, after all. She spent her days re-shelving books, straightening shelves, things like that. But the library didn't feel like a workplace.

It felt like home, if your home had a steady stream of people going in and out while strangers sat around reading.

It wasn't long before Theresa knew who the regulars were, if only by their name and the number on their library card. Mostly she identified them by the books they read. There was Mrs. Science Fiction. Miss Romance. The mysterious Mr. Philosophy and Eastern Religions.

Even the demure and quiet Mrs. Erotica.

One of those regulars was a twelve- or eleven-year-old middle school girl who was all knees and elbows with unkempt, eggplant-colored hair and a permanent slouch beneath a hooded sweatshirt at least two sizes too big. Theresa recognized the posture and the look, mostly from mirrors and her own school pictures that Millicent hung alongside the staircase, minus the combat boots, safety pin earring, and fingerless fishnet gloves.

"Are you looking for anything special?" Theresa asked.

The girl shrugged but didn't say anything.

"What's your name?" Theresa asked.

"Elizabeth."

"Well, Elizabeth, come with me." Theresa didn't look to see if the girl followed. She knew she would.

They walked past the table marked "New Arrivals," past "Staff Picks" and "Bestsellers" and on to the back of the library. She stopped at a row of paperbacks.

"This is one of my favorites," Theresa said. "It's not about solving crimes or having a boyfriend or having a house on the prairie, wherever that means."

Theresa offered Elizabeth a well-worn copy of *Harriet the Spy*. First her fingers, then her entire hand emerged from the dangling right sleeve of the sweatshirt. Elizabeth held the book and looked at the bright red cover.

"She's a spy?"

"Sort of," Theresa said. "Not like a James Bond spy. She just watches people around her and writes everything she sees in a notebook."

"Does she get in trouble?"

"She does," Theresa said. "Big trouble."

"Like me," Elizabeth said.

"Well, I don't know what kind of trouble you get into, but Harriet is always in trouble for something," Theresa put her hands on her hips. "She gets into so much trouble that my mom wouldn't even let me read this. She said it was 'inappropriate'."

Elizabeth looked confused. "I thought you said this was one of your favorites?"

Theresa crouched in front of the girl. "I hid beneath the covers and read it with a flashlight so I wouldn't get caught."

"Really?" Elizabeth's mouth was caught somewhere between a jaw drop and a smile.

"Really. And if you like that one, there's three others."

"Is it?" she asked.

"Is it what?"

"Is it, you know, *inappropriate?*"

"Only if you think girls shouldn't be smart and think for themselves."

They walked to the counter. Elizabeth didn't have a library card, so Theresa got one for her. She stamped the return date and handed the book back to Elizabeth.

"Okay, Harriet, er, I mean Elizabeth. You're good to go."

Theresa thought she saw just the trace of a smile. She definitely heard a thank you.

Elizabeth was still looking at the book's cover as she left.

Theresa put the date stamp and the ink pad back in their spot on the checkout desk.

For the first time since the fire, her life was exactly where she wanted it to be. Then she saw Millicent standing at the checkout desk with a large stack of books and a single sheet of goldenrod paper that looked like a shopping list.

"We're asking you to remove these books," Millicent told MaryElla. "If you don't, then we'll go to the Library Board and have them removed."

"Let me know how that works out for you," MaryElla said. She smiled broadly. "I was at the School Board meeting."

"That wasn't a meeting." Millicent was almost shouting as her face turned bright red. "That was an ambush." She lowered her voice. "And it shows how even good kids, kids with good parents, good upbringing, can be led astray by these raunchy, defiant, *sinful* books." She paused as if to take a breath. Theresa knew it was for dramatic effect.

"I lost my daughter," Millicent said. "I pray that other parents don't lose theirs."

"I don't think it was the books that drove your daughter away," MaryElla replied.

Theresa kept listening from between the bookshelves. *Oh please don't let her see me.*

"The School Board was a temporary setback," Millicent explained. "We're going to get rid of those books one way or another. And we'll do the same thing here."

"Like I said, let me know how that works out for you." MaryElla started stacking the books on the cart to be reshelved. "We'll be right here."

Theresa took *Zen and the Art of Motorcycle Maintenance* home that night and laid it on her kitchen table, face up with the title clearly visible. She started reading it when she went to bed.

No covers.

No flashlight.

No fear.

47

The Ozarks get snow in December. Memphis, with its lower elevation, higher temperatures, and constant humidity, gets rain. Sometimes ice, which can be a problem because native Memphians have no idea about how to drive on ice, but mostly rain. Almost every day. The gray drizzly days made it hard for Jeremiah to get into the Christmas spirit, despite the proliferation of Styrofoam snowmen and aluminum Christmas trees inside the mall.

To Tamika, who grew up in Memphis and in malls, it all felt like Christmas, from the gaudy street light decorations to the Black Santa doing the live remote on WDIA radio from the Ebenezer Community Center.

"We should bring that guy in here," Tamika joked, except she wasn't really joking.

"Can't," Jeremiah said. "The mall sent out this big memo saying that there was only *one* Santa and he would be in his little house near the food court. They're afraid kids will freak out if they see more than one Santa in the same mall. Said they would fine stores that had their own Santas."

"Yeah," Tamika said. "We'll go with that."

Tamika had come in on her own late Thursday night, after Thanksgiving had faded into just another Thursday, and built a display she was calling "Books That Deserve To Be Given."

Tamika's smile beamed. "You like it?"

Jeremiah smiled and shook his head in disbelief. "I take it you know about my old store."

"I do," she said. "There was a story in a magazine somewhere about your parents speaking at a book protest in Alabama. Now, *they* sound interesting."

"As opposed to their uninteresting son?" Jeremiah asked. "Yeah, they're interesting."

Tamika smiled and looked at Jeremiah. "Oh, Jeremiah. I'm sure you are interesting too. You're just better at hiding it." She went back to straightening books on the display. "That article talked about your display at the bookstore. Great name."

"Clear Spring Books and Electronics?" Jeremiah smiled and shrugged. "I never really thought of that as a great name."

"Not the store," Tamika said. "The display. 'Books That Deserve To Be Read'."

"And did the article talk about what happened to our store?"

"No. It was an older magazine."

"It was burned down. Because we sold banned books."

Tamika shook her head like she was shaking off an electric shock. Or a hard left hook to the jaw.

"You're kidding me."

"I am not. That's how I ended up here." He left out the part about wanting out and not wanting to be a crusader like his parents.

"Still, though." She stopped. "Wow. Burned it down."

"Burned it down."

"Still." She smiled. "Great name. If you sold records, you could have had a display called 'Voices That Deserve To Be Heard'."

Jeremiah nodded in agreement. "You could use that name for a book display, if you wanted. Be read. Be heard. Be seen. Same thing." He walked around Tamika's display.

"What all do you have on here?"

"Well, there's *The Prophet.* She held up the small, khaki-colored book.

"Nice," Jeremiah said. "And *Jonathan Livingston Seagull.* And *The Little Prince.*" He looked at Tamika. "Were you just on a philosophical bent when you built this?"

Tamika ignored him. "There's all the Winnie the Pooh books." She looked back over her shoulder at Jeremiah. "The original A. A. Milne books, not this homogenized Disney stuff. And *Velveteen Rabbit.*"

"Also nice." Jeremiah still had his Winnie the Pooh books from when he was a kid. He read them to Zachary sometimes.

Jeremiah picked up a book and flipped it over in his hand. "And *The Outsiders.*" He tucked *The Outsiders* under his right arm as he picked up other books from the display. "And *A Wrinkle in Time.* And *Harriet the Spy.*"

"*Harriet* was one of my favorites when I was a kid," Tamika said.

Jeremiah laid the books on the table with the display.

"McKay isn't going to like this," he reminded Tamika. "Remember? 'No banned books on the displays.' Those were his exact words."

"But these are *good* books, Jeremiah. Bestsellers."

"Which is why we have them in the store," Jeremiah replied. "We just can't have them on the display."

"Should I send them to the kitchen before somebody sees them?" she asked. Her voice was heavy with sarcasm.

"No." Jeremiah ignored the reference to kitchen help. "I kind of like having them out here. And McKay's probably not coming by today. Let's keep it up for the weekend and then see where it goes from there."

"Thank you, boss." Still sarcastic.

"Thanks for building the display." Jeremiah smiled. "It looks great. We'll see if we get away with it."

The new bookstore's first holiday shopping season went very well, outselling the Little Rock location by more than twenty percent. Best of all, from Jeremiah's perspective, this happened without any visits from McKay.

Until Christmas Eve.

Christmas Eve could have been marketed as "Guy's Day at Riverside Mall." Riverside was full of last-minute shoppers, mostly men, desperately seeking something they could give to their wives or girlfriends. Young mothers had long since bought, wrapped, and placed under the tree all their Christmas presents for their kids.

Despite the best efforts of Jeremiah, Tamika, Darnel, and Stacy, the shelves of The Corner Bookstore looked pretty picked over. Most of the books on the "Books That Deserve To Be Given" display had already been given, or were about to be. One of the few books that remained was *Our Bodies, Ourselves.*

And that was the book that caught the attention of Thomas McKay when he walked in. He reached the display as Jeremiah was putting a customer's books into a Corner Bookstore bag.

"What's this?"

Jeremiah stepped out from behind the counter and made his way to the display. McKay wouldn't pick up the book. He only pointed to it on the table, like it was some unclean, unholy thing.

"Looks like *Our Bodies, Ourselves,*" Jeremiah said. He dreaded what he already knew was coming next.

"And what is this doing on my Christmas display?"

Jeremiah tried to diffuse the situation. "You mean sex isn't a gift? That's what they told us in Sunday School. 'Sex is a gift.' I distinctly remember that."

McKay was not amused.

"I told you no banned books on the displays. I'll agree to have them in the store, but not on displays. Not recommended by staff.

And certainly not for Christmas. This is *Christmas,* for God's sake. *Christmas!*"

Jeremiah picked up the book. "I'm sorry. I'll put it back where it belongs."

"Did *she* do this? Did she… whatever her name is… your Assistant Manager. Did *she* put that book on this display?"

"It was my decision," Jeremiah said. "I thought this was a good idea."

Tamika walked out from behind the counter and looked at Jeremiah. Then she turned to face McKay.

"I put it there."

"You're here?" McKay's temperature was rising to a slow boil. "Who's watching upstairs?"

"Darnel and Stacy are upstairs," Jeremiah said. "We get more traffic down here. With everything going on, I thought we should both be on the main level."

McKay looked like he was trying to stare down Tamika. "Young lady, this is very inappropriate. It's downright offensive."

Tamika said nothing. Jeremiah spoke up.

"I apologize, sir. This is my mistake. I approved the display."

"She built it and you approved it? Is that how it went?"

Tamika and Jeremiah answered at the same time.

"Yes."

McKay huffed. He looked at Jeremiah.

"I told you…" he began, but then stopped, his voice disappearing into anger.

"Both of you will be getting a written warning for poor judgement and insubordination. I gave you specific instructions and you ignored them."

"I understand," Jeremiah said. "But you should know, we've sold a lot of copies of that. There are colleges here," Jeremiah said, as if he had to remind McKay of that fact. "A lot of college-age women have requested that book. Older women, too."

McKay's retort was vicious. "And one of the biggest Southern Baptist Churches in the country is also here. And one of the most vocal preachers. The Baptists were here long before Memphis State. We don't need this."

"I apologize," Jeremiah repeated. "This is on me."

"This is on both of you," McKay said. "I'll write up your warnings when I get back to Little Rock. Merry Christmas." McKay walked away but stopped right outside the door.

"I was going to congratulate you on your numbers," he said. "That is impressive. But…" His voice rose again. "I am *not* impressed with you not following specific directions. That will not happen again."

"Yes, sir," Jeremiah said.

They watched Mr. McKay walk away.

Jeremiah put *Our Bodies, Ourselves* back on the display.

"Tomorrow's Christmas," he said, as if Tamika needed another reminder. He looked at the clock behind the counter.

"It's almost time to close. We'll take this down when we come back. Then, you can start working on what you want to do for New Year's and January."

Closing time came with all the excitement, decompression, and collapse of retail workers at the end of the Christmas season.

"Can you hang around for a minute?" Jeremiah asked Tamika as Darnel and Stacy left for the evening.

She smiled. "Was going to. I have something for you."

Jeremiah went back to the safe in the office while Tamika ducked into the break room. She emerged with a pie pan covered in foil.

"I thought you and your son might like this," she said.

"Thank you!" Jeremiah lifted a small part of the pie pan's foil cover and inhaled deeply. "This smells great."

"It's sweet potato, not pumpkin," Tamika said. "Pumpkin pies taste like Piggly-Wiggly. Sweet potato pie tastes like home." She watched Jeremiah set the pie on the counter and carefully crimp the foil cover back into place. "I hope you like it."

Jeremiah smiled. "I'm sure we will. Here…" He picked up the gift-wrapped, book-size package he'd retrieved from the safe. "I thought you might like this."

"Wow," Tamika said. "Let's see. I wonder what it could be?" She smiled as she unwrapped the book. Then she opened it to the title page.

She blinked, stunned. She stared at the book and then at Jeremiah.

"It's a little burned because it was in the fire," Jeremiah explained. "And there's a little water damage on the back cover. It's one of the books I saved when I found it." The book was *The Bluest Eye*. Inside, on the title page, was the blue ink signature of Toni Morrison and the inscription, "Thank you for what you do."

"My mom got this a long time ago at some rally they went to. Toni Morrison was there so my mom asked her to sign it."

Tamika groped for words. "Your mom doesn't want it?"

"I was going to give it to her, but I thought you might like it more. She said it was fine. I actually think she has another signed copy of this same book. She kind of collects these things. And she thought it'd been burned up in the fire anyway."

Tamika put the book on the counter and hugged Jeremiah.

"I just wanted to thank you for everything you've done around here," Jeremiah said after they had hugged. "So, thank you. My mom said that Toni Morrison wrote what most folks were too afraid to say out loud. That reminded me of you."

Jeremiah thought about Tamika's display and McKay's response as he drove to pick up Zachary and then headed home. He wondered, on the scale of Corner Bookstore consequences, just how serious "an official written warning" really was. It probably wasn't as serious as the McCarthy hearings that destroyed his parents' careers—more like something between a stern finger-wag and a formal tongue-lashing.

They'd sold a lot of books. Tamika was happy. He decided it was worth it.

Jeremiah picked up Zachary, thanked Patricia, and went home to enjoy his pie. George and Tammy would be arriving later that night. They'd decided that since Jeremiah only got one day off for Christmas—the only thing bigger than Black Friday was the day after Christmas when everyone returned things—they would drive to Memphis. Besides, they wanted to spend some time with their grandson. Tammy was planning on taking Zachary to the zoo, provided it stopped raining long enough.

Christmas morning was a good old-fashion celebration of American consumerism, with Fisher-Price toy sets, Tonka trucks, and a View-Master with reels of cartoons, Disney characters, and, because George liked them, two sets of reels from national parks.

Tammy handed Jeremiah his present while George watched. They both looked very proud of themselves.

"I wonder what this could be?" He echoed Tamika as a joke to himself but also to make his parents laugh. He tore an open a corner of the paper and immediately knew what it was.

Where the Wild Things Are, complete with some burn marks on the edges of the papers and fairly substantial water damage on the back cover. Jeremiah was not the only one to sift through the ashes of Clear Spring Books & Electronics. He wasn't even the first.

That night, after his parents had gone back to the Peabody Hotel, Zachary curled up in his dad's lap while they read about the naughty but beloved Max, the King of all the Wild Things.

48

There was no snow in Clear Spring that Christmas. The clouds, while seasonally heavy and gray, were stingy with their frozen precipitation treats that year. One more disappointment in what, for Theresa, had been a promising but ultimately heartbreaking year.

Theresa looked forward to the arbitrary turning of the calendar, although she understood that her problems would not disappear because the year changed. She predicted it would take longer to solve the problem than it would take people to get used to writing the correct date when they wrote a check.

The calendar moved, but the problem left a forwarding address. Theresa was fairly sure Jeremiah had given his forwarding address to Ruthanna. So far, she had resisted the temptation to ask Ruthanna for his phone number.

That particular problem was on hold for now.

"This has always been kind of a dead week," MaryElla said as she unlocked the library at the usual time on December 26. "People are busy. Kids have new toys to play with. Readers have new books to read."

"We've got the story time thing," Theresa said. "That should help." She wasn't thrilled about the idea of reading to little kids, but it would at least be a distraction from the loneliness and forced cheerfulness of the holiday season. She'd called Millicent but there was no answer. Messages she'd left on her machine were not returned.

Ruthanna was kind enough to invite her over for Christmas lunch, but it wasn't the same as Mom's. She had hoped—slightly, wishfully—that Jeremiah would come back to Clear Spring for the holidays.

But why would he? His store was gone, his parents were either in Florida or, maybe, visiting him in Memphis. She hoped for Jeremiah's sake they were in Memphis. She never really understood the relationship between Jeremiah and his parents, other than the extent to which it mirrored her own relationship to her mother.

There was nothing in Clear Spring for Jeremiah now. Probably just as well. He probably had to work, anyway.

She was right. Jeremiah was having another busy day. December 26th was an explosion of book returns, exchanges, and shoppers who hoped to get a discount on books about Christmas since the holiday was over, as if Christmas books were perishable goods with an expiration date close to that of ripe bananas. Jeremiah got tired of telling people that *The Night Before Christmas* cost the same on December 26th as it had on the 24th. At his request, Darnel had all the displays down and the Christmas books off the shelves and boxed up in storage by noon.

Tamika was already working on new displays with self-improvement books, diet books, and "Read The Bible In A Year" devotionals. After the scene with McKay, she was playing it safe, for now, with an eye towards committing major violations of company policy in February's Black History Month displays.

Theresa was building her own display for the library, "New Year, New Books, New You!" It felt right, not just for the library, but as a statement about her own life. New look, new apartment, new job. Still, she couldn't help wondering whether Old Theresa was waiting in the wings, hoping for New Theresa to fail.

Millicent certainly was.

Elizabeth came in for another *Harriet book*, sporting black buttons with large white letters proclaiming: "READ BANNED BOOKS" and "HARRIET WAS RIGHT!!!"

"Christmas presents?" Theresa asked.

"Yeah. From me to me."

Theresa's face lit up. "How would you like to read for story time this week?"

Elizabeth tried to suppress her excitement.

"Cool," she said. "But what would I read? Will people even show up? It's no fun if nobody shows up."

"Good questions," Theresa said. "As it turns out, *I* was going to read so I already have the book picked out." She handed Elizabeth a flyer advertising the story time schedule. "And we've been giving these to parents that come in. It's been in the newspaper, too." She couldn't believe she was saying something positive about *The Dixiecrat*, but Whitely had run their ad for free. Probably to get back at Millicent. Theresa was afraid she might throw up a little, but it passed.

"That could be cool," said the nonchalant Elizabeth. "And did you already tell them what you would be reading?"

"*There's a Monster at the End of This Book!*" Theresa walked to the checkout desk to retrieve it. "Can you do a Grover voice?"

Elizabeth had to smile. In her best Grover voice, she said. "You want me to talk like Grover? Like this?" Her face lit up like a marquee. "I was just in a school play."

"Really?" Theresa said. "What part did you play?"

Elizabeth rolled her eyes. "I was backstage. And I did makeup."

"Sounds like fun," Theresa asked. "And like art. I could never do that."

"They wouldn't give me a speaking part." Elizabeth said. Her face broke into a wide smile. "I think I scare them too much."

"Well, here's your chance to do a one-woman show of your own," Theresa said. "The kids will be here at 2:00."

Elizabeth and her well-loved Grover puppet arrived at 1:30 to prepare for their performance. Theresa smiled at the juxtaposition of the cheerful blue monster and a female Alice Cooper with a puppet.

"I thought Grover could read the book. I could talk like me. I mean, the character Elizabeth. Not the real me. A character based loosely on me. Don't want to freak out the kids *too* much."

"I'm glad you took their little sensibilities into consideration," Theresa said.

An impressive crowd showed up for story time, despite it being the day after Christmas. Theresa herded them into a circle while Elizabeth hid in a back room.

"We have a special treat today, ladies and gentlemen," she told the crowd of assorted little people and most of their parents. MaryElla had warned her about the parents who dropped off their children so they could have a break from all the holiday happiness. She wasn't kidding.

"Today's book will be read by the one and only—ta da!!!—Grover!"

Elizabeth stepped out from behind the checkout desk and greeted her audience in her best Grover voice.

"Hello boys and girls. I am Grover. And I am going to read for you!"

She momentarily juggled the puppet and the book. "Look! Grover's skeleton!" Elizabeth wiggled her fingers as she moved Grover from her right hand to her left so she could better manage the book.

"Just kidding." The kids laughed. The shy kids giggled.

Theresa couldn't tell who got the most attention, Grover or Elizabeth, with her safety pin earring, heavy mascara, and torn fishnet stockings below her torn cutoff shorts.

Grover began reading. Elizabeth tried to position the book so the children could see the colorful text: "Did that say there would be a monster at the end of this book?"

Grover froze and looked at Elizabeth. She stared back at him. Grover turned back and forth between her and the kids sitting on the floor as if he was watching a high-speed tennis match.

"Me no like monsters," Grover screamed as he banged his head against the open book. Children were rolling on the floor.

Elizabeth paused and looked at the kids. "He's being really dramatic, right? I mean… not that I would know anything about that." The kids and some of the parents laughed. Others looked like they weren't sure how to respond.

Millicent walked in about halfway through the performance. She watched a few seconds, shook her head in obvious disgust, and went to the circulation desk.

"I wanted to drop these off." She pushed a stack of goldenrod flyers across the counter to a rather perturbed MaryElla who was enthralled with the puppet show and the kids' reactions.

"What's this?" MaryElla asked.

"We're holding a meeting to make the library a safe place for kids." Millicent looked straight at MaryElla as she pointed to Grover and her dramatic puppeteer.

"Case in point," she said. "We would appreciate it if you would give these to people when they check out a book."

"Right." MaryElla stretched the word as only a Southerner could. "And this is about?"

"Protecting children." Millicent's reply was accented with a "you should know this" inflection.

"The school let you down so you're coming here?" MaryElla smiled her best "Aren't you special?" smile.

"The School Board was ambushed," Millicent sneered. "I'm hoping the Library Board is more courageous and is willing to do the right thing."

"I'm not sure the Library Board would agree with you about what's the right thing on this." MaryElla studied Millicent's face.

"I'll be honest, Millicent. If you leave those here, they will be in the trash before you're out the door. You might have more luck with somebody else. Somewhere else. Like maybe in your church."

"It's sad that no one seems to care about the stuff we put into kids' minds these days."

Across the room, Grover screamed, "You turned another page!". The puppet looked at Elizabeth, then at the kids. "How could you do that? Don't you know there's a monster at the end of the book?!!"

Theresa noticed the departure from the written text and smiled. This wasn't a reading. This was a performance.

Millicent took one last look at Elizabeth and stormed out of the library. She went straight to *The Dixiecrat* and Whitely's desk.

"Whitely," she barked as if it was her office and she was in charge. "I'm going to write a letter to the editor and you're going to publish it."

The newspaper man folded his arms across his chest.

"I am?" He squinted his eyes and shrugged from behind his typewriter.

"And why would I do that?"

"Because you get it, Whitely. You can see what's going on around here. You know what's happening."

Whitely got up from his desk and closed the office door.

"What I know is you used my newspaper to get support for you and your church and then threw my son under the bus."

"I had nothing to do with what happened to Malachai. He's the one who decided to confess to a crime he didn't commit."

"Uh-huh. He was trying to protect that girl and you didn't do a damn thing to stop him. You can't tell me you didn't know what was going on, Millicent. I know better."

"I'm sorry you feel that way."

"Don't give me that, Millicent. You should be sorry for what you did to my boy. I don't need your apologies for how I feel."

Millicent held her hands palms up and took a step back. "Please here me out. The books at that library are even worse than the books at the school. And you should have seen what I just witnessed over there. They've got some kind of devil worshipper reading a book about monsters to the kids. Wearing fishnet stockings, Whitely. Fishnet."

Whitely's face was still beet red, but he was listening.

"Go on."

Millicent took a careful step forward. "We need to put a stop to this, Whitely. Now. Publish my letter and let's move on."

"Do you have it with you?"

"I don't," Millicent confessed. "I just found out about this. I guess they thought they could sneak it past me, but I saw it with my own eyes. Just now. I was on my way home to write the letter but I wanted to talk with you first." She smiled. "You have always been the voice of reason around here, Whitely. You've used your paper for good. Please don't stop doing that because you're angry at me."

"I am very, very mad at you, Millicent. I don't think you understand how mad I am about this."

She ignored Whitely's anger and kept pushing. "I know you're upset. And I'm sorry. But we are a team, you and I, Whitely. We've accomplished a lot together. Let's not end that now, just when our town needs us the most."

"OK. Bring in your letter and I'll think about it." He raised his voice. "That is not a promise. I may write the editorial myself. I don't need you to write or speak for me. But bring it in. I'll look at it, and we'll see where to go from there."

49

Millicent picked up her copy of *The Dixiecrat* from her driveway at about 6:30 that morning, as she was leaving to walk to the Cozy Kitchen for coffee and conversation. At one time, Theresa would have walked with her.

She missed those walks. She missed those times.

She went inside and took her usual seat facing the window. At one time, Laura would have sat with her. Before that, it was Laura's parents.

Now Laura was in jail and Laura's parents weren't speaking to her.

She missed those conversations.

She opened her paper. She ignored the front-page headline (*RISING GAS PRICES PROVE END TIMES ARE HERE*), went past Miss Doris's "Around Town" column on page two (*"Our neighbors had the loveliest Christmas light this year…"*), and the weather report (*"Cold"*) and went straight to page three, Opinions, Editorials, and Observations in search of the Letter to the Editor that she'd written yesterday afternoon, a scathing rebuke of inappropriate books and, now, inappropriate book readers at the library. She'd slipped the typed page into the mail slot just as the bell at the Clear Spring Methodist Church chimed 5:00, technically closing time for Whitely, but Millicent knew for a fact that he usually worked until 9:00 printing the paper.

Her letter wasn't there. In its place was a letter congratulating Susy Dennison for her award-winning Christmas light display.

Beside that was a new editorial from Whitely:

Right Vision, Wrong Voice.

Millicent started to read.

Millicent Spate…

She would never admit it, but Millicent always smiled when she saw her name in the newspaper like that. Just something about seeing your name in the paper.

…has spent almost twenty years fighting to keep inappropriate books and other filth out of our schools. If newspaper articles, flyers, speeches, and presentations scored points, she would have won this battle long ago.

But speeches don't score points. Presentations don't always lead to action.

And Millicent hasn't won anything.

Twenty years after Millicent's crusade began, we are still fighting to keep Socialism, Darwinism, Feminism, and all the other isms they try to shove down our collective throats out of our schools. Books play a big role in this indoctrination.

Millicent has failed. As her daughter said to her at the School Board meeting, "I love you, but you're wrong."

Millicent's face froze as she stared at the paper. She quietly folded it up, placed it on the table, and slammed the napkin dispenser on top of it when it wouldn't stay folded.

One half cup of coffee later, she opened to page 3 again.

But our mission to clean up our schools continues to be necessary.

Sadly, her loss to the professional liberal activists at the School Board meeting is only one of Mrs. Spate's multiple failures in the school and in the community.

You might say she's gone down in flames.

Police and fire officials knew immediately that the fire at Clear Spring Books & Electronics was not an act of God, although, as we noted at the time, one could be forgiven for assuming God had seen enough. Now, information has come to light that seems to say that Millicent Spate was either directly or indirectly involved in the bookstore fire. Worse, while the police are still investigating the cause of the blaze, it appears that Millicent permitted and probably persuaded a young man (name withheld to protect this innocent individual) to confess to a crime he did not do in order to protect another of Millicent's followers. This woman is the arsonist who ultimately lit the match.

"Would you like some more?"

Millicent blinked and wondered why the waitress was shouting at her. Then she realized she'd heard the question three times before she realized the woman was even talking to her.

"Yes, please."

Let me be blunt: It's no secret that I have wanted to put the Malone family out of business since they built their display about books that should be forgotten. I wanted to win that fight. I cheered when they left in shame. But I want to win it with ideas, not arson. Not violence. I want to win because our ideas and our values are better, not because somebody burned down your business.

And I certainly don't want to win if it means an innocent young man might be asked to go to prison as a sacrifice for someone's movement.

As a sign of my commitment to our cause, I have scheduled a meeting in the high school gym

Millicent felt her chest rise. "He didn't."

to discuss removing inappropriate books from our public library. It's the same problem as the school. Why should your tax dollars be used to buy books that question our history? Our morals? Our faith?

The editorial ended with the time, date, and location of the meeting Millicent had arranged. Whitely had taken the information from a flyer she'd left.

Millicent shook her head. She should have known there was a problem when he refused to print her flyers. She'd had to drive all the way to Calico Rock to get those printed. At full price.

She thought about what was unfolding.

Whitely wasn't just stealing her thunder. He was taking her flock.

At least she hadn't distributed any of the flyers about her meeting. People wouldn't know that Whitely had upstaged her with his editorial and was hijacking her plans. She'd been angry that she had allowed herself to be so distracted by that Satanist reading in the library that she'd gone straight to *The Dixiecrat* and then home to write her letter, for all the good that did. Turns out that was a good thing. People would be talking about Whitely's editorial. That meant people would be talking about her.

She needed to make sure she controlled that conversation. She had to one-up Whitely.

She paid for her coffee, left the waitress a to-the-penny ten percent tip, and walked at a pace just short of a run to the Courthouse.

"I need to get on the agenda on the next City Council meeting," she told the receptionist.

"Council meetings are on the second and fourth Thursdays of the month," the receptionist said flatly. "You're too late to make the second Thursday meeting, so you'll have to wait for the last Thursday of the month." She looked at the puppy calendar hanging on the wall. "That would be the 29th."

"Fine," Millicent said. She was disappointed it wasn't that very night, but at least she would have time to prepare.

The receptionist reached under her desk and pulled up a bright pink form. "Fill this out and bring it back to me. Be sure to press hard because you're making three copies. If you want to be on the next meeting, then you need to get this to me tomorrow. If it's after that, you'll just have to wait."

Millicent snatched the request from the receptionist's hand and stomped off to the waiting area. She completed the form before she left.

On the line marked, "Reason for your request", she wrote, "To protect our children from evil influences by defunding the library."

"Thank you." The receptionist placed the completed form in the basket. The receptionist waited until she heard the elevator ding. Then she picked up the phone and dialed 411.

"Information? Yes, in Clear Spring. Please give me the number for Theresa Spate."

"Yes, it would be a new listing."

Millicent hurried home to make an important phone call of her own.

"Pastor Kettle," she said. "I need to ask you a favor."

Theresa was also making phone calls. After she got off the phone with her friend from the courthouse, she called Ruthanna.

It was time.

50

Theresa met Ruthanna at The Cozy Kitchen at 6:00 the next morning.

"I hope this wasn't too early," she said as Ruthanna slid into the booth.

"Honey, when you reach a certain age, God blesses you with an alarm bladder. I couldn't sleep later if I wanted to."

"Oh—wait." Theresa stood. "You should sit on this side. That way I'm facing away from Mom…"

She pointed to Millicent's table in the corner, facing the front window. Millicent's spot reminded Theresa of a book Elizabeth said she wanted to read for story time:

"I'm Yertle the Turtle! Oh, marvelous me!

For I am the ruler of all that I see!"

"What can I get you?" asked the waitress.

"Just coffee," Ruthanna said.

"I'll have a cinnamon roll," Theresa said. "And some milk."

"You're playing mind games," Ruthanna said after the waitress left.

"I prefer to call it psychological warfare," Theresa said.

The waitress brought their order but said nothing.

"At least you admit it." Ruthanna doctored her coffee with three packages of non-dairy creamer and four packs of sugar and began to stir.

Theresa's eyes moved from the coffee mug to Ruthanna's face.

"That's not coffee," she said. "That's dessert."

"And that isn't?" Ruthanna smiled from across the table. "Maybe I like dessert." She put her elbows on the table and leaned forward.

"Would you like to tell me why we're really here?"

Theresa turned to look over her shoulder at Millicent's empty table. "I will. But, honestly, I only want to say this once and I want her to hear it."

"So you're waiting for Millicent." Ruthanna stirred her coffee. She nodded towards the table. "She just walked in."

Theresa resisted the temptation to turn around and look while Ruthanna smiled and did the same kind of head nod wave that all Clear Spring drivers did when they met at an intersection.

"She's sitting down, just like you said she would," Ruthanna whispered. "Does she do this every morning? She always sits in the same booth?"

"Millicent likes her routines."

"What if someone else had been sitting there?"

Theresa chuckled. "The waitress wouldn't let someone else sit there. What about her newspaper?"

Millicent's newspaper was on the table alongside her cinnamon roll and coffee.

Ruthanna slid her glasses down her nose so she could see better.

"Still rolled up with a green rubber band."

"Good," Theresa whispered. "That means she's listening."

Theresa sat straight up against the back of the booth.

"I'm going to Memphis," she said, loud enough for Millicent to hear but, hopefully, not so loud that she would think she had been targeted.

If Ruthanna was surprised, she didn't show it. Theresa arched her eyebrows as if to ask Ruthanna if Millicent had heard. Then she smiled slightly.

"You're going to bring him back?" Ruthanna asked.

"I'm going to remind him who he is," Theresa said.

"I think he's forgotten," Theresa said. "Or he's trying to."

"And you want him to remember?"

"Yes," Theresa said. "I'm going because Millicent isn't done. She's going to ask City Council to not give any money to the library unless they remove some books." She paused and watched Ruthanna's face for any sign of a reaction from Millicent.

Millicent appeared to be focused on unrolling a bite-sized portion of the cinnamon bun, but Ruthanna could see she was listening. She nodded for Theresa to continue the performance.

Which she did.

"And you want backup," Ruthanna noted. "You don't want to face Millicent alone."

A self-assured smile flashed across Milicent's face but quickly disappeared. She stared into her coffee mug and stirred.

"I want someone who has something to lose, even if he doesn't know it yet."

Ruthanna leaned against the back of the booth. "He's lost his store. What does he have left to lose?"

"His legacy." Theresa momentarily forgot about Millicent. "Whether Jeremiah likes it or not, his name means something. *He* means something. People need to remember that once, someone stood up to Millicent Spate. Jeremiah stood up when it mattered—in the gym, at the School Board meeting, and in his bookstore."

Ruthanna nodded. "I'm glad you understand that this wasn't over when the School Board agreed with you. That was probably just the beginning."

"I know," Theresa said. "That's why she's going to City Council. She thinks she can win there."

Ruthanna stirred her coffee. "Millicent is going to do whatever it is she's going to do. There's nothing we can do about that. This is about us and what we are willing to do for what we believe."

Millicent asked for a box for the uneaten two-thirds of her cinnamon roll. She made it halfway to the door before she stopped, turned around, and strode over to the table where Ruthanna and Theresa were sitting.

"Hello, Ruthanna," she began. "Always nice to see you."

She turned to face her daughter. "I see you got a job. Are you responsible for inviting that Satanist I saw reading to the children?"

Theresa froze just as the milk she was drinking hit her tongue. She slowly returned the glass to the table.

"What are you even talking about?"

"That creature I saw reading to the children about a monster. The one with the weird clothes and the jewelry. And that hair."

"Elizabeth?"

"Is that her name? I figured it was Delilah or Jezebel or something like that. She's clearly a devil worshipper."

"She's a theater kid stuck in a town with no real theater," Theresa told her mom. "She's isolated and alone, something I can relate to, by the way." She unpeeled a sticky section of the cinnamon roll, then put it down in disgust.

"The only devils here are the ones in your head."

"She's been deceived," Millicent said. Then she turned to walk away.

"Seriously?" Theresa turned to look over the back of the booth as Millicent made her way towards the door.

"*You're* talking about deceit?"

Millicent did not look back.

The hush that followed Millicent's exit wasn't peaceful. It was heavy in the air, like a musical scale that stopped before it reached the last note. The kind that makes you want to run to the piano and pound that last key.

"It's okay," Ruthanna said. "But you never answered the second part of my question. That's why you want Jeremiah to come back. Why does it matter that he remembers?"

"Because if he forgets, the people who want to rewrite the past—the people who want us to *forget* and resent the fact that we remember—win."

She pushed the cinnamon bun to the edge of the table. "Nobody alive today was in the Civil War. Look at how they've rewritten that. You'd think the South played a better game but the North won on a technicality."

Ruthanna shrugged. "I know. Now they're trying to rewrite things that happened since I was born. People are being told that what they remember, what they saw and lived through, didn't really happen that way."

"There used to be people in Clear Spring who cared about learning and feelings and facts. George and Tammy Malone cared about the books that showed us those things, even when they were hard to face. Jeremiah still cares, even if he doesn't know how to say it."

She looked out the window.

"You and I know that we're fighting. MaryElla is fighting. In her way, Elizabeth is fighting. But it feels like the town has gone silent. Clear Spring needs its voice back. Too bad the one we need left."

She stopped.

"Sorry. Didn't mean to sound so melodramatic."

Ruthanna smiled. "But it's true."

"That's what scares me."

Theresa slowly reached for the cinnamon roll she'd previously pushed away. Ruthanna waited for her to tear off a piece and take a bite before she said anything.

"And why wouldn't they remember how much you care about those things?"

"They will, I hope." Theresa smiled and leaned back. "They were chanting my name that morning, weren't they?"

"I wasn't there, remember?"

"Oh, right. Well, they were." Theresa allowed herself a moment to revel privately in that memory. "So they know. But they need to know it's not just me. It's not just Jeremiah. People need to know they are not alone, that they aren't just blindly following some self-anointed leader. They need to know a lot of people think like they think. They have to remember Jeremiah so they don't forget their past."

"Fair enough," Ruthanna said. "Now, why are *you* going to Memphis?"

That question was as difficult as it was unexpected. True, she could call and save herself the trip and the face-to-face rejection. She was curious about the new store and what Jeremiah might have done with it, but she'd be lying if she said that's why she wanted to go.

"I asked him if he loved me, Ruthanna. And he said, 'Now is not the time for this conversation.' That's it. He said Zachary loved me, which is nice, I suppose, if I suddenly wanted to be a babysitter. But he couldn't bring himself to even answer my question."

"It's a hard question to answer," Ruthanna said. "Someone asked me that question once. Right here, in the good ol' Cozy Kitchen. During lunch rush."

Theresa's eyes were as big as the cinnamon roll. "What did you say?"

"I said the same thing Jeremiah said. *Now is not the time to talk about this.*"

Theresa's eyebrows arched, the better to frame her dilated pupils.

"Why?"

"I was afraid."

Theresa smiled and leaned in closer.

"Who was he?"

"Stephanie." Ruthanna slowly picked up her mug and took a long sip. "I have regretted that ever since. But, unfortunately, my instincts were correct."

"How?"

Ruthanna put down her mug. "A week after the meeting, I got a registered letter from the elders of Clear Spring Church of Christ. I actually had to sign for this thing. They said I was being disfellowshipped for, and I quote, 'deception.' Said I could return to the church only after I'd have repented of my sins and have renounced the sinful lifestyle that I'd hidden from them for so many years."

"Wow." Theresa was shocked. "I didn't know they could do that."

"It's their club. They can do what they want." She looked out the window so Theresa wouldn't see her tears.

"I had to smile at the 'sinful lifestyle' line. I've been celibate my entire life."

"Yeah, well…." Theresa smirked. "Join the club."

"Honey, I've got a few years on you. And nobody joins that club by choice."

She explained how she always made sure she looked as feminine as possible. Dresses, skirts, soft blouses, conservative women's hair styles. She couldn't really wear jewelry because she was always handing babies, but when she did, it was minimal but definitely feminine. She had certainly never been seen in the company of another woman, at least not in a context that might imply anything romantic.

"There were times, especially after Stephanie died, when the loneliness felt like a deep, physical ache. People think this is about sex. It's not. It's not that simple."

"How did you deal with that?"

"You learn to suppress it. To accept it and go on." Ruthanna looked out the window again, remembering all the days and nights she'd spent alone, with no one's touch, no whispered words or private smiles. No family, no children of her own. Now the lonely feelings were back, like a metastatic cancer, eating away inside her with messages of unworthiness, guilt, and shame.

Feelings of fear.

Messages of sin. All revived by a single registered letter.

Her thoughts were interrupted by Theresa.

"And nobody knew?"

"I suspect that Tammy Malone figured it out. She's pretty sharp that way. But she never asked. And I never had a reason to tell her."

Theresa reached for Ruthanna's hand. "That's why you said that at the Board Meeting?"

"Yes," Ruthanna said. "I owed Stephanie that much." She leaned forward. "I think I have a pretty good idea what Jeremiah is feeling right now. He needs to answer that question for his own sake. You need to hear his answer, yes or no."

"And," she said, "I think you know that and that is why you are going to Memphis."

Theresa and Ruthanna looked at one another. There was understanding.

"You're telling me I should ask him again?"

"I'm telling you that you deserve to ask him again. For both of you."

51

"There's a woman up there came to see you," Tamika told Jeremiah.

"Does she have a name?" Jeremiah pushed the book cart aside so it wouldn't block the aisle while he was away. He started walking with Tamika.

"What does she look like?"

"I don't know," Tamika said. "White girl. Does that narrow it down?"

"More so here than it would in Clear Spring." They both laughed as they made their way to the front of the store. Whoever it was must have been hiding behind a bookshelf. Jeremiah scanned the area but didn't see any familiar faces. Other than the regulars who came in for their daily newspapers, but they never came to see him.

He stopped in his tracks. Tamika saw his face, smiled, and gracefully turned away.

"Wow."

"I know," Theresa said. She did the little jazz hands move Elizabeth had shown her.

"Surprise!"

Jeremiah moved in for a hug. Theresa stepped back before he landed.

"I came to ask you to come back to Clear Spring," she said, as if she was hiring a plumber to fix a stubborn toilet that would not yield to any plunger. "Millicent is on the rampage again and we need your help."

"But, I didn't really do anything. The School Board meeting was all you. Well, you, Ruthanna, and Ethan. I was about as useful as a right-hand glove."

It took Theresa a moment to catch the reference, but she had to smile when she did.

"That is truly horrible."

"What's the point of being an amputee if you can't cut people off?"

"Again. Horrible."

"I know. I can do this all day."

Theresa tried not to smile. "Funny as that may be, I didn't come here for a comedy routine. We need your help. You don't realize what you represent. What that bookstore represented."

"I know where this is going," he said. "So I'll just say it for you. 'What your parents represent'."

"No offense, but your parents are old. Clear Spring needs you to show them this isn't an old person's fight. That it still matters. Your parents can't do that. You can."

"So can you," he said. "I think we've established that."

"Yes, I could," Theresa said. "And I am. But I'm not a symbol, Jeremiah. Not yet, anyway." She paused to think about what she'd just said. "Maybe someday, but we don't have that kind of time right now. Clear Spring doesn't have that kind of time."

She looked into Jeremiah's eyes and hoped he could understand what she was saying.

"What you represent is bigger than anything you or I might say. Bigger even than what your parents could say."

"But I have nothing to say, Theresa." He stopped and smiled. "Although, I've already managed to tick off my boss about a display with banned books. You would have been proud."

"So you do have something to say."

"I didn't build it." He nodded at Tamika behind the counter where he should have been. He wondered who was upstairs. "Tamika built it. I just told her it was okay."

Theresa was not going to stop.

"Some people would say that's leadership, Jeremiah. Some people might even say that was inspirational. Which is exactly what we need in Clear Spring."

"I don't know about all that. She built it and I told her she didn't have to tear it down. Not sure how much leadership or inspiration went into that."

"You've inspired people in Clear Spring. You weren't there to see it, but people left flowers and books in front of that store for weeks after you left." Her voice drifted off for a moment. "Then it snowed and they got all nasty until I couldn't stand it anymore and had to clean

441

it up." She paused for just a moment as she remembered how the makeshift memorial looked before it was buried in snow.

"If nothing else, you made them believe they could be heard."

It was Jeremiah's turn to smile. "They certainly heard me when I told them books were fifty percent off."

"Yes, they did," Theresa agreed. "And you sold a lot of books that next week or so."

"They heard us at the School Board meeting," Jeremiah added.

"Yes, they did."

"And then they burned my store down." *Checkmate.*

"And the ones who heard you came back the next morning." Theresa's voice was as intense as her pinpoint pupils. "They were there for you, Jeremiah. They need you to be there for them."

She took Jeremiah's hand. "That bookstore inspired people and now it's gone. You are all that's left of that. We need you to remind them of what once was before they forget and it's gone forever."

Jeremiah took a step back. He let go of Theresa's hand.

"And what about us, Theresa? What do we need?"

Theresa blinked and swallowed hard.

"When I was a little girl, hiding beneath my covers so I could read, I used to dream that a handsome Prince would come and rescue me. He'd take me away to a place where I didn't have to hide beneath the covers. A place where I could not only read books, but talk about them with friends. No hiding. No fear. Just a place where being able to choose what I wanted to read was a real thing."

She blinked back a tear.

"I had that dream a hundreds, maybe thousands of times. Never once did that prince ask me to babysit his son while he went off to work."

Jeremiah froze.

Theresa spoke more softly. "We just need you to help us shut down Millicent before she does permanent damage. That's all I'm asking."

Jeremiah wiped his eyes. He tried to smile but ended up with nervous laughter. He tried to discreetly wipe the tears from his cheeks.

"The answer is yes, by the way," he said.

"Yes, you'll come back?"

"Well, that too. But, to your original question, 'do you love me?', the answer is yes."

He reached out for her hand.

"I love you."

She took his hand. They stood in the afterglow that only a near miss can create.

They didn't stand there long.

"Mr. Malone!" McKay bellowed from the counter. "Could you *please* check out these customers so they can go home and read their books?"

Jeremiah looked at the counter. Tamika had a customer at the first cash register. Three more were lined up behind that one. No one was working registers two or three.

"Is that your boss?" Theresa asked.

"Yes," Jeremiah said. "And a wonderful boss he is."

Theresa's face formed a sarcastic, questioning smile. "Does he not know how to run a cash register?"

"I've got to go," Jeremiah said. "Take a look around. Let me know what you think."

Jeremiah went to register number two. "I'll help whoever's next," he announced from behind the counter. He checked out five customers before he was able to step away. McKay watched the entire time. Jeremiah waited for Tamika to finish with her last customer before he spoke to her.

"You should probably go upstairs and see how Darnel and Stacy are doing."

"Not yet," McKay interrupted. He looked at Tamika.

"Stay here." He held up a book, *Natural Beauty for All Seasons*.

"What's this?"

"It's about—".

McKay interrupted her before she could finish. He waved the book in Tamika's face.

"And what's it doing on a display in my store?"

Tamika looked at Jeremiah and took a calming breath. "It's by Naomi Sims. She's very popular." Tamika turned to Theresa for a sign, any sign, that she was not the only person in the room who knew who Naomi Sims was. Unfortunately, there was none.

"I don't really follow fashion," Theresa said blushing. "Black or white." Theresa smiled and opened her arms wide as if to confirm her statement. "But it sounds like the kind of book I wish my mother had given me when I was fourteen. Not for Black girls, but for skinny fourteen-year-old girls who hated mirrors."

Tamika nodded as if she'd been there, too.

"Naomi Sims is the first Black supermodel," Tamika tried to explain to McKay. "I put her book out with all the diet books, makeup books, and other self-help stuff people always buy in January.

"I said nothing controversial on the front displays," McKay said. "I thought I was very clear about that."

"It's not controversial," Jeremiah said. "It's a health and beauty book. We've got an entire shelf of those on upstairs."

"An entire shelf just for Black women?" he said.

"No," Tamika said. "Although, that wouldn't be a bad idea." Tamika laughed nervously. "Just saying." She immediately took on a more serious tone and expression.

"All of our beauty books are for white women. And that's not just us." She turned to Theresa in hopes that at least she would understand. "Do you know how hard it is for a Black woman to find anything about hair styles or makeup for her?"

Theresa nodded. She could only imagine.

The Assistant Manager turned back to McKay.

"This is the first real book like this that was written for Black women. With Black hair. Black complexions. Makeup for Black faces. Women think about that kind of thing this time of year."

"So Black power?"

Tamika didn't budge. "No. Black beauty."

"If it's a beauty book," McKay sneered, "then why don't you have it back there with the other beauty books?"

"It's there with the other beauty books," Tamika tried to explain, "but Black women are so used to not seeing books written for them that they never think to look for it there. Or anywhere, for that matter."

"And that's where it should stay," McKay said. "We do not want our customers to get the wrong impression."

"We have Black women customers," Jeremiah reminded him.

McKay did not appreciate being corrected. "We have Black shoppers," he said. "Customers actually buy things. Shoppers shop; customers buy. Shoppers take up space and move things around so you have to put them back later. Customers take their books to the cash register and pay for them."

McKay held his hands as if he was shaping a pot. He turned to his right.

"Customers pay the bills."

He kept his hands the same and turned to the left.

"Shoppers shoplift."

He looked at all three of them, including Theresa, to make sure everyone had heard.

"Am I making myself clear?"

"Loud and clear, sir." Jeremiah resisted the urge to emphasize "loud".

Tamika held out her hand. "I'll take it upstairs," she said.

Theresa watched McKay as he watched Tamika walk all the way up the stairs. Her side-eyed expression made it clear to Jeremiah that she thought McKay watched a little too long, with a little too much interest, and a little too much of what she'd come to expect from men like him since she was in high school.

"I told you to keep an eye on her," McKay said. "But if you're not going to do that, then I will. Or." He paused for intentional dramatic effect. "Better yet, I'll let her go."

"Today?" Jeremiah said.

"Not today," McKay said. "This kind of thing isn't explicitly spelled out in the handbook and I don't want her to sue me. But the next time there is an infraction." He turned his head slightly and twisted his mouth. "The next time she puts something up there that she knows isn't supposed to be there, I want you to fire her immediately. Don't wait for me. Just do it."

"And if I don't?" Jeremiah asked.

"Then you can leave with her."

McKay stomped out of the store.

"Nothing punctuates a sentence like leaving," Jeremiah said. "Sorry you had to see that."

"It was…interesting." Theresa said. "Yeah. Interesting. Let's go with that."

Jeremiah checked the clock. He had just over three hours before he could leave.

"I get off at six," he said. "You should stick around and we'll do something. Zachary would love to see you."

"You don't have to stay later?"

"Tamika is scheduled to close tonight," he said. "I'm the boss now, remember? At least when McKay's not here." He held out his arms. "It's good to be the boss."

"Right," Theresa said. "OK. I'll meet you back here at 6:00. Don't run off without me. I don't know anything about Memphis."

Theresa followed Jeremiah to his house that night. They left her car there while they picked up Zachary from Patricia's and then went to Garibaldi's.

"I've heard that everyone here is either a music major or a theater major," Jeremiah said. "I just know that the pizza's good."

They returned to Jeremiah's house after dinner.

"It's still early," Jeremiah said. "You might as well come in."

"Early for you," Theresa said. "I've still got a four hour drive to get home." She looked at her watch. "It'll be midnight by the time I get home. And that's if I leave now."

"Then don't go home," Jeremiah said. "Stay here."

"Yeah!" Zachary seemed to think that was a good idea. "You can stay here. We could have a sleepover."

Theresa shot a playful look at Jeremiah.

"Oh, really? Does your dad have a lot of sleepovers?"

Jeremiah laughed.

"No," Zachary said. "You're the first person to come to our house since we moved here."

Theresa's face returned to normal. Jeremiah exhaled. Zachary was more of a writer of fiction than he was a reporter. Jeremiah was glad he hadn't fictionalized his love life.

Jeremiah pointed to the backseat. "Don't forget your book." Zachary climbed into the backseat to get it. "He took a book to school today to read. He was pretty excited."

"Oh really," Theresa said. "What book did you take?"

"Where the Wild Things Are," Zachary said. "But she didn't read it."

She looked at Jeremiah. She'd heard the story of how the same thing had happened to him and how it lead to the creation of Books That Deserve To Be Read.

Jeremiah tried not to overreact. "That happens sometimes."

"You could read it to me," Zachary said.

"Or you could read it yourself," Jeremiah said as he looked at Zachary in the rear-view mirror. "You know how to read."

Zachary flipped a few pages while they drove the short distance from Garibaldi's to the house.

They went in and sat side by side on the couch. Jeremiah picked up TV Guide.

"What do you want to watch?" he asked.

"What do you think, Zachary?" Theresa asked. "Know what I think? I think your dad should read that book to us." Theresa's smile was as wide as the smile of the Wild Things on the book cover. At least some of them. Some of them were just toothy.

"Us?" Jeremiah repeated.

"Yeah." Theresa smiled and put an arm around Zachary. "Us."

The three of them settled into the couch. Jeremiah sat in the middle, between Zachary and Theresa, ostensibly so everyone could see the colorful illustrations while he read but actually because he wanted to sit close to Theresa.

Theresa smiled at Jeremiah's subtle manipulation of his child.

They huddled together as Jeremiah turned the first singed, water-damaged page.

"Miss Patricia said Max was naughty," Zachary announced before Jeremiah began.

"Really?" Jeremiah said. "Is that why she wouldn't read the book?"

Zachary thought for a minute. "That's not what she said. She said we were out of time. But then she read another book after that."

Jeremiah remembered this same conversation from over twenty years before.

"But what did Max learn?" he asked his son.

"Not to wear his wolf suit to dinner," Zachary said. Theresa covered her mouth and quickly converted a laugh into a coughing fit.

"Well, there is that," Jeremiah said. "But Max also learned that being wild didn't make him happy." He looked over Zachary's head just as Theresa was turning to face him.

Jeremiah recalled this conversation vividly. "He learned that being loved meant more to him than being wild."

"His mom loved him." Zachary looked at Jeremiah. "He didn't have a dad."

"Well, he had to have a dad somewhere," Jeremiah said. "And I bet that wherever his dad was, he still loved Max very much."

"Max's dad was gone," Zachary said.

"The book doesn't really say, does it. I guess we don't know." Jeremiah tried to remember if the idea of Max having a dad even entered his mind when he was Zachary's age.

Then Zachary asked the question that Jeremiah had been dreading since the day Susan left.

"Like my mom?"

Jeremiah blinked and tried not to react in front of his son. Theresa's audible gasp made that almost impossible.

"The other kids at daycare have moms," Zachary said quietly.

"I'm sure they do," Jeremiah said. "But in our family, it's just us. You and me." He handed the book to Theresa and put Zachary on his lap.

"You are getting so *big!*" Jeremiah said. "Your mom had to do something to take care of herself," he explained. "She didn't feel well, so she went to live with her mom and dad. But I'm sure that wherever she is, she still loves you very much." Jeremiah hugged Zachary until the boy began to squirm. He crawled off his dad's lap back to where he was.

"There's one more thing," Jeremiah said.

"And then we can read the book?"

"Yes, but this is very important, so listen. Besides learning that he shouldn't wear a wolf suit to dinner, Max also learned that even the Ruler of the Wild Things can always come back home, no matter how wild he might have been."

"Why would he think he couldn't come home?" Zachary asked.

Theresa smiled and nodded. "Yeah, Dad, why would he think he couldn't come home?"

"I don't know why he thought that," Jeremiah conceded. "That is kind of silly, isn't it?"

Zachary nodded in agreement. "Silly Max."

They finished the book. Jeremiah made some popcorn while Zachary changed into his wolf suit pajamas.

They turned on the TV and watched what was left of Monday Night Football. Jeremiah sat next to Theresa. Zachary sprawled across the rest of the couch and rested his head on Jeremiah's lap. Jeremiah stroked his son's hair as he slept.

And that's how they were when they woke up the next morning.

52

Theresa wasn't the only book-loving person from Clear Spring who was reaching out for help. Ruthanna called Tammy with a very specific request.

"I'd like to buy the bookstore," she told Tammy almost as soon as Tammy answered the phone in Florida. "I mean, unless you and George were planning on rebuilding. Are you going to rebuild?"

"And good morning to you!" Tammy laughed. "We've talked about it. I'm not sure Jeremiah's heart is in it. It might be best for us to let it go."

"So you and George aren't coming back?"

"Probably not," Tammy said. "I mean, we miss you. I miss you a lot. These Florida people are mostly transplanted New Yorkers. Florida has all the efficiency of the South and the hospitality of New York City."

"Didn't Kennedy say that about Washington?"

"Something like that. I see you're still a stickler for accurate citations." Tammy laughed again. She'd missed her friend. "Are you planning on selling books?"

"No, but I'm afraid someone else might be." Ruthanna's tone became more somber. "I want to get it before Millicent gets it. Theresa thinks she's going to get that Pastor Kettle guy to help her put something there. Probably as some kind of ultimate revenge against us heathens."

"She's talked about that since we first moved in," Tammy said. "But we would never sell it to her, Ruthanna. You have to know that."

"You wouldn't, but somebody else might." Ruthanna listed the potential disasters. "Some follower we don't know about. Some shell company that this Kettle guy sets up to hide his involvement. Anybody, really, who might buy it and then be persuaded to sell it to Millicent."

"Is she still in search of demons to conquer?" Ruthanna could hear Tammy blowing on her coffee. "You'd think burning down our store would have been enough."

"I wish," Ruthanna said. "She's going after the library now. You'd think they were one of those nasty adult bookstores the way she's coming after them. She's on the agenda for the next City Council meeting."

"Same song, second verse," Tammy said.

"Exactly," Ruthanna said.

"And you're looking for the bridge."

"Cute," Ruthanna said. "Right now, I'm still trying to figure out the chorus."

"What did you have in mind?"

"First of all, can you even sell the store yet? Are they still investigating?"

"Well," Tammy said as she sat down at her kitchen table. "The police have a confession but they're waiting on the judge to officially declare her guilty and do all that. But"—her voice changed to a more hopeful, more optimistic tone—"as far as the insurance company is concerned, the case is solved. We got the check last week."

"Not to be nosey," Ruthanna began, "but was it enough?"

"More than we thought it would be, honestly. First, you know we paid cash for that, right? We had enough money from selling our place in California that we didn't need to get a loan for that or the house."

"Wow." Ruthanna never thought of George and Tammy as rich, probably because they never acted like how she thought rich people would act. "I had no idea."

"Yes, we were millionaires once." Tammy shuddered and rolled her eyes. "That lasted about six months. Then we bought the store, and the house, and the cars, and the rest of it. It wasn't exactly a vow of poverty, but we spent a lot of money back then."

"But that was what?" Ruthanna did the math in her head. "Twenty five years ago? How much is that worth now?"

"That's the thing: George got insurance for the *replacement* value of the business, what it would cost for us to rebuild in case a tornado hit or something. We didn't think about a fire, but it still applies. The check we got was for what it would take to clear the lot, rebuild the store, replace the books, and pay our salary while that was happening."

"So do you have to rebuild?" Ruthanna asked.

"Nope," Tammy said. "I hate that the store burned. We lost so many memories, so many things that can't be replaced. But it was an unexpected profit."

"Well, good for you." Ruthanna let her congratulations ring for a moment before she popped the question.

"So, with all that, do you want to sell the lot?" she asked. "I'll still pay for the cleanup."

"Let me talk to George, but I don't see why not." Tammy paused. "Not that it's any of my business, but what are you planning to do with it?"

"I want to build a Center for Free Speech," Ruthanna said. "Kind of a headquarters for what you and George have been doing. A place where people could find books, talk about books, and maybe even publish books that people like Millicent don't want people to read."

Tammy's smile was audible. "I like that idea. George is out doing something. I'll talk to him when he gets back."

George wasn't the only one Tammy talked to. She started calling her old Hollywood friends—the writers, actors, and producers who once used her scripts and partied in their home before McCarthyism destroyed their world. Other blacklisted writers gave their blessings and their money. Some were gone, but many were still around. They called their friends—sympathetic editors, set designers, composers—people who had suffered when the writers disappeared. Those friends called *their* friends, in Hollywood and wherever else they'd ended up.

Rolodexes spun like roulette wheels—and most of the spins were winners.

Ruthanna reached out to Ethan, who contacted all the musicians and songwriters he knew. He reached out to artists whose work had been banned from radio play. Everyone except Cleetus Bowman and his unholy brigade thought it was a good idea. They agreed something needed to be done to protect history and new ideas. To defend new voices from attack.

She contacted the ACLU and other civil rights groups to see if they would be interested. She called colleges. She called every place she found that had been threatened by book banning groups or, even sadder, places that had books removed because of book bans.

What's more, she, Theresa, and the others made all this happen before the next City Council meeting.

At George's insistence, Ruthanna hired an attorney to set up the corporation. George and Tammy insisted on one more thing, without which the deal was off.

"We will donate the lot," George said. "I'll keep the money, so you'll still have to pay for the cleanup, but the land is yours for free."

Ruthanna was stunned. "That's a lot of money, George. I was going to offer whatever the going rate is for that kind of thing. Are you sure we can't come up with a compromise that won't cost you so much?"

"This was the compromise," he said. "I wanted to pay for the cleanup. Tammy reminded me that we have to live on this money for the rest of our lives."

Ruthanna heard Tammy scream "George!" in the background.

The attorney listed Ruthanna, George and Tammy, and Theresa as Board members. Ruthanna was named Board President by almost unanimous decree. She refused to vote for herself.

"Why not put Jeremiah on the Board?" Theresa asked.

"Have you heard from Jeremiah?" Ruthanna said. "Because I have not."

"Fair enough," Theresa said. She had, in fact, been hearing a *lot* from Jeremiah. They were talking on the phone almost every night. She'd made another trip to Memphis in January and was looking forward to visiting again soon.

They just hadn't talked about this.

Jeremiah's ambivalence was clear. Stirring the waters was not going to help.

53

Theresa used her trips to Memphis to gradually erase Jeremiah's objections to coming back to Clear Spring. It wasn't a neatly drawn linear process. Had it been a notebook, there would have been erasure marks, scuffs, and plenty of crossed-out words, circles, and rewrites all over the page. But his resistance to leaving faded as his frustrations with Mr. McKay and the various forms of corporate censorship grew.

She happened to be in The Corner Bookstore when Tamika asked Jeremiah about building a display for February, Black History Month. The idea of a month dedicated to the history of Black people was new at the time; so new, in fact, that it had yet to be named an official national event.

"And someone thought it was a good idea to choose the shortest month of the year?" Theresa joked.

"They thought it'd be a good idea to choose the month when Frederick Douglass was born," Tamika told her. "And Lincoln."

"Sure," Jeremiah said. "Let's do this. Build the display. Use books we already have and let me know if we need to order anything we don't have in stock. If we're going to do this, let's do it right."

Tamika cocked her head and half-squinted with one eye. "What about the Grand Cyclops from HQ?"

"I'll deal with him," Jeremiah said. "Just don't put it in the front of the store. That's the rule, right? 'No banned books in the front of the store?' So we'll go with that."

"Speaking of banned books," Tamika said, "a lot of these Black writers have been banned at one time or another. A lot still are. Toni Morrison, James Baldwin, Malcolm X, Angela Davis. Banned literature tends to be Black literature."

"Which is why we're not putting the display in the front of the store." Jeremiah imitated McKay's substantial Southern drawl. "I said nothing controversial on the *front* displays. I thought I was very clear about that. This is a direct order from your manager and you are expected to do it."

Tamika laughed and replied with her own version of a Mississippi drawl.

"Yes, sir. You're right, sir. Very clear. I'll get right on that."

Theresa knew it was time to talk to Jeremiah. He was ready.

Jeremiah's favorite food court lunch was the Chinese place. He ordered his usual, shrimp lo mein, very spicy.

"How many stars hot?" the lady behind the counter asked.

"A galaxy," he said.

Theresa had sweet and sour soup and an eggroll.

"There's something I need to talk to you about," she said while she tried to figure out how to use the bowl-sized porcelain spoon without spilling soup all over her chin. Or, even worse, slurping.

"You realize that for me, that term has historically not been followed with happy news, right?"

Theresa gave up on the lovely porcelain spoon and grabbed the plastic spoon that came along with Jeremiah's chopsticks.

"I'll be quick," she said. "We need you." She hated how much of what she was saying was true, but Jeremiah's presence would bring something that no one else could bring. He would be the spark.

Theresa told him about Ruthanna's idea for the Center for Free Speech, how his parents' had already donated the land—this was news to Jeremiah—and that she, as a member of the Center for Free Speech Foundation, was in the position to offer him a job as Executive Officer.

Jeremiah dropped his chopsticks.

"So, you would be my boss?" he asked.

Theresa smiled. "I suppose, technically, that would be the case."

"This is all very, very nice," he said. "Incredible, really. But— and I hate to say this—I have a child who likes to eat. I, myself, enjoy the occasional sustaining meal. Not to mention having a roof over my head."

He broke character. "Seriously, this is very nice, but how would I make a living? There aren't any jobs in Clear Spring that would pay what I'm making now, especially if I'm also doing this Center for Outrageous Speech."

"Free speech," Theresa said.

Jeremiah picked up his chopsticks but put them right back on his plate.

"You say free. Millicent will say outlandish. At least. And probably more than that."

Theresa ignored him and went on with what she had to say.

"We are prepared to offer you the same pay that you are making now," she said.

"You don't even know what I'm making now."

"Doesn't matter," she told him. "You don't know how much money we've already raised." She smiled like the Cheshire Cat. "And how much more we could make. We plan to protect books, book writers, and book readers. That's a given. But we also plan to sell books, to publish books, and to do other things that'll bring in the money we need. And you would not believe how many people have asked if they could make regular donations every month. We're not going to get rich, but this will work."

Jeremiah smirked. "I believe those donors would be called 'Patrons'," he said. "That's all very Renaissance of you."

"Yes, we will have patrons." She corrected her verb tense. "We have patrons. What we don't have is an executive who can run everything. That means day to day stuff but also big picture stuff. The Board is there to help, but the ideas will mainly come from you." She gently touched his hand.

"And me. Because, after all, I will be your boss."

"You really love saying that, don't you?"

She smiled with a tight-lipped but very satisfied grin.

"I do," she said.

"Again." Jeremiah shuddered dramatically. "Another phrase with which I do not have positive associations."

"Oh, sorry. My bad."

Theresa left Memphis after she finished their lunch. She had to meet with their attorney early the next morning and didn't want to be late. Jeremiah went back to the store and Tamika.

"Build the display. Now."

Over the next week, Tamika built a shrine to Black literature in the middle of the History and Biographies section. She pulled books from every Black writer they had in the store. She ordered new books from writers recommended to her by teachers at Memphis State and Ole Miss, none of which were submitted to McKay for approval. She included historical facts about the authors, their work, and whether their book had been banned anywhere.

She called it, "Readers Who Deserve To Be Seen."

Jeremiah looked over the finished display.

"Not exactly subtle, is it?" he said. "I like it."

McKay showed up a week later with Jeremiah's weekly sales report in hand.

"These numbers are impressive," he said. "I told you things would work out if you did what I said."

"That's all Tamika," Jeremiah said. "Those sales are all from her display." Jeremiah caught his mistake as soon as he said it. "The display I told her to build. It was my idea and her labor."

McKay smiled and nodded. "Good managers know how to delegate and then take credit for it," he said. "I like that."

"And I did."

"Well, let me see this display that's doing so well," McKay said. "We should be doing this in all the stores."

Jeremiah saw Tamika coming down the stairs. He discreetly motioned for her to wait.

"Here it is," he said. "The display that doubled our sales last week."

McKay gasped. "I did not approve these books."

"No, you did not," Jeremiah told him. "I did."

"I thought we talked about that," McKay snarled. "Do you know what kind of problems this could create?"

"I do and I did it anyway." Jeremiah softened his tone to be a bit less confrontational. "I wanted to show you the potential for this market." He pointed to the report that McKay was slowly and, by all appearances, involuntarily compressing into a small paper wad in his hand. "Probably ninety percent of those sales are from Black customers."

"I doubt that," the older man replied. "How would you even know that?"

"We tracked it." Jeremiah was glad Tamika thought of that. "Those are the sales marked with a 'B'."

Jeremiah looked at the stairs and motioned for Tamika to join them. He continued as she walked towards them.

"I didn't ask for your approval because I knew you wouldn't approve. Going with the 'easier to get forgiveness than permission' theory here." He silently noted that McKay did not look amused at his joke. "And I ordered the books, not Tamika. But everything else about this display meets your rules. It's not in the front of the store. We're not advertising these books outside of the store."

McKay said nothing, but Jeremiah could see he was not happy.

"All of this is word of mouth," Jeremiah told him. "We spent zero dollars advertising this."

McKay dragged one foot on the floor in front of him, like a bull getting ready to charge the matador.

"This isn't the kind of store we operate here, Jeremiah."

"You're right." Jeremiah folded his arms across his chest and nodded. But maybe it should be."

McKay ignored the comment.

"I gave you explicit instructions and you deliberately ignored what I said. More than that, you ignored the spirit of this store. There's no telling how many good customers you've chased away with this thing."

"Then maybe you need to reconsider who you think of as a customer," Jeremiah said.

It was becoming clear that the apology McKay was looking for—the apology he expected to hear—was not coming.

"You're not giving me many options here, Jeremiah.

"And you haven't left me with many options either," Jeremiah said as he removed the name badge from his shirt. "I would strongly recommend you make Tamika manager before she goes to some other store. He handed his name tag to McKay. "When other stores see this sales report, I'm sure she'll have plenty of offers."

McKay was indignant. "Why would I do that?"

"Because I quit."

54

It took Jeremiah less than one day to box up everything in his house. Zachary packed his own toys and books. Darnel helped put some of the bigger things on the truck, the couch and other things that Jeremiah couldn't carry with only one hand. He arrived in Clear Spring two days after he quit.

Ruthanna knew the fight wasn't over, but she enjoyed watching the show. The City Council meeting was still a week away, but public opinion seemed to be moving away from Millicent, especially after Whitely's repeated editorial dragged her through every mudhole in the county. In the Cozy Kitchen, people were excited about "that new thing they're doing with the bookstore".

Theresa and Ruthanna told Jeremiah the same thing. George and Tammy repeated the mantra over dinner with Jeremiah and Zachary.

Even Ethan, who arrived the day before the ceremony, seemed to have been told what to say.

Jeremiah was not to touch the tarp. He assumed this instruction applied to everyone, but it seemed to be especially aimed at him.

Whether it was because of paint fumes or concrete curing—or some other excuse depending on who told him—they'd done everything short of hiring an armed guard to keep him away.

The groundbreaking ceremony was set for Monday of the week after Jeremiah arrived. The anticipation in the community was so great that even Whitely was obliged to acknowledge the event in the *Dixiecrat*.

"Ladies and gentlemen," Ruthanna said to the crowd assembled in the street. "As President of this organization, it is my honor to break ground today for…"

There was a pause while Ethan and George struggled to remove what seemed to be a child-safety lock on the tarp covering the sign.

Jeremiah's jaw dropped when he saw the inscription.

"The Malone Center for Free Speech."

As he listened to the applause, Jeremiah remembered what Theresa said to the School Board only a few months before. How she'd sacrificed so much so others could have what she didn't. He thought about Ruthanna sharing her deepest, most private feelings for Stephanie because she believed it was important for people to know they are not alone.

But mostly he thought about the people who were not there. The Stephanies who never saw themselves in the books in their classrooms or, even worse, those who saw themselves and then watched as those books were banned and those mirrors disappeared. The Tamikas who uplifted others even when it meant possibly losing their job. His parents, who fought to keep what happened to them from happening to anyone else. He looked at the crowd as he approached the small stage.

"I am Jeremiah Malone," he said.

"I want to talk about books."

THE END

From the author

This one is personal.

I started writing *The Bookseller's Son* after my first novel, *The Band Room*, was removed from our local high school library. I had donated copies of all my books—*The Band Room, Dad, Drawn to Murder,* and *Portrait of a Murder*—to the school where I taught. I enjoyed seeing students carrying them in the halls. Students who read the books seemed to enjoy them.

And then one day, *The Band Room* was gone. It was and remains the most political book I've ever written. I guess someone in our deeply conservative community didn't like my politics.

The other three books, as of April 4, 2025, are still there.

I'm not alone. In the 2023–2024 school year, over 10,000 instances of book bans were reported—nearly three times the number from the year before. Most of these bans targeted authors of color, LGBTQ+ voices, and stories about race, gender, and identity. States like Florida and Iowa have led the charge, backed by new censorship laws.

This isn't just about protecting books, although that would be reason enough. It's about who gets to tell stories and who gets to read them. It's about speaking truth to power, answering falsehoods with facts, and refusing to be silent in the face of censorship. It's about who has the power to decide which ideas will be read and which ideas will be silenced.

If you care about free expression, if you believe young people deserve access to a wide range of voices, then now is the time to speak up. Donate banned books to schools and libraries. Support teachers and librarians who resist censorship. Ask your School Board what policies they follow. Vote. Enlist help from groups like the ACLU, the American Library Association, and other groups that are committed to free speech and truth.

Silence is not neutrality. It's permission.

Other books by Bob Seay

Literary Fiction

The Band Room (2020)

Angel enjoys his status as a star high school football player. But some bad luck changes that. Rejected by his coach and teammates, Angel finds himself in a place with new people and new ideas. In his first novel, Bob Seay pits tribalism, anger, and hate against diversity, acceptance, and compassion while reminding us that everyone is doing the best they can.

- 2021 Readers' Favorite Gold Medal Winner

Dad (2021)

Jacob Martin's life is not going well. His marriage is falling apart, his job is on the border of legal and illegal, and he's living in what could generously be described as a dump. Now Dad, whose memory and mental faculties aren't exactly what they once were, has decided to drive from Cincinnati to Colorado for a surprise visit. At least that was the plan, until John got lost along the way. Forced into an unplanned road trip to retrieve his father, Jacob finds love, enlightenment, and ultimately himself along the way.

- Winner Colorado Authors League 2022 Literary Fiction Award
- Winner of 2021 Indie Reader Discovery Award

Cozy Mysteries

Drawn to Murder- a Gabriella Alegré mystery Book 1 (2022)

Gabriella Alegré draws caricatures and portraits of visitors on Pearl Street. It's a fun place to be – until someone is murdered.

Now, Gabriella must use her powers of artistic observation and attention to detail to find the killer. She is helped by Pearl Street's living statues, musicians, a reclusive psychic who isn't what she seems, and other street performers.

A cozy mystery packed with more tricks than a street magician, DRAWN TO MURDER draws you into the story and the busker community of Pearl Street.

You're going to want a cupcake!

Portrait of a Murder- a Gabriella Alegré mystery Book 2 (2022)

They hired her to paint a family portrait. They didn't tell her there was a killer in the picture!

Gabriella Alegré is no ordinary street artist. After solving the murder of a fellow street busker, Gabriella tries to focus on her art and her future in Colorado, but when she gets commissioned to paint a portrait of one of the most prominent and mysterious families in Boulder, something is destined to go wrong.